A FOUR POINTS IRISH MAFIA BOOK

IT WILL ALWAYS BE YOU

SHANNON JADE

Published by Jade's Publishing
Copyright © 2025 by Shannon Jade

Cover art and formatting by Aurelia Dunbar (@mayonaka.designs)
Editing by Alexa at The Fiction Fix
Proofreading by Elizabeth Carmichael and Paris Browne

CONTENTS

PLAYLIST

Little Bit Better – Caleb Hearn, ROSIE
Who's Afraid Of Little Old Me? – Taylor Swift
loml – Taylor Swift
Ice Cream Man – RAYE
you'd never know – BLU EYES
Healing hurts – BLU EYES
Who Am I – NEEDTOBREATHE
something I can't afford – Cian Ducrot
The Golden Years – Joshua Bassett
Compromise – ROLE MODEL
Sweet Oblivion – David Kushner
Shadows – Bryce Fox
SHREDS – Chi$tian Gate$
Day Is Gone – Noah Gundersen, The Forest Rangers
Why Why Why – Shawn Mendes
Love You Right - Chanin
Love The Hell Out Of You – Lewis Capaldi
Remembering Sunday – All Time Low
Troubled Waters – Alex Warren
The Prophecy – Taylor Swift
Kept Me Alive - Grayscale

Home Is Where the Hurt Is – The Script
dead the day ur gone – Matt Hansen
You Could Be Happy – Snow Patrol
Shelter – from the room below – Sleep Token
Let Me In – Dermot Kennedy
Always Been You – Michael Sanzone
Ends With You – David Kushner
Empty Bench – David Kushner
I Wanna Get to Heavan – David Kushner
Safe in My Arms – David Kushner
Old & Grey – Darren Kiely

AUTHOR'S NOTE

Thank you for picking up It Will Always Be You. This is book three in The Four Points, and while it can be read as a standalone, you will get the best overall experience reading the series in order.
This is **much darker** than the previous books, so please check the trigger and content warnings below.

On page sex trafficking (not by the MMC)
On page sexual assault (not by the MMC)
Sexual violence including murder (not by the MMC)
Forced body modification (not by the MMC)
On page death of a parent
On page death of a sibling
Mafia-related violence including torture
Praise kink
Breeding kink
Cum play
Office romance
Second chance
Secret tattoos
Hate to love
Forced separation
It's always been you
BDSM elements as healing

JONATHAN

As the heir to the Four Points, control has always been my weapon and my shield. Enemies are everywhere, and weakness is a luxury I can't afford. But then she came into my world.

She was an obsession I never saw coming—dangerous, intoxicating, and impossible to ignore. The worst possible timing… yet I was already in too deep.

My existence had always been dictated by legacy, duty, the cold weight of blood and power. But in an instant, she shattered all of it. She consumed me in ways I can't explain. A force I couldn't fight.

I never saw the darkness lurking in the shadows, not until it was too late—until they took her.

Now, I'll burn everything down to bring her back—and protect the empire that's mine to claim.

HELEN

For years, I lived in the shadows, the perfect mafia daughter—silent, obedient, unseen. But the moment they threatened my sister, that life was gone in a heartbeat. I vanished into the darkness, becoming someone else, someone who could survive. Until a job brought me right back into this hellish world—and into his orbit.

My new boss was a storm of darkness and desire. Cold, ruthless, and impossible to escape. Every glance from him pulled me closer to the edge. Every word dragged me deeper into his dark and dangerous world.

He didn't understand the word no, and I could feel the walls I had spent years building slowly crumbling.

For so long, I'd sacrificed everything. And just when I thought I might finally have a taste of happiness, it was ripped from me—brutally, violently.

Now, I'll make them pay. For everything.

And maybe… maybe I'll let myself believe there's still something worth fighting for. Something worth saving — even if it's just the pieces of us we left behind.

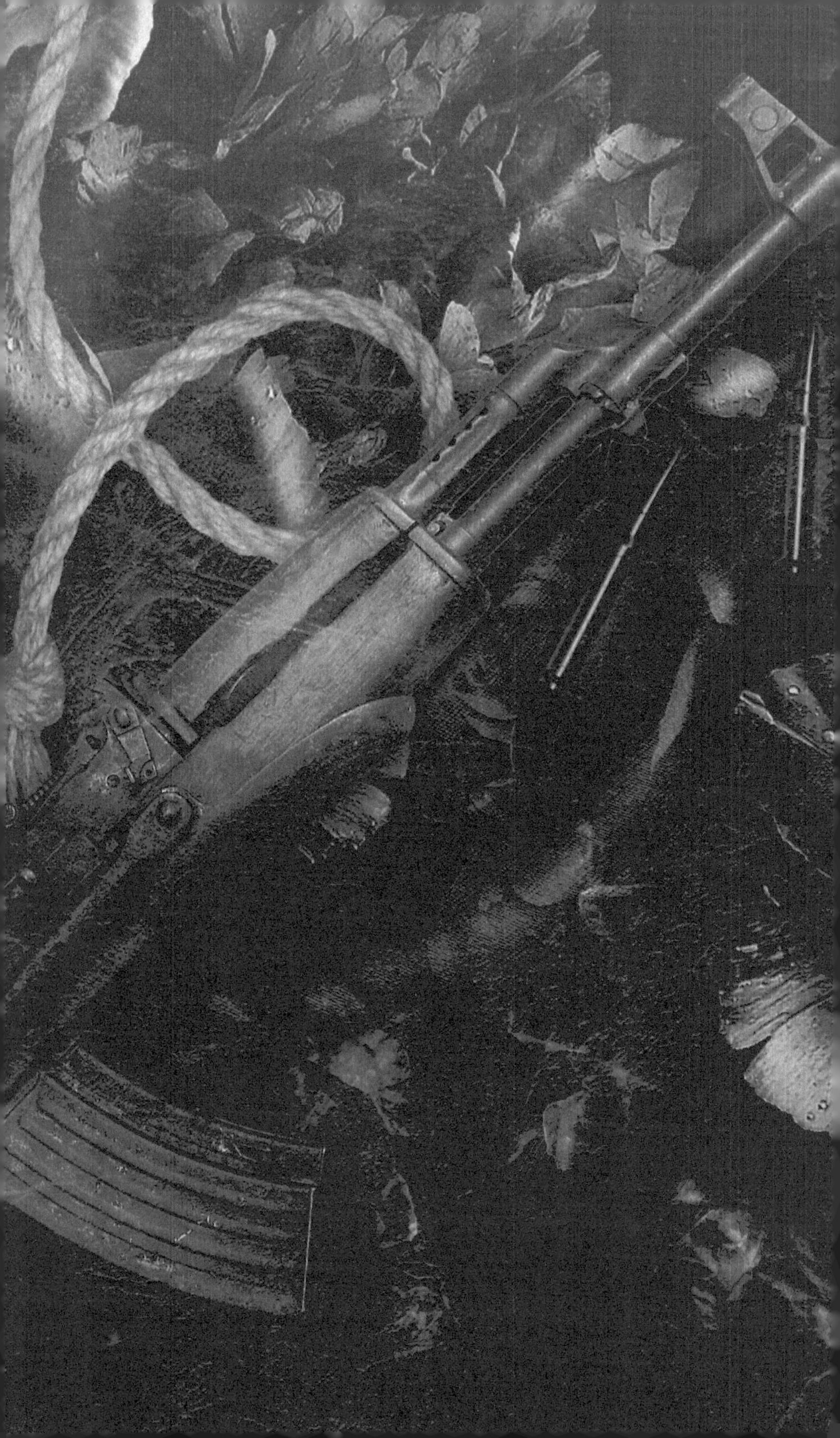

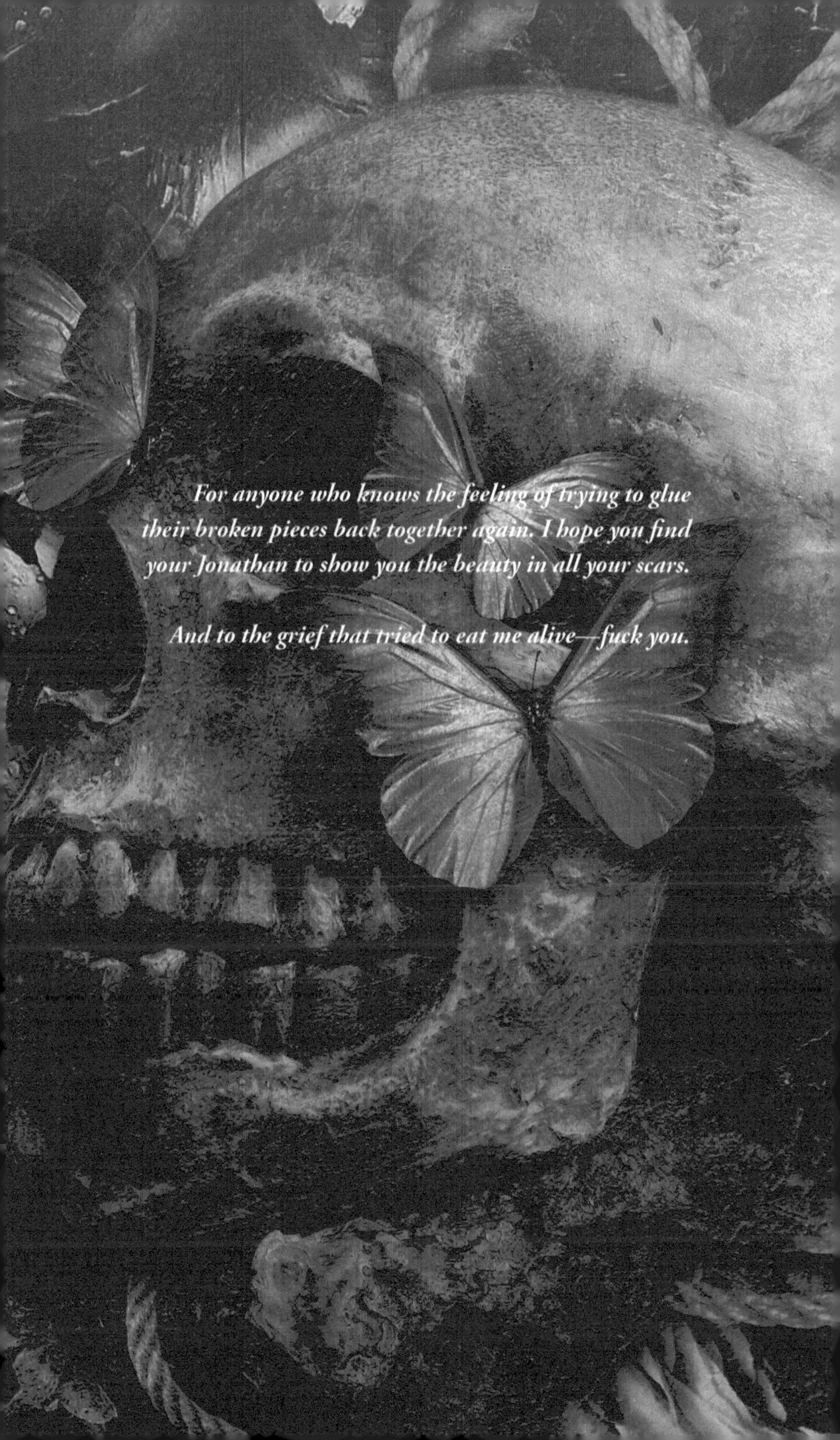

*For anyone who knows the feeling of trying to glue
their broken pieces back together again. I hope you find
your Jonathan to show you the beauty in all your scars.*

And to the grief that tried to eat me alive—fuck you.

Falling

HELEN
CHAPTER 1

I'm going to die tonight.

The thought ricochets through me, beating against my skull like a drum as I go through the motions of getting ready. A coat of mascara and a dusting of blush mixed in with a pinch of trepidation. A glance at the clock ticking down the seconds to my funeral.

My childhood bedroom feels like a cage, and I'm the animal seconds away from turning feral as I pace the length of it. The dress I've been instructed to wear tonight—a red scrap of fabric with a plunging neckline—mocks me from where it hangs on my wardrobe door. The irony that, only a handful of weeks ago, wearing something so revealing would be rewarded by a date with Father's belt isn't lost on me.

I don't even know why I'm wasting time pacing. Actually, that's a lie. It's because if I sit still, my thoughts will catch up to me, and I'm not ready to deal with them. Soon, it won't matter if I'm ready or not.

I yank my shirt over my head, slide off my knee length skirt, and then remove my bra before I slip on the dress better suited for a night on the town than a family dinner. But what Angus wants, Angus gets.

Screw questions or social norms. In this case, what he wants is to see what he's buying, which my parents were only too happy to facilitate. Tonight is one big façade, and it simultaneously makes me sick to my stomach and pisses me off beyond measure that they could do this to their own daughter.

"Helen, hurry up. Angus is waiting for us," Mother tuts from my open doorway, clear disapproval and distaste making her features pinched—features so similar to mine, it makes me wonder why she can't place herself in my shoes. Is it sheer unwillingness to acknowledge her wrongdoing? Or have the pills she thinks we don't see her popping altered her brain chemistry beyond repair?

"Coming, Mother," I tell her, taking one last look in the mirror as I steel myself for what lies ahead. The girl looking at me looks far from excited, and I can't say I blame her. Forcing a fake smile onto my face, I fiddle with the hemline of my dress and brace myself to sit through one final charade.

Months of planning has gone into tonight, and I'll be damned if anything will stop me from escaping the death sentence my parents have laid at my feet. Because make no mistake: letting Angus Graham dub me wife number five and giving him complete control over my life, my body, and everything in between feels like a death sentence.

It shouldn't cut me so deeply that they would do this to their barely legal daughter. Somewhere along the way, between being handed off to nannies and then tasked with raising my younger siblings, I came to the bitter understanding that my parents are far from the loving kind. Raised voices and things breaking were a far more common occurrence than loving comments and family meals, which had me thankful we were shipped off to boarding school for months at a time. Still, this is a new low, even for them, that has me questioning everything. If they can sell me, what won't they do to achieve their sick, twisted goals?

Are there any lines they won't cross?

Anything they won't let Angus demand?

I'm not about to stick around to find out, that's for sure.

Taking a fortifying breath, I brace myself for the night ahead and make my way downstairs. Peter, my baby brother, Father's pride and joy, stands in front of a mirror, frowning at that one strand of hair refusing to be slicked back, looking more concerned with his appearance than the obvious tension in the room. Typical. Mother and Father gather near the door, wearing matching expressions of frustration as they exchange heated words. It's my younger sister who catches and keeps my attention, though.

She's huddled in a corner, baby blue eyes clouded with fear as she wrings her hands in front of her and fidgets with her dress every couple of seconds, her fear bleeding from her pores like a physical entity. Any hesitation I had vanishes as we lock gazes. If I don't do this, God knows what will await her. Tearing my gaze from her before I draw Father's attention, I'm met with his assessing stare. He takes me in, from the fancy up-do I'd wrangled my wayward curls into, to the high heels I'd squeezed over my protesting feet. They're already throbbing with pain, but I know better than to show weakness around him. For a breath, I think I might just pass his inspection, but then his eyes narrow, and his lip curls as he focuses in on my throat.

Shit.

"I thought I told you to remove that cheap piece of crap." His voice is a low snarl that has Freya flinching and shrinking in on herself, even though his ire isn't aimed at her. Instinctively, I reach up to touch the shell necklace I never take off. It's the only reminder I have of better days, days when things were carefree, less life or death. It was a gift from a boy I'd spent one summer flirting with, and while the boy may be long gone, a part of me longs for the reminder of happier times.

Swallowing past the lump in my throat, I reach behind me to undo the clasp before handing it over. With a smirk, he curls his hand into a fist, shattering the delicate necklace just like he shattered my freedom.

"You insolent girl," he snarls, spit flying into my face as he leans closer. "Tonight is the single most important night of your pathetic life, and you want to show up wearing this tacky thing? Are you trying to insult Angus?" In a split second, his hand is flying towards me, and before I can duck, it lands across my cheek. The pain is instantaneous, and my eyes well with tears as I lock eyes with Freya. A bitter understanding passes between us; this is what it means to be a woman in this godforsaken Clan.

The sooner I die and set us both free from this curse, the better.

"Gary, we need to leave," Mother interrupts him, taking a step forward as her eyes flick over my face. Annoyance flares to life as she purses her lips in distaste, as if the redness blooming on my cheek is my fault. I suppose, to her, it is. God forbid Father ever take responsibility for his actions.

"Control your children better in the future," Father sneers at her before buttoning his jacket and charging out of the house, leaving us in his wake. Tonight is shaping up to be even worse than I anticipated.

Peter tosses a smirk at me over his shoulder as he follows Father like the good little soldier in training he is. The temptation to lash out at him is like fire in my veins, but as we cross the threshold out into the compound, the feeling of being watched has me biting my tongue and reaching out to grab Freya's hand. At fifteen and the youngest daughter, she's been pretty sheltered until recently. The only thing Mother and I ever saw eye to eye on was keeping her out of Angus' sight, but apparently, that ship has sailed.

"Hel, what's going to happen?" she whimpers, leaning into my side, looking up at me with wide eyes. I would do anything to reassure her, but I also swore to never lie to her. As I take in her pale features and the way her whole body trembles, it's clear I need to settle her nerves before Angus lays eyes on her. Men like him prey on weaknesses, and I'll be damned if I give him have any opportunity to so much as look at Freya.

"Nothing. It's just dinner, right? Father has probably done something to earn favour. If we just keep our heads down, it'll be over before we know it." It's not a complete lie, and hopefully, it's enough to keep her calm while I work to stop this car crash in its tracks, or at least shelter her from the fallout as much as possible.

"Pinky promise you'd tell me if you knew more?" Holding her pinkie out to me, I'm reminded just how young at heart she is. Living a sheltered life will do that to a girl, and her innocence is something I'm determined to preserve, no matter the cost. Crossing my fingers behind my back, I link pinkies with her, giving her a forced smile.

"Come along, girls. We don't want to keep him waiting. Angus is a very busy man," Mother calls, her perfect society wife smile painted on her face as she turns to look back at us. While her smile says one thing, the look she gives me — all tight-lipped rage and denial, coupled with the vein throbbing in her forehead, says another. I wonder if she would be so quick to look at me with barely concealed rage if she knew tonight was the last time she'd see me. Would she even care?

"Coming, Mother." Painting an equally forced smile on my face, I quicken my pace, pulling Freya along with me. As we near the steps up to the main house, her palm grows damp in mine, her inhale sharp as the door opens to reveal the man of the hour.

Angus Graham has a reputation that precedes him, and rightly so.

Despite his best efforts to portray a welcoming aura, with his neatly styled hair, crisp, three-piece suit, and the wide grin stretched across his face, it's all a dirty lie. This man is Satan, and everyone who has spent any amount of time with him knows it. The vast majority just chose not to challenge him, not after what happened to the last person who did.

Rumour has it, they never did find all the pieces of him.

"Welcome, Gary. How lovely to see your wife with you tonight. And these must be the infamous Campbell children back from St Andrew's. Come, come. Let me take a look at you." His smarmy smile makes the hairs on the back of my neck stand up, nausea rising in my throat. I follow Peter, who is positively beaming as he shakes the older man's hand, and it's not long before I'm standing in front of him, Freya trying to hide behind me.

His grey eyes roam over me, darkening as he takes in my exposed décolletage and legs. His tongue darts out to wet his lips as he looks me over, and while it disgusts me, it's a price I'd happily pay a thousand times if it keeps his eyes off Freya. Unfortunately, she whimpers behind me, drawing his attention to her. As his eyes flick between us, like a predator weighing up who will be his prey first, I swallow down the urge to step in front of her. Doing so would only result in drawing even more attention to her.

"Why, you girls could be twins! How fascinating." He smirks before turning his attention to Father. For a blissful second, I get a lungful of air without his attention or cloying cologne clogging my senses. As we follow him inside, the door clicking closed behind us, the walls start to feel like they are closing in around me. Fighting back my rising anxiety, I remind myself I just have to get through this dinner. After this, it'll all be over. Just get through dinner. It's only a few hours. I can do this.

I don't know who I'm trying to kid. Any hope of this being just a dinner was snuffed out the moment Angus' name was thrown into the mix. As we file into the dining room, Angus and Father help themselves to the seats at the heads of the table, leaving us to fill the spaces between them. Mother and Peter are quick to take the seats closest to Father, forcing me and Freya to sit beside Angus. So much for one final meal.

"Gary, remind me again why I asked you here?" The thinly veiled glee in Angus' voice would alert even the most oblivious person to the fact that something is brewing. Grinding my molars, I keep my gaze fixed squarely on the table, my thoughts to myself. Maybe if I remain quiet, they'll forget I'm here.

"I believe you wanted to discuss how I plan to repay your, ah... generosity." Father clears his throat. If it wasn't for what's looming, I would take great joy in his obvious discomfort for once. Why should he get to be comfortable while my life slips away in front of my eyes?

"That's right. How silly of me to forget. If memory serves, you cost me quite a lot of money, Mr Campbell, more than you can afford." At his raised eyebrow, Mother shifts uncomfortably while Peter watches the back and forth with wide, glee filled eyes. Before either of them can say anything else, a server comes in carrying our starters—salads for the women, and soup with a hearty bread roll for the men. The toxic masculinity in this place never fails to amaze me.

The tension in the room does little to Father or Angus' appetite, their bowls cleared in minutes while I push my dry lettuce around my plate. The thought of trying to push anything down around the lump in my throat sounds as appetising as eating dirt. I'm jerked out of my thoughts when a heavy hand, adorned in gold rings, lands on top of my own. Freezing my movements, I look up to meet Angus' stare head on. I might be sick to my stomach to be near him, but I'll be damned if I show him that.

"Something wrong? Your mother assured me Caesar salad, minus that awful dressing, of course, is your favourite." I barely hold my snort in. As if she would know what I like. I can't even remember the last meal we had together as a family.

"Of course not. I'm just not overly hungry. I thought I'd be best saving room for the main course." I smile at him, all prim and proper, like the perfect mafia daughter I've been raised to be. With a self-satisfied smirk, he sits back in his seat, eyes pinned to my chest.

Considering he's at least twenty years my senior, and my eighteenth birthday wasn't even a week ago, the act is disgusting. What's worse, however, is when he turns his attention to my woefully underage sister. Breathing through my nose, I count to five in my head. Stabbing him with my fork is not an option, no matter how much I want it to be.

"Sir. If there's something…other than money I can offer, I would be happy to," Father's voice cuts across the room, drawing Angus' attention back up to him and away from Freya, who trembles in her seat.

"Hmm, well now that you mention it…I am in need of something quite special." The emphasis he puts on special as he looks at me is enough to seal my fate, even before the next words are out of his mouth.

"I need an heir. Young Helen here would make a wonderful bride and mother, don't you think?"

HELEN
CHAPTER 2

Any fragile hope I had shatters in an instant. The room feels too small to contain my raging emotions. The weight of Angus' words weighs down on me too heavily, squeezing the air from my lungs. For a moment, we are all suspended in a silence so thick, it clogs the air, as if Angus' words have sucked all the life out of the room before it explodes into a cacophony of sound.

Mother gasps and drops her fork with a clatter, clutching the pearls at the base of her throat as her eyes shine with emotion. The fakeness makes me want to roll my eyes. As if she wasn't in on this. As if she herself didn't tell me this was on the table weeks ago. Freya lets out a sob as she shoves her chair back and bolts out of the room. Meanwhile, Peter joins Father and Angus in letting out a hearty laugh filled with a sick kind of glee no ten-year-old should be able to express. It hammers home just how lost to me he is. Long gone is the little boy I tried to steer away from following in Father's footsteps.

And me? I don't make a noise. No, I watch my sister as she runs, cataloguing every inch of her for memory's sake. The hardest thing about knowing tonight is my last night is knowing I'll never see her again. I'll never get to hug her tight or help do her hair. I'll miss out on her first love and first heartbreak. But none of that matters more than getting her out of Angus' clutches. The second I'm gone, Freya will be sent back St Andrew's and Angus will turn his focus onto finding my replacement, setting her free from his web of perverse intentions. That is worth paying the price, no matter how steep. Drawing in a deep breath, I lift my chin to look around the table. I knew this day was coming, but no amount of preparation could soften this blow.

What kind of father is all too happy to send his eighteen-year-old daughter into the hands of a nearly forty-year-old creep? Especially with the reputation Angus has.

There's a reason he still has no heir. His wives never survive long enough to produce one. And now my father, *my flesh and blood*, is handing me over to be the next?

Over. My. Dead. Body.

Steeling my spine, I thrust my shoulders back and hold my chin up high with a dazzling smile as I bat my eyelids and channel my inner airhead. "Wow. Me? What an honour that would be."

As his focus returns to me—and away from Freya's empty seat—I embrace the anger burning through me. Let him think the sudden heat in my cheeks is simply a flush of excitement. If only he knew I was plotting a hundred different ways to murder him. Surely, that would wipe the smirk off his face. Or maybe not, given the kind of sick bastard he is.

Before anyone can comment further, the next course is brought out. This time, we all get the same roast dinner, just in varying degrees of portion sizes. Glancing once more at Freya's empty seat with a furrowed brow, Angus issues a sharp command. "Helen, be a dear and retrieve your sister. It would be such a shame for her to miss the celebrations."

Not one to pass up an out when it's so freely presented, I excuse myself and follow the sounds of her soft cries. It's times like these I realise, despite there only being two years between us, the differences are far bigger. Maybe I've sheltered her too much, resulting in her becoming such a fragile, sensitive soul. But then again, maybe that's just the way she was destined to be. Either way, I pray she's never forced to shed her softness in exchange for a tougher shell.

Pushing the bathroom door open, I find her sitting on the closed toilet lid, her head in her hands. She flinches at the sound, like a wounded animal expecting the next blow, her panicked gaze meeting mine before she visibly relaxes.

"You can't marry that…that monster!" she spits out, jumping up to grab me by my shoulders, as if her shaking me can change anything. We're just pawns on a bigger chessboard. Our opinions and objections aren't worth shit here. Yet another reason to get the hell out of here before it's too late. Before irreparable damage is done.

"Breath for me, Frey. In and out. Now, listen. I have a plan, okay?" Brushing an unruly curl back from her face, I do my best to calm her before she works herself into a panic attack. Now is not the time, nor the place.

"How are you so calm? You've heard the stories, how not one of his wives could stomach being married to him for more than a few months before they… I can't lose you to him." She sobs, throwing herself at me, burying her face in my shoulder. It's all I can do not to cry with her. Instead, I inhale the familiar scent of her vanilla bodywash and run my hand over her hair before tugging her back so I can lock eyes with her.

"Just trust me, okay? When have I ever let you down, huh? All we have to do is get through tonight, and then we can sort this out. We'll be fine, I promise." Holding out my pinkie for her, I watch as a hundred questions dart behind her eyes before, with a shaky exhale, she links pinkies with me.

The last thing I want to do is subject her to even a second longer in Angus' presence, but we all have a part to play. For the moment, I need to play the part of the perfect, obedient mafia daughter like my life depends on it. It may grate on my nerves and make me sick to my stomach, but I don't have a choice. Tonight is very much do or die.

Thankfully, the rest of the dinner passes without incident or any more talk of my impending nuptials to Satan himself. As we wrap up and the countdown begins for my plan to come to fruition, Father hangs back to join Angus in his study while Mother ushers us home before disappearing into her bedroom without so much as a backwards glance.

Oh, don't worry about me, your daughter, you just sold off. I'm fine, thanks for asking.

As soon as I'm sequestered in my room, I set my plan in motion. Pulling up the loose floorboards underneath my bed, I pull out the supplies I've been hoarding. A backpack. A few hundred in cash. A fake ID. Blood bags. A butcher's knife. Growing up as a daughter of a member of the Clan, the Scottish mafia, I've always feared this day would come. I've watched countless peers get paired off with a man old enough to be her father, and with each wedding I was forced to attend, I knew it was only a matter of time before the gauntlet was thrown down for me. I may not have known who I would be given to, but one thing I did know was that I would never go quietly.

With a grimace, I exchange my pathetic excuse of a dress for a dark hoodie and jeans before putting my plan into motion. Soon enough, my room looks like something out of a slasher movie: blood everywhere, upturned furniture, sliced bedsheets. A quick look at the time tells me it's now or never. Father will be on his way back soon, and the last thing I need is to bump into him while making my great escape. Adding the final touches, I take one last look at what was once my childhood room, now prison, before easing open my balcony doors and making the short jump down into the back garden. Leaving Freya behind has a lump forming in my throat, but I push it down and focus on slipping out unseen. She's safer at St Andrew's than she would be if she were on the run with me. Both of us vanishing would have Father spending every waking moment hunting us down until he could drag us back to this hell.

Not allowing myself to delay the inevitable any longer, I make a quick dash to the gates with my hood pulled up, purposely leaving a trail of blood behind me. Approaching the gates that, in theory, are there to protect us but are really here to keep us prisoner, I use the random soldier's ID I pickpocketed earlier on the scanner. Holding my breath, I pray he hasn't noticed and reported it missing yet, but when the little light flashes green and the gates swing open, I exhale with relief.

Despite growing up here, this place was never a home. I won't miss it or most of the people behind these gates. I know they won't miss me either. When they stumble across my blood-soaked room and bloody balcony doors, they'll assume someone took me, and the chances of any of them sending out a manhunt for me or even caring is slim to none. The biggest inconvenience will be that Angus has to find a new bride, and while I wouldn't wish that fate on anyone, better them than me.

Keeping Freya far away from his clutches is the only thing that matters.

Phase one: get out of the compound undetected. Complete.

Phase two: vanish and make a new life, one I can eventually bring Freya into. Let's go.

JONATHAN
CHAPTER 3

Call me a cocky bastard, but striding into an office with my name on it never gets old. It doesn't matter if I'm heading into one of the smaller offices across town or the main O'Neill's Corporation Headquarters in the heart of Canary Wharf—it's always a heady feeling. Every day here is a glimpse of what's to come, a glimpse at the power that will one day be at my fingertips. It's tangible proof of my future; one I can't wait to grab by the bollocks and make my own. As I stride up the few steps to the doors, the mantle I wear every day falls over my shoulders.

My posture eases into something less threatening, more alluring. Behind these walls, I'm the guy who can charm a deal out of even the most reluctant customer, not a gangster who will do some wanker's kneecaps in to get what I want. This office is the respectable side of the family business, what we can present when questions arise as to how we make our billions. It's a way to keep the pigs off our backs and the less-than-legal dealings under the radar.

Dipping my chin at Tina, the front receptionist, I step into my private lift and take one last deep, centring breath. From the moment this lift spits me out on the executive floor, the day stretches in front of me like a long, winding road with no rest spots in sight. I thrive best when I'm *this* close to burnout out and, as such, every day is jam packed.

"Good morning, Mr O'Neill. Your coffee is on your desk, as well as this morning's analytics report." Brenda, my executive assistant, appears at my side the moment the doors open. She rushes to keep up with my long strides through the office, used to my aversion to slowing down or stopping by now.

"Perfect. Anything I should know?"

"No, sir. Profit margins look good, and enquiries are flowing in steadily. Mr Jameson requested a lunch meeting, but other than that, no changes to the schedule." At my nod, she jots my approval down in her ever-present notepad before breaking off to go to her desk while I continue my path to my office. An office that I've painstakingly put my stamp on and made my own. Alright, fine. I got Brenda to put my stamp on. Same difference if you ask me.

In most of our other offices scattered across the city, Da has the corner office reserved, even if he hasn't set foot in the building in years, and the clubs, while fun to run, don't provide anything beyond a dark and seedy room to work in. So, as soon as I had the keys to this kingdom, I wasted no time in putting Brenda to work. My first, and arguably favourite, order of business was designing it so that Brenda's office is attached to mine. It gets rid of the inconvenience of having to go out into the hall any time I need her and has the added benefit of making it impossible for people to bypass her and storm into my space.

Letting out a groan, I loosen my top button and collapse into my chair. Last night was a long one. Running a successful empire was never going to be easy, but doing all the heavy lifting and getting none of the credit is starting to grate on me. Over the last year or so, Da has increasingly stepped back, leaving more and more of the day-to-day business up to me. Which is *fine*, except I'm out here busting my balls without so much as a thank-you, while he skulks around his mansion, shutting me out both figuratively and literally.

Shrugging my suit jacket off and draping it around the back of my chair, I crack my neck before logging on. Immediately, the ping of a dozen emails makes me want to turn the damn thing off. Clenching my jaw, I down my espresso before I get started on answering the people waiting for my attention. The morning passes in a blink, and before I know it, a knock on my open door draws my attention away from the computer screen and up to the figure in the doorway. Dark, cropped hair and green eyes dancing with mirth greet me, a smirk planted firmly on my oldest and closest mate's face as he strolls into my office like he owns the place.

"Oh, sure, make yourself at home," I drawl with a shake of my head. The jab rolls off Seamus' back as he pours us both a measure of whiskey before turning to face me with a smirk planted firmly on his face.

"I'd have thought you would be a wee bit more relaxed this morning," he taunts with a salacious smirk, tilting the bottle at me in question. At my refusal, he shrugs and helps himself to a top up before pouring me one anyway.

"Yeah? Why's that?"

"Well, I heard through the grapevine you were seen getting close to one of our girls last night at Alibi." It's a statement, not a question, one that makes me roll my eyes. Seamus should know better than to listen to gossip.

"Diamond's ex came sniffing around. What was I meant to do? Let that fucker hit her again?" I throw back, leaning back in my seat and crossing my arms behind my head. Tipping my chin at the chair in front of my desk, I watch as he throws himself into it, looking every inch the relaxed, recently reformed playboy he is. He slides one of the whiskeys towards me as he sips his.

"You and your martyr complex. You should be living it up, taking one for the team, not locking yourself in this office all day and then the office over there all night. Come on, mate, live a little. Any one of the girls would jump on your dick in a heartbeat if you so much as winked at them." He snorts, pumping his eyebrows at me. If he was anyone else, he'd have lost a limb by now, but Seamus is my right-hand man and fellow businessman. By businessman, I don't just mean behind these shiny walls. No, he's my brother forged in blood in a way only Four Points men can understand, and one day, he'll be my underboss. That doesn't mean he can get away with running his mouth unchecked, though.

"Fuck off. Not all of us let our dicks rule us."

"How about you let me set you up with one of Fiona's friends?"

"How about you take a hint? Now, why are you plaguing my office today?" I snap, trying to get him off this insane crusade. Just because he's got himself a ball and chain doesn't mean I want or need one. Life as the heir to the Four Points is chaotic enough without throwing in a woman who expects me home in time for dinner and demands my undivided attention.

As he crosses his foot over his knee, his gaze grows serious as he ponders, "Any update from Senior?"

"No. He's rejecting my calls again," I grunt, distaste coating my tone. Seamus is one of the few I dare be so candid around. There's no one I trust more than this bastard, all jokes and teasing aside.

He clicks his tongue, a thoughtful look on his face. "We're going to have to do something about that. There's unease amongst the ranks. No one has laid eyes on him in months."

"I'm working on it," I snap before changing the subject to more urgent matters. "Any more updates on Graham?"

"It's suspiciously quiet down there. Word is, he's getting married soon, so maybe that's why they've been quiet. Though it does beg the question: how the hell are they keeping the cash flowing?" he muses, voicing my thoughts. Normally, Angus is the first to leap at any cash flow opportunity, but the last few drug and gun runs haven't drawn any kind of response out of him. It makes me wonder if Da was right in thinking there's more than meets the eye going on with him.

"Keep your ear to the ground. Something's not right with that fucker," I mutter before my phone rings, cutting off his response. Unease sinks in. Brenda knows better than to interrupt me unless it's urgent.

"Yes?" I clip, picking up on the second ring.

"I'm sorry to interrupt, sir. There's someone on the line, a house-keeper? She says your father needs you—urgently." Her rushed words send a jolt of dread through me. With a curse, I thank her and hang up, my jacket already half on as I gather my things.

Seamus is hot on my heels as he asks, "What can I do?"

Meeting his dark gaze, I fill him in as we leave the office with little more than a barked command at Brenda to clear my schedule and hold my calls.

"Make sure this doesn't leak. If anyone asks, I had an urgent ap-pointment I forgot about. If they keep pressing, make up an excuse that keeps the focus on me," I instruct him as we make our way to the underground car park. With a clipped nod, he dips into his car as I get into mine. Letting out a breath to centre myself, I peel out of the car park, heading for Da's house. Sheila, his housekeeper, wouldn't call the office looking for me if it wasn't urgent. He wouldn't let her. That, coupled with his disappearing act lately, worries me. Who the hell knows what I'm about to walk into.

Pulling into his driveway, I abandon my car and have the front door open before Sheila can even move. She's been our housekeeper since I was a kid. She is by no means a stranger to the violence and hor-rors that go hand in hand with being Irish mafia, so the frantic look in her eyes as she ushers me in has a rock wedging its way in my rib cage.

"He's in his room," she explains as she leads the way, only to stop outside his splintered doorway. Turning her hazel eyes on me, she places her hand on my arm. Motherly concern radiates from her as she warns me to brace myself. Swallowing past the lump in my throat, I dip my chin and ease the door open.

Jonathan O'Neill Sr has always been a force to be reckoned with, but the man in front of me is a shadow of the man I idolised growing up. Gaunt, dishevelled, bed bound in the late afternoon—words I never thought I would use to describe the man who taught me how to dismember a body on my thirteenth birthday. His wheezing breaths have me freezing at the foot of his bed as he struggles to open his glazed eyes.

Frail is not a word I ever thought I'd use in conjunction with Da, but as I take him in, it's the only word that comes to mind. Guilt slams into me. I should have demanded to see him before now. Whatever plagues him should never have gone unchecked for so long.

"Son? Is that you, Junior?" he rasps, eyes looking through me rather than at me.

"I'm here, Da. Why didn't you tell me things weren't going so well? Let me phone Doc." Before I can pull my phone out, he's already shaking his head, his hands trembling.

"No. The men can't know. They'd oust me. We can't risk it, not now. Not with Angus spiralling out of control. We can't let that son of a bitch know. He'd use it to his advantage. Bastard is already up to no good," he spits.

"Trust me, okay?" I plead. The thought of letting whatever's wrong with him go unchecked a moment longer has me grinding my teeth. No fucking way am I risking his health over his pride. Rather than answering me, he just rests his head back against the pillows and lets sleep pull him under. Slipping out of the room, I catch Sheila's eye, indicating for her to follow me further down the hall.

"What the hell is going on?!" I demand in a hushed whisper.

"He barricaded himself in his room a few weeks ago, but he accepted his meals and left the trays outside his door. I just assumed he was attending to urgent business and didn't want to be disturbed. Then, this morning, I knocked but got no answer. When I came back up to collect the tray, it hadn't been touched, so I tried again. Still no answer. That's when I forced my way in," she confesses, heat rising to her cheeks as she explains why the door to his room is damaged, though that's the least of my concerns.

"Your niece is a nurse, isn't she?" I frown, mentally flicking through our limited options. Normally, everything medical is dealt with by Doc, and then we go from there, but news of us calling him will travel through the ranks like wildfire.

"Yes…but only just. This might be a bit complex for her. She only graduated last year," she rushes to explain, but I've already made up my mind. This is the way we'll get him outside help without alerting the masses.

"Then get her to bring a doctor she trusts. They'll be heavily compensated for their time." As I raise an eyebrow at her, she catches my drift and scampers down the hall to make her call. Slumping against the wall, I let out a sigh before pulling my phone out.

Time to call in reinforcements.

JONATHAN
CHAPTER 4

"Run that by me again, this time like I'm some pimple faced teenager fresh from St Theresa's," Ciaran drawls, leaning forward to brace his forearms on his knees. His slightly less psychotic but way more neurotic twin, Brennan, hovers behind the sofa, looking equal parts confused and intrigued.

"Jesus Christ. Did you hit your head? What's so fucking hard to understand? It's the same shit we've been doing, just to a higher degree. Johnny needs our help picking up the slack while Senior's busy. If we can find out what the hell Graham is up to at the same time? Even better." Seamus' blind trust is both a curse and a blessing. There are days the weight of it threatens to pull me under, but then the next day, it'll have me feeling higher than an addict after their latest fix. Responsibility may be my birthright as much as the Four Points empire, but that doesn't make it a comfortable skin to wear.

"Where the hell will Senior be while we run the show?" Bren drawls, eyes narrowed in on me. Fucker always was too suspicions for his own good. Or, in this case, *my* own good.

"Busy. Now, can we focus, or should I let him know you're questioning his orders?" I throw back.

"This is fucking bullshit. We're expected to break our backs running this shitshow while he, what? Fucks some whore? And gets all the credit at the same time? Fuck that," Ciaran fumes, destroying the last remnants of my patience. In seconds, I have him shoved against a wall, fist pulled back, ready to unleash the pent-up emotions that have had me in a chokehold for longer than I care to admit.

"Calm the fuck down, both of you. Jonathan, you know damn well we're on your side. Always have been and always will be. Ciaran, pipe the fuck down for once, would you?" The frustration dripping from Jack's tone as he wedges his way between us, breaking my hold on Ciaran, says it all.

"If you can't give us, *who are on your side,* an answer, then how the fuck do you think you'll stand up to being quizzed by the others? It's already suspicious that he wouldn't tell them he's preoccupied himself, never mind when you factor in his disappearing act lately. You can't afford to be overly defensive," Declan adds, ever the voice of reason. Letting out a grunt, I begrudgingly step away from Ciaran.

"He's out of the country, okay? That's all I'm at liberty to say." I exhale slowly, tossing him the letter I had Da sign and date earlier. Silently, Declan scans it before passing it back to me with little more than a nod of acknowledgement.

"Great. Now, what's the first thing you need us need to tackle?" Seamus cuts in, trying to wrangle us back on track.

"We need to split up. I'm needed back at O'Neill's HQ, but I can work on fielding his emails and staying on top of all things Four Points while I'm there. Bren and Jack, take the clubs. Make sure the girls are safe, and the men are happy, yeah? Ciaran, keep an eye on our new recruits. Weed out any who either won't make it or seem suspicious; get Dec to help you. Seamus, you take the restaurants. In the meantime, keep your ears to the ground. If you hear so much as a whisper of discontent, tell me. If you hear anything about what Angus is up to, dig as deep as you can without getting caught." With muttered agreements, they clear out, leaving me to my thoughts for the first time in days.

After getting Sheila's niece to come to the house, things have been chaotic. It only took Dr Hawkins a few tests to determine the worst: stage 4 lung cancer. Before the news had even sunk in, they were talking about treatment plans and begging me to get him to agree to a trip to the hospital. Easier said than done. Da is determined to keep this under wraps until the bitter end, consequences be damned.

Thoughts of the fallout this will cause for the Four Points is enough to give me a headache. Sure, I'm his only heir, and he has been training me since before I could walk to follow in his footsteps, but the fact remains: currently, I am not his underboss, his consigliere, or anything else, nor have I been recognised as his successor. Right now, it would be easier to get a seat at the royal family's dinner table than claim what's rightfully mine.

Heading into the kitchen to grab my keys and briefcase, I pull out my phone to check in with Sheila. As much as she's promised updates, I can't help but worry.

"Good morning, Mr O'Neill," she greets, sounding harried. Knowing Da, he's probably making her life a living hell. Sitting still and taking orders is as foreign to him as stepping into his size nines is to me.

"How is he?"

"Nothing's changed. The oxygen tank seems to be helping, but he's still struggling without it, and his appetite has yet to return. So far, the shakes seem to be going well, but he's still got a lot of weight to regain. Sharon and Dr Hawkins are taking turns keeping watch over him." Her run down does little to comfort me, but at least things aren't worsening. With a gruff reminder to contact me—night or day—if anything changes, I hang up before dipping into my Bugatti and making the short commute to HQ.

It's not until I'm walking the executive floor alone that I realise there's a sense of quiet that feels out of place. I've never once entered this building without Brenda ready to flank me to my office, giving me a summary of things with a coffee either in hand or waiting for me on my desk. Yet today, nothing but silence greets me.

Frowning, I set my things on my desk before heading back out to find out where the hell my assistant is. It's not like her not to communicate with me if she's not going to be here—I can count on one hand the number of times that has happened over the last three years. Finding her desk cleared out and all her personal touches missing, I head out to the hallway on the hunt for answers.

"You. What's your name?" I bark at the first person I see, some terrified kid who looks like he just left school. Granted, we're probably only a few years apart, but I doubt this kid has ever so much as killed an insect, never mind something a little more…living.

"S…Sa-ul, sir," he squeaks, going fire engine red at the crack in his voice.

"Where's Brenda?" Jerking my thumb back at my office, I watch as his eyes grow impossibly wide while he struggles to stutter out a response.

"She's not here," he finally chokes out. Feeling a headache coming, I pinch the bridge of my nose and let out a breath before I snap this kid's neck.

"I can see that. What I want to know is where she is and when she'll be back," I retort, watching him shrink in fear as he scrambles for something to say. Poor kid wouldn't last five minutes in the Points.

"Jonathan." The sharp click of high heels and the even sharper snap of my name draws my attention away from Saul. Turning to face the fierce redhead currently stalking my way, I hold my hands up in mock defence. Donna is our head honcho up in HR, not someone you want to fuck with. She's also Jack's soon-to-be wife. It's unclear which taught her to be a chief ballbuster, but I know I couldn't run this place without her.

"Yes?" I drawl, quirking an eyebrow at her as she advances on me until she's only a few feet away.

"Let's walk and talk, shall we?" It's not really a question, but I humour her by nodding along and following as she leads us back to my office.

"Cut to the chase, Donna. Where's my EA?" Sighing, I hold my office door open for her before following her in. It's barely even eight and, already, today has been far too fucking long.

"Brenda no longer works for us."

"What? How did this happen? I was only out of the office a couple of days." I frown, trying to recall if she had mentioned being unhappy. "Did we offer her a raise? More annual leave?"

"All of that and more, but she wanted to be at home to look after her grandkids, and her son in law was willing to pay her. She didn't even hand in her notice, forgoing her final pay check in her hurry to get out of here." Her words are a well-aimed arrow that have me grabbing my chest, feigning being wounded.

"I did nothing, your honour. You have my word."

"Likely story. Either way, you're down an EA until I can get you a replacement. The plan was for Saul to step in, but I can see that's not going to work," she muses, taking a seat in front of my desk.

"That kid? How'd he even get a job here?" I snort, moving my chair so I can take a seat.

"Watch your tone. He's only a year younger than you, so I'd lay off the kid remarks. And he's surprisingly good at what he does. But moving on from him: how about Ella? She could make a good stand in," she offers, naming her executive assistant.

"Fine, but how long is it going to take to get a replacement? This is the last thing I need right now." I blow out a breath, trying to do the mental maths of the hiring process. I need someone competent, and I need them now. I've no doubt Jack will have shared some of our meeting with her, so surely, she understands the why without me having to spell it out to her.

"Hopefully, not too long. I have the first batch of interviews scheduled for later today, with the last few wrapped up by Friday afternoon.

We should have it narrowed down to the top candidates for you to review by Monday afternoon, and then we'll expedite the pre-employment checks," she reassures me before pinning me under her mother hen look and asking, "Now, enough about all that. How's the family situation?"

"Stressful, but what family situation isn't?" I toss her a smile. "I want to sit in on the interviews."

"That's not a good idea. Don't you remember the last time? You scared them half to death," she reminds me with an eye roll before chucking the pen that's always wedged either in her hair or behind her ear at me.

Dodging it with a chuckle, I hold up my hands. "And weeding out the ones who wouldn't last a week is a bad thing?" At her pointed glare, I concede. "Fine. I won't say anything, you'll hardly notice I'm there."

"Give me your word," she demands, her eyes narrowing into slits.

"You have my word." After assessing me for a moment, she gives me the details with a roll of her eyes before leaving me to catch up on what I missed.

HELEN
CHAPTER 5

A lot can change in two years, and yet, at the same time, some things never do. I might have spent the last year keeping a low profile, trying to shake my accent and working a myriad of agency jobs, but the second I saw a job opening as an executive assistant at O'Neill's Corporation HQ, I had the application filled out before I'd even finished my morning coffee. You can take the girl out of the mafia, but turns out, you can't take the mafia out of the girl. Working for a rival mafia might be a recipe for disaster, but at the same time, where better to hide than in plain sight? Or at least that's what I'm telling myself. Desperate times call for desperate measures, and the state of my bank account, thanks to a sudden lack of temp work, says it all.

But still, this interview is little more than practice. It doesn't truly count if they turn me away. It's highly unlikely my paper-thin résumé will land me the job. Honestly, I'm shocked it even landed me an interview. Sure, I need the job, and I absolutely need the money, but there's bound to be a hundred more qualified people interviewing.

During my time in the waiting room, I've seen two other candidates come and go. The confidence in their strides alone had me questioning why I'm putting myself through this. Interviews are a form of torture, and anyone who enjoys them is a psychopath. Letting the agency hook me up with a new temp post would be the smart thing, the responsible thing. The *safe* thing. If I leave now, it's no harm, no foul. Edging forward, I have one hand on my bag, ready to bolt, when a serious-looking redhead enters the room, clipboard in hand, a professional yet polite smile on her face.

So much for dipping out of here.

"Helen Mongomery?"

"That would be me." I offer her a smile, following her as she leads me down the corridor. From the moment I crossed the threshold, it has been clear no cost has been spared—chandeliers, lush cream carpets accented by oak hardwood floors and marble surfaces, high-end brands scattered around like it's nothing. This place screams money in a way I should be used to, and yet, it still takes my breath away. There's a distinct difference between buying lavish things you probably can't *actually* afford to show off your wealth, and the casual-yet-undisputable evidence of it, this building has. I can only imagine how luxe the executive floor is.

Entering the interview room behind the redhead, I'm still taking in the impressive décor when my eyes land on the imposing figure in one of the chairs on the other side of the table. Even without my upbringing, I would know this man radiates power, danger, and more red flags than should be normal. It's more than just his clenched jaw, muscles tensed like he's ready to leap into action at a moment's notice, and the glower on his face. It's in the way he commands all the energy in the room without so much as moving a muscle. It's the way he has perfectly placed himself near the exits. A man like him would never be cornered. Even before the introductions happen, I know in my very soul he is no doubt a member of the Four Points. To my great disdain, he's undeniably handsome, that classic kind of attractive that stabs you in the heart and sends you to your knees. His eyes are so blue, they put the ocean to shame, and his jaw is something angels would weep over. He drips effortless perfection and oozes confidence from his very pores, all from a seat behind a table. I fear I wouldn't be able to cope if I were cursed with the full vision him standing would provide.

Swallowing is a challenge, but I manage it—barely.

As the redhead rounds the table, taking her seat beside him, I take the only chair on this side of the table. It puts me directly in front of him, and I have to fight the urge not to shuffle it over a few inches to face the woman instead. Unfortunately for my nerves, showing such a weakness isn't in my marrow. Father made sure of that.

"Welcome. I'm Donna. This is Jonathan. You're Helen, yes?" Her brisk, no-nonsense tone helps me shake off the unease and focus my attention on her.

"Pleasure to meet you. Yes, I'm Helen," I confirm, noting that, while Donna looks prepared to take notes, her pen poised above her clipboard, Jonathan looks like he'd rather be anywhere else. If he leant any further back, he'd be horizontal, and the bored look on his face looks like it's glued there.

What an asshole.

"Tell us a bit about yourself. Your résumé was a bit on the thin side; can you expand on that for us?" Donna prompts, pinning me under her stare. I bet she's normally intimidating beyond belief, but beside Jonathan, who demands all the attention without even trying, she seems like the safer option. I look solely at her as I recite my now-well-practised story.

"Of course. I was raised in a very traditional household, so it's only in the past year or so, since I moved out, that I've been able to secure work for myself. My father, the old school gentleman he is, was a huge believer in women staying home to be wives and mothers, being the homemaker while the men bring home the bacon." The words taste like ash on my tongue, but it's better than the alternative. This is one of those times in life when the truth is not the answer. My words have their desired effect, the corners of Donna's mouth turning down, lips pursing like she tasted something sour. Jonathan scoffs from his seat beside her.

"How outdated," he mutters, much to my pleasant shock. Maybe he's not a total asshole after all. It would be such a shame for looks as good as his to be wasted, a true crime against womankind.

"I wholeheartedly agree. That's why as soon as I was able to secure new living arrangements, I got straight to looking for work and, as you can see from my résumé, I've done a lot of temp work as a secretary or personal assistant covering sick leave, maternity, that type of thing."

"Any reason they were all temp roles?" Donna probes, jotting something down in her notes.

"Due to my lack of experience, my options were a bit limited. I'd love something more permanent, the opportunity to get into the swing of things and find a rhythm that works, both for me and for whoever I'd be reporting to," I supply, doing my best to convey how serious I am about getting a permanent post. Temp work is great when you're in a fix, but the instability of it leaves a lot to be desired.

"And how soon would you be able to start?" Jonathan inserts himself—much to Donna's irritation, if her side eye and scoff are anything to go by. Seems like my kind of woman. I wonder if she'd be up for getting a coffee even if I don't get the job. God knows I'm in desperate need of friends, even if I do have to keep secrets from them.

"Immediately. My last position finished up a couple of weeks ago." Basically, please hire me, because I am beyond desperate. Bills are calling my name, and there's only so far I can stretch that last pay check.

"How do you feel about long hours?" he demands, leaning forward and closing the distance between us. The bite in his words and the fire in his eyes have me biting back the retort on the tip of my tongue.

"Ecstatic. Will there be notice if I need to stay past six?" I throw back, watching his eyes darken even further, and a muscle jumps in his jaw as he grinds his teeth.

"Why? Have a hot date to get to? If so, I can't see this being a good fit for you." His lip curls in distaste, and I so desperately want to slap that look off his face. A face as handsome as his should never have such an ugly expression painted across it, nor should such ugly words leave a mouth as kissable as his. It truly is a sin.

I wonder if knocking him down a peg or two would cost me the job? It might be worth it. Asshole clearly needs it.

"No, but I would appreciate knowing so I can bring dinner with me," I throw back, just about keeping my eye roll to myself.

"Dinner can be expensed," he rebukes, looking ready to launch into his next attack when Donna cuts him off with a sharp glare.

"Okay, well, I think that about covers it. Thank you so much for your time. We'll be in touch." Reading the clear dismissal, I offer her a smile and a muttered thanks before gathering my things and getting the hell out of dodge.

Talk about a domineering asshole. God help anyone unfortunate enough to have to deal with him on a daily basis.

JONATHAN
CHAPTER 6

"**A**bsolutely not." No fucking way this is going to work. That was my initial thought when Helen, in her tight skirt with her big blue eyes, followed Donna into the meeting room. She's a distraction of the highest order, which is the last thing I need right now when my Da's legacy rests heavily on my shoulders and all eyes are about to be on me, even more so than usual. Never mind the fact she's woefully underqualified and overflowing with attitude. There's no way we could work together. We wouldn't last a week before she'd be bent over my desk, getting her ass spanked raw to knock the brat right out of her.

"What the hell is the issue this time?" Donna sighs, capping her pen and slotting it into her ponytail before giving me her full attention, arms crossed, lips pursed, tapping her foot. All signs of my impending doom.

Pointing at her, I respond, "You know what! Don't give me that. Playing dumb doesn't suit you. The girl has no experience."

"Jonathan. You shot down the last nine interviewees for reasons ranging from their lack of availability to not having the balls to stand up to you. Now, it's your turn to listen." She blows out a breath, rustling her bangs. Plucking her pen out of her hair, she pokes me with it as she continues. "We're fast running out of options. She's perfect for the role, and we both know it. Now, pick: her or Saul?"

"Fucking hell, woman. That spineless piece of shit wouldn't last an hour. Fine. But if she sets one foot out of line, she's gone. No second chances, you hear me? I will not be babying her." Ignoring the smug look of satisfaction on her face, I take my leave.

As much as sitting in on these interviews has been a pain in my ass, it's also been a nice reprieve from the bigger storm brewing. But with no more excuses or distractions available, I head to the carpark while dialling Seamus.

"Anything?" I demand as soon as the call connects.

"Other than painful small talk, a few underhanded deals, and, oh! They ran out of the salmon… Nope."

"Cut the crap and be serious for a second. You know what I mean."

"I am being serious. That salmon is insane. Have you tried it?" The mirth in his tone would normally have me laughing, but these days, laughter is a foreign concept.

"I put it on the menu. What do you think? I meant anything about Angus," I clarify with a roll of my eyes as I peel out of the car park and head towards our underground torture chamber, nicknamed the Pit, to meet Ciaran.

"Nope." He pops the p. "Maybe they have access to oil or diamonds or something up there."

"You know as well as I do that the arms deal he was chasing after was easily worth five figures a month. How much oil would it take to be raking that in?"

"Shit, I don't know. Why does this even matter?"

"Because Da says it does. Because there's a rumour that whatever he is up to isn't Table approved." The implications of that hang between us like a thread neither of us want to pull. There's only one thing the five heads of the most powerful and deadly mafia factions agree on wholeheartedly, only one rule they must abide by to keep their seat at the Table. If Angus has gone against that and gotten involved in the flesh trade? God help him, for he will be spared no mercy.

The silence stretches between us for a moment, heavy with bitter understanding, before Seamus rasps, "Roger that. I'll get Brennan to do some digging for us. Speaking of the twins, you headed to meet Ciaran?"

"Yeah. Any idea what he caught?" I enquire. Ciaran's tendency to be vague at best is one of those qualities that drives me up the wall while also making him the best at sniffing out intel most would never get their hands on.

"None. He just said it was something juicy. Fill me in later?" With a grunt, I hang up on him and continue making my way to the Pit. Pulling into the car park, I abandon my car before clearing security and heading to the basement.

"You catch me something, O'Malley?" I call, strolling into the all-too-familiar room. At this point, this place may as well be my second home for the number of hours I've spent here. Spying him reclining against the wall, one foot crossed over the over, a smug smirk on his face, I make my way over to him. The quietness has me quirking an eyebrow at him in question.

"Oh, you could say that," he taunts, jerking his head for me to follow him deeper into the room. All around us are tools of the worst kind, and the urge to stretch my muscles and put some of those to good use has me salivating, wondering where the fuck his captive is.

I swear, if he dragged me out here to chat…

"Stop edging me like I'm your wife and tell me what's going on." He stops walking suddenly, and I nearly run into his back. Whirling around to face me with a manic look in his icy blue eyes, he says, "Look down, Johnny."

Noting we've approached the edge of the Pit, I glance down to see one of our new runners, bound and gagged as he thrashes widely.

The whites of his eyes are visible as he locks eyes with me and starts fighting even harder to get free.

"And what do we have here?" I drawl, prowling around to the other side of the hole, crouching down so I can see the kid better. Kid truly is the only way to describe him—he looks young as fuck.

"We have a wannabe rat. Isn't that right?" At the kid's increased mumbling and frantic head shaking, Ciaran continues, "Oh, so it *wasn't* you I saw trying to break into Senior's house? It wasn't you who was about to go in all guns blazing like some pathetic rookie hit man?"

Spitting on him, Ciaran steps back, looking at me with glee. "I caught him crawling around the house all sketchy like, a mask on and his hood pulled up. He was packing heat, too."

With a curse, I ponder aloud, "Now, what would give someone like this the idea that was a smart thing to do?"

"Probably someone whispering in his ear, full of false promises."

"Question is, who?"

"Only one way to find out."

Sharing a dark look, we act at the same time, reaching to grab the kid by his ankles and armpits. Ignoring his wiggling, we wrangle him over to the meat hooks and get him hooked up just how we like them: Immobile. Helpless. Stretched to the point of pain. All their vulnerable areas exposed.

"Here's how this is going to work. We're going to ask you questions. If you answer them, we'll only beat you up a little. If you don't or you lie, we'll start removing body parts," I drawl, unbuttoning my cufflinks and rolling up my sleeves. Slipping one of the black rubber aprons we keep down here over my white shirt, I pick up a rusty knife from the array of tools beside me. Ciaran lets out a cackle as he joins me in getting ready, shouldering his hatchet before joining me in front of our captive.

Reaching up, he yanks the gag out to a steady stream of pleas and apologies that fall on deaf ears. I jerk my chin at Ciaran. With a manic chuckle, he lands a punch before prowling around to take his place behind the captive, resting his chin on his shoulder and muttering, "Now, now, enough of that. You heard the man. All we want are some answers out of you. Easy peasy, right?"

Watching him struggle not to let out more noise, I tip his chin back with edge of my knife.

"Let's start easy, shall we? What's your name?"

"Co…Colin, sir," he stutters, his Adam's apple bobbing with his struggle to swallow around his nerves.

"See how easy that was? Now, Colin, what were you doing outside Senior's house? Surely, you've been told that's off limits to specks of dirt like you by now." I curl my lip in disgust as he whimpers, and his eyes glow glassy. Fucking pussy. Whoever recruited him needs to relearn what it takes to be a Four Points member, because this sure as shit isn't it.

"I…I didn't know… I thought it was a random house." The thing about this job is, you learn how to weed out liars early on. Everyone has tells, and detecting those tells is all too easy when you've clocked as many hours down here as we have. Between the frantic, almost skittish expression on Colin's face to the way he can't maintain eye contact, he gives himself away instantly.

"You thought a house in our gated community, with our emblem engraved on the front fucking door, was a random house?" I snarl, spit flying as I apply pressure to the knife currently wedged under his chin.

"That sounds like a lie to me." Ciaran sighs, that manic look in his eyes returning. Quicker than Colin can flinch, I draw my knife down and slam it into his thigh, listening to him howl in pain.

Little does he know, that's nothing compared to what he has coming his way.

Stepping back, I wipe the blood on my hand on the apron and grab a pair of pliers. While he's busy whimpering about his stab wound, I clamp the pliers around one of his fingers, relishing in the crunch as I rid him of the useless digit. For a second, he goes silent as all the blood drains from his face, and then he lets out a noise only dogs should be able to hear.

"Let's try that again, shall we? *What the fuck were you doing at my Da's house?*" I roar, taking great pleasure in his flinch, only to freeze as he realises that just presses him even closer to Ciaran. With a chuckle, Ciaran swings his signature hatchet to the ground, taking great joy in the kid's whimper at the clang.

"It was just meant to be a quick in and out," he cries, glancing between us as if he doesn't know who to fear the most. That's the smartest choice he's made so far. Depending on the day and circumstances, the answer to that varies. Right now, though, we're pretty neck in neck and equally sick of this bullshit.

"We're going to need more than that, kid," Ciaran chimes in, making a show of reaching for his hatchet again.

"No, please! I'll…I'll tell you everything, just not that. Please!" It's always amusing to watch realisation sink in that the Butcher Brothers isn't some cute nickname Ciaran and Brennan have. Seeing either one of them handle a hatchet always serves as a surefire way to loosen tongues.

"Then. Talk," I growl, wrenching my knife free and wiping the blood across his cheek, pressing the tip into it to draw his eyes back to me.

"I was meant to see if he was really out of the country, that's it! No one was meant to get hurt," he explains frantically, looking between us for a scrap of mercy he won't find.

"Who sent you?" I growl, spitting directly into his face and watching it land beside his eye.

"My dad!" he damn near squeals like a pig. Scanning my mental memory of the ever-growing family trees of the Four Points draws me a blank. When I look at Ciaran, he just shrugs, equally as lost. It's impossible to keep up with everyone when half these fuckers are popping out a new kid every year like it's going out of fashion.

"And just who the hell is your dad?" I bark, slicing into his cheek and relishing the scream he lets out.

"Billy Hayes," he finally confesses, looking at me with wild eyes, begging for this to be the end of his suffering. I'm too frozen in shock to deal with him. Looking behind him, I meet Ciaran's gaze, who, for once, looks horrified. And for good reason—Billy is our current underboss, my dad's second. If he's sending his son to snoop around then, shit just hit the fan even quicker than I was expecting.

Fucking perfect.

JONATHAN
CHAPTER 7

With the weight of Colin's confession hanging in the air, we work in silence to rebind, gag, and secure him before making our way outside. This is the absolute last thing I need right now. I'd already been working on the best way to make it clear, under no uncertain terms, that the Four Points would be staying in the family. With Billy being Da's second, he stood to be my biggest obstacle or biggest supporter. Guess we know which way he's leaning now. There's no way in hell I'm letting him take over. I've been raised for this my whole life, sacrificed more than most. I'm not letting that be in vain.

"What now?" Ciaran muses, lighting a cigarette as we exit the building

Wrinkling my nose at the offensive smell, I grouse, "That shit will kill you."

"I'm more likely to die on the job," he rebukes with a roll of his eyes as he props a foot up on the bumper of his car. Conceding his point, I let it drop.

"I need to schedule a meeting with Billy and iron this shit out. But first, I need to pay a visit to Da's house. Someone needs to make sure Sheila has everything under control," I answer his original question, leaving out that I also want to see how Da's doing with my own eyes and up his security measures.

"Need backup?"

"Not yet. Head back to Dec and continue vetting the new recruits. I'll link in with you later." With little more than a dip of his chin, he watches me leave. It's getting clearer by the day. I need to nip this rising discontent in the bud before things get out of control. At face value, it should be simple: a few beat downs, a show of power or two. But when you factor in keeping the legal front running and the sixty hours a week that takes, it's not quite so straight forward. And of course, the timing of everything had to coincide with my EA problem. Fucking typical. God forbid I catch a break.

Pulling up in front of my childhood home, I push thoughts of things I can't change for now to the side. Even on his sick bed, Da is all too likely to pick up on it, and stress is the last thing he needs right now.

Growing up, this place always felt like a safe haven from the madness outside these walls. Da was adamant about keeping our home life as separate from everything as possible. But now, everything feels cold and hollow. Lifeless. Still in a way it never was. When I call out for Sheila, only silence greets me. Frowning, I head up to Da's room, wondering where she is. My question is soon answered when I spy Sheila sleeping, a book in her lap, at his bedside as he watches her with a soft look on his face. Looks like the old man still has a soft spot for her after all these years. I used to wonder why he never made a move, but as age opened my eyes to what goes bump in the night, that question answered itself.

"Son," he rasps before letting out a rickety cough, startling Sheila awake. Seeing me standing in the doorway, she jumps up. A blush heats her cheeks as she stumbles through her excuses before brushing past me and leaving us.

Walking over to take her place, I tease him, "Better be careful, old man. Sheila has the hots for you."

"Stop talking out of your ass and get over here," he grumbles with a heavy sigh, rolling his eyes at me.

"Ah, I see. You're still living in denial." Flipping the chair around, I straddle it, hanging my forearms off the sturdy wooden back while I take him in. He's lost more weight, and that cough still doesn't sound good, but there's more life in his eyes than there has been.

"Why are you here? Or is your sole purpose in life to test me?"

"I came to see how you are, if you must know."

"I've told you, I'm fine." His statement would be a lot more convincing if he didn't have to stop to cough into his handkerchief. We both avert our eyes, pretending not to notice it's stained red now.

"Come on, Da. Stop bullshitting me. I'm on your side. I'm doing everything I can to keep this ship sailing but I need you to be honest with me, or it's never going to work." I sigh, bracing my elbows on the back of the chair and running a hand over my jaw. Frowning at the stubble that scratches my palm, I make a note to shave later.

Taking pity on me, he sighs. "I'm as fine as I can be. There're bad days, but there are also good days, son. Sheila is taking good care of me. You'll look out for her for me, won't you?"

"Of course. She's family. But you're going nowhere, okay? You need to help sort out this mess before you get to skip out on your responsibilities," I joke, drawing a dry laugh from him before he turns serious on me.

"When you get to my age, son, you'll realise it's the little things that are the most important, not power or money. Promise me you'll give some thought to finding a nice girl one day? I want you to be happy; to know the comfort only a woman can bring to your life."

"Da..." I trail off. We've had this same tired argument time and time again. I'm no closer to changing my mind than I was the last time he tried to persuade me.

"Johnny. I know you're young now, but you won't always be. Just humour an old man, will you? Please." Hearing my Da, the Boss of the Irish Mafia, utter a plea is so out of the ordinary, I'm helpless but to dip my chin as my walls crumble a little under his insistence.

"Okay, fine, I'll think about it…if you think about making that will before you can't," I implore, only for him to wave me off like he did the last time I brought this up. Stubborn fucker. And he wonders where I get it from.

"Da, I'm serious. If you don't, who knows what will happen to the Four Points?" I toss out there, hoping the mention of his pride and joy will make him see the severity of things.

"What do you mean, what will happen? It'll stay within the family, as it should. This is the family business, son. Why the hell do you think I've had you shadowing me since you could walk and talk, huh?" he snaps, looking more like himself than he has in months. There's fire in his eyes, as if he's ready to leap out of the bed and into action at a moment's notice. Fuck, how I'd kill to see him do so.

"I know that, but *they* don't. And we both know they won't take my word for it," I tell him, the same old argument we've had on and off for years now. Da's always been a stickler for the old ways, even as the rest of the Points has moved into the twentieth century.

"Then you fight for it. You grab it by the bloody throat and make it yours. This is the fucking mafia, son, and you'll do it the mafia way. None of this legal shit." He sniffs, shifting against his pillows and looking one wrong move away from launching into a lecture.

"Humour me. Write it up, but I'll still do you proud and fight for it. Deal? It's about time Billy was knocked down a peg or two anyway." At his reluctant nod and dropping eyes, I tell him I'll get the lawyer out here tomorrow and leave him to give into the tiredness he's no doubt been fighting. When I catch Sheila in the hall, she offers me a tentative smile, which I return by pulling her in for a quick hug before making my exit.

Cracking my neck, I let out a sigh before once again hitting the road—this time on my way to a sit down with Billy Hayes. No time like the present to put him in his place, and what better place to do it than at O'Neill's, my very own pride and joy?

As I'm led into through the doors to the VIP area, I mentally prepare myself for the war of wits that's bound to be waiting for me. By design, I'm first to arrive, so, taking my seat, I order a bottle of McCallen twenty-five for the table and two glasses while waiting for my guest to show up. Billy has been at my Da's side since before I was born, but that doesn't give him any right to send his son snooping, to challenge my father's orders, or to question me. It's my job to remind him of that tonight. Whether he likes it or not doesn't matter. People like him can be replaced in a heartbeat if necessary.

It's about time he learnt just how replaceable he is.

Ten minutes later, five minutes late to our impromptu meeting, Billy strides in, puffing out his chest and acting like he owns the place. Funny—I don't see *his* name on the door.

"Nice of you to join me." I nod to the chair in front of me for him to take a seat. He doesn't deserve a respectful greeting. Maybe if he was on time, but then again, after today, probably not even then.

"What can I do for you?" he asks, leaning back in his seat and helping himself to the whiskey between us without so much as asking or offering me a top up. Rude bastard.

"It's funny you should ask. You'll never believe who I crossed paths with today," I muse, catching the waitress' eye as she makes to approach the table. With a subtle shake of my head, she turns and leaves us.

"It wouldn't be your father, would it? I've been meaning to give him a call. He must need my help with whatever is keeping him so occupied." Not bloody likely.

"Oh no, much closer to home. Your home, at that. Say, I wasn't aware your son had joined our ranks," I muse, watching him freeze for a split second before he launches into his lies.

"My Colin? Well, not yet, but as soon as he's eighteen, I'll be putting him forward. He's an excellent shot already. Taught him myself. He'll make a great addition to our ranks," he blusters, a bead of sweat forming at his temples that he dabs away.

"That's odd. If he's not one of us, then how come he was found outside my father's house today?" I drawl, watching the colour leave his face as his eyes frantically scan the room. If he's looking for an escape, he won't find one, nor will he find any lies to feed me.

"You know, now that I think about it…Colin has recently joined. You know what it's like to keep track of who's doing what. I'll talk to him, see why he was there. Don't you worry—I'll get to the bottom of this." He laughs, adjusting his shirt collar and avoiding my eyes.

"I imagine that might be rather difficult," I drawl, a smirk tugging at the corners of my mouth as I draw a circle on the table in the ring of condensation from my glass.

"What…what do you mean?" He dabs at the sweat beading along his forehead again, flicking his eyes between me and the room behind me.

"Well, you see, as you are aware, we don't take trespassers lightly. Or rats. Things like that need to be delt with swiftly. I'm sure you understand." Emotions fly across his face: confusion, horror, fear, disbelief before he tries and fails to school his features into something a mask of cool disinterest.

"You don't mean…" He trails off, as if not speaking it into existence can change things.

"I fear I do. Your Colin is in the Pit and will remain there until I'm sure you can be trusted. *If* you can be trusted. Now, care to confess why you sent him snooping? That's right—he squealed like a little pig. It only took three removed fingers." God, I wish I could tape this moment. Ciaran would love it.

"Why, you little-" He tries to lunge across the table for me, sending the perfectly good whiskey flying. But before he can wrap his hand around my throat, I twist his wrist behind his back, leaning closer to snarl, "I can, and I did. Now, confess your sins, William, or your son will pay for them."

Releasing him, I watch as he falls to a puddle on the floor. Brushing himself off, he stands and glares at me as he sneers, "You're not the boss and never will be, you little shit. Now, get Senior on the phone so the real men can talk."

"I wish you could stick around long enough to eat your words, but I fear that won't be possible," I muse, clicking my fingers. In a split-second, Seamus comes strolling out of the shadows with Jack and Brennan in tow.

"Why don't we reunite you with your son for now? There's plenty room in the Pit for one more," I taunt as we make quick work of binding him and carrying him out a back entrance and throw him into the boot of the waiting SUV. His protests and smack talk fall on deaf ears. He's a bigger idiot than I gave him credit for if he thought he could take my Da's position, my birthright, right out from under our noses.

HELEN
CHAPTER 8

After that car crash of an interview, the last thing I expected was a call from Donna hours later, congratulating me on my new job. Questioning the hows and whys would be looking a gift horse in the mouth, and I may be blonde, but I'm not stupid. Instead, I thanked her and told her I couldn't wait to get started. With instructions to meet with her at seven a.m. sharp on Monday, we hung up. I then spent the weekend panicking over what to wear and ruined my new manicure by biting my nails.

By the time Monday crawled around, I was no less nervous, and as the intimidating high-rise office came into view, the reality that I'm about to be a sheep in the wolf's den has me questioning if I shouldn't run and hide before it's too late.

Breath, Helen. Lift your chin, push your shoulders back, and smile.

Smoothing my hands down my navy pinstripe skirt and tugging at the matching jacket, I take a deep breath in. It's just a job. I can do this. I doubt I'll even cross paths with any of the O'Neill's themselves. Angus would never be caught dead doing a day's work, so I can't see why other factions would be any different. All mafia men are the same: entitled wankers, through and through—though maybe I should have picked the sensible black pantsuit just in case. But alas, the urge to look my best and make a good impression on my first day won out.

Pushing open the heavy glass door, I'm immediately assaulted by the hustle and bustle. While the streets outside might be filled with commuters, half asleep and guzzling down coffee, here, it's like people have been awake for hours, and everyone is on a mission. Getting a visitors pass, I make my way over to the bank of lifts as clipped conversations float around.

Following Donna's instructions to meet with her first and get my new hire paperwork squared away has a fresh ball of nerves settling in my stomach. No matter how often I hand over my falsified documents, the dread this will be the time I'm caught and my life implodes never lessens. The fact she still hasn't shared with me who I'll be reporting to doesn't help my rising anxiety. Still, the general camaraderie I've witnessed so far has me excited to find out. Everyone seems genuinely happy to be here, which speaks volumes.

Knocking on the open door to her office, I pop my head in with a smile.

"Nice and early. He'll love that. Now, let's get this paperwork sorted, shall we?" It's a rhetorical question, so with a smile in place and hands folded in my lap, I don't offer any comment as she shuffles some papers on her desk until she finds what she's looking for.

"I trust you brought the hard copies of your qualifications with you?" she asks, quirking a brow at me.

"Here they are," I offer, handing them over before wiping my sweaty palms on my skirt.

"Perfect. I'll get these scanned onto the system and returned to you today." Setting them to one side, she settles into her chair before launching into the typical new hire speech. Wrapping up her information overload, she lets out a laugh at the lost look on my face.

"Don't worry. If you have any questions, you can send me an

email. Now, let's show you to your desk and introduce you to every-one." As I follow her through the busy office space, it's clear that in the time we've been doing my induction, morning chatter has settled into something distinctly more work focused. Hardly anyone looks up as Donna strides past with me in her wake, and I can already tell I'm going to fit right in. There's nothing worse than an office full of slackers who rush to look busy when management appears.

"If you'll recall from the ad, you'll be reporting directly to our CEO. He can be a bit of a hard ass, but he'll warm up to you as long as you keep on top of your duties. Pay attention to how he likes things done, and you'll be fine. And the best perk about reporting to him is, this is your office," she explains, leading me into a glass office before I can even clarify that, *no,* I did not know that. Any word of protest is stolen from me as I take in my new space. It screams pure luxury, and having my own separate office, albeit with a connecting door to my boss', feels like a massive leap up the corporate ladder. It sure as hell doesn't hurt that, as the door closes behind me, the noise from outside gets muffled. Pure and utter bliss.

Setting my bag on the desk, I take in the open space with visions of leaving my stamp on this place. With three glass walls, the lighting is fantastic and offsets the dark grey of the fourth wall perfectly. Before I can get lost in my head, Donna makes her way over to the solid oak door connecting my office to my new boss'. She raps her knuckles against it before entering a code and pushing it open, indicating that I should follow her.

As my eyes lock on that head of dark hair, five o'clock shadow, and dark expression, I know I am utterly screwed. His presence fills the room just as efficiently as his cologne, blanketing it in a dark cloud of barely-contained emotions as he lounges in his chair like a king on his throne. Of course, the asshole from my interview is the damn CEO. Cold dread creeps in as the implications of who I'm staring at sink in. Jonathan *O'Neill.* Heir to the Four Points.

The need to keep my identity a secret has never been more urgent.

The storm brewing in his eyes has me shuffling my weight from foot to foot, trying not to wince at the dull throbbing already starting to kick in. I knew I should have stuck to flats.

"Jonathan, you remember Helen, your new EA. Helen, this is our fearless leader. I'll leave you two to get settled. Someone from IT will be down shortly to get Helen all set up. Jonathan, play nice." With that warning, she leaves me to the wolves with little more than a pat on the shoulder as she strides away like a woman on a mission. Her ability to walk so effortlessly in heels that high truly is an accomplishment. I wonder if she could give me pointers.

"I don't have time to baby you, so keep up. Any questions, don't ask me unless you've exhausted all options. Once IT gets you set up, check your emails. Your to do list is there." Disdain drips from each word, and the dismissal is clear even before he drops his eyes back to his computer, waving me away.

So, this is how it's going to be? Fine.

If he thinks he can intimidate me, he's got another thing coming.

I didn't survive eighteen years in the Clan under Angus' rule and two years on the run by being weak or spineless. Time to show Mr CEO just who he hired.

Game, set, match.

JONATHAN
CHAPTER 9

"**F**uck me." I exhale slowly. Running on three hours of sleep after another night in the Pit, means that dealing with my new EA is the last thing I have the time or patience for. I'd much rather poach someone from another department and leave them to deal with training someone new. According to Donna, that's a hard pass, something about ethics. The irony is not lost on me.

At the sight of Helen standing in my doorway, in that too tight skirt hugging every one of her sinful curves, and those God damn heels making her legs a mile long, my belief that she's the perfect distraction was hammered home. She's the kind of woman you lose hours thinking about and then lose sleep fantasising over, the kind you wind up just to see her creamy skin flush with anger while you dream about bending her over your desk and putting her in her place.

The kind I absolutely cannot afford right now.

Maybe in another life, I could have scratched that itch and got her out of my system. But not in this one. I don't have time for a hookup, and I certainly don't have the time for anything more. Dragging my palm down my face – fuck I still need to shave-, I push thoughts of her to the back burner.

After delivering Billy to his new temporary home on Friday, I've been trying to come up with a plan. I need to nip this rebellion in the bud before it spirals into something more, but at the same time, it's a careful dance of how to go about it. The men can't know Da's sick, and issuing a formal challenge for Billy's seat, while not impossible, will raise questions. Da's absence from something like that is unheard of, but it's shaping up to be the only option. It's time I remind everyone just who they answer to. This is my crown to inherit, and it's about damn time I stake my claim.

It's times like this, I wonder if Da doesn't have a point. Having someone to come home to, to relax with and forget about all the stresses of the day would be nice. But the thought of painting a target on their back soon cures me of that notion.

My phone ringing draws me out of my thoughts, and with a bitten off curse, I answer. "Yes?"

"Ryan from IT is here. He needs your signature on something before he can leave." Helen's slightly husky voice coming through the line causes me to simultaneously narrow my eyes in frustration and adjust the sudden hardness in my slacks.

"And what? You're too good to walk him in here and instead expect me to come to you?" Honestly, the nerve of this girl. She's practically begging to be put in her place—on her knees. With my cock down her throat, teaching her some manners. *Fuck.* What I wouldn't give to make that fantasy a reality.

"No, but you failed to give me the code to get into your office," she snips, hanging up on me with a huff. Her defiant nature has me fighting to hide my rock hard cock before shoving my chair back. Walking through our connecting door, I freeze at the sight that greets me.

Fucking hell is she trying to kill me?!

"What the hell is going on?" I demand, watching her jump from her bent over position looking like a deer in headlights. As she should.

At the same time, Ryan quickly averts his gaze and shuffles his feet. Fucker shouldn't have been looking in the first place. I make a note to have *Ryan's* manager made aware of his wandering eye. I also make a note to have him taken off this floor's rotation.

"I was trying to reach this stupid switch," she snarls, blowing a wayward curl out of her eyes and glaring at me. Her pale skin is flushed a delicious shade of pink. I bet she turns the same colour when she comes, and, fuck, do I want to see that. I want to find out how far down it travels and trace it with my tongue, only to turn her ass the same colour before claiming it as mine.

"How about next time, you walk around the desk rather than bending over it in that ridiculous excuse of a skirt and causing a scene?" I growl, snatching the pen out of Ryan's hand and sending him on his way with a glower. He scampers off with stuttered apologies.

"Men," she huffs, rolling her eyes and walking around her desk. Not a moment later, she finally gets the switch turned on with a little squeal of victory.

"See what happens when you listen to me?" I gloat, watching as she fights to keep the fury off her face as I lean against my doorway. Looks like things are shaping up to get interesting around here.

"Oh, I'm sure someone as great as yourself is always right. Thank you for that wonderful insight. Now, what's the code so we can bypass this in future?" Her sarcastic tone has me itching to make my earlier thought a reality.

Shaking that thought off, I roll my eyes as I tell her, "It's in your emails." Then, I leave without a backwards glance at the distraction that is my new PA and her ass in that skirt.

"Do you really think we'd accept that? You're low balling us, and we both know it," I drawl, winding the phone cord around my finger and leaning back in my chair as I listen to the man on the other end rush to defend his offer. Marketing doesn't come cheap, and you'd think people would understand by now that you get what you pay for. If you pay for cheap, you'll get cheap results. Alan here has been trying to weasel out of coughing up what we quoted him, demanding to speak to whoever crafted 'these ridiculous prices', which landed him a phone call with me. He probably thought this would be the kind of call where I try to smooth things over, offer him a deal, and promise to handle his case directly. He'd be sorely mistaken. One thing about me: I'll always double down on what my employees said. Even if they're wrong, I'm not going to admit that to people like Alan. No, I'll get them to cough up and then talk to whoever I need to internally to make sure the staff member doesn't make the same mistake again.

Midway through his pathetic excuses, my computer pings with a message. Wedging the phone between my shoulder and ear, I continue making listening noises as I click to open the chat.

Helen.Montgomery:
Permission to take a lunch break?

Jonathan.O'Neill:
Permission granted. Use the company card, get me a sandwich from the shop across the road. They know my order.

Helen.Montgomery:
Yes, sir. Three bags full, sir.

Biting back a laugh at her use of the classic childhood rhyme, I tune back into the conversation just in time to hear him concede and offer to pay our original quote. Smirking, I seal the deal, passing his information on to the next cog in the wheel before picking up my phone.

"Brennan, any updates?" I ask as soon as he answers.

"No one is looking for either of our little friends, not even the wife.

The chatter about Senior seems to have lost a bit of traction, at least for now. And all's fine with the clubs. How the fuck were you pulling these shifts plus the office and not collapsing?" He lists off with a groan. Sounds like the exhaustion that's been my best friend for years now is catching up to him. Welcome to the club.

"Don't remind me. That shit was killer." I snort. "That's not odd at all."

What kind of family are the Hayeses if both her husband and son have disappeared, and Mrs Hayes doesn't even bat an eyelash? The husband, I can understand, but the son? It makes no sense.

"Do some digging into the Hayeses. See if you can't find out why she doesn't care about their disappearances. And pass a message to the others to meet at Seniors after nine tonight, yeah?" At his confirmation, I hang up just as my door swings open. Looking up with a reprimand on my lips, it dies in my throat. Helen has given up on attempting to control her hair, and seeing her curls loose around her shoulders for the first time is a sight to behold.

Her arms are full of our lunch, and she's using her hip to hold the door open. Clearing my throat, I make my way over to her, relieving her of the burden of my lunch. As I do, I graze the skin of her wrist with the back of my knuckles, and we both freeze at the contact. Her eyes flash as they meet mine. It's a standoff, both of us caught in the grasp of the electric current zapping through us. Neither of us blink; hell, I don't think we breath for a solid thirty seconds as we silently weigh each other up before she mutters something about eating at her desk and excuses herself.

I almost reach out, wanting to drag her into my office, to eat with her, to catalogue her likes and dislikes. I shake that stupid notion away and watch her hips sway with her steps instead. Watching her go is both a blessing and a curse, a tease and a torment at the same time.

JONATHAN
CHAPTER 10

"**Y**ou want to issue a public challenge?" Seamus says the words slowly, drawing out each syllable like it's possible he misheard me. I can't blame him. It's practically unheard of these days and runs the risk of creating an even bigger mess for us to contain. But no matter what way I twisted the facts around in my head, I couldn't see an alternative. Protecting Da and keeping the Points in the family are the two most important things, and if killing Billy is the only way to do that, well…hand me a gun.

Glancing around the room, I take in my mates and their varying degrees of "what the fuck". It's clear they think I've lost the plot once and for all.

"It's the only way forward."

"Senior approved this?" Declan presses, bracing his elbows on his knees as he pinches the bridge of his nose. He's no doubt trying to weigh the pros and cons; fucker lives and breathes by a pro and con list.

"One better: he's going to be on video call during it." It's going to require a bit of finesse and team work to do so while keeping his health a secret, but there's a reason Brennan is considered our computer whizz. I just need to feed him enough info to help without compromising everything.

Easy.

And then maybe, I'll go out and buy a winning lottery ticket.

"How can we help?" Jack might be the one saying the words, but he's echoed by sighs and grunts of agreement that make it clear he's speaking for all of them.

"Right now, all I need is Brennan's help with some IT shit while we spread the word. Saturday, noon, at the Pit, I'm claiming Billy's spot." Shared looks of determination pass through us as we make plans to take the first steps toward our collective future. For as much as it's my seat I'm fighting for, we all know I'll be bringing them to the top beside me.

The days blur into an endless, monotonous rhythm of meetings, preparing for Saturday, and avoiding Helen as much as possible. Before I know it, everything's in place, and it's show time. Bren is at Da's house, with strict instructions to monitor the video call and interfere if the falsified background so much as glitches. Our men may be loyal to a fault, but weakness isn't something they'll take lightly. And neither is the fact we've hidden it for so long. It won't matter that he's the Boss or that I'm his heir if they think we've betrayed them.

Sheila is at Da's bedside, ready to hit the mute button if he so much as sniffles, and all the medical equipment is out of shot, with Sharon on standby to get it all back in place as soon as the call disconnects. Still, the margin for error is wider than I'm comfortable with—all it would take is one tiny slip up for everything to crumble down around us like a house of cards.

But on the other hand, a fight sounds like the perfect way to rid myself of the tension brewing to boiling point. Helen has been a test of resistance in and of herself. From her tempting outfits, which have been nothing short of a distraction for half the workforce, to her snarky attitude, it's a wonder we've made it through this first week working together. Even with Donna's warnings ringing in my ears for me to play nice, it's been far too much fun to rile her up and get a rise out of her. With every snarky demand from me, her cheeks flush, her eyes narrow, and I feel like I'm seconds away from getting a tongue lashing, only for her to let out a huff and bite back what she really wants to say. I'm dying to see if I can't make her lose her control once and for all. I bet it would be a sight to see.

Shaking off thoughts of Helen as I pull into the Pit, I pull on my leather gloves and exit my car. Rounding the corner to the back of the building with anticipation pounding in my veins, I see my mates already hard at work. I'm sure by now, they have their suspicions about what's going on, but none of them have outright asked me. For that, I'm grateful; I've never had to lie to them, and while I'd hate to start now, I'm not about to break my promise to Da.

Ciaran and Jack are in the process of laying out the rest of the tools while Seamus and Declan wrangle a spitting, furious Billy into the metal chair waiting for him. They quickly bind him to it, and if they spit on him in the process, that's between them and him. I'm sure as shit not going to tell them not to when I'm about to do a hell of a lot worse.

"Everything ready?" I ask, striding forward, glaring at Billy as I come to a stop beside him. Fuck, I can't wait to unleash all my pent-up frustration on the bastard. It's the least he deserves.

"Almost. Just need to hook up the projector to the laptop, and then we'll be sorted." Walking over to where Seamus is working on the projector, I give him a hand before sending Brennan and Sheila the green light to get things sorted on their end.

Just as we've ironed out all the kinks, the men start entering with looks ranging from confusion to bitter understanding. The older generation has never been one for asking redundant questions, so it doesn't surprise me when they just shuffle forward, brace themselves, and wait.

Equally, the confused mumblings from soldiers I went to school with, as they gather in clusters, don't come as a surprise.

"I'm sure you've gathered why we're here by now. But in case you haven't shaken off last night's hangover yet, let me spell it out for you. I, Jonathan O'Neill, challenge William Hayes for place as second, as your underboss." I have to bellow to be heard over the immediate outcry of questions and demands.

"Where's Senior?"

"What gives you the right?"

"What the fuck is going on?"

With a sigh, I nod at Seamus, who cocks his gun and fires a shot into the sky to get them to shut their traps long enough to listen.

"First, my name gives me the right, more right than Billy ever had. Second, if you would all pipe down, I'd explain what's going on. And third, Senior is here." Like a well-oiled machine, as the words leave my lips, Declan connects the video call. I have to hand it to Brennan: it's a beauty what he can craft with a few clicks of a button. Looking at it, I'd never suspect Da wasn't really on a balcony backdropped by the ocean, colour in his cheeks and light in his eyes. The picture of health and strength, a leader to his core. The fact that it's all an illusion sits heavy in my gut like lead.

"Son." He tips his head at me. We'd agreed to keep his speaking to a minimum, lest we blow our own carefully crafted story.

"As you can see, he's here, or as close as he can be, given the business he is travelling for, which dear old Willam here thought was okay to question. He sent his son on a mission to spy around Senior's house, as if he had any right to question his Boss. Turns out, that's not all he's been up to. Dear old Billy here likes to take his temper out on his wife." I spit at his feet, circling him and meeting everyone's furious gaze one by one. "Given this betrayal and the fact he's broken our code of honour, Senior thought it time to update his will. Can't have someone like that thinking they can just walk into his role, *my role*, after all. What's to stop him offing Senior to get a pay rise if he thinks it'll grant him a seat at the top?" The outrage on everyone's face encourages me to continue.

Stopping in the middle of the group, I splay my arms wide as I declare: "You're officially looking at your newly backed heir. It's no secret Da has always wanted this to stay the family business, so why Billy boy here thought he could rob me of my birthright is beyond me. Therefore, I challenge him. If he can beat me fair and square, he can remain second. For now. But if I beat him… Well." With a dangerous smile, I let the bloodthirsty energy in the air feed the beast inside of me begging to be set free.

"Is this true, Senior?" Jo, one of our most senior members, asks, gaze narrowed on the screen behind me.

"Yes. Jonathan is my heir, and there is no one else I'd rather see take the reins. One day." He manages to keep his voice sounding strong long enough to get that sentence out, but if the way his shoulders jerk afterwards is any indication, it's obvious Sheila has had to mute him. Praying no one was paying enough attention to pick up on it, I shift the focus back to what we're all here for.

"Well then, let's get this show on the road." As cheers ring out around us, I whirl to face Billy just as Jack frees him of his restraints. As soon as he's free, he lunges to his feet, spitting out his gag as he kicks the chair out of the way and makes to attack me.

Feigning left, I dodge right until I have him dizzy and confused. Using this to my advantage, I lunge for him from behind. Wrapping my hands around his throat, I drag him back into my hold, only to slam him to the ground and kneel on his back while I reach into my waistband for my knife.

Digging the tip of it into his cheek, I taunt him, "Do you think this is the same knife I used to slice and dice your boy? Wouldn't that be poetic." After tracking down Mrs Hayes and seeing for ourselves the damage father and son had done to her, dear old Colin didn't last the night. Now, it's time for Billy to meet the same fate.

With an outraged cry, he tries to overthrow me, but in his frantic motions, my hand slips down to his neck, and one wrong move on his end has my knife embedded in his carotid, blood spraying my face. As cheers rain out and satisfaction flows through me, I look up at the crowd gathered with a bloody smirk.

"Does anyone else want to challenge my father's rule? Challenge me?" When all they do is shake their heads before letting out cheers and chants of my name, I let their praise wash over me. I might a long, bloody way to go to prove my worth, and there may still be a shitstorm brewing outside this Pit, but a win is a win.

The rest of the shit calling my name can wait; tonight, we celebrate.

HELEN
CHAPTER 11

It's amazing the difference a couple of months can make. My first day jitters have long since been replaced by a quiet confidence. After a few weeks, it became glaringly obvious that Jonathan couldn't care less what I wear, just so long as I'm presentable. The days of wearing heels and attempting to style my hair are long gone. My desk is loaded with hair tools, and a pair of heels are ever present under my desk for the occasions I need to play the part of polished executive assistant and sit in on a meeting. And thank heavens for that, because running this place like a well-oiled ship is a hundred times easier when I'm not trying to pretend my feet aren't killing me.

"I need that report, Saul, and I needed it fifteen minutes ago. You don't want Jonathan breathing down your neck, do you?"

"Cecilia, since when do we not refill the coffee pot after ourselves? It's called manners, people. Use them."

"Deborah, get IT down here. The printer is still broken."

Commanding people doesn't come naturally to me, but I quickly learnt that to thrive, not just survive, it's a necessity. The best way to keep Jonathan from breathing down my neck like a pissed off dragon is to be at least five steps ahead and ensure anything that can be handled without him never crosses his desk. It's all basic maths, really. A happy CEO makes for a much happier work environment for everyone.

He's still a major asshole ninety percent of the time and grumpy to the extreme, but learning his quirks and how he takes his coffee—black, just like his soul—has done wonders in making this more bearable. It doesn't hurt that the pay more than makes up for dealing with his irate behaviour.

"Helen." Hearing my name in that deep rumble of his never fails to send shivers down my spine. Turning to face the bank of lifts, I clock his all-black ensemble and the tension radiating off of him in waves. As he makes his way across the office floor, I'm helpless but to admire the sight of him. Unfortunately, two months of working under him has done little to desensitise me.

His long strides speak to the confidence he seems to have in spades. His perfectly tailored three-piece suit, and silk shirt, look like sin against his lean frame, which is emphasised by the way he carries himself. It's a raw kind of power that speaks to me on a primal level. It makes my stomach tighten with want while my core tightens with need. Even in his bespoke suits, it's clear Jonathan is the kind of man who can make you see stars without even trying. And if he did try? You would never be the same again.

Channelling my mother, I tilt my chin up so that, despite our height difference, it looks like I'm looking down my nose at him. With a haughty tone and raised brow, I drawl, "What can I do for you?"

"You can start by explaining what the hell you're wearing." He doesn't so much as slow his stride down as he brushes past me. He's already pushing open the door to his office when I catch up with him, and, with an eye roll, I follow him as I answer.

"What, this old thing? It's called a dress," I coo, looking down at the black midi dress I picked out this morning. It cinches in at the waist and has cap sleeves with a modest neckline. It's workplace chic, certainly nothing to write home about.

"I can see that. What I can't see is any colour," he drones on as he practically inhales his coffee before getting settled behind his desk. Watching this process is a guilty pleasure of mine. First, he shrugs off his jacket before he painstakingly rolls up the sleeves of his shirt, cracking his neck, and taking a seat. Something about the whole display feels sinfully private and intimate in the most delicious way. All it's missing is a sexy as fuck slow-mo belt removal.

"Pot, meet kettle." I laugh, indicating to his own wardrobe choice with a roll of my eyes.

"Do as I say, not as I do. You're meant to be a pretty, welcoming face, not look like you're playing a widow," he replies, his gaze sweeping over me with clear distaste.

"Oh, I *know* you did not just imply I'm only here to look good," I growl, crossing my arms under my chest, only to drop them with a huff when the movement draws his eyes lower. Men.

"Just…don't let me see you wearing that again, got it? Now, what's this talk about a party tomorrow?" He frowns, scanning the Post-it note I left on his computer.

Rolling my eyes, I take a seat in front of his desk as I remind him about the fundraiser for the children's cancer charity tomorrow night. "It's taking place at that fancy hotel across the road, so no need to worry about transport. All you have to do is show face for an hour or two, shake some hands, get some photos, sign a cheque, and then you can crawl back to your bat cave."

"I certainly hope you have a better dress picked out." His muttered words cause me to frown in confusion.

"Me? I wasn't planning on going." I point to myself with a freshly manicured nail.

"Nonsense. My assistant can't not go. How would that look?" He scoffs, before sliding a card across his desk. "Use that. Get yourself something fitting for your role here. And while you're at it, get some new work wear. I'm sick of seeing the same outfits on rotation. People are going to think we don't pay you enough."

Before he's even done talking, he's turning his computer on, making it clear he's done with this conversation and on to the next thing. Having never been one to say no to something when it's free, I pick up the card, twirling it between my fingers as I toss a thanks over my shoulder and leave him to his brooding.

"What about this?" I hold up a floor length navy dress. Donna caught me as I was leaving, and the minute the word shopping came out of my mouth, she had her phone to her ear, barking commands for someone to pick up the slack while she joined me. And so, what was originally going to be a quick errand to the closest high street store quickly turned into a trip to a high-end department store with lunch on the company card as well. Any time I've brought up Jonathan needing me back, she's brushed it off with a wave of her hand, deeming this far more important. And really, who am I to argue with the head of HR?

"Do you want to blend in with the catering staff? Absolutely not. Speaking of, what on Earth are you wearing?" She frowns, looking me over from head to toe, her head cocked to the side, like she can't make sense of what she's seeing.

"Ugh, not you too. Where in the employee handbook does it say I can't wear black?" I huff, placing the dress back on the rail and hunting for another option. Honestly, you'd think I was breaking a rule with the way these two are acting.

"Technically, it doesn't —"

"Exactly! So how was I meant to know Jonathan would nearly have a heart attack at it?"

"Interesting. Well, anyway, you know now, right?" She tosses a sparkly silver dress at me, and my jaw nearly hits the ground as I catch the minuscule bunch of fabric.

"Donna, we're shopping for a work charity event, not my audition for a strip club," I hiss, shoving it back at her and making my way deeper into the store.

"We're getting nowhere with this. You! Pick out some dresses fitting for a formal event." Donna turns her attention to one of the sales associates and starts rattling off a list of demands that go over my head before she turns her green eyes back on me. Narrowing them, she cocks her head to the side.

"What bra size are you? A 32 D? Double D?"

"Donna!" I gasp, looking around, mortified, fighting the blush that wants to take over. With a roll of her eyes, she shoves me into the changing room with instructions to strip and leave it all up to her. She's a chaotic whirlwind, but I think I'm in love.

Hours later, we're seated in a private booth in a fancy restaurant, both of us a glass of wine deep, with more bags than I want to admit—and yes, the sparkly mini dress made the final cut.

"Lay it on me: how's working with the boss man going?" Donna's blunt nature still makes me jerk back in surprise, so foreign to what I grew up around. Mother would have a fit if she spent a single second with Donna. I can already hear her outcries about me being corrupted.

"It's going…fine." I shrug, swirling the dregs of my wine around the glass. With a scoff, Donna finishes her glass and tops us both off before flicking her hair over her shoulder and rolling her eyes at my diplomatic answer.

"Darling, cut the bullshit. I know that man almost as well as I know my husband. He can be an utter bastard to work for, so think of this as your chance to offload. Now, lay it on me."

"I swear, now that I've worked out what makes him tick, it is fine, but good God, is he infuriating. And stubborn. It's like he's never heard the word no! Take this fundraiser, for example—he's insisting I have to attend even though there is literally zero reason or need for me to do so." I huff, throwing my arms up in defeat.

"Oh, honey, that's *nothing*. He made Brenda, his old EA, attend my wedding as his plus one when I threatened to set him up with a friend of mine." She laughs, shaking her head fondly as she tells me countless stories about Jonathan. It's clear she's trying to help make me see him as more than just the scary CEO, but little does she know, I view him as something a hundred times worse: someone capable of blowing my whole cover story if only he dug a little deeper. Every time his attention lingers a little too long, I get cold sweats just thinking about what would happen if I was found out. What would happen to Freya, to me, to everything I've worked for. Everything I'm working towards. It's a risk I can't afford to ever take.

JONATHAN
CHAPTER 12

I could list a hundred things I'd rather be doing than attending this fundraiser and a thousand more that I *should* be doing. Yes, it's for a good cause, but my time is stretched thin as it is without wasting precious hours there. Hours I won't get back. Yet, here I am, waiting in Helen's office, looking at the time on my watch for the fifth time in as many minutes. She's late. Of course she is.

I'm in the middle of straightening my cuff links when the sound of heels on the tiled floor draws my eye. Over her two month-long tenure here, I thought I'd seen every version of Helen Montgomery there is to see. I've seen her with her curls flying wild and I've seen them tamed. In skirts and dresses that drive me wild. With and without makeup. All fired up and ready to rip me a new one or cool, calm, and collected. But the woman striding through the door like she owns it is one I've never seen before. She's fucking stunning, and what she's wearing… My gaze should not be roaming everywhere at once, but I can't fucking help it.

If I wasn't going to hell already, I'm going there now. That's where they send sinners who lust over their employees, isn't it? But fuck me. The way the maroon dress clings to her every curve, a deep vee between her breasts, is testing my strength by the second. She's done something different with her makeup as well. It's darker, edgier. It makes the blue of her eyes shine in a way I haven't seen before. She looks like a succubus ready to claim her next victim, and it's all I can do not to throw myself at her feet in offering.

This isn't my whip smart and sassy assistant I've come to tolerate and begrudgingly respect. No, this is a woman used to the finer things, who should be dripping in jewels. Anyone lucky enough to have her on their arm should be thanking a God they don't believe in that she deigns them worth her time. Visions of draping jewels around her delicate throat only to later give her a different kind of pearl necklace have me clenching my fists to stop myself from tearing that dress off her and showing her all the filthy things I want to do to her.

"Cat got your tongue?" Her red lips tip up in a knowing smirk as she sweeps her eyes over me. Entering the room, she plucks her clutch from her desk and wedges it between her arm and chest before advancing on me. I stop breathing when she reaches up to straighten my tie with narrowed precision. Her close proximity has my cock impossibly harder.

"You scrub up nice," I mutter gruffly, stepping back to put some much-needed distance between us. There's only so much a man can handle, and with all the blood rushing to my other head, being able to see the delicate curve of her breasts down her dress while inhaling her perfume is above my limit. Clearing my throat, I point to the door. "Shall we?"

We make our way to the hotel across the road, an easy, if heated, silence between us. I've never been so glad to see a room full of people demanding my attention as I am when we step foot in the function room. It's a welcome distraction from my tease of an assistant. I need to shift gears before I do something I shouldn't. The room is filled with a mix of good Samaritans, businessmen looking to cut a deal, and socialites looking to be on the front page.

Flagging down a waiter, I take the offered champagne, downing it and taking a second before glancing at Helen. Mirth dances in her eyes as she tries to keep her laugh to herself. Thoughts of leaning down, claiming her laughter for myself, and stealing her breath flood in. What I wouldn't give to taste her, to hold her, but I can't. She might drive me insane in a way that makes me want to make her mine, but that doesn't mean she deserves to be brought into the firing line of my life.

"Thirsty there, boss?" Her teasing tone would normally be something I try to snuff out, but when it comes from her…I find myself encouraging it, egging her on. Our battle of wills and sarcasm is my favourite thing about coming into the office these days.

"Something like that," I murmur, looking at her and watching her eyes droop to half-mast. Her eyes flicking between mine and my mouth, her want is clear. It's dripping from her every pore, but before I can forget myself and dip down to claim her mouth, she jerks back with a sharp inhale.

"Well. Now that you're hydrated, it's time to mingle." With that, she strides further into the room, confident I'm following, and for once in my life, the thought of following doesn't grate on my last nerve. How could it, when the view is as good as this one? I'd be a fool not to admire the gentle sway of her hips as she leads us across the room, everyone parting for her like the red sea. That dress is doing sinful things to her ass, and it's clear I'm not the only one to notice. Something hot simmers in my veins, but before I can act on it, she's linking her arm through mine. Whether she knows it or not, she's essentially branded herself as mine for the night. I should warn her what her actions imply to this room full of vultures, but instead, I embrace the feeling of her pressed against me like the selfish bastard I am.

The night passes in a blur of faceless handshakes and meaningless conversation, and before I know it, she's shoving me towards the larger than life cheque that's here purely for the photo op. The real thing has long since been cashed. Before she can dash away, I wrap my arm around her waist and tug her beside me, ignoring her gasp and the way heat rushes through me at the contact.

"If I have to suffer through this, so do you," I rasp in her ear, ignoring the shiver that races through her and her soft protest. Realising there's no easy way out, she poses beside me with a hand pressed to my chest, the sharp tips of her nails digging into my flesh as she hisses at me through gritted teeth, "You'll pay for this one, boss."

"Bring it on, sweetheart," I croon, just to watch her shiver once again as the cameras flash all around us. Da's advice echoes in my mind, and, as I look down at the top of her head, I can't help but wonder if it would be worth the risk. As she glares up at me, heedless of the cameras documenting our every expression, I shake that thought off.

Before the night is over, I leave Donna a message to get a copy of the pictures from the photographer.

Da prepared me for a lot of things in life. How to effectively run the Four Points while also running multiple businesses and understanding why the hell we bother doing so. The importance of knowing when to get your hands bloody versus when to delegate. Hell, he even taught me how to knot a tie ten different ways, and which is suitable for what occasion. But what he didn't teach me, what he could never have prepared me for, is this: watching him fade away before my eyes, knowing there's not a damn thing I can do about it. Sprinkle in the fact he's sworn me to secrecy, despite the glaringly obvious signs something's wrong, and you have a clusterfuck waiting to happen.

It's with that thought ringing in my head, I make my way up the stairs to visit him. Sharon and Dr Hawkins have been getting increasingly concerned about his lack of improvement. He's not responding to the medication the way he should be. The problem is, short of overruling him and exposing our lies, there's not much I can do. Call me a fool, but I want to honour his wishes for as long as I can. I know it might not be long before that option is taken out of my hands, but for now, I'll cling to it.

Pushing his door open, I pause to take him in. He's lost more weight, and his breathing still isn't right, but there's a dash of colour in his cheeks today. That's got to be progress, right? A sign we're doing something right. I hate seeing him like this. Jonathan O'Neill Sr should not be lying in his bed, struggling to breathe, pumped full of meds and hooked up to a dozen machines to monitor his health. He's supposed to be unstoppable, untouchable, but…here we are.

"Hey Da, how are we feeling today?" I greet him, making my way over to his bedside and reaching over to squeeze his hand.

"Same shit, different day. Have you given any thought to what I said?" he wheezes, referring to our daily battle of wills. Ever since the photo of Helen and me made the papers over a week ago, he's been like a dog with a bone.

"Depends. Have you given any thought to my counter?" At his nonanswer, I probe him. "Because the offer still stands. One hospital appointment in exchange for one date."

For once, he doesn't shoot me down immediately. Instead, he ponders it for a bit. A coughing fit later, he finally gives in. "Fine, but I want to meet this girl. Humour an old man, will you?"

"That can be arranged, but Da, keep it clean, yeah? She doesn't know about the Four Points," I remind him, only for him to wave me off like I'm an idiot for reminding him about something he drilled into me from I was no age: We take our secrets to the grave, or they'll take us. It's the Four Points way.

"How's business been?" I ask Seamus, dropping into a seat beside him in the VIP area of one of our more lucrative clubs, Alibi, hours later. They've been shifting around the tasks I assigned them. Right now, Seamus is leaning into the party-boy persona, keeping an eye on our clubs and the girls in them with Jack's help. Meanwhile, Brennan is busy digging into Angus' finances. As for the other two, there's no chance in hell of pulling them away from the Pit.

"Busy as hell. Apparently, no matter the economy, people want to party and look at pretty girls." He watches the floor below us lit up with strobe lights.

"I hope, for your sake, you're not looking; Fiona would have your balls," I quip.

"Fuck. Don't remind me. I came home the other night after helping Diamond into her car, and she swore she could smell perfume on me. She was this damn close to kicking me out. I had to ring Diamond to get her to confirm my story, and even then, she wanted to see the tapes to be sure. She's a feisty one, but you know I love that shit." He smirks, adjusting himself.

"Enough of that." I deliver an elbow to his side. The last thing I feel like dealing with is my best friend having a hard on beside me while thoughts of his better half run wild in his head.

"Wanker. Anyway, how's that assistant of yours? Jack says Donna's half in love with her, never mind you." He smirks, pumping his eyebrows. A group of women make to approach us, flirty smiles on their faces and heat in their eyes. It's a look I've seen a hundred times before. Hell, it's one I've entertained before, but with a shake of my head, I dismiss them and refocus on Seamus. With a smirk and knowing eyes, he looks between me and the woman who's already moved on to her next target.

"Shut up," I grouse, looking away from him and back out at the floor. Bodies grind against one another to the beat of the music. Everyone is here to let go, to be wild for a night, to hell with responsibilities. I can't remember the last time that was me. Life as a businessman by day and mafia heir by night doesn't leave room for much else. But tonight, I've carved some time out to shoot the shit with Seamus, drink a few whiskeys, so that's exactly what I do. If thoughts about Helen and what treat she's going to have for me tomorrow trickle in well…

that's no one's business but my own.

HELEN
CHAPTER 13

Morning people are psychopaths. Legitimately. Like, one day you'll be watching the news, and they'll be wanted for murder, and you'll wonder why until they mention that they were a morning person and then you'll be like 'ah, say less'. And people who are morning people on a Monday? They're even more insane. Morning people simply can't be trusted; clearly, their judgment is miles off. Or maybe they just don't have to deal with the joyous thing that is an alarm clock jolting you out of your dreams—and if those dreams feature my criminally hot boss, then that's between me, myself, and I. With a groan, I scramble to turn my alarm off before dragging myself out of bed.

It's been over a week since the fundraiser, and in that time, the photo of me pressed up against Jonathan has been plastered everywhere. Seeing myself on the front page of all the major newspapers had a ball on anxiety lodged in my throat, the fear that at any moment, I would be ripped from my life and thrust back into Angus' orbit made it impossible to focus on anything else. Even the beauty of the picture couldn't pull me from my worries, but as the days passed without any signs of being caught out, that anxiety has died down to the gentle simmer that's my norm.

At this point, there's nothing I can do about it. What's done is done, and all I can do is hope that by some miracle, I'm still coasting by under his radar. Surely enough time has passed for him to have found his next victim and forget I ever existed. I would bet my entire pay cheque the only person who still cares is Freya. Thinking about her is like a stab to the heart, one I'm well used to at this point. Tucking her memory back into the box I guard with my life, I focus on getting ready for the day ahead. I can fall apart later, but for now, I've a part to play.

Pairing a fitted white blouse with a black pencil skirt and securing half my hair back with a claw clip, I call it a day. Jonathan can suck it up if it's too basic for him; Mondays are the epitome of doing the bare minimum. With an iced latte in hand, I make the now familiar commute to the office. While the early hour leaves much to be desired, the hush of the lazy morning is always something I enjoy. It's the calm before the storm; the last chance I'll have to savour my coffee in peace before I get to the office and hit the ground running in an attempt to stay ahead of Jonathan's demands. While he's more bark than bite, his bark is still annoying enough to want to avoid it at all costs.

Exiting the tube, I'm immediately assaulted by suits, ties, and ego. The sun hasn't even fully risen, but Canary Wharf is a hub of activity already, with everyone shaking off the remnants of sleep, guzzling their coffees, and getting ready to make their billions. Making my way through the office, I wave at Tina before heading to the lift and heading up to the top floor.

I'm in the middle of firing off a few emails and sending things to the printer to prepare Jonathan's morning briefing, only to freeze in my tracks when he comes strolling in a full forty minutes earlier than scheduled. I make a show of looking at my watch as I quirk a brow at him.

"Who kicked you out of bed?" I tease, springing up to get his coffee, only to just about lose my shit when I clock the coffee cups from the cute artisan place across the street in his hands. Coffee cups- plural.

"Here, you'll need this. I've got to be across town for the meeting with Alan and Sons at eight, and you're coming with me," he says without even pausing his stride into his office. Trailing after him, I watch as he picks papers up, seemingly at random, before he looks up at me with a frown. "Well? What are you waiting for? Get your stuff gathered. We're on a time crunch."

"I know you're the big boss and all that but, Jonathan, it's not on my schedule. I'm meant to be here, getting that research for tomorrow's meeting finalised and fielding your calls. If I go with you, then…" I trail off, watching as he picks up his phone without removing his eyes from me.

"Donna? Get Saul to cover Helen's to do list. She's coming with me." Without even waiting for an answer, he hangs up and raises a brow at me in silent challenge. I should be pissed at his domineering behaviour, but something about a man taking charge to get what he wants is unfairly sexy. Heat rushes to my core despite my best efforts to remind myself this man is firmly off limits. Holding up my hands, I back out of the room with a shake of my head and make quick work of switching out my shoes and checking for flyaway hairs.

"You look perfect. Let's go."

Where did my grump of a boss go, and who is this in his place? Perfect? Since when does he lay compliments at my feet? God damn, this whole morning has been a whirlwind, and it's not even eight. He wasn't wrong when he said I was going to need the extra caffeine.

I hurry after him as we make our way to the car park. Leading me over to his sleek black Bugatti, he clicks a button on his keys to unlock it and holds my door open. Something about a man holding doors open scratches an itch in my brain just right. Not looking at him, I duck under his arm and get in. Watching as he rounds the car to get in, I use those precious moments to take a few deep breaths and centre myself. Big mistake. Now, my lungs are full of his cologne—musk, cigars, and cedarwood. The combination makes me want to roll around in it like a dog in heat.

What would Father say if he saw me now, I wonder? Here I am, in the enemy's car, more at ease than I ever was at 'home'. The irony that the safest I've ever felt is in Jonathan's presence is not lost on me, nor is the danger. This whole thing could explode in an instant. All it would take is one wrong move, one slip up, but God, do I pray it doesn't happen. I'm not ready to give this up just yet.

The morning passes in a blur of marketing talk I only half understand while I scribble down notes. By the time Jonathan wraps it up with handshakes and promises of a follow up call, the morning is long gone. As soon as we're back in the car, I'm past the point of caring, toeing off my heels the second Jonathan closes my door. Mother would have a heart attack if she saw me doing something so crass in public, which just makes it all the more satisfying to stretch out my stocking-clad feet in the footwell and relish in the satisfying crack as I roll my ankles.

"I don't know why you bother wearing those if they hurt so bad," he grumbles from the driver's seat, putting an arm around the back of my chair as he reverses. The sexiness that one action possesses should be studied.

"I don't always wear them, only when the day calls for it. Flats hardly send the same message," I try to explain.

"And what message is that? I'm suffering, but at least I'm a few inches taller?" he mocks with a teasing glint in his eye and a playful smirk tugging at the corner of his mouth. Seriously, who is this guy, and where's my grumpy, monosyllabic boss?

"There's a reason they say beauty is pain. It's a power thing; you wouldn't understand. I mean, why would you? It's a man's world. I doubt you've ever had someone doubt your abilities just because of what's between your legs." I scoff at the unfairness.

"You don't need any of that shit. And the next time someone questions your abilities, you come to me, got it?" The barely concealed threat in his tone has me clenching my thighs and praying he doesn't notice. Now is not the time to get the hots for my boss. And even if he wasn't my boss, Jonathan is firmly off limits to me. Forever. He has to be, for my self-preservation. And yet, I find myself looking at him through new eyes. Today has shown me all kinds of sides to him I'd never seen before, and the urge to dig deeper, to learn more, is eating at me. Shaking it off, I offer him a smirk and a 'Yes, sir,' taking great joy in the way a muscle in his jaw clenches.

"You hungry?" He changes gears both figuratively and literally, and I don't know whether to look at his veiny forearms or the unfamiliar road he's taking us down.

Frowning at the sudden change of subject, I shrug. "Sure. I could eat."

"Good," is all he says before making an abrupt turn down a side street. As far as I can tell, we're going in the complete opposite direction to the office. Surely, there are lunch spots closer to the office.

"Would it not make more sense to head the other way? Save a bit of time and all that."

"Sweetheart, I'm the CEO. I make the rules, but I sure as shit don't adhere to them. Plus, didn't you hear? Rules were created to be broken." The dark promise in his words speaks to more than lunch. Sinking lower in my seat, I watch the scenery blur by, listening to the music playing softly on the radio as a cool autumn breeze floats in my rolled down window. It's not long before he's pulling up to a quaint little café and once again holds my door open for me.

"This is where you wanted to come?" I frown, looking around the place as we make our way in and seat ourselves. None of the men back home would be caught dead somewhere so common. Father would have a fit if he knew I was about to eat somewhere like this. It's absolutely perfect.

"What, not up to your standards?" he snickers, settling into the booth opposite me, the black vinyl creaking as we get settled. It's strange to see him so carefree, like the weight he normally carries has been lifted. It suits him a bit too well for my sanity.

"Oh, you know me. I only dine in places that hide their prices," I quip, scanning the laminated menu.

"Well then, this should be an experience." He laughs. The fact that he doesn't even crack open his menu speaks volumes, and even before the waitress greets him, it's clear this is far from his first time here.

"Now, who have you brought me, Johnny?" the middle-aged waitress asks as she strolls over to us. Her whole demeanour screams motherly, and the laugh lines around her eyes speak to a life well lived. Her use of Johnny, a name I haven't heard anyone call him, has my eyebrows disappearing into my hairline.

"Angie, this is Helen. I dragged her here to educate her on life's finer things," he teases.

She tosses her head back on a laugh before asking him, "The usual, son?" At his nod, she turns her gaze to me.

"Oh...um... What's good here?" I ask, not having a clue where to start.

"Angie, make that two of the usual. And toss in two milkshakes when you get a chance," he interrupts, and my core tightens at the bold move. Old world manners are my kryptonite, and I need to remind myself that this man is firmly off limits. Not only would getting with him blow up my secrets, but he would want nothing to do with me if he knew the truth. I won't risk Freya's safety by getting myself caught up in this world again. I *can't*. No matter how hot a night with Jonathan would be, it's not worth the risk. Thinking of my sisters is like dousing myself with ice cold water. Instantly, the steady thrum of lust that has been burrowing under my skin is snuffed out.

"A girl like you should never look so forlorn," Jonathan murmurs, bringing my attention back to the man across from me. His suit jacket has been abandoned in the car, leaving him in a black shirt that looks like silk against his tan skin. A strand of his dark hair has fallen forward from his slicked back style. My fingers twitch with the urge to push it back. I wonder if it's as soft as it looks.

"Hmm, try telling that one to life," I mutter, fiddling with the coaster in front of me.

"That pesky thing? She's stubborn, isn't she?" he remarks. I can feel his eyes drilling into me, but I refuse to meet his gaze.

"You can say that again."

"On a serious note, I owe you an apology." At his softly spoken words, I jerk my eyes up to meet his.

"Oh yeah?" I prompt, raising my eyebrow at him and taking joy in his expression.

"I judged you before I even gave you a shot. That was wrong of me. You've been an absolute godsend these past few months." He looks bashful as he confesses what I already knew. Still, hearing him admit it is beyond satisfying. Show me one person who doesn't crave the reassurance of a job well done.

"You wouldn't be the first. However, you've heard the saying don't judge a book by its cover, right?"

"I have, and I should know better. Patience isn't my strong suit at the best of times, and training a new start takes a lot of that. I should have reserved my judgment until I'd spent more than five minutes with you, and for that, I'm sorry."

Before I could unglue my tongue from my suddenly dry mouth and formulate a response, Angie came back with two vanilla milkshakes and a jug of water for the table. Thanking her, I take a sip before turning my attention back to Jonathan.

"How about we move on and focus on the here and now?" I offer an olive branch. He lets out a relieved sigh before aiming a crooked grin in my direction and giving me the full effect of those molten baby blues.

"Sounds like a plan. Now, why don't you tell me a little about yourself," he prompts, leaning back in his seat, tossing an arm along the back, and giving me his undivided attention. Shit. Maybe I should have continued playing hardball.

"There's not much to know." I shrug.

"Uh-huh," he replies, eyeing me dubiously. "You do realise I can tell when you're bullshitting me, right? No one seems to know anything about you, despite working for us for nearly three months. You don't go out with the team on Friday nights, and you don't strike up small talk with any of them."

"Are you stalking me now?" He better not be. I don't care how hot it is in dark romance books; that shit is not something I need right now.

"I don't need to. It's all anyone is talking about in the break room, which you also never make use of," he points out with a self-satisfied shrug.

"I like my space," I deflect, flicking my hair over my shoulder. It's obvious he has no intention of dropping it that easily. Luckily, Angie picks that moment to appear, arms laden down with food. Two plates are piled high with the juiciest looking burgers, fries, and not so much as a lettuce leaf in sight. The differences between Jonathan and Angus couldn't be any more obvious. We eat in comfortable silence, and it's not long before I'm sitting back, feeling more satisfied than I have in a long time. I can't remember the last time my metaphorical cup was quite so full.

"Don't think I've forgotten you dodged my questions," he quips, dabbing at his mouth before sitting back and looking so at ease, it should be a crime. Surely, a man with an empire to run shouldn't look so relaxed, never mind one with whatever illegal shit is calling his name on top of that.

"My secrets are earned, not handed out like candy."

"I guess I'll just have to work on earning them then, won't I?" So much heat in such a short sentence, it's a wonder I don't melt then and there. So, when he suggests I take the rest of the afternoon off, it's all I can do to nod and offer him my address when he asks for it.

If you were to ask me anything about the ride home, I wouldn't be able to answer you, as I was too wrapped up in the comfortable silence and stifling tension to pay attention to anything else. However, as soon as I reach my flat, the blissful joy of the day is soon wiped away. Among the random junk and bill mail sits an unmarked envelope, and in it, a clipping of the photo from the fundraiser. The damming evidence of my betrayal speaks volumes, and even without a letter, I know a threat from the Clan when I see one.

In an instant, my tentative hopes of building a stable life—one where I could eventually return and sneak Freya out of the Clan's clutches—are snuffed out. In their place, the overwhelming realisation that I am utterly doomed sinks its claws deep into my bones.

JONATHAN
CHAPTER 14

The sterile smell and eerie silence of hospitals never get less unsettling. It makes every breath heavier, every nerve ending stand on edge. Death and despair cling to the air, and while that's something I deal in, and dish out, daily, I still can't stop my foot from tapping nervously as I sit in the hard plastic chair in the waiting room, the fluorescent lights buzzing and flickering overhead.

Sitting here, shit hitting the fan from all directions, while Helen is at the office handling both our workloads isn't my idea of fun or time well spent. But since the only way to get Da to come was if I accompanied him, of course I came, no questions asked. To distract myself while they run some tests on him, I ring Brennan.

"Yeah?" he answers on a yawn; he's been back to the clubs this week, so, at most, he's probably had two or three hours of sleep. I should feel bad, but I can't find it in me to do so right now. Bastard better get used to being tired. The higher up the ladder I climb, the higher up I drag them with me, the less time we're going to have for luxuries such as sleep.

"Any luck getting access to his bank account?" I don't bother wasting time on pleasantries or names.

"Christ. No, I told you I'd tell you the second I did," he grunts, sounding as close to pissed off as Bren ever gets.

"And I thought I told you this was urgent? Senior wouldn't send us down this rabbit hole if he didn't have reason to," I remind him with a growl in my voice as I pace the length of the waiting room.

"I know, and I'm working on it, day and night. Why the fuck are we wasting so much time on this anyway?"

"Because if he's not going through the usual channels, that means something's afoot. I highly doubt it's something harmless." I exhale slowly while pinching the bridge of my nose. This phone call is only serving to make the pounding in my head worse.

"Fine, I'll get some of the new guys to help me. More manpower might be the secret to this," he mutters before hanging up. If he was anyone else, I'd make him pay for that slight, but him and the rest of my inner circle are like brothers. While they might mouth off to me in private, I know they'd cut the tongue from anyone else who dared.

With a groan, I take a seat in the plastic chair again. Taking a sip of the lukewarm, weak as piss coffee the vending machine spat out at me, I can't help but long for the perfectly brewed espresso Helen makes, which leads me down the rabbit hole of thinking about her. I can't shake the feeling there's more to her than meets the eye. I don't know if it's just my Da's voice ringing in my head, but the more I think about her, the more I wonder what she would say if I told her about this side of things. If I made her mine and said fuck the consequences. Would she run for the hills? Or has my sneaking suspicion that she'd stay got roots?

"Mr O'Neill?" Looking up at the nurse calling my name, I dump the subpar coffee and stride over to her.

"That would be me." I offer her a charming smile. It's not her fault the coffee here is shit or that Da needs to be here in the first place.

"If you'll follow me, the doctor would like you to sit in on the results." With that, she indicates for me to follow her. A few months ago, I'd be chatting her up, fishing for her number and details of when her shift ended, but now, I don't offer her so much as small talk as I dutifully follow her. Knocking on the door, she pushes it open before leaving me to enter alone and make my way over to Da's side. The doctor fiddles with something on his computer screen before sighing and turning his grim expression on us.

"As I'm sure you both know, the prognosis isn't the best. As it stands, your lungs are working at less than half capacity. I really wish you had come in sooner. But the good news is, we do have a few options to make things more comfortable." Comfortable, not curable. The difference is glaringly obvious to me. The words land like a blow, and Da flinches under their impact.

"How long do I have?" he rasps, asking the question that plagues both of us, the question I long to bury and ignore for as long as possible.

"These things are always hard to pinpoint, but if I had to make an educated guess...I would say a few months," he answers, looking remorseful. But no matter how the words are delivered, they don't ease the burden or the impending grief that hits me. Someday soon, far sooner than I ever dreamed, my Da, the person who has been by my side my whole life and weathered his own grief when my mum died in childbirth, will soon be gone. Soon, I won't be able to ask him for advice or hear the same old stories I've rolled my eyes at hearing for the thousandth time.

I only half listen as the doctor lists our options, and it's only when a pile of paperwork is being pressed into my hand do I realise I'm expected to do the impossible: put my own feelings on the back burner and shoulder the weight of the world while I take care of him. The time for him to be the strong one has come to a crashing halt; it's my job now. The time for keeping things on the down low is quickly slipping out of our fingers.

We're both silent, running on autopilot as I get us home. Wordlessly, I help Da back into his bed and leave him in Sheila's care before calling a meeting. The time for keeping secrets from my brothers has long since passed. If I'm to make it through this, I'm going to need them, in more than one way.

Letting Seamus into my flat, I lead him into the living room, where the others are gathered. Silent and watchful, it's clear this isn't just a social call—especially when the twins arrived, and I didn't even react to Ciaran's ribbing. A well-placed elbow from Brennan had him reining in the mania that usually clings to him like a second skin, opting instead to watch me pace back and forth. I rake a hand through my hair, trying to figure out where to begin.

"Senior isn't really attending to some urgent matter elsewhere, is he?" Jack's careful probing makes me turn to face them—my five best friends, my brothers in every way but blood. I should have told them months ago. We don't keep secrets—we never have—so why did I start now?

"No, he's at home. I got a call a few months ago at the office. Sheila was frantic." I hesitate, searching for the right words. There are two stages to knowing someone has cancer: before and after. Right now, these guys are living blissfully unaware in the before, and it's up to me to drag them into the after with me.

Senior has been like family to all of them, shaping them as much as their own fathers. Half the time, he's the first person they'd turn to for advice. The one who gave us direction when we needed it most. Now, more than ever, I feel the weight of his legacy pressing down on me—suffocating me—as the inevitable stretches ahead, grey and bleak.

"Stage four lung cancer." The words slice through me as I choke them out, and instantly, their expressions shatter. Declan and Jack exchange looks of disbelief while the twins shake their heads in denial. Seamus rubs a hand across his jaw, his eyes clouded. The impending grief is like a boulder tied to our ankles, dragging us underwater as silence stretches between us.

"What can we do?" Declan's hoarse words aren't a question—

they're a statement. The Four Points has always been, first and foremost, a family. We look out for our own, no questions asked, no matter the cost.

"For now, let's focus on keeping this under wraps while we dig up answers about Angus. I'll work on solidifying my place with the other ranks, and we'll keep doing what we've been doing. Maybe Brennan can work some IT magic to feed them evidence he's fine? And the sooner we fully vet the new recruits, the better."

Murmured agreements ripple through the group as they slip into planning mode. Seamus presses a drink into my hand as he comes to stand beside me.

"You should have told me."

"I know, but would you have disobeyed a direct order if you were me?" I challenge.

"No—but this goes beyond that, and you know it." He sighs before clipping me on the shoulder.

Looking around the room at the men I call brothers, I can't help but acknowledge how lucky I am to have them ready to go to bat for me in a heartbeat. Not everyone has this, and I'm all too aware of how fucked I'd be without them, especially now.

HELEN
CHAPTER 15

Whatever fragile progress we made over lunch that afternoon has since been overshadowed by a strange mixture of the daily photo clippings I've been receiving, and Jonathan going missing. Fine, he's not *technically* missing. According to Donna, he's been working from home. Which, fine, maybe he is. But it's not like him. Not in the slightest.

If it weren't for Donna, I would probably have thrown in the towel by now. Being an EA to a CEO who has decided to work from home is hard enough. Throw in the fact he's gone no contact, and you have me trying to step into his size tens, which is absolutely not what I signed up for and *way* above my pay grade. Hip checking my office door open, arms laden with my coffee and today's reports, I nearly drop everything when I spy the dark, brooding figure behind my desk.

In all my time working for Jonathan, I've never seen him look anything less than perfectly put together: hair always slicked back, stubble carefully trimmed, suits pressed, shoes polished. And yet...here he is—hair a mess of dark strands falling across his forehead, well on his way to having a beard, and, most shockingly, he's in a tight black tee shirt...and are those *jeans*?

Who the hell is this impersonator, and where's my mafia boss who doesn't know I know he's in the mafia? It's complicated, I know.

"Jonathan?" His head snaps up, and those beautiful blue eyes are red rimmed in a way that breaks my heart and shatters my self-control. Closing the door behind me, shutting the rest of the world out, I make my way over to him. Dumping everything on my desk, I round it until I'm standing at this side.

He turns in the chair to face me, and I take the opening to inch closer, standing between his spread thighs as he looks through me. It's like he's not even on this planet. The urge to do anything I can to help him courses through me. Conscious of the glass walls and the eyes watching us, I keep my expression as composed as possible. "What's going on? Are you okay?"

"What a question." He snorts, looking lost as he gazes up at me. His eyes fixate on my hair, and before I can react, he's reaching up to tug at a loose curl, watching as it springs back into place. Reaching up, I grab his wrist, anchoring him to me as I scramble for a way to help him.

"Jonathan, I want to help you, but you need to give me something to work with here. *Please*," I beg. My usually effortlessly powerful boss has been replaced by this shell of a man; he looks haunted, like he's one wrong move away from spiralling out of control. It doesn't add up. What the hell happened after our lunch? Who do I need to deal with?

"You should never beg. You're too good for that." He frowns, and it's then I catch the hint of whiskey on his breath.

My eyebrows fly up into my hairline as I gape at him. "Are you seriously drunk right now?"

My words are a hiss that seems to wash over him without landing until, suddenly, he stands, making me take a step back. Something flickers in his eyes before he shrugs, brushing off my concern. The utter desperation clinging to every inch of him has me fighting the urge to reach up and brush my thumbs over the lines that don't belong on his face.

"Fuck it. Life's too short," he whispers, almost as if he's talking to himself rather than me. Before I can ask him what the hell is going on, he's palming the back of my neck, drawing me closer. I open my mouth to object, only to lose my breath in an instant as he claims my mouth as his with a fierceness that should terrify me. And it does, but not for the reasons it should—no, it terrifies me because I want more. I want everything he has to give me, fuck the consequences.

Even with all the reasons we shouldn't be doing this ringing in the back of my mind, I can't bring myself to tear myself away from his touch. The brush of his tongue against mine sends heat coursing through me. With a whimper, I cling to him, digging my nails into his neck as I lose myself in the moment. This moment should be all we will ever have. It's all we can afford, and yet, I'm desperate for more.

Pulling back, he scans my eyes. "Let me take you to dinner." It's not a question or a plea but a demand, and as sexy as it is, I can't say yes. *I can't.*

"We can't." As much as there's no point in hiding the truth from myself any longer, my guard has been sky high for as long as I can remember, and while he makes me want to let it crumble around us, I can't. There are far too many risks, far more than just my future and safety at risk.

"Give me one good reason." Warm palms cup my face, forcing me to meet his eyes. Seeing my own desire reflected at me causes a perfect storm to explode inside my mind. Air catches in my lungs—lungs that refuse to do their job—as he holds me captive, helpless to do anything other than lean into his touch.

"You're my boss," I whimper, gesturing blindly to the glass wall behind him.

"There's no anti-fraternisation policy in place. Next." His determination has my resolve weakening despite my best efforts.

"You don't even like me. You've been drinking. When you sober up, you'll regret this." I'm grasping at straws at this point, but I don't care. I need him to give up before I cave in. Reaching up, I take hold of his wrists and try to pry them off my face.

"False. Just give me a chance, Helen. One date, that's all I'm asking." God, hearing my name on his lips never fails to send shivers down my spine. There's something in the way he rasps it that has me half feral every time. It has me crumbling at his feet before I've even weighed up the consequences. So much for my self-preservation skills. Seventeen-year-old me would be rolling over in her grave if she knew we escaped one mafioso's clutches only to fall into the arms of a different one.

And when I arrive home to another letter, this time with a note on the back, I know my time is fast running out. One date before I disappear again. That's what I promise myself as I read the hastily scrawled text on the back of the photo.

Freya says hello.

JONATHAN
CHAPTER 16

"**A** meeting? Here? Has he lost his fucking mind?" This is the last thing I need to deal with right now. I'm already spinning enough plates without throwing Angus fucking Graham into the mix as well. Between covering for Da, running the Four Points, and keeping all our businesses afloat, it's a wonder I haven't dropped the ball yet. Or maybe I already have, considering the date I have planned for tonight.

Heading into the office wasn't a conscious decision— and probably not one of my smartest moves, considering the dent I'd put in that bottle of whiskey. One moment, I was in my flat; the next, I was in Helen's office, more intoxicated by her presence than alcohol had ever gotten me. Kissing her was easier than breathing. And damn—the taste of her on my tongue had me throwing all caution to the wind.

Even now, days later, sitting in the office at Alibi with Declan, I can hear her moans and whimpers as clear as day. Not even the news that Angus has been sniffing around our borders is enough to wipe her from my mind.

"Apparently, he said the only reason he's here is to ask a favour. Something about a misunderstanding," he explains, though the frown on his face tells me exactly what he thinks of that.

"Fine. Set it up," I concede with a sigh.

"Funny you should say that…" He trails off, looking guilty as sin. With a curse, I say goodbye to the idea of getting any work done today before indicating for him to lead the way. It shouldn't surprise me. Angus makes me look like a saint when it comes to patience.

Making our way outside, Declan leads me over to the heavily-guarded SUV before dropping back. Nodding at the soldiers as I dip into the back seat, I brace myself. I've sat in on enough meetings to know you never quite know what you're getting with this unhinged bastard. His smug smirk is the first thing to greet me, soon followed by a handshake that's more like an arm-wrestling contest. Eventually, he stops trying to break the bones in my hand and sits back in his seat, his beady grey eyes watching me like a hawk. For someone who is firmly on enemy territory, he looks awfully comfortable. Time to change that.

"You wanted to talk, so talk," I drawl, making a show of looking at my watch.

"It's quite simple, really. You have something that belongs to me."

"Do we now?" I lift a brow. I wonder where the hell he's going with this.

"Yes. As I'm sure you can understand, I'd quite like it back. Word on the street is, you're looking after business at the moment, so all I need is you to look the other way while I retrieve her," he explains, looking ten shades of self-assured, as if this is a formality and I'm about to roll out the red carpet for him. Not bloody likely.

"Her?" Shit just got interesting.

"Aye. It seems we have a little runaway problem. You know how these mafia brats are." If he thinks he's doing anything other than solidifying my desire not to help him, he's sorely mistaken. Anyone who felt the need to run from the Clan no doubt has their reasons. More power to her for managing to get away, if you ask me.

"Indeed. Well, unfortunately, I can't do that. If you gave me a name, I could pass along a message, but I'm not going to give you free rein on our turf. I'm sure you can understand." Checking my watch once more, I make to leave.

"I feared you'd say that. Fine, I'll let her father know." The lack of fight is odd, even odder when you consider he travelled here himself. All for some runaway…that he's fine with going home without? I smell trouble. Leaving him to stew, I unfold my body from the SUV and make my way over to Declan. In a low tone, I give him instructions to keep an eye on Angus, a very close eye, before leaving him to tidy up this mess and focusing on what's important.

Which would be my five foot nothing assistant. She might not know it yet—she might even believe this will be our only date—but tonight, the first night of the rest of my life with her. Maybe my method of asking her out was unprofessional, but if there's one thing Da made sure to teach me, it's that O'Neill men get what they want, no matter the cost or method.

I'm no longer afraid to admit that what I want is Helen. Seeing just how easily everything can be ripped away from you soon cured me of that. I want her sassy attitude. I want to earn my way behind her prickly self-defensive mechanisms. I want her moans ringing in my ears and those little dresses and tight skirts discarded on my bedroom floor. But most of all, I want her secrets. I want to be someone she trusts and confides in, to be her safe place to land. I'll do anything to become that person for her.

I get ready with her in mind. I've seen how her eyes take me in every day at the office. It's clear she likes the suited and booted look, and so I've pulled out one of my favourites: a dark navy suit, tailored to my exact measurements, paired with a sky-blue silk shirt. According to Donna, the colour brings out my eyes, whatever that means. I'm in the middle of putting my silver cufflinks on when my phone rings. If it were anyone else, I would let it go to voicemail, but seeing Da's name flash across the screen has me thumbing the answer button before the second ring.

"Da? Is everything okay?"

"Just inching closer to dying, but other than that, I'm fine." His dark sense of humour makes me snort despite myself.

"Shut up, Da. You're not dying, I won't let you. Now, why are you ringing me?"

"I heard you have a date tonight."

"How'd you hear that?" I ask.

"You think my son booking out O'Neill's wouldn't flag up? Come on now." He tsks, pausing to cough before continuing, "I want to meet her, this girl who's made you change your mind. She must be special."

"Of course they rang you. She *is* special, but it's incredibly new…" I always intended to honour his request, but I wasn't banking on doing this on the first date.

"Well then. All the better for me to vet her for you." Realising there's no way out of this, I concede with a grunt, promising to bring her by before the date.

JONATHAN
CHAPTER 17

Pulling up in front of Helen's rundown flat, I make a note to talk to Donna about giving her a raise so she can move somewhere safer, preferably closer to my penthouse, ideally with a doorman and armed security.

Getting out of my car and making my way over to her front door, I'm robbed of the honour to knock when she comes striding out with a smile in place and the world's tallest heels on her feet. She looks stunning, her hair in big, beautiful curls I want to bury my hands in and mess up, not to mention the red lipstick I can't wait to smudge. Advancing on her, I place my hand on hers, stilling her movements as she goes to lock up.

"I thought we talked about this. You don't need to suffer in those things you call shoes for me. Change into something more comfortable. I'll wait."

Her eyes narrow into slits, and for a moment, I think she's going to give me a piece of her mind before her expression softens, her mouth dropping open on a stuttered breath. Without a word, she dips back inside as I lean against the wall, not wanting to miss out on the chance to escort her down the steps for a second time.

When she comes back out in red ballet flats that match her bag, she looks far more comfortable and at ease. Perfect.

"That's my good girl. You look fucking stunning," I murmur, a dark note to my words as I take her hand to help her down the steps. "We have a slight detour to make on our way to dinner. I hope you don't mind, but my dad really wants to meet you."

I lead her to my car. Holding open the door for her, she ducks under my arm to get in.

"Meeting the parents already? You could have warned a girl." She lets out a stilted laugh before meeting my gaze. Something on my face must give away how important this is to me, to him, because she drops the sass for a moment, her face softening as she responds.

"This means a lot to you, huh? Well, go on then. Show me where you grew up. I bet it's ten shades of fancy and massive." She's not wrong there. Growing up, money was never an issue or a second thought. Da did all he could to keep me humble, reminding me everything could slip away in a heartbeat if we took our feet off the gas pedal for even a second, but it doesn't change the fact that the wealth I grew up with is far from normal.

"Wow," she breathes as we pull up to my childhood home. I try to see it from her eyes. Settled behind the gates of our gated community and set up on a hill overlooking the other houses, I have to admit it, is pretty impressive—a three story, old school, stately home that, at times, seemed excessive for just the two of us.

"Yeah, I guess it is kind of…a lot," I say, getting out of the car before making my way to her side. Never in my presence will a woman open her own door. With my hand on her lower back, I lead her up to the door, letting myself in. Making our way up the stairs, I turn back to look at her. She's still taking everything in with a sense of wonderment, and it's with a grim sense of dread I place my hand on her cheek. Drawing her eyes to mine, I wait for her to focus on me before speaking.

"There's something you should know before we head in. My dad isn't exactly…himself at the moment. No one knows."

Confusion darts across her face before understanding lights behind her eyes. "Of course. You can trust me. I would never dream of sharing your secrets."

A sense of connection flows between us, and it's with a tightness in my gut that I lead her the rest of the way. Knocking on the door, I push it forward and try to take it in from Helen's point of view. Da is propped up on a mountain of pillows, dressed in black silk pyjamas, with a greying beard and hair that's seen better days, an oxygen tank and medical shit all around him. He looks nothing like the strong mafia leader I always idolised or the ruthless businessman millions feared.

Her shocked inhale and tightening grip on my hand are the only outward signs she shows before replacing them with a calm, cool, and collected mask. She lets go of my hand to stride forward like she's been here a million times, a blinding smile in place as she introduces herself. Watching Da's face light up as she talks away to him like it's second nature hammers home just how special she is. Maybe this is the right move after all. Maybe Da had a point this whole time, that the risk can be worth the reward.

"I see why you tried to keep her to yourself, son. Scared I'd steal her away from you, huh?" Seeing him so carefree, even for a brief moment, is reassuring, more than I could ever have dreamed of. Maybe I should bring Helen around more often if it brightens his day so much. He could do with the uplifting of his spirit.

"You caught me. But can you blame me for wanting to keep her to myself?" I tease, walking over to stand beside her and place my hand on her waist. She leans into me, and Da's eyes track the movement with a soft smile on his face.

"Well, if my son here messes up, just know I'm waiting in the wings," he teases her, and she lets out a laugh. Something about the light, carefree sound has my gut clenching.

"Oh, stop teasing me." She laughs again, shaking her head at his antics.

"I think that's my cue to whisk her out of here before you show me up on my own date, Da," I joke with a laugh. With promises to bring her for another visit, we take our leave.

As we settle back into our seats in the car, she asks the question I dread hearing the most these days. "How long has he got left?"

"We don't know for sure…but not long." It's all I manage to get out, and she reaches over to squeeze my knee before making an effort to switch the subject to something lighter. Before she can take her hand back, I twine her fingers with mine as I put the car in gear.

"So, where exactly are you taking me?"

"Now, why would I spoil the surprise? You'll just have to wait and see." I smirk at her annoyed huff. Luckily, O'Neill's is only about ten minutes' drive from my childhood home, so it's not long before I'm parking the car while she lets out a low whistle.

"This place is supposed to be impossible to get a reservation for," she comments, looking at me with a raised brow and questions dancing in her eyes.

"Hmm, I've heard that," I hum as I get out and open the door for her, placing my arm around her waist and guiding her to the door. Pushing the door to the dimly lit restaurant open, we're greeted by the soft notes of classical music and the hostess.

Eyes solely focused on me, she looks me over from head to toe as she gives a sultry smile. "Jonathan, so good to see you again. Please follow me, and if you need anything, *anything* at all, just give me a shout."

Helen grows tense at the woman's openly flirtatious behaviour and thinly veiled innuendo—looks like someone is more affected by me than she wants to let on. I'm a sick bastard for it, but damn, if her jealousy doesn't turn me on. As we're led through the restaurant, Helen lets out a gasp as she sees the candles and flower petals leading to our table in the middle of the room.

"What the hell is this…" I'd be lying if I said I wasn't smug about the fact I rendered her speechless.

"This, sweetheart, is the benefit of letting me wine and dine you." I guide her over to the table, pulling her chair out for her. As she sinks into her seat, I round the table and take my own.

"But how did you manage this on such short notice..." After a moment, she answers her own question. "Of course. This is your place, isn't it, Mr O'Neill?"

I wonder if I can get her to call me that with her thighs around my face and my tongue buried in her cunt.

With a groan, I discreetly adjust myself as I answer her with a filthy smirk. "As I said, sweetheart, there are benefits to being on my arm. This is just the tip of the iceberg." Before she can come up with a response, we're interrupted by the waitress. Once again, she's young, blonde, and needs to keep her eyes to herself. She doesn't even look at Helen, instead treating me like the only customer as she hands over the leather-bound menus. Placing both in front of me, she bats her eyelashes, as if that's going to do anything for me when I have Helen sitting right there, looking like my every fantasy come to life.

"I'm Amy, and I'll be your waitress tonight. What can I do for you tonight, sir?" Her husky tone implies she knows me, implies she's done something for me before, and it makes me want to strangle the fuck out of her. It causes Helen to grow frosty across the table and cut in with a snarl that makes me proud.

"Excuse you. I'll take a glass of Chardonnay. That's the white one." Goddamn, her jealousy is sexy as hell.

"Make that a bottle for the table. And get me a MacMillan twenty-five on the rocks." I dismiss her without taking my eyes off Helen, and after a moment, she struts away with a huff.

"Something wrong?" I tease Helen, taking satisfaction in her darkening gaze and quirked eyebrow.

"Why, of course not. I just *love* it when my date has the whole female staff dropping their knickers at his feet. It's a real turn on."

"Oh, is that what they were doing?" I lean back in my seat as I drawl the words, watching her eyes track my every move, once again admiring the view in front of me. She truly is beautiful without even having to try, a classic Hollywood beauty if I ever saw one.

"You know it is. Do you make it a habit to fuck your employees?"

"That's an ugly accusation, one that doesn't suit you, Helen," I rebuke.

"Well, you can thank *Amy* for that." The venom dripping from her voice when she says the other woman's name says it all. As much as teasing her is fun and seeing her riled up has me hard as steel, I'll be damned if I fuck this up on the first date. Time to switch gears and do damage control before this spins out of control.

"You know, my dad has always encouraged me to date, to make time for something other than work and my responsibilities. Up until *very* recently, I've always scoffed at that idea. I can assure you, Amy has no reason to be flirting with me. As the owner of this place, I will be sure to handle this. But for now, can we forget about her and focus on us?" The anger simmering in my veins makes my words come out in a near snarl, but despite the harsh edge to my tone, my words have the desired effect of softening her defences. Her mouth parts, her pupils blowing wide as she struggles to come up with a response. Before she can, we're interrupted by Amy returning with the drinks.

She places my drink in front of me, making sure not to spill a drop, before practically throwing the wine at Helen. Having had enough of her shit, I snarl a demand to speak to her manager. While she struggles to come up with an answer, I turn to Helen.

"I'm sorry about this. I'll just be a moment. Why don't you look over the menu, and when I'm back, I'll see if I can't guess what you've picked out?" Standing, I cross the table until I'm beside her. Leaning down, I press a kiss to the side of her head. "You look absolutely ravishing tonight. Jealousy suits you, sweetheart."

With that, I straighten my jacket as I stride after the positively quivering Amy as she leads me to the staff room. Entering it, I spy a middle-aged man scrolling his phone, his half eaten dinner in front of him. At the sound of the door closing behind us, he glances up, only to grow pale when he sees me.

"Jimmy, how's things?" I ask as he comes over to shake my hand, his confused glance flickering between myself and Amy.

"Things are good. Business is good. How can I help you?"

"Well, that's the thing, Jimmy. It seems we have a slight attitude problem going on."

"An attitude problem?" He frowns.

"You know I booked this place out tonight, correct? And asked for the candles and flowers? That would imply it was a romantic occasion, would it not?" With every word, he gets more and more nervous. Good.

"Why yes, of course! Did we not deliver?" He frowns, looking thoroughly confused.

"Everything is wonderful, but do you care to explain why two members of your staff thought it appropriate to not only openly flirt with me, but this one nearly threw my date's wine at her? That's after blanking her existence and handing both menus to me."

At that, Amy starts to stutter out excuses and denials, but Jimmy is having none of it. His eyes cut to her, and he snarls for her to shut up before turning to me. "I'm so sorry, sir. Please accept my sincere apologies. I'll handle this immediately."

"See that you do. I'd hate to have to look for a new manager as well as a new waitress and hostess." With that, I spin on my heel and make my way back out to Helen. From this moment on, I will not stop until Helen Montgomery is mine, and I'll fight anyone and anything who tries to come between me and my woman.

HELEN
CHAPTER 18

I've always thought a man taking charge was the epitome of attractive. So, seeing him not only reassure me that these women were meaningless, but take action here and now to cut out the bullshit, has me so distracted, I don't so much as even open the menu in the time he's gone. I'm far too busy fantasising about him taking control in other areas. Does he like to command in the bedroom as well? Please say so.

This whole evening so far has been a fever dream. If I didn't know better, I'd think he'd read my mind to discover what makes me tick before making it a reality. It's making me second-guess my resolve to disappear after this. But no matter how good this date is going; it's not worth the risk. I can't afford to fall for anyone right now, least of all the heir to the Four Points, who is closer to taking over than I first anticipated, if his dad's health is any indicator.

"Sorry about that. Now, where we?" I'm shaken out of my thoughts by Jonathan's return.

"Hmm, I believe we were reading the menu."

"Funny. I thought we were discussing the reason for my very recent desire to date. But if you're sure…" His words are taunting and deliberate, but I don't rise to the occasion.

"Oh, I'm very sure. You were saying you liked the," I quickly scan the menu before blurting out the first thing I see, "feta cheese salad."

"Ahh, yes. I'm a big fan of it," he jokes before shifting his gaze back to the menu, glancing over it and then snapping it closed.

"You already know what you want?"

"Perks of owning this place. I crafted the menu, which means I know what's best and what's just middle of the road," he answers as he lifts his drink to his mouth.

"Care to share with the class?" I enquire, taking a sip of my wine. God, this is the good shit. Before he can answer, a man comes over to take our orders. In comparison to Amy, this man is all smiles and has a welcoming aura as he addresses the table.

"I'm Jimmy, and it's my pleasure to look after you two tonight. What can we get started for you?"

"We'll do the seafood sharing platter to begin with, and then a medium rare steak for me and a truffle pasta for the lady," Jonathan says, handing Jimmy our menus, once again taking swift control and making my knickers wet. At this rate, it will be a wonder if I don't leave a damp spot on the leather chair. As Jimmy leaves us, Jonathan turns his attention back to me.

"So, tell me about yourself. Forewarning, this time, I won't let you escape without answering." *Fuck.*

"There's not much to know. I've lived a pretty sheltered, boring life." I shrug.

"Any siblings? Hobbies?" he probes, and without even pausing, I make the decision to lie to him. I'd happily throw Peter under the microscope, but doing so would increase the risk of him finding out more and endangering Freya.

"No, I'm an only child. And who has time for hobbies when they're working full time? My boss is a real hard ass. All kinds of late nights and early starts." I brush him off with a teasing smirk.

"Is that so? Maybe I need to have a word with him for you. Everyone should have time for something that brings them joy. What do you do when you go home from work?" he pushes, not giving in to the distraction I tried to dangle in front of him.

"You mean other than having a glass of wine and watching a horror film?" I joke.

"So, horror movies are your guilty pleasure. I'm more of a thriller man myself."

"No way, they're too scary!" I gasp, clutching the stem of my wine glass.

"Isn't that the whole point?" He laughs.

"No! The point is to be entertained, not to scare yourself shitless," I rebuke, and with that, we delve into a debate of which is better and our favourite films. We talk about everything and nothing at the same time—it flows seamlessly, effortlessly. We hardly even stop talking to eat, and before I know it, the food is done, I'm a bottle of wine down, and there's just us and the stifling tension that has been building between us all evening. It's a living, breathing thing between us. My walls are hanging on by a tether. This kind of ease so soon isn't normal. I shouldn't feel relaxed enough that I have to remind myself not to mention Freya. I haven't so much as dared utter her name aloud when I'm alone, never mind share her with someone else. But Johnathan has me wanting to spill my every secret, my every hope and dream.

"Thank you for humouring me and letting me take you out tonight," he murmurs.

"It's been a beautiful night, but I'm still not sure this is a smart idea," I confess, looking up at him from under my lashes.

"What can I do to convince you to let me prove to you this can work?" He leans his elbows on the table, imploring me to give him a shot, and it's with a twist in my gut I realise I want to. I want to take this for myself. I want a chance to be wined and dined again, to feel like I'm the only thing he sees.

"We'd have to keep things quiet. I don't want the office talking about us." The words have barely crossed my lips before he's nodding along.

"That can be arranged. We'll have to tell HR to keep things above board, but that doesn't mean it has to go any further than Donna. Secret is her middle name."

"True." I fall silent, weighing my options.

Is it so wrong to want something for myself for once? For so long, my life was controlled, my freedom non-existent. Even now, when I'm technically free of the Clan's control, I've still spent more time hiding than living. Isn't it time to live a little?

"Fine. I'll give you a chance. But I'm warning you now, Mr O'Neill: I won't be easily won over." The heat in his eyes as I tease him has me curious to know what would happen if we were truly alone right now. Would he make a move? Tease and taunt me some more?

"Sweetheart, I'll have you begging for mercy soon enough. Just remember, you're the one who issued the challenge." With that dark promise, he rounds the table. Bathed in candlelight, he leans down, caging me between the chair and him as he claims my mouth for the second time. More than a little eager, I reach up and circle my arms around his neck as I open for him with a moan. The chemistry between us is unlike anything I've ever known. Everywhere he touches me feels like I'm on fire, like I could burst from my skin at any moment. If this isn't worth the risk, then what is?

CHAPTER 19

The way life passes in a blur when things are going well truly is a crime that should be studied. For the first time in my life, I wish I could hit the pause button to soak up every second of it. But every day since our first date has flown by, and before I know it, a month has passed. A month filled with secret looks, heated touches, and all manner of luxury dates. A month of Jonathan carving a space for himself inside my walls. A month of shared laughs and not an ounce of regret for my choice. But like all good things, it comes to a screeching halt in the most abrupt way.

The morning started like any other, with the largest coffee mug I could find while answering the influx of emails that appeared overnight. No matter how empty I leave my inbox at the end of the day, it's always bursting at the seams by the next morning. But as time ticked on, and eight turned to nine and nine turned to ten with no sign of Jonathan, unease started crawling through me.

Not showing up is not his MO. Being late is *definitely* not his MO. Not texting or ringing me to tell me he was making a detour or had a last minute of site meeting? Highly unlikely. Something's not right. Firing off the last of my emails, I head up to Donna's office. If anyone here would know what's going on or where he is, it would be her. Only, her office is empty too, and going by the scattered paperwork on the floor of her otherwise meticulous office, it wasn't a planned exit. With anxiety crawling through my veins, I run back to my office to grab my phone. I'm already halfway to the exit by the time Jonathan answers.

"Helen… My Da…" Three words, and yet they convey everything. The pain in his tone, the broken whisper, says it all. Something is drastically wrong. I need to get to him. *Pronto.*

"I'm on my way. Just please hold on," I beg as I flag down the first taxi I see. Stumbling my way through giving the man Jonathan's father's address, it's all I can do not to shout and demand he hurry. The last thing we need is to be pulled over by the police, but Jonathan needs me, and he needs me *now*.

As the car pulls into the driveway, it dawns on me I don't have any cash, but before I can work out a plan, the car door is being yanked open to reveal a frantic Donna. In my four months of working for the firm, never once have I seen her look anything less than polished perfection. Yet, here she is, her hair looking like she's been running her hands through it for hours, her feet bare, throwing cash at the driver as she pulls me after her.

"Thank God you're here. I should have known to grab you when I got the call. Go on up. He's in Senior's room." Her words are a hoarse whisper that speaks of her own grief, and, not for the first time, I question just how she's connected to the Four Points. It's glaringly obvious that she is, but that's a question for another day.

Bracing myself, I head up the stairs, following the path we took the last time I was here. As I brush my fingertips over the framed photos that tell the story of a happy childhood, my heart breaks for what I know lies ahead. The grief clings to every corner of this house like a weighted blanket, determined to suffocate everyone inside. I draw closer to the bedroom, the eerie silence solidifying what I'm walking in to. There's no wheezing breaths. The gentle whir of the oxygen tank is silent. When I cross the threshold into the room, the sight that greets me nearly sends me to my knees. Grief is something I've never been exposed to, and as I take in Jonathan, on his knees at his father's bedside, with his head resting on the sheet while clutching his father's motionless hand, I pray I never have to experience it firsthand. This is gutting enough, and as my heart breaks for Jonathan, my resolve to be there for him in whatever manner he needs it only strengthens.

"Hey there, handsome," I breath out as I edge closer to him, laying a hand on his shoulder and feeling him lean into it with a whole body shudder. He reaches up to link his hand with mine, drawing strength from me.

"Thank you for coming. I'm sorry, I..."

"You have nothing to be sorry for," I cut him off, using my other hand to run through his hair. Sometimes, soothing touches is all we have to offer, and while they won't fix everything, they can take the sharp sting away.

"I knew this day was coming, but I still wasn't prepared," he confesses, his attention focused on his dad's prone form.

"I don't think death is something we can ever be prepared for. But at least he's not in pain now, and you know he's proud of you and all you've achieved." He lets out one last, ragged breath before getting to his feet and pulling me into his arms, burying his face in my neck while I run my hand through his hair. We stay like what for what could be minutes or hours until a knock on the door forces us to separate. Donna stands in the doorway with a man behind her. He looks as wrecked as Donna, but underneath all that, I can tell he's most likely a hardened criminal. Something about the hardness to his features tells the story that his mouth may never speak.

"Sorry, Jonathan, but it's time."

"Give us five minutes, Seamus," Jonathan says, and with little more than a tip of his head, Seamus steers Donna away from the open doorway.

"We should clear out; you don't want to witness this," I murmur, stepping back so he can detangle from me and say his goodbyes before he threads his hand with mine and tugs me out of the room. Down the hall, he pushes open the door to what must have been his childhood bedroom, stumbling over to the bed with me in tow. I barely have a chance to take in the school trophies lying about before he's pulling me down and into his side.

"It's ironic. He would be so thrilled to know I finally brought a girl into this room."

"Are you telling me this *isn't* where you bring all the girls? I'm shocked." I fake gasp, curling into his side and tilting my head so I can look up at him. His blue eyes link with mine and as silence takes over, heat builds between us. After seeing how fragile life is, how temporary and fleeting, the urge to feel connected to him on a baser level is almost more than I can handle. I want to crawl inside his skin and live there, meld us into one so thoroughly, we can never be separated.

His eyes flicker between mine before trailing down to my mouth. Tilting my neck up, I fuse our mouths together. I pour all my conflicting, desperate emotions into this kiss, trying to tell him without words what this means to me. With a hungry groan, he soon takes control, thrusting his tongue into my mouth and battling for dominance that I willingly hand over. Curling my hands around his neck and playing with the hair at his nape, I cling to him, scared that if I let go, he'll vanish. I want his kiss more than my next breath. I need his touch more than air. Soon, he rolls us over so he's looming over me, bracing his arms either side of my head so I'm surrounded by him, his scent, and the heavy weight of him pressing me into the mattress, all while he smoulders at me with a look fit to make me explode. I bite back a whimper as I try to pull him closer. His need is plain as day as he rests his forehead against mine. "Are you sure?"

It's a fair question. So far, I haven't let us progress past make out sessions, scared of giving myself over to him so completely. But that fear has evaporated in the face of our fragile reality and left a burning need in his place. "I've never been so sure. I want to be yours, Jonathan. In every way. Please, make me yours."

"I'll make you mine. I'll claim you so thoroughly, no one will ever doubt who you belong to, so deep, you'll never forget what it feels like to have me buried inside your pretty pussy," he says on a hungry groan, nipping his way down my neck. The thought of him leaving marks for all to see has me fisting his hair and holding him against me, encouraging him to mark me up. God, the thought of wearing his marks on my skin is so hot. As he makes his way lower, I've never been so glad I picked out a blouse. Linking eyes with me, he deftly undoes the buttons, revealing my black lace bra to his gaze. With a muttered curse, he kisses my heaving chest above the lace. He leaves hot, open mouthed kisses across my breasts, before enveloping my nipple in his mouth over my bra, causing me to moan and clench his hair even tighter in my fist.

Fuck, I wish there wasn't a barrier between his mouth and my skin right now.

At my whimpers, he smirks, asking me, "Does my needy girl want more? Hmm?" When all I do is moan, trying to pull him back down, he tsks, saying, "Good girls use their words, and you are such a good girl, aren't you?" The praise dripping from his words has me melting into a puddle beneath him as heat licks up my spine and lights me on fire.

"I want your mouth on me," I beg on a whimper.

"My mouth is on you, sweetheart. See?" he croons, dipping his head to lave at my nipple through my bra again.

"I need to feel you, please," I beg him, getting more desperate by the second. If he doesn't hurry up and give me what I want, I might just lose it.

"That's my good fucking girl," he growls, reaching under me to undo the clasp and letting out a groan as he sees my bare flesh for the first time. His reverent gaze has me feeling like I'm floating. Nothing could ground me now.

"You are perfection, an absolute goddess who deserves to be worshipped daily," he vows, circling each nipple with his tongue before pulling back to look at me as he shrugs off his own shirt. My mouth nearly drops open as my eyes take in his sculpted muscles for the first time. He truly is a work of art. His skin is flawless except for an intricate tattoo of a skull encased in a four-leaf clover over the right side of his chest. The fact he's been hiding this sight from me beneath his suits is a sin.

Leaning back down, he claims my mouth in a sensual kiss, working me up to a fever pitch in record time. Digging my nails into his neck, I cling to him as he makes me feel things I've never so much as dreamed of feeling before. Heat unfurls in my stomach, need climbing my veins, making me want things I can't even explain, foreign desires I've never let myself feel or explore before. I want to belong to him. I want his claim on me to a soul deep level. I want there to be no mistaking who owns me and who owns him. In a hundred years, when scientists are looking at our bones, I want our DNA to be so melded, it's a medical mystery.

Pulling back, he looks at me with his heart in his eyes as he confesses, "I need you, Helen. I need this." And in that moment, it's clear to me my desires are his as well. His need for human connection, for something grounding after his world has just been shattered, isn't something words can explain. Nor are there words to convey how much I want to be that person for him. Instead of trying to find the words that don't exist, I press a soft kiss to the corner of his mouth before guiding him back down. I reach between us to undo his belt.

Reaching between us, he rucks my skirt up before moving my underwear to the side as he runs his knuckles through my wetness with a heady groan. Climbing off the bed, he rids himself of his trousers and underwear until he's standing in front of me as naked as the day he was born, with a look so full of fire in his eyes, it's a wonder the room hasn't gone up in flames around us. Reaching for me, he pulls me off the bed and holds my eyes as he drops to his knees. Sliding his hands up my calves, he works his way up under my skirt. Following his touch with heated kisses, he pauses as he reaches the edge of my underwear.

"Please don't stop." I whisper, reaching down to card my hand through his hair.

"Never," he vows, leaning in to draw my underwear down with his teeth. At the same time, he reaches behind me to undo the zipper on my skirt. With a wiggle, it pools at my feet, leaving me naked in front of this man who I'm realising has my heart in the palm of his hand. I've never felt more powerful than in this moment, having the newly crowned Irish Mob Boss kneel at my feet with a look of adoration on his face.

Nudging my legs wider, he reaches up with one hand to tweak my nipple while he uses the other to spread my pussy before licking a line up my slit. The sensation causes me to throw my head back on a moan and tighten my grip on his hair. With a sinful chuckle against my pussy, he does it again, this time nipping my clit and thrusting his tongue inside me. The noise he lets out could rival a starved animal. Abandoning my nipple in favour of gripping my hip, he pulls me closer and guides me to balance a leg over his shoulder. With a curse, he flicks my clit and slips two fingers inside me. The added sensation is more than I can cope with, and it sends me hurtling over the edge with a sharp cry as I hold his face against my pussy and pleas fall from my lips.

"Oh my God. Jonathan, please don't stop," I cry out as my pussy clamps down on his digits. He just keeps working me over with a hungry moan, and another orgasm races in on the heels of the first one, quicker than I can process what's happening. Only when he makes me come a second time does Jonathan pull pack. The blue of his eyes is nearly completely swallowed by his pupils as he raises to his feet, keeping a firm grip on my ass. Considering my knees are still shaking, it's lucky that he is.

"You taste divine," he rumbles, dipping down to kiss me, and the taste of me on him is like an aphrodisiac. Instantly, I'm desperate for more. As he presses himself against me, I twine my tongue with his.

Pulling back, the expression on his face should have me nervous as he demands, "Get on the bed. Now." Instead, I find myself eagerly obeying, craving his praise nearly as much as his touch. And when I'm rewarded with a growly 'Good girl', I melt for him as he follows me down onto the mattress.

Crawling between my thighs, he cradles my face between his hands. "I'm going to make you mine now. After this, there is no going back. You belong to me, Helen. Do you understand? I'm never letting you go."

"I don't want you to. I'm yours, Jonathan, and you're mine." Looking into his eyes, I reach between us to guide him where I need him most. With a growl, he takes over. Fisting his cock as he wedges his thick head at my entrance, he holds my gaze as he presses himself inside me. My breath stutters at the overwhelming fullness as he presses in all the way, until his hips are nestled against mine.

"You're so fucking tight. You're absolutely perfect, sweetheart. My pretty girl, you feel so good," he praises. "Look at you. You're taking my cock like such a good girl. Every inch of me is buried inside you. How does it feel?"

"Soo…full," I manage to gasp out over the wave of emotions coursing through me. The few times I'd dared to risk it, sex never felt like this. I never imagined it could. Jonathan continues to mutter praise and curses as he drives both himself and me over the edge, and I know this is something special. Nothing could or ever would compare to this utter feeling of belonging that only he can give me. He vowed to claim me, and claim me he did, both figurately and literally. He tenses before burying himself deep inside me, and the feeling of him coming in me is enough to trigger one last bone-melting orgasm from me.

I was never meant to let myself fall for someone, let alone someone so tied up in what I'm trying to escape, and yet here I am, holding his head against my chest as we try to catch our breaths and bathe in our afterglow. As I make silent vows to help him through his grief, an entirely different fear to the one I'm used to consumes me. Instead of fearing for my life, I'm fearing for the day he's ripped away from me.

JONATHAN
CHAPTER 20

For a few moments, I forget. I forget the chaos on the other side of the door, the ramifications of what's just happened, the pain and grief that threaten to swallow me whole. For one moment in time, I just bask in the feeling of having my woman curled up beside me, her cheek on my chest and her legs twined with mine. The title I was itching for is now mine, but at what cost?

I might be twenty-two years old, but that's the cruel truth about losing a parent—you're never truly ready. Not today, not in twenty years. I've inherited an empire, more money than I'll ever need, and taken on the weight of being the Boss. But all of it came at the cost of losing the best man I've ever known. No matter how I try to frame it, the reality doesn't get any easier to swallow.

Running my hand along Helen's back, twining my fingers through her hair, I close my eyes for a moment and try to soak up the comfort she's offering me. Shit is about to change drastically, and the question of is it worth risking her safety is going to need answered, sooner rather than later. But for now, I let myself get lost in stroking her silky smooth skin and the feeling of her head on my chest, listening to the soft snores she's letting out.

A screen flashed on, illuminating the room and jerking me from my thoughts. Glancing over at my discarded clothes, I find the culprit and reluctantly detangle myself from Helen without waking her. Seeing Seamus' number flash across the screen, I'm more than a little tempted to let it ring, but knowing my luck, he'd just keep ringing or come let himself in. Slipping out to the hall, I answer it.

"About time you answered."

"The fuck do you want?" I seethed, beyond pissed that today of all days, he's interrupting the brief moment of peace I've manged to carve out for myself.

"You need to get to the Pit."

Eyes flashing, I rasp, "You aren't the fucking Boss, or have you forgotten that?"

"I know I'm not, which is why we need you here. It'll only take an hour or so, and then I'll make sure you're left alone," he tries to placate me. With a curse, I pinch the bridge of my nose to fight off the impending headache.

"Fine. I'm on my way." Hanging up on him, I head back into the bedroom. Helen's curled herself into a ball around my pillow, and the vision of her in my bed has me itching to climb back into it and curve myself around her back. Fucking business. Quietly, I get dressed, lean down to press a kiss to the crown of her head, and leave.

Catching sight of myself in the hall mirror, I pause. For so long, this has been Da's city, but now, it's mine. I make the rules now. Shrugging off my jacket and undoing my tie, I drop them to the ground before undoing the top few buttons and rolling up my sleeves. It'll do. Tomorrow, I'll buy some new shit fit for the new king of the Irish fucking Mafia. Wearing a three-piece suit past midnight to the Pit, of all places, is going to be a thing of the past. Hell, if it wasn't for Helen's obvious appreciation of them, I'd burn them all and start from scratch.

Grabbing my gun and holster from the unit in the hall, I grab my keys and hit the road. Less than twenty minutes later, I'm soaked through as I make my way to the back of the Pit. Rounding the corner to see all our men gathered with sorrow etched onto each of their faces, I realise I got it wrong earlier—this affects more than just me and my brothers. Everyone from the bottom of the ranks to the top will have their own grief to weather over the coming days and weeks.

When I meet Seamus' gaze, an understanding of what he's done passes between us. He's taken the load of telling everyone off of my shoulders, sparing me from having to put into words what I can't even fully comprehend yet. He dips his chin at me, a soft shrug his only comment as I make my way to stand beside him, with Declan, Jack, Brennan, and Ciaran flanking us.

"We've lost one of our own today, the best man many of us have ever known. There's a shitstorm of things we'll need to address, but before any of that, we need to honour him. Senior was more than just my father. He was our leader, our king, and I'll be damned if we don't give him the best fucking send off this organisation has ever seen!" At once, all the men stomp their feet and let out cheers loud enough to raise the dead.

"To Senior!" Seamus chants, and soon, they all join in, the show of unity driving home why we deal with the bad parts of this life. This brotherhood makes every long day, every bloody deal and broken bone worth it. Knowing that, at the end of the day, each and every one of them would have my back, would go to war without thinking, makes it all worth it.

Glancing at my brothers, the reality that I was wrong hits me again.

This isn't just my city now.

It's our city.

And God help anyone who gets in our way.

HELEN
CHAPTER 21

Grief does strange things to people. For some, it renders them motionless, the mere thought of getting out of bed being too much, but for Jonathan, it seems like he's determined to run himself into the ground. Long gone are the days of me beating him to the office, of him insisting on cutting our days short to make time for dates. Now, he's here long before I come in and long after the rest of the office has trickled out. Enough is enough. Pushing my chair back, I straighten my skirt and undo the top couple of buttons of my shirt before striding over to his office and letting myself in.

"What did I say…" His razor sharp words die on his lips as his eyes snap up and take me in.

Cocking a brow, I kick the door shut behind me. "About interrupting you? If memory serves, you said not to unless it was urgent. And this, Mr O'Neill, is *very* urgent."

"Oh yeah?" he drawls, leaning back in his seat and cocking a dark brow at me as hunger dances across his face.

"Mhm. You see, my needs haven't been met in quite some time, and as my boss, I would like to think employee satisfaction is a top priority." Slowing, I start toying with the idea of undoing another button as I make my way to his desk. His eyes stalk my every move, and as I round his desk, he moves back, making room for me to perch on the edge.

"Hmm, we can't have that," he murmurs, eyes glued to my hands as I work another button free before snapping to my thighs as I cross my legs, causing my skirt to inch up and tease him with a glimpse of the straps of my garter belt. "Is my pretty girl feeling needy? Do you need me to look after that pretty pussy? I bet you're dripping for me like the messy girl you are. My messy, needy girl."

Before Jonathan, I never would have pegged myself as having any kinks worth talking about, but praise drips from his lips so sinfully, it has my core tightening with need and a whimper crawling up my throat. His voice is like pure silk as he rolls his chair closer, trapping me between him and his desk. Looking down into his molten eyes, I see the challenge there. Am I really going to do this *here*, in our place of work, and flirt with the idea of getting caught?

In answer, I cock a brow and finish unbuttoning my shirt, shrugging it off. His eyes flash with allure as he takes in my exposed flesh, the black lace demi bra struggling to contain my chest. The air between us feels charged with unspoken questions, questions neither of us want to face right now. Reaching between us, I grab his hand from his lap, placing it on my inner thigh. Taking that as the challenge it was, he trails his pinkie up towards the lace edge of my underwear as he opens that filthy mouth once more.

"Are you going to be my good girl, sweetheart? Will you let me show you just how sorry I am for neglecting this perfect fucking cunt?" With every word out of his mouth, he edges his pinkie closer and closer to where I need him before, on the last word, he plunges two fingers inside my dripping core. With a cry of his name, I clamp around his digits, the suddenness of the motion shocking me in the most sinful way.

"Look at you, doing such a good job for me. You can take anything I give you, can't you?" he praises, his eyes glued to what he's doing to me. My head is spinning, raw, unfiltered need overwhelming me in the best way. Everything blurs except for the man between my spread thighs and the sinful smirk he flashes my way.

"Anything. I need more. Prove just how sorry you are." My words are breathy at best, and a positively starved look flashes across his face before he reaches up, collaring my throat with the hand not buried in my pussy.

"If you can think clearly enough to do more than whimper and beg for more, I'm not doing a good enough job." As he tightens his grip and thumbs my clit, my eyes roll back in ecstasy. I need something to ground me before I float away. Reaching up, I dig my nails into his wrist. He doesn't flinch—no, instead, he tightens his grip and doubles down on his efforts to make me come all over his hand.

"Be a good girl and come for me. I want to lick up the mess you make before I make a mess of you all over again. You can do that, can't you, baby girl?" At the new nickname, I shatter in an instant, just as fuzziness starts to creep in at the corners of my vision. With a moan, he lets go of my throat in favour of working my knickers down over my thigh-high stockings. At the sight of my bare, glistening pussy, he curses as he urges me to lay back before taking my thighs in hand and tossing them over his shoulders.

"You smell like mine." He groans as he nuzzles his nose along the inside of my thigh before bestowing a trail of hot, open-mouthed kisses in his wake as he makes his way closer to where I need him most. The second his tongue makes contact with my clit, I see heaven. He's relentless in his ministrations, licking and sucking and making a meal out of my pussy. My back arches, my fists clenching in his hair as he tirelessly works me over—and work me over he does. His determination to make me come is second to none, and oh my God, the humming, the vibrations as he groans into my pussy and rains down praise as he works me up to a fever pitch has me ready to tumble over the edge.

"Jonathan," I cry. "Jonathan, please…"

"When you're seconds away from coming for me on my desk, you call me Mr O'Neill." His gritted words, spoken into my pussy, are followed by him sucking my clit into his mouth and driving two thick fingers inside me, and I'm coming with a shout of his name. My head flies back, thunking against the desk below me, my mouth wide, ragged sounds tearing loose from somewhere deep inside me, somewhere only he can reach.

"That's my good fucking girl, coming all over your boss' desk like the needy little thing you are. Come here," he demands, sitting back in his chair and patting his lap. Eyeing the obvious bulge, I slide off his desk on shaky legs, wiggle out of my skirt, and straddle him, clad in only my bra and garter. The second I'm within his reach, he cups the back of my neck, pulling my mouth down to his. In seconds, he's licking into my mouth, sharing the taste of my cum with me and swallowing my whimpers. In return, I reach between us, snapping his belt open and palming his hard length.

"Fuck it," he mutters before taking himself in hand and notching the thick head at my entrance. Leaning back, he gives me a cocky smirk as he folds his arms behind his head. The juxtaposition between him being fully clothed and me being the needy EA half naked in his lap, his hard cock filling my dripping pussy, is like an aphrodisiac. It has me reaching back to balance on his knees as I slowly rise before sinking back down, watching his eyes grow hooded at the slow roll of my body.

"A needy, desperate brat like you can do better than that. Coming in here, demanding I pay you attention; well, you've got my attention now, sweetheart. Show me what you were missing, what made you interrupt me," he drawls, looking every inch the cocky bastard I took him for after our first meeting. Flicking my hair over my shoulder, I make a show of rising until only the tip of his cock is inside me and staying like that as I squeeze around him. His nostrils flaring is the only warning I have before he's collaring my throat and pulling me closer. "Stop being a tease. You can take me, so fucking take me like a good girl, or I'll show you what happens to brats who bite off more than they can chew."

"Hmm, but it's fun to tease you, Mr O'Neill. After all, you kept me waiting. *For. So. Long.*" I moan as I grind down on him, earning some friction against my clit as he tightens his grip and darkness creeps in. I'm seconds away from shattering around him when suddenly, he pulls himself free and stands, taking me with him. My back meets the cool glass of the window a split second before he hammers himself home so hard, my eyes roll back. He sets a punishing pace that has me wrapping my legs and arms around him to hold on as I beg for more.

"Teases don't get to come. Are you sure you still want to play this game?" he taunts, reaching between us to pinch my clit. Whimpers and pleas for more fall from my lips as I struggle to form coherent sentences.

"Harder."

"Now, now…how do good girls ask for what they want?" He slows down to the point of stopping.

With a huff, I roll my eyes. "Please."

"That's better." He nuzzles his mouth along my collarbone, leaving open mouthed kisses in his wake as he makes his way up to my mouth. In one swift move, he claims my mouth as his own, invading my every sense as he drives his hips into me at a pace that will bruise and tightens his grip on my neck. The combination of not being able to breath and him stealing what little air is left in my lungs as he kisses me is enough to have me writhing against him and my pussy clamping down around him.

"Oh, no, you don't." He spins us around, pulls out of me, and bends me over his desk, delivering a swift slap to each cheek before curling himself around me as he notches himself against me again. The heat of his chest against my back, the feeling of him stretching me open—it's heavenly. And when he fists my hair, tugging my head back? I'm helpless to do more than let out a breathy moan.

"I'm going to come in this little cunt, and then, and only then, will I make you come. Got it?" The bite in his words should scare me, but instead, it has me arching back into him and clenching down, desperate for him to make good on his threats.

"Harder. I can take it. I promise," I beg, urging him to take what he needs from me. With a curse, he straightens up, but before I can mourn the loss of contact, he's palming my ass cheeks as his pace increases. With every thrust, he's getting more and more desperate, and so am I.

"Fuck, that's it. Take my cum inside your cunt. Keep it there," he demands as his hips stutter and his release floods me. Before I have time to process what's going on, he drops to his knees behind me, his big palms spreading me open and his tongue pushing his cum back inside me. My eyes roll back as I scramble for something to hold onto as he picks up where he left off, flicking my clit and thrusting his fingers inside me until, with a cry, I come all over his hand and mouth.

"Mmm, that's my good fucking girl, keeping my cum exactly where it belongs." With a final kiss to my clit, he scoops me up and takes a seat in his chair again, with me curled up on his lap, careless of the mess I'm leaving on his thousand pound suit.

"Thank you, sweetheart. I needed that," he murmurs, pressing a kiss to my forehead. With a hum, I curl in closer, fisting his shirt in my hand and basking in the afterglow with him. Soon, we'll need to move and clean up, but for now, holding each other close like this is all we need to do.

HELEN
CHAPTER 22

"**R**emind me again why I let you drag me here?" I quirk my eyebrow at Donna as she weaves us through the busy streets of London with a single-minded determination that has people jumping out of her way.

"Because you know there's no point fighting me. I'd beat you in a heartbeat, never mind with the backing of my girls. Now come. We're running closer to being late versus fashionably late." Looking at me over her shoulder, she winks before linking arms with me and leading the way to O'Neill's. Hardly what I would call a casual work lunch location, and if I had known this was where she was bringing me, I'd have at least attempted to tame my curls and touch up my makeup. You'd think that after close to a year working with her, I'd know better than to take her offers at face value.

Waving off the hostess, she leads me to a set of doors to a separate, more intimate dining area. When Donna proposed I join her for lunch, I'd assumed she meant nipping out to the sandwich shop across the road, not coming halfway across town to Jonathan's Michelin star restaurant. I certainly hadn't expected to be blindsided into meeting more people tied up in the Four Points. Taking a deep breath, I push my shoulders back and follow Donna's lead.

Pushing the door open reveals a darker, more private section of the restaurant. Peering around the empty room, I clock the two women waiting for us. Looking at them is like night and day. Where one is polished to perfection, the other has a slight dusting of flour across her cheeks and arms. Both are absolutely stunning in an old money kind of way, the same way Donna is, and as someone who grew up in mafia circles, it's clear to me that these women aren't just dating mafia men—they've been raised in the life.

"Donna, how lovely of you to deign to join us," the elegant one drawls with a smirk on her face.

"Why, Una, you know you can never rush a good thing. And honey, I *am* the best damn thing," Donna retorts, making her way over to the table and giving Una an air kiss on each cheek before turning to the other woman and placing a kiss on her flour-dusted cheeks. Interesting. The dynamics between these three have my guard up even higher than usual, and that's saying something.

"Is your little friend planning on joining us, or is she just going to lurk in the doorway?" Una turns her eyes to me. The ice cold look in them reminds me too much of my mother for me to do anything more than fire a snarky response back.

"I'm used to a much grander welcome, but I suppose I'll humour Donna." Feeling three sets of eyes on me as I prowl forward has me repeating my teenage mantra in my head.

Shoulders back, chin up, tits out.

Smile pretty but don't show them your teeth before you attack.

As I reach the table, Donna reaches out to link arms with me again before taking over mediator duties.

"Una, Fiona, meet Helen. Helen, meet Una and Fiona. Una's all bark no bite. Don't mind her." Una's scoff and eye roll would indicate otherwise but, wisely, I let that subject drop.

Shifting my gaze to Fiona, I ask her, "You don't happen to bake, do you?"

That seems to break the tension a fraction as stilted laughter breaks out, and soon enough, we're all taking a seat and placing our drink orders when the young waitress comes to take them. Given the knots of anxiety that have been making me sick more often than not lately, I was planning to stick to water, but my plans are soon thwarted as Una switches my water glass for a wine glass, and Donna fills it with a healthy pour. The movement is so slick, it makes my head spin. Choosing my battles, I let the movement slide with little more than a raised brow.

"So, Helen, tell us. How awful is it being Jonathan's assistant?" Una drawls, that haughty tone in her voice like nails on a chalkboard.

"She runs that place like a well-oiled machine these days, like she's been there for years," Donna chimes in, pride shining in her green eyes.

"He's pretty much all bark, no bite. Or should I say, all grumble under his breath. Once I nailed down his routine, it was simple enough, and now I can step out for a lunch with Donna with no fear about what I'm going back to. It truly is a gift of a job." I shrug, letting my quiet confidence shine through. I conveniently leave out the decidedly unprofessional nature of our relationship these days and how that no doubt influences things. What we have is ours and ours alone.

"Jonathan? Our Jonathan is all bark, no bite?" The disbelief in Fiona's tone, coupled with her calling him theirs, has my hackles rising with the urge to claim him as mine then and there. Before I can out us, Donna swiftly inserts herself.

"Office Jonathan is a whole different beast. It's true." Donna's slight slip of the tongue would have her facing all kinds of consequences if we were back on the compound, but as the food and wine flows, it's clear these three have never once felt the fear that clings to everyone back home.

Thoughts of the differences between there and here follow me throughout the rest of my day. It's only as I'm slipping off my shoes and locking the door do I spy the letter waiting for me. I've almost become numb to the newspaper cut outs, with their varying degrees of threats. But when the photo in front of me is instead a zoomed in snap of me entering Jonathan's dad's house, the nauseous feeling I've been fighting only gets worse as dread curls in my gut.

Flicking it over, I see a message waiting for me: ***Tik, tok. You can't run forever.***

At once, the bile I've been pushing down comes rushing forward, and it's by pure luck I manage to make my way to the bathroom. I'm still clutching the cool porcelain when my phone chimes. With a groan, I drag myself back out to the hall and fish it from my bag. Less than five people have this number, and anyone who would be calling me on it immediately gets bumped up the priority list. I flip it open with a muttered greeting.

"Hello?"

"Helen? Is now a bad time? I can call you back…" Jonathan trails off, and immediately, all thoughts of self-pity and worry get placed on the back burner as I focus on him.

"No, of course not. I just got home." I drag myself over so I can lean against the wall as I search my bag for my water bottle. Taking a drink, I listen as Jonathan lets out a ragged breath.

"I was just ringing to see if you could come over tonight. Or I can come to you, if that's easier?" The uncertainty clinging to his words is so foreign to the man I was getting to know that every time I hear it, it breaks me a little bit more. Weighing my options, I tell him I'll pack a bag. With the promise that he's on his way, he hangs up, and I bang my head against the wall with a curse before heading to the bathroom and erasing all evidence of my vomiting. Spying the little pink and blue box that's been taunting me for days, I pick it up with shaking hands.

Between his dad's death and the sudden power shift, Jonathan more than has his hands full right now without my shit adding to that. But it's becoming clear the time to control the narrative is running out, and if my suspicions are true…I'm either going to have to confess everything or vanish. The problem is, I can't work out which is going to hurt less, and my growing feelings don't help matters. I can admit I'm falling for him, but that doesn't change things. Love doesn't equal safety or reassurances of understanding or happy endings. Sometimes, love means walking away, but the thought of leaving him when he needs me the most threatens to send me to my knees.

JONATHAN
CHAPTER 23

Having Helen by my side has been the only salvation to the otherwise never-ending nightmare that has taken over my life the last few months. It's been an endless cycle of meetings and proving myself worthy of the crown placed on my head. Most of these men have watched me go from awkward teenager to a cocky little shithead, but now they need to view me as their leader—which is proving to be a harder task than anticipated. Every move I make, every deal I negotiate, is met with more questions than they would ever dare have thrown at Da. The only bright spots have been when I've had Helen in my arms. Not having her by my side at the funeral gutted me, but keeping her sheltered from the limelight was the best call. Knowing she was waiting in my flat was the only thing that got me through the day.

And now, after a long day full of meetings, I just want to hold her and forget about my never-ending responsibilities; to soak up every inch of her goodness so maybe it'll mellow out the evil crawling inside me. But from the moment I picked her up, it's been clear she's a thousand miles away, any gentle probing on my end met with half-assed smiles and lacklustre reassurances. Even now, as she takes the penthouse in, her usual awe is diluted. With a frown, I cup her elbow. Turning her to face me, I link eyes with her as I try once again. "Sweetheart, what's wrong? Did the girls say something at lunch?"

"Nothing's wrong, I promise. It's just… Everything's so *heavy* at the moment. I want to be here for you more than anything, but I don't know how to help you other than being here when you need me." It's a half-truth at best, but with a kiss to her forehead, I let it lie. She'll confide in me when she's ready. Until then, I just want to hold my girl. Threading my fingers through hers, I continue down the path to my room. As the door closes behind her, she tugs me to a stop. Turning to face her, I raise a questioning brow.

"Please. Give me some guidance here. What do you need?" she blurts, looking up at me with her bottom lip trapped between her teeth. Reaching up, I tug it free with my thumb, only for her tongue to dart out and lick me. With a groan, I adjust myself as I watch her suck on my flesh. "You. All I need is you in whatever capacity I can have you."

"I'm yours, mind, body, and soul," she vows, leaning up to hook an arm around my neck, drawing my mouth down to hers.

Burying my fist in her hair, I haul her closer to me as I devour the taste of her. She slots against me perfectly, like this is what we were made for. With a breathy moan, she digs her nails into my neck before tipping her head back, exposing the delicate column of her throat to me. Letting go of her hair, I palm the curve of her perfect ass with both hands. She circles her legs around my waist as I use my grip to lift her up. Fusing our mouths back together with a curse at how good she feels, I walk us over to the bed before laying her down on the silk sheets.

"Please, Jonathan." I've barley taken a step back when her whimper reaches my ears. The sight of her laying there, blonde hair contrasting with my black sheets, chest heaving with each breath, pupils blown wide, has my cock rock hard. With a smirk, I take my time rolling up my sleeves and basking in her whimpers.

"What does my pretty girl need?" I croon, watching the shiver that passes through her as she clenches her fists in my sheets.

"I need you to touch me," she whimpers.

"Hmm, yeah? Where? Here?" Trailing my fingers along her ankle does little more than wind her up. With a huff, she shakes her head as I get rid of her shoes before pressing a kiss to each ankle.

"Higher," she pants, reaching for my wrist. She tries to drag me further up her body, but with a click of my tongue, I unravel her fingers before gathering both her wrists in one hand and pin them above her head. Leaning down, I nip her bottom lip.

"Use your words, pretty girl. Tell. Me. Exactly. What. You. Want." Between each word, I kiss my way down her neck, skip past her enticing cleavage, and return to my spot on my knees at the edge of the bed.

"I need you to fuck me. To claim me. I need your cum. *Please* give it to me. Fill me up. Claim me as yours." Goddamn, does she look pretty with tears in her eyes as her skin takes on a rosy hue of desperation.

"That's my good fucking girl," I praise her, watching as her back arches at the words. Huh, looks like my girl likes a little praise. Good to know. Running my hands up her legs and under her dress, I hook her underwear around my fingers before pulling it down.

"Looks like someone is a needy, dirty fucking girl," I growl, inhaling the sweet scent of her arousal from the damp spot on her thong.

"Needy for you," she confesses with a blush heating her cheeks. As a reward for being so fucking perfect, I crawl up the bed and push her dress out of my way. Letting out a curse at the sight of her wet pussy, I hook my arms under her legs to raise her hips off the bed before licking her from slit to clit. Her moans wash over me as I eat her like a starved man, circling her clit with my thumb and rocking my hips down into the bed. I need inside her now, before I blow and waste my cum. It belongs inside her, coating her insides, claiming her as my fucking woman in every way.

"Come for me, pretty girl. Come all over my face, and then I'll fuck you so full of my cum, it'll be dripping out of you," I growl, thrusting two fingers inside her and watching her face as pleasure ripples over her and she cries out my name. Fuck, I could watch her come all day.

"Jonathan, please, I need it," she whimpers, reaching down to fist my hair. With a groan and one last taste of her, I work my way up her body, kissing her stomaching and sucking her nipples along my way. I might be fit to burst, but my woman is always going to feel like the queen she is, and I'll be damned if I don't worship her the way she deserves. Every. Fucking. Time.

As soon as I'm level with her, she's wrapping her arms around the nape of my neck and drawing my mouth to hers with a hungry groan. Reaching between us, I free myself before notching my head at her entrance. Pulling back, I take in the sight of her wet pussy gripping at me. With a groan, I watch as I sink inside her before locking eyes with her again.

"You feel so fucking good. So perfect for me, aren't you? Look at you, taking every inch, my perfect, pretty girl," I ramble, mouthing at her neck as I build a rhythm that has both of us cursing. Pulling back to look at her, I cup her jaw.

"Who does this pussy belong to?" When she takes too long, I slap her tit. Her mouth drops open on a gasp before her eyes roll back into her head.

"Ahh…you!" she squeals, back arching into the pain. With a curse, I spit on her pussy, the need to come almost more than I can handle. Reaching between us, I thumb her clit until she's a whimpering, pleading mess beneath me and her pussy has me in a vice grip.

"Be a good girl for me. Come all over my cock. Show me how much you want it, and I'll give you my cum. You can do that for me, can't you?" Rather than answering, she arches her back and cries out my name as she does exactly what I asked. With a curse, I follow her over the edge, giving her everything I have before pulling back. Her eyes are glazed over as she smiles up at me, and not for the first time, my chest tightens with emotion. Pulling myself free, I push my cum back in her, where it belongs, before laying down beside her and pulling her into my arms.

I may have tried to fight this, and now might be the worst possible timing for it, but there's no denying my feelings anymore. Helen is it for me. She has my whole heart in the palm of her hand. She's my obsession, one I don't want a cure to. I didn't think I could have something so pure—so good—until she stormed into my office and my life. The words are on the tip of my tongue, only before I can say anything, she utters two words that shatter the peaceful moment and abruptly force us to crash back to reality.

"I'm pregnant."

HELEN
CHAPTER 24

Raw fear explodes inside me as I wait with bated breath as Jonathan freezes beside me. As soon as the confession left my lips, all movement stopped. His hand running through my hair, the gentle kisses he was pressing across my face — hell, it even feels like he's stopped breathing.

Pulling back to put a little bit of space between us, I call his name softly. When he turns his attention back to me, his shell-shocked look is still all over his face but, blooming like a flower, is a small tendril of awe. Of tender wonderment. And it's that sliver of emotion that gives me something to cling to.

Sitting up, I twist so I can look at him as I explain. "I've been incredibly nauseous lately, which I put down to anxiety, but then I missed my period, so I took a test, and well…" I break off on a watery laugh as he reaches for me, cupping my face in his palm. I lean into his heat and soak up the comfort he's offering me.

"I guess that's what happens when we take a risk or two, huh?" He laughs, offering me a sheepish smirk before his gaze drops to my still-flat stomach.

"Yeah," I breathe as emotions fly across his face, too quick for me to pin down.

"Have you been to a doctor? Do you know what we're having yet? Have you heard the heartbeat? What about those little photographs they give you?" His shock gives way to a series of frantic questions. The obvious care in his voice has me reaching up to cup his face between my palms.

"I love you," I blurt out, unable to contain it anymore. With a smile so wide, it's a wonder he doesn't pull a muscle, he claims my mouth in a searing kiss that lights my soul on fire and wipes away the worry that's been niggling at me since I first suspected I was pregnant. The fear of what we do now, where we go from here, has been eating me alive. The sea of secrets and half-truths between us, the odds being stacked against us… The reasons to be worried far outweigh the ones not to be.

"I love you so much, pretty girl. So fucking much. There's so much we need to sort out, to talk about. You'll need to move in here, we'll need to come out publicly. Not to mention, I'll need to find a new assistant." He mutters things to himself as his mind goes off a million miles an hour, the same way mine has been for days now, as suspicion settled into my bones. Reaching up, I press my hand on his mouth to shut him up before catching his gaze with my own again.

"Press pause. Be in the moment with me, handsome. We are having a baby." I implore him to let that sink in. All the worrying and planning that will plague us both can hit the back burner for a second. There will never be another opportunity to have this moment again. The moment where we find out we're having a child, that our love has bloomed into a physical thing in the most beautiful way. Right now, there's a baby who's the perfect mix of both of us growing inside me. It's a magical moment, and one that should be treasured.

"You're right, pretty girl. I'm sorry. There's so much to do, but I'm all in, I promise you. We're in this together, you and me against the world." He rests his forehead against mine, and silence blankets us, him and me and our little surprise. Hours or minutes could pass before I talk myself into confessing my sins to him. Letting these secrets lie between us for another second longer didn't feel right. While I know it's far from a pretty conversation, it's one we *need* to have, but the moment I open my mouth to lay myself bare, he beats me to it.

"There's something you need to know, and I'm not entirely sure how to tell you." Oh shit. He's not really going to…is he? I remain quiet with my eyes closed as he speaks the words into the top of my head, praying I don't give myself away.

"There's a lot more to the O'Neill empire than business holdings, and not all of it is above board. As far back as history goes, my great-whatever grandfather has had his toes dipped in all sorts of pots. One of those happens to be the Irish Mafia."

I pull back to look at him, and the determination on his face has me biting my tongue, letting him explain all about the Four Points and the criminal world he thinks I know nothing about. As he spits Angus' name out with hatred, the fear of revealing my secrets returns tenfold, and rather than confessing my sins, I dig a deeper hole for myself by continuing to uphold my lie.

"This is…a lot," I settle on after a moment. "I mean, this kind of thing just doesn't happen to girls like me."

"I swear, you're safe. More than safe. I give you my word," he vows as the opportunity to come clean slips through my fingers like quicksand. It's all I can do to act shocked while my mind races with *what the fuck have I done.* But it's too late to backtrack now. Instead, I have to commit to the façade of being new to the mafia world, let him teach me all about it, and pray that Angus never finds out and blows it to smithereens.

Even as I say nothing, the guilt gnaws at me, carving into my chest like a dull blade.

I had a plan—I swore I would go back for Freya, pull her out of the Clan's grasp, and make sure she was safe once and for all. But now,

I'm tangled in lies, sinking deeper into a world I swore I'd never return to. And yet…two little lines changed everything.

I'm so sorry, Frey. I can't risk it. Not now

JONATHAN
CHAPTER 25

Two months later

While the timing could do with some work, the news that Helen's pregnant was far from a bad thing. Sure, becoming parents in our twenties wasn't on our agendas, but the feelings between us aren't going anywhere, so why the hell should it matter if we have kids now or in a few years? And the way she took the news about the Four Points just cemented my belief that she couldn't be any more perfect. Keeping the fact that I have a pregnant girlfriend on the down low has been close to impossible. If not for Seamus and Donna, I doubt we'd have pulled this off for so long.

Keeping her and our child a secret grates on me. All I want to do is be able to shout it from the rooftops, but at the same time, the last thing I want to do is open up Helen and our unborn child to an attack. It's a huge part of why moving her out of that rundown flat and into my penthouse was one of the first things I did. No one and nothing gets in or out of here without my express permission and knowledge.

Now, as she creeps past the four-month mark, she's starting to show in a way that drives me crazy with both want and fear. The time for keeping this to ourselves is fast disappearing, and soon, the choice will be out of our hands. But for now, I focus on getting her ready and out the door before we're late.

"Do I look fat in this?" She's tugging at a purple maxi dress and frowning as it clings to her newly rounded middle.

"Sweetheart, you look as radiant as always. Now, please, we need to get going, or we'll be late." I come up behind her, wrapping my arms around her waist and kissing her neck. Her hitched breath and bitten of whimper are enough to have me smirking as I make her a deal. "If you're a good girl and come with me now, I'll forgive you for insulting yourself. That means we can skip the punishment and get right to the fun part later."

"Mmm, what if I want a little punishment?" she teases, pressing her ass back into the cradle of my hips. With a groan, I detach myself from her with a swat to her ass before leading her out of the bedroom and into the lift before she has a chance to delay us any further. Crowding her against the back wall of the lift, I silence her protests with a kiss, and soon, she's melting like butter in my hands. Good. I've big plans for after this appointment, which means we don't have time for any more delays. We make the drive in comfortable silence but, as we get closer to the clinic, she grows tense, frowning to herself as she looks out the windows.

"What's put that frown on your pretty face?" I ask, reaching over to lay my hand on her knee.

"Hmm? Oh, nothing. It just hit me. This isn't just any baby—it's your heir. What if it's a girl?" She worries her bottom lip. Her words give me pause. My natural instinct is to reassure her, but the truth is, I don't know what will happen if our child is a girl. There's never been a woman at the head of the Points before, but at the same time, I know my men. I know their hearts.

"It'll be okay, Helen. While it hasn't happened yet, there's no rule saying a female can't be in charge. Plus, that's years away from being a worry. We have time to figure it all out. Together." I squeeze her knee in reassurance as we pull into the clinic. Making my way around to help her out of the car is second nature, and as I guide her inside, I can't help but note how right it is. She belongs in my arms, by my side, and in my life. I can't believe I ever thought otherwise. I'd be lost without her sarcasm keeping me on my toes.

As we're led into the examination room by a friendly nurse, I keep my hand steady on her back before helping her up onto the exam table. Once she's settled with a death grip on my hand, the doctor comes in with a warm greeting and gets to work checking over the baby before turning to us with a smile on her face. "Would Mum and Dad like to know what they're having?"

"Absolutely. Please, I can't handle one more moment not knowing." Helen laughs, clutching my hand as the doctor takes note of a few things on the screen before pointing out something to us.

"See that? That's the head, the torso, and that…is a clear indication it's a little girl."

A girl. We're having a little girl. A daughter. As I stare at the blur on the screen, I already feel her wrapping me around her tiny, invisible finger. Helen looks equally awed, clutching the printouts in her hand. She lets me help her into the car, still lost in thought, and we're already halfway to Southend before she glances up with a curious frown.

"I thought we were headed home."

"Soon. I wanted to take a walk along the beach with my girls first."

God, that feels so right to say. Of course, it's a girl. It could hardly be anything else. I hope she looks just like her mum—or maybe not. I'll have my work cut out for me, warding off unworthy boys.

With a sharp inhale, she reaches across to thread her fingers through mine on the gearstick as we make our way to the beachfront.

"I hope this isn't your form of punishment," she teases as we make our way toward the walkway.

"Of course not. I know your preferred methods of torture. This is just a trip to get some fresh air," I reassure her. We walk in comfortable silence for a while, until I spy an older couple on a bench. I squeeze her elbow gently to get her to stop before I head over to them.

"Excuse me, sir. You wouldn't do me a favour and take a picture of us, would you?" I ask.

"Young love. How sweet, Bob. Take the photo for the young man," the lady prompts, and with a hearty laugh, Bob gets up, following me back to Helen's side and taking a few pictures before heading back over to his wife and leaving us to look out at the sea.

"I wanted something to commemorate today with."

"Hmm, yeah? And what makes today so special?" she teases me, leaning up on her tiptoes to place a chaste kiss against my lips. Pulling her in close, I wrap a fist in her hair, tilting her head back as I take her in. She's been glowing lately—our baby is doing amazing things to her.

As she looks at me, love shining in her eyes, I know then that my Da was right. The love of the right woman is worth the risk, and Helen Montgomery is that woman for me. From the moment I laid eyes on her, this was inevitable.

"Because today we found out we're having a little girl and..." I trail off as I thumb the box in my pocket and take a step back, getting ready to drop to one knee when screams ring out behind us. The sweet older couple I approached before are being held at knifepoint by two men, and an SUV with blacked out windows pulls up.

"Jonathan, we should leave," she hisses, tugging at my sleeve. A quick scan of the area tells me the time for making a run for it has vanished, so with a curse, I push her behind me, trying to shield her from sight.

"Just trust me. Stay behind me, okay? And if anything happens to me, run," I snarl just as the door opens, and out strolls none other than Angus. I'm getting sick and fucking tired of him showing up on my turf uninvited.

"What the fuck do you think you're doing here?" I spit as he strolls towards me like he doesn't have a worry in the world, like it's his right to be here. I don't bloody well think so.

"Awk, well, I asked for your help, and you denied me. So, here I am, taking matters into my own hands. Really, this is all your fault, Johnny boy." That damn accent makes me want to drive my fist through his skull. Slowly, so as not to draw his attention, I reach behind me to put one hand on my gun, ready for action.

"Remind me again: what is it you're looking for?" I try and distract him as I search for an out. He has men stationed all around us. Without risking Helen, there's no easy way out of this. Fuck.

"Now, don't play dumb. It doesn't suit you. I had a little runaway problem, you'll remember," he drawls, daring to get into my personal space. Something to the right of me catches his eye, and he freezes and zeros in on it before a sick smirk takes over his face.

"Well, what do we have here? Come forward, girl. No need to hide." Fucking hell. No way is he getting anywhere near her. Over my dead fucking body.

"Leave her out of this. She's just a random civilian. Now, how about you get in your car, clear your men, and I'll join you when we can talk some more?" I try to placate him, and it seems to work. With a sharp whistle at his men, they scatter. Once they are all out of sight, he heads back to the car. Looking back at me, he cocks a dark brow in question.

"I'm coming. Just let me get rid of this girl. We don't want witnesses, do we?" As he ducks into the car, I turn to face a nearly hyperventilating Helen.

"Sweetheart, listen to me. Ring Donna. Tell her it's a code red and then get the fuck out of here. Take the keys and just drive. Don't stop until Seamus finds you. I love you, so fucking much. Remember that." Without waiting for a response and not daring to hold her the way I want to in fear of who's watching us, I leave her, saying a prayer I can manage to distract Angus long enough for her to get out of here and out of his line of sight.

HELEN
CHAPTER 26

Coming so close to Angus after all this time has my heart pounding in a way that can't be good for the baby, and watching Jonathan disappear into the car with him does nothing to resolve that issue. All I can do is hope Angus didn't recognise me, because if he did, I know there is no way in hell I'm getting out of this carpark unharmed.

Making a mad dash for the car, I dial Donna at the same time.

"Code red," I gasp as soon as she picks up. Flinging myself into the car, I slam the door and yank the seatbelt on before pressing as hard on the accelerator as I can. Peeling out of there and leaving half of my heart behind feels wrong, but guarding this half is more important. Jonathan can defend himself, my baby girl cannot. She needs me to do it for her.

"Shit. Okay, deep breaths. We've got you. Just keep driving. Don't stop for anyone or anything who isn't Seamus or Jonathan, okay? That's the only two people you trust, you hear me?"

"Yes, I hear you. Just please, I need to save her," I sob, and, in that moment, something passes between us. Over the past few months,

Donna has been the rock I never knew I needed. From holding my hair back as bouts of morning sickness had me rushing to the bathroom, to confiding in me about her own pregnancy, I don't know how I would have kept my sanity without her.

"Helen, I promise you, nothing is going to get anywhere near your baby. We will not let that happen." The fierce determination in her words should soothe me, but nothing can, not until Angus is gone and Jonathan is back in my arms. Disconnecting the call, I focus on the road in front of me. I've no idea how long passes; all I know is, I'm beyond turned around. I have no clue where I am, never mind anyone who may or may not be tailing me. Hitting the brakes, I check my phone to see if I somehow missed any calls while I was playing fast and furious. Seeing nothing, I curse before looking up, only to swallow a scream.

Because all of a sudden, a car has appeared, and the driver is fast approaching me. With a curse, I try to turn the engine on, but the damn car refuses to start. Slamming all the locks down and praying the tinted glass will be enough to deter him, I keep quiet. I sincerely hope this guy is as dumb as he looks; otherwise, I'm fucked. He leans in close, bracing his hands on the window to get a better view.

As he reaches behind him, I see my life flash before my eyes. Freya. Jonathan. My unborn baby. All the lies and what ifs wasted. This is the moment I have been running from, and now, it's too little, too late. I'll never get to hold my baby, never get to tell Jonathan I love him one more time. Wetness trails down the side of my face.

But as he goes to withdraw his weapon, someone twists his arm behind his back, forcing a pained grunt and muffled shout. And there behind him, covered in blood, is Jonathan, pain etched into every crevice of his face. In that moment, a bitter, heartbreaking understanding passes between us.

The immediate threat may be gone, but the damage is irreparable. In just minutes, Angus tore through everything we had, shattering the fragile peace we'd built and ripping our happiness out from under us.

There's no undoing the devastation he left behind—no taking back the fear, the anguish, the suffocating grief.

It's too little, too late. No amount of time, no amount of pretending, can salvage what's been lost. Our hearts have already drowned in the wreckage.

JONATHAN
CHAPTER 27

Angus Graham can burn in hell.

Not only did he lure me into the car, holding me at gunpoint while his men gunned their engines to chase after Helen, but he also wasted precious moments—moments we'll never get back. He talked in circles until I knocked him out. Time lost. Time stolen.

Today should have been a celebration. Finding out the gender of our baby was meant to be the start of forever—not the end before it even had a chance.

We should be celebrating our engagement, making plans to go public. Instead, Helen is sobbing in my arms as we scramble to make plans to hide her, to ensure her safety—and that of our unborn child.

Angus just cost me the love of my life and my unborn daughter. I'll be damned if he lives a peaceful existence after tearing my world out from under my feet.

Watching Donna and Seamus pack Helen's things into boxes feels like watching my future unravel before my eyes. And when Donna gently pulls Helen away, the heartbreak etched into her face as she cradles her swollen belly will haunt me for the rest of my days. Angus Graham will pay for this—if it's the last thing I do.

Suffering

JONATHAN
CHAPTER 28

"**S**et up a meeting with Jianyu Li. We need to get this deal on the move. The sooner we get the drugs out of here, the better. How's finding new girls for Alibi going?" Exhaustion and frustration bleed into my voice. If I thought taking Da's position would come with more freedom, I was a fucking idiot. I may not have to answer to anyone, but every decision I make now carries consequences more severe than ever. One fuck up could cost us everything, and not a day goes by when that doesn't weigh heavily on my shoulders.

It's a never-ending cycle of problems. As soon as we get one issue ironed out, something else creeps up. Someone always wants more: more drugs, more guns, more money. You name it, they want it. I can't even remember the last time I was able to roll up my sleeves and get my hands dirty in the Pit.

From his seat opposite me, Seamus lets out a grunt before responding with an eye roll. "Finding girls is the easy part. They're practically gagging for the prospect of being under our safety net. The hard part is making sure they're up to Una's standards."

Ciaran's ex is proving to be a thorn in all of our sides these days. Why he ever gave her the time of day, never mind had a child with her, I'll never know. She was always an unsufferable bitch at the best of times, never mind now that she can lord their son over him. The only good thing that came out of their marriage was Matt—the kid's shaping up to follow in his dad's footsteps with a knack for torture.

"Tell her to remember her fucking place. Any power or control she might have had got halved the minute she filed for divorce. She should be grateful we found her a job after what she did," I spit. Ciaran might be an unhinged fucker, and I'll be the first to admit he's a piece of work, but he gave that woman everything and more, only for her to fuck her guards behind his back and then have the nerve to accuse him of cheating. If it wasn't for their son, she'd be where she belongs: in the Pit. But alas.

"Roger that." His dark expression promises retribution.

"What about Owen? Do you think he's ready?" I shift the subject to something we've been dancing around for a few years now. Somehow, the kid's turned into a bit of a golden retriever, even with everything he's been privy to or involved in. Considering his role in our hierarchy, it unnerves me. One day, he'll need to be ready to step into his dad's shoes, and while I love the kid like my own, I have my doubts. Business is business at the end of the day. We're only as strong as our weakest member, and no matter who that weak link is, they need to toughen up, or they'll be cut loose.

"Honestly? I'm not sure. But he knows how important it is. Now that he's finished his time at St Theresa's, I'll get him up to par one way or another," he reassures me before looking at his watch. "Speaking of which, I should head out. Fiona will have my balls if I make us late."

"Graduation day already, huh?" I muse. Thinking of my own child never fails to send a pang of longing through me. I should be there, picking her up and celebrating her results and future with her. Holding her and Helen. Taking them out and spoiling them like they deserve. To this day, Seamus and Donna are the only two who know Helen was pregnant, but even they don't know the gender. The fact that I have a daughter is a secret I've held close to my chest. A secret pride I've never let cross my lips.

If we couldn't be a family, then it only felt right to keep that to myself.

"Feels like only yesterday we dropped him off for the first time," Seamus reminisces with a fond look on his face before freezing and shooting a guilty look my way. Ignoring it, not wanting to get into this again, I dismiss him before pouring myself a double measure of whiskey. Swirling the amber liquid around, I let my mind wander.

Today is one of those days the missing out hits me even harder, the could've, should've, and would've of everything haunting me even more so than usual. Keeping my girls safe is worth the sacrifice a hundred times over, and I would do it all again if it kept them out of Angus' reach, despite the heartache. Time has dulled the razor sharp longing into a dull ache buffered by the fact I used my resources to keep tabs on them and make sure they're looked after. It's no coincidence Helen stumbled across a house just beside our gated community in her budget, nor is it a coincidence Cora ended up in St Theresa's surrounded by children of my men. I lived for the updates that would land in my email inbox every Monday, without fail, from my hired security team, even if sifting through the photos of them always felt like a knife to the chest. Knowing even if one day we find our way back to one another, these are moments and years that can never be recreated is a bitter pill to swallow, but I'd do it all over again to keep them safe.

Their safety is paramount – my happiness is not.

Shaking off my dark thoughts and throwing back my drink, I shift my focus to the mountain of issues on my desk. Maybe I should delegate some of this, but keeping busy is the only thing that works to keep my mind focused on the here and now, so I throw myself into it with gusto. I'm in the middle of drafting an email to send to Angus when my phone rings. The fucker wants to encroach on Four Points territory to access a transport route for his latest party drug for free.

Not on my fucking watch. If he wants to peddle that shit further afield, he's going to have to find a different way or cough up a percent.

Seeing the number of the security firm I outsourced to watch over my girls flash across my screen has my gut clenching. With sweaty palms, I hit answer as I shove back from my desk, already on my way to the lift.

"What's happened?" I growl, dreading the response. Our contract is clear: phone calls are reserved for emergencies only.

"Sir, there's been an accident."

My world narrows into a fine point, and white noise fills my ears, blocking out what else he's saying. Those five words are on repeat in my ears, whittling down to one. One word capable of sending me to my knees. Of ending my world.

Sir, there's been an accident.

There's been an accident.

Been an accident.

An accident.

Accident.

"Where?" I manage to grit out and, after getting a location, I give in to the urge to hurl my phone across the room. When that doesn't even so much as take the edge off my roaring emotions, I whirl around, planting my fist through the wall beside the lift. I smash the down button several times before it finally opens. Jabbing the button for the carpark repeatedly and ignoring the throbbing in my knuckles, I barely even notice the bloody trail I'm leaving behind me as I make my way to my car. I'm on autopilot, making my way to the scene of the crime.

The crime scene where my heart and soul lays.

As I get closer to the motorway, the roaring sounds of sirens great me, telling me all I need to know and everything I never wanted to hear. This isn't a bad dream or a hallucination. I'm not about to wake up with Helen in my arms.

The car I'm looking at looks like a squished can—Helen's car. I'd know that number plate anywhere. I'm still on autopilot as I stumble out of my car and head for Jake. Clocking me, he meets me halfway with a grim look on his face.

"Boss. It was a freak accident. We called the ambulance immediately, but..." He trails off just as the ambulance gurney rushes past us. The sheet is completely pulled up, telling us without words that the worst has happened.

Denial. Rage. Helplessness. Devastation. The weight of a hundred different emotions hits me, all of them washing over me at the same time, threatening to send me to my knees. I can't fucking breathe. Can't move. Can't think. The only thing I can do is stare at the wreckage in front of me. It was all for nothing. Years of denying us happiness and a family, and for what?

The love of my life, the woman I've never gotten over and never will, is gone.

And in that moment, on the side of the motorway, the last shreds of my tattered soul die too.

HELEN
CHAPTER 29

Awareness trickles in like slow waves lapping at the shores of my reluctant conscious. The phantom feeling of holding my baby girl in my arms is ripped from me as my hazy eyes focus on the grimy ceiling of my cell. Time has lost all meaning in this hell hole, but every morning begins the same way: with dreams of Cora and Jonathan haunting me, teasing reminders of everything I've lost. Screwing my eyes closed until the point of dizziness does nothing to alleviate my reality.

Plans of picking Cora up, and spending the summer making memories to carry us through yet another period of separation while she continued to chase her dreams at university, came to a crashing halt in a flurry of screeching tires and blinding lights.

My life flashed before my eyes in a blink: the fleeting moments with Jonathan I would sell my soul to have had more of, the heartbreak that nearly crushed me until Cora came screaming into the world. Becoming a mother may have scared the absolute shit out of me, and doing it alone was certainly not how I ever envisioned embarking on that chapter of life, but in an instant, she became my whole world.

And in an instant, I was torn away from her and thrust into the depths of depravity.

I've spent seventeen years protecting Cora with every fibre of my being, both from my past and her dad's present. I've shouldered my heartache like a badge of honour, because it meant she was safe. And if enduring this pain and torture somehow protects her from it? I'll take it all with gritted teeth and pray she never knows about the true underbelly of the crime world she was born into or the crown of thorns that awaits her.

Blinking back the wetness in my eyes, I inhale through my nose as I envision a steel wall slamming down between thoughts of Cora and Jonathan and my reality. I tuck them safely behind that wall, where they can't be tarnished.

I refuse to let these vultures pick apart the only good things I've ever had.

Over my dead body.

Trailing my gaze from the ceiling to the door, I brace myself for what the day holds. If the creaking floorboards overhead are anything to go by, I won't have to wait long. Keeping my eyes trained on the door, I work to retreat somewhere far from here, where what's coming can't touch me, can't penetrate me. By the time the door crashes open, I'm so far removed from my body, I don't even flinch.

"Rise and shine, 103." Long gone are the days of hearing my name. Now, I'm just a number, and that's if I'm lucky. Being addressed as 103 beats being called bitch or slut or whatever oh so creative name he can come up with. I wonder if he's aware of the small mercy calling me 103 truly is. I don't dare allude to it, in fear he'll start using my name. Not having to hear my name cross his lips as he rolls over every boundary I ever had makes separating myself from the here and now easier. Being a number makes it easier to say these things are happening to 103, not me.

103 was the one paraded naked in front of a roomful of vile, hun-

gry men. They were the one sold to the highest bidder. It was 103, not Helen, who was medicated and moved to this basement of horrors. 103 is the one being dragged from her metal cot by her hair and thrown into a porcelain tub that's seen better days.

Helen is blissfully unaware, locked away in concessions far away from this, away from the grimy hands that touch her body like it's theirs and the hot breath beating down her neck as evil eyes devour her whole.

"Today is a big day, 103. We're having a very important visitor, so I need you on your best behaviour. You'll be a good pet for me, won't you?" At first, remarks like this would draw a response from me, but I soon learnt that's what he wants.

He wants me to flinch, to cry, to scream and fight back. Because then, that means his actions are just. As if anything I could ever do would justify what's been done to me since I was sold like a piece of meat to this sick fucker.

I'll be damned if I give him that get out of jail free card.

Now, I just stare at a spot on the wall in the distance and imagine I'm somewhere else, maybe on a sunny beach sipping a cocktail. Sometimes, I'm back in Jonathan's arms, but usually, I'm braiding Cora's hair as she tells me all about her day. Those moments are what gets me through each day in this hell hole while I keep my eyes and ears peeled for a way out, for a weakness I can exploit. If my captor thinks he's managed to break me…well, he's got another thing coming. I have far too much to fight for, to hold on to. Giving up isn't an option.

With a hard yank on the chain attached to the collar around my throat, I'm dragged out of my hazy dreams and back to the here and now. With my morning 'bath' done, I'm left feeling grimier than when we started, as I'm dragged back over to my cot, where my wrists and ankles are shackled once more. I guess that's what I get for trying to claw his eyes out one too many times.

As he paws at my naked body, his excitement evident, I focus on the blood-spattered ceiling above.

As his hands trail lower, I let my mind flutter away.

I'm not here when he cups my breasts, pinching my nipples to the point of pain.

Not here, when he touches between my legs, tutting at the lack of arousal that greets him.

I'm far away as he shoves himself inside my dry and unwilling channel. As he grunts and moans above me, I think of Jonathan instead. All we ever had were brief moments together, and even if I manage to crawl my way out of here, I doubt that will change, but still, my mind wanders to him. To my safe place. I picture him the way I knew him and wonder what time has done for him. Time might have been a bitch for me, but I bet he's aged like a fine wine.

Is he living the life we always dreamed of? Has he moved on or does he still think about what was stolen from us? Does he miss his daughter? Will he have heard the news about my death? If so, is he helping her through her grief? Or is she alone? That thought is like a hot poker to my insides, a blow even worse than the sensation of my captor shuddering with his perverse enjoyment as he reaches his climax.

"I'll be back soon. Be a dear and don't go anywhere." With that sarcastic remark, my tormenter leaves me chained to my cot, the sticky condom laid across my stomach as a reminder of what just happened. Sick fucker. The day I get to enact my revenge can't come soon enough.

JONATHAN
CHAPTER 30

Little surprises me these days. I've come to always expect the worst. Not that there's much 'worse' left to experience after losing Helen so utterly, but when my office is flooded with blinding light, I flinch before glaring at the offender. I take another swig from the whiskey bottle clenched in my fist.

I've been sitting here alone, cloaked in a hatred and rage threatening to swallow me whole as day turned to night, the city lights below the only light penetrating the penthouse. Another day Helen's not here to see. Another night our daughter is spending thinking she has no one in this world. If I could snuff them out and plunge the whole city into darkness, I would. With no answers or outlet in sight, the rage simmering in my veins has turned venomous, like a viper ready to lash out at the first unfortunate soul who stumbles across its path.

"What do you want?" I slur as Seamus stands in the doorway with his arms crossed. His stance screams defensive, but I can't say I blame him. The last time he came here uninvited, he left with a broken nose and a shattered casserole dish. Given his obsession with Fiona's cooking and reluctance to share in the first place, I'd bet my net worth on the fact I won't be getting any more care packages anytime soon.

"It's time to pull your head out of your ass and stop being a moody wanker. Drowning your sorrows isn't going to change fuck all, and leaving your child to handle this on their own goes against everything we stand for. Family above all else, remember? What the bloody hell are you waiting for?" His words have me itching to lash out, to demand to know just how peachy he would be if it was his wife who had died, if he was the one having to grieve in secret because as far as the world knows, he has no reason to be anything short of normal. But one look at the pinched look on his face has the words freezing in my throat. His concern is like an ice-cold shower, waking me up from the fog I've been sleepwalking through.

"What I'm wating for is for you to get the fuck out of my office and back to work," I snap, pointedly ignoring the less-than-impressed look on his face. His reaction to my words isn't my problem.

My problem is Angus wanting to encroach on our territory.

My problem is keeping my daughter safe without her knowing me, because knowing me is a curse I wouldn't wish on anyone right now.

Everything else can go fuck itself.

Days later, the guys have dragged me out to O'Neill's under the guise of needing to show me something. Turns out that something was the new hostess. Apparently, being chronically single is a red flag that they feel the need to rectify. They can go fuck right off. If it's not Helen, I don't want to know.

"Come on, man. Lighten up and go get some. She was definitely checking you out," Jack grouses with a wag of his eyebrows.

"Maybe if you got your dick wet, you'd chill out," Ciaran chimes in, leaning back in his seat, his eyes firmly glued to our waitress' retreating ass.

"Pig." I snort, chucking my napkin at him. "How about I tell your new missus you're checking out our waitress's ass?"

"Feel free. Jen said it herself; I can look without touching as long as I'm coming home to her. And coming *in* her." He smirks, dodging Seamus as he reaches up to clip him around the ear for me. While some organisations might not give a fuck what their men do in their personal lives, Seamus is right. Family has always been the driving force behind everything we do, and Ciaran's remarks toe the line a little too far south.

"If the only reason you fuckers dragged me out was to try and slip me the number of one of my staff, then I'll be seeing myself out." With an eyeroll, I start to stand, only for Jack to shove me back into my seat without even looking up from his phone.

"Sit your ass down. You've been icier than usual over the last few months, and if it wasn't for Seamus, we'd have dragged your grumpy ass out sooner. Now, this is what's going to happen: you're gonna eat some food, shoot the shit, and relax for one fucking night, got it?" Bren drawls from across the table, pinning me under his challenging stare.

"Fine. But if you fuckers think I won't get my own back on you for tricking me, you've another thing coming."

"Wouldn't expect anything less." Dec laughs before downing his drink and flagging down the waitress. She makes a valiant effort to ignore the heated looks from Ciaran and Brennan while she takes our orders, and I make a mental note to leave her a hefty tip. Trust the twins to be so stereotypical and have the same type.

Dinner passes in a blur of small talk and comparing war stories from their weeks. Jack swears he has the shortest straw: dealing with new recruits. But the guys are quick to interject with their own woes. I'm only half listening, most of my focus where it always is these days: on death and destruction, retaliation and vengeance.

As the food is cleared and the drinks continue to flow, I'm swirling my drink around my glass as I muse, "I'm telling you, this shit doesn't add up, no matter which way we twist it."

I'm met with groans and muttered curses, my obsession nothing new to them.

"Bren has checked everything he can hack into, and there's nothing to write home about," Jack counters, his brows a dark slash across his forehead at the change of topic.

"And we've been sniffing around as much as we can without being caught. Other than the fact their compound is like a prison and no one seems to have a mind of their own, there's nothing out of the ordinary," Declan summarises, not for the first time. It's the same old story every time we discuss this, but I can't shake the feeling we're missing something.

"Well, clearly, we're missing something." Call me a dog with a bone, but there are too many red flags to ignore. I'll be damned if I let him continue whatever bullshit he's up to. He may not have been driving the truck that crashed into Helen, but he alone bears the weight of her death.

Because of him, she was fending for herself.

Because of him, she wasn't by my side, guarded by my soldiers.

And for that, he will pay.

Hours later, I've ditched the guys and stumbled my way into a tattoo studio. I'm sure they'd love to turn my intoxicated ass away, but my name means no door is closed to me in this city. So, the gruff artist who drew the short straw pulls on his gloves and sets up his station as I lay back on his table. I can already picture what Seamus would say if he knew I was branding my soul as Helen's so permanently, but luckily for me, he's home with his wife and son. Lucky bastard. If passing on being the Boss meant I got to go home to the same thing, I'd burn this whole organisation to the ground in a heartbeat.

"Ready?" the artist grunts at me, gun in hand just above my heart.

"Get it done." I grunt and close my eyes as the sweet pain floods my system. I might not be able to hold her in my arms again, but she will forever own my heart and soul, so it's only fitting I ink her there for the world to see.

HELEN
CHAPTER 31

365 days in captivity

An indeterminable amount of time later, I'm ushered up the stairs, naked and blindfolded; wearing clothes is a ghost from the past. As I'm pushed to the ground, the impact of the cold, rough floor on my bare knees sends a shockwave of pain up my spine. I know better than to react. Instead, I embrace the pain for what it is: a reminder that I'm still alive.

The telltale sounds of gravel kicking up outside alerts me to our company arriving. Any second now, a fresh wave of hell will descend upon me. Screwing my eyes closed behind my blindfold, I count backwards from ten. Days when we have company are always the worst. Never once has a visitor resulted in anything good. The last time we had one, I couldn't move for a week. The time before that, it was a month. Taking what might be my last pain free breath for a while, I brace myself.

Remember, it's 103 who's here, not Helen.

Raucous laughter booms from outside. The mere sound makes my skin crawl with the need to get out of here. *Now.* But if being blindfolded and naked wasn't enough of a hindrance, having my wrists tied behind my back ensures the chances of me making a run for it while my tormenter welcomes his guest is impossible. I learnt that the hard way.

"It's been far too long, Kyle. I'd hoped for an invitation sooner than this. After all, you wouldn't even have such a delicious pet if not for me." The all-too-familiar Scottish lilt sends a wave of terror through me as the front door closes behind them. The control I've fought so hard to hold onto is slipping through my fingers like quicksand as my mind races to find alternative explanations. My ears are deceiving me. I'm imagining things. I *have* to be. The alternative is more than I'm prepared to face.

"You'll have to forgive me. I'd meant to have you over sooner, but my dear pet here took quite a bit of breaking in before she was up to standards. I didn't want to insult you with a subpar offering," Kyle blusters. The panic lacing his words, so far from his usual cocksure attitude, tells me I'm not imagining things. A tremor of fear races up my spine as I hold my breath, hoping, praying I'm wrong.

"I do hope she still has some fight in her. The feisty ones are always the most rewarding. When you feel the fight leave them as you make them come on your cock. Seeing the light dim as you tear them apart. There truly is nothing better, don't you agree?" His taunting words sink into my bones, weighing me down and trying to force me to bow under their weight as he stalks closer. He's so close, the woodsy cologne that haunted my childhood burns my sinuses as he crouches down and removes my blindfold.

"Why, hello there, my runaway bride. Miss me?" The salacious expression on his face as his eyes drop to my exposed chest tests my resolve to remain dissociated from what's going to happen. At my silence, Angus chuckles, a mixture of amusement and condescension. Hot breath fans across my face as he leans closer, his coarse beard scraping across the side of my face as his venom seeps into my pores.

"Freya made a beautiful bride. She was positively glowing, though that might have been thanks to being pregnant. I couldn't take any risks a second time. You understand." His words land like a physical blow. *Please, God, no.* Everything I've done, everything I sacrificed… It was all in vain. I thought running away would force him to turn his attention on some other family, and yet, if his words are to be believed, I grossly miscalculated. How could my parents have allowed this?

He leans back, his cold grey eyes searching mine. What is he waiting for? For me to congratulate him? Say I'm sure it was a lovely ceremony, sorry I missed it? Go fuck yourself, you piece of paedo shit?

None are words I can let pass my lips, not unless I want to risk his wrath or, God forbid, him taking it out on Freya. Sweet, innocent Freya, who only ever wanted the freedom to chase her artistic dreams. God, I let her down so spectacularly, it burns. I should have done more; I should have brought her with me. I should have done something, *anything,* to protect her from this monster. Why the hell did I ever believe she was safe being the walls of St Andrew's? I should have gone back for her at the first opportunity. Instead, she's been paying the price for my own naivety.

Flicking my gaze slightly to the left, I count the tiles on the wall behind him until I can shove my temper back into the lockbox I keep it in, where it can fester and grow until I'm free to unleash every scrap of anger I've been forced to swallow.

"Nothing to say? How disappointing." He tuts, rising to his full height and disappearing out of my line of sight. I don't have long to wonder where he's disappeared to. Wrapping my hair around his fist in a cruel grip, he yanks my head back before continuing his taunting.

"What do you say we put her through her paces, Kyle? See if we can't get her to show us some of that famous Scottish fire, hmm?" The glint in his eyes would have terror licking up my spine if I wasn't so numb to my body being abused at this point. Not a day has gone by in this hell hole when my body has been my own. Pain has become my closest confidant. So, while Angus' taunting words have my stomach revolting, they float over me, skimming me but not quite sinking in.

After all, what harm can his words do in the face of what's to come?

What are words and taunts compared to searing pain and intrusive touches?

Kyle must agree as, with a sharp tug on my hair, Angus draws me to my feet and turns me to face him. Kyle closes in behind me. The sick excitement that coats his features has my stomach twisting into a knot of unease. *Please, God, let me get through this.*

"It's about time you give me what should have been mine. What do you think your Johnny boy would think if he could see you now? Naked and at my mercy, where you belong. Irish loving slut." Spittle flies into my face. Flinching back, I stumble into Kyle, whose grip on my wrists stops me in my tracks. The suffocating feeling of being trapped seeps in as Angus trails one knuckle across my cheek before gripping my jaw and tilting my head up.

"Now, now, be a good girl, and I won't have to hurt little Freya. And you wouldn't want that, would you? Or maybe you do. Maybe you want her to join you, hmm? I can arrange that, you know. Gift Kyle here another pet to train." One look in his manic eyes tells me the sick cocksucker would do it a heartbeat. The mere thought of my baby sister in that basement of horrors with me is more than I can handle.

"Leave her the fuck out of this," I snarl, thrashing against my restraints as all rational thought vanishes. Instant regret floods my system as his face lights up with glee a split second before he lashes out, circling my throat and applying pressure until black spots dance across my vision. I'm wheezing for breath as he leans in, that damn cologne choking me almost as successfully as his fist.

"I want to see you covered in blood, dripping with it, as the re-alisation you've just sealed your sister's fate sinks in," he sneers before jerking his chin at Kyle. For a moment, it's me and him, frozen in a staring contest so full of hatred, it's a wonder the building doesn't alight around us. Then, Kyle is back, joining Angus in front of me and pressing a meat cleaver into his open palm.

I can't tear my eyes from the knife, in fact, I can't move at all.

There's nowhere to run, even if I could. The one time I tried, I made it as far as the front lawn, only to discover we're truly in the middle of nowhere, no neighbour in sight. So yeah, I could try to run, but how fast can I run across gravel with bare feet? Not fast enough.

"Sir, if I may? Why don't we move this downstairs, where you'll have more room to…enjoy my pet," Kyle interjects, standing off to the side, shifting his weight and looking a second away from pissing himself.

It's ironic. Up until now, he's seemed like the big bad wolf, but in comparison to Angus and the threat hanging in the air since he arrived, Kyle feels like the safer option. Better the devil you know. Kyle, as sick and cruel as he may be, clearly wants a living pet, someone to torture and fuck when and as he pleases. But to Angus, I'm disposable. He replaced me once; who's to say he can't and won't do it again?

With a grunt of agreement, Angus wedges the knife into his waistband before tossing me over his shoulder with his hand firmly planted on my backside. His wandering hand as we make our way back to the basement is the least of my worries. Tossing me down onto my cot, he follows me down with that damn knife in his grip once again.

"Now, why don't we play a little game? Let's see how many cuts it takes to make you squeal like the rat you are." He cackles as he presses the tip of the knife against my collarbone, his beady eyes glued to the blood that swells up. Over his shoulder, Kyle shifts his weight from foot to foot, the same sick desire dancing across his features.

Time blurs as my skin turns red and pools of blood seep into the threadbare mattress. His erection presses into my hip, his enjoyment more than evident. Bile threatens to escape at the implications of what's to come. The clicking of his belt buckle is soon followed by pressure against my entrance. A whimper escapes me as I feel him push himself inside, and wetness I refuse to let fall gathers in the back of my eyes. Somehow, this is even worse than when Kyle uses my body for his pleasure.

"You like that, don't you? A slut like you is only good for spreading her legs, isn't that right?" he jeers from above me in between groans of pleasure. Biting my tongue against the venom that wants to spew out, I focus on the ceiling, counting the blood spatters once more. I wonder how many of those were here before me, how much of my own blood stains the walls of this place now.

Not satisfied with my nonresponse, he digs the tip of his knife into my chin as he demands, "Kyle, make yourself useful and get the poker. I'll get this bitch to cry out one way or another."

The implication of that threat has me frantically shaking my head as I plead with the devil between my thighs. But no amount of pleading or begging is going to stop him, that much is clear, from the euphoria painted across his face to the way he picks up his pace, thrusting himself deeper into my body with every movement, regardless of the pain he's causing.

"O'Neill will never want to touch you again, not after we ruin you for good," he taunts before stuttering to a stop with a shout. As he climbs off me, the weight of his body is replaced by the weight of his words, and the tears I've been holding back slide down my cheeks in silent agony.

He works to shackle my ankles and wrists to the bed while raining down more taunting remarks, but I'm not here anymore. I'm so lost in my head, in my heartbreak, it's like I'm floating above my body, watching.

Watching as they make good on their threats to ruin me.

As Kyle joins Angus at my bedside with the red-hot poker at the ready.

As Angus holds me down and Kyle presses the brand into my hip.

As they take and take and *take* what they want from my body until no part of me remains untouched.

As the tattered remains of my heart crumble with the pain coursing through my body.

Please, let this hell end.

JONATHAN
CHAPTER 32

A Table meeting is neither a good nor bad sign—it's simply a measure of time. Da used to say these meetings were integral to keeping the ever-fragile peace between the five most powerful crime families in the UK and Europe. That, without these meetings, tensions would have room to fester and boil over. Personally, having all that ego shoved into one room seems like the perfect way to tempt fate. One wrong move—hell, one wrong *look*—and an all-out war could start.

It's never used to discuss the regular shit either. Extortion, drug deals, illegal weapons—those kinds of discussions are our common ground in the same way our disgust for dealing in the skin trade is. It's as natural to us as dealing in the stock trade is to investors, or drafting up a contract is to a lawyer.

So, no, none of that is grounds to call a Table meeting. Considering every man in this room has his own mile long list of crimes he's wanted for, with at least two different agencies actively hunting him down, wasting time is the last thing we can afford to do. What is also a given is the fact that none of us will ever see the inside of a jail cell—we'll never pay for our sins. Call it corrupt. Hell, I'll be the first to hold up my hands and concede that fact. That's the perk of having the connections and wealth the crime world provides.

As the heir of the Four Points, this status quo has suited me quite nicely. Why the hell wouldn't it? Never having to worry about the consequences of my actions was something I took for granted. Then, Helen entered my orbit, only to be ripped from it just as swiftly. And so now, as I sit here surrounded by the leaders of the Italians, Russians, Chinese, and Scots, all I can think about is how different things would have turned out if not for this shitshow. If it weren't for this never-ending war I was born into, would she still be mine? Would we have stood a chance if the odds weren't stacked against us from the start? A man could go insane pondering all the what ifs.

The rapid sound of gunfire, followed by exclamations, draws me back to the here and now. And here and now, Angus has officially lost the plot. The whole damn point of these meetings is we're all disarmed to stop shit exploding. Yet there he is, pointing his gun at Salvatore as he rants and raves. Ivanov clutches his shoulder, the once-white shirt stained red, while Jianyu Li has ducked under the table. Fucking coward.

"What do you want to do, boss?" Seamus mutters under his breath from behind me. Sharing a look with him, I jerk my chin at the door. Our best bet is to get out of here while Angus is caught up in his issue with Salvatore. If we can just make it to the other side of the double doors, we'll be able to reclaim our weapons and even the playing field. Silently, I slide my chair back and make to move, only to freeze when movement to the right catches my eye.

Slipping in a side door, crouched low to the floor with determination lining his features, is Angus' son, Logan. Last I heard, he was practically an outcast, all but disowned. It's clear there's no love lost on his side either as he rugby tackles his father to the floor and swiftly disarms him before using his forearm to apply pressure to his windpipe.

"Sorry to interrupt. If you'll excuse me, I'll get rid of the trash and leave you to your meeting." With a tip of his chin, Logan disappears as quickly as he appeared, dragging his father's body along with him.

"What the fuck?" Salvatore mutters, breaking the stunned silence. *You can say that shit again.*

"He's gone too far this time," I spit out. I always knew he was an unhinged bastard, but opening fire at a Table meeting is too damn far. He may as well spit on everything we stand for. Shared looks of anger and muttered curses float around the room before Jianyu Li chimes in.

"He needs to be stopped," he mutters, dusting off his suit with narrowed eyes.

"Agreed. Next time, why don't you step up and help instead of hiding like a coward?" I demand, ignoring Seamus' warnings as I advance on him. Jun Weng, Li's second, quickly steps in front of Jianyu, crossing him arms and puffing out his chest in an effort to look bigger than he is.

Quirking an eyebrow, I drawl, "You do know relying on Weng to fight your battles does little to disprove my point, right?"

"I'd like to point out that I was the one shot, and you don't see me taking part in this pissing contest," Maxim mutters as his second makes a tourniquet on his arm to stop the blood flow. He knocks back his drink with a wince before turning his icy glare on us.

"Dry your eyes. I get worse injuries just working in our clubs half the time," Seamus adds with a roll of his eyes.

"Gentlemen. How about we bench this childish behaviour and focus on the issue at hand?" Salvatore drones as he dusts off his suit before taking a seat again. Raising an eyebrow in challenge, he waits for us all to grudgingly take our seats again.

"What do you propose? We have a heart to heart about his evil ways?" I snort. Maxim does an awful job at covering his laugh with a cough to my left, drawing a glare from Salvatore before he continues.

"What I propose is that we handle this little problem before it spirals any further." At his calm words, the room freezes. I glance at Maxim first, his heavy brows a dark slash across his forehead. Given he hasn't outright scoffed at Salvatore's suggestion, I'd say he's leaning towards being on board. Fucker never could control his bloodlust; he's worse than a drunk trying to control their bladder. Li, on the other hand…

"I don't have time for this shit. You three might have time to burn, but I do not. I've a cocaine empire to run." He sneers, making to get up, only to be stopped by Salvatore's next words.

"And I've a heroin empire and numerous vineyards to take care of, yet I still have time to get rid of a threat. It's called delegating, or is the Triad so weak, you can't do that?"

"Come on, Li. Face it. Your precious cocaine isn't what it used to be, and everyone knows your heroin and wine are the best in the business, Salvatore, but let's be real for a second. They're out of most people's price ranges, and don't get me started on how niche the weapons trade is. Angus might be a bastard, but his party drugs rake in more than our endeavours have in years. Now, if we took him out…" I drawl, leaning back in my chair and flicking my eyes over each man in turn. I watch as my words land, seeds taking root.

"I'm in. When do we do this? I can set one of my snipers on his tail." Trust Maxim, a Bravata Pakhan to his core, to be the first to sign up for bloodshed.

Sighing, I shake my head before continuing. "It's not that simple. We need to go about this the right way, unless you want his men gunning for us. We also need to get to the bottom of what shit he's involved in before it blows up in our faces."

"So, we take it slow. We investigate, keep our ears to the ground, keep each other updated on anything we find and revisit this next quarter, yes?" Salvatore's suggestion is met with some grumbles, but at the end of the day, it's the best plan we have. With a dip of my chin, I raise my glass in silent agreement.

"Let the games begin," Jianyu declares gleefully before tipping back his drink, nodding at Jun, and leaving.

Angus' takedown is long overdue.

Let the games begin, indeed.

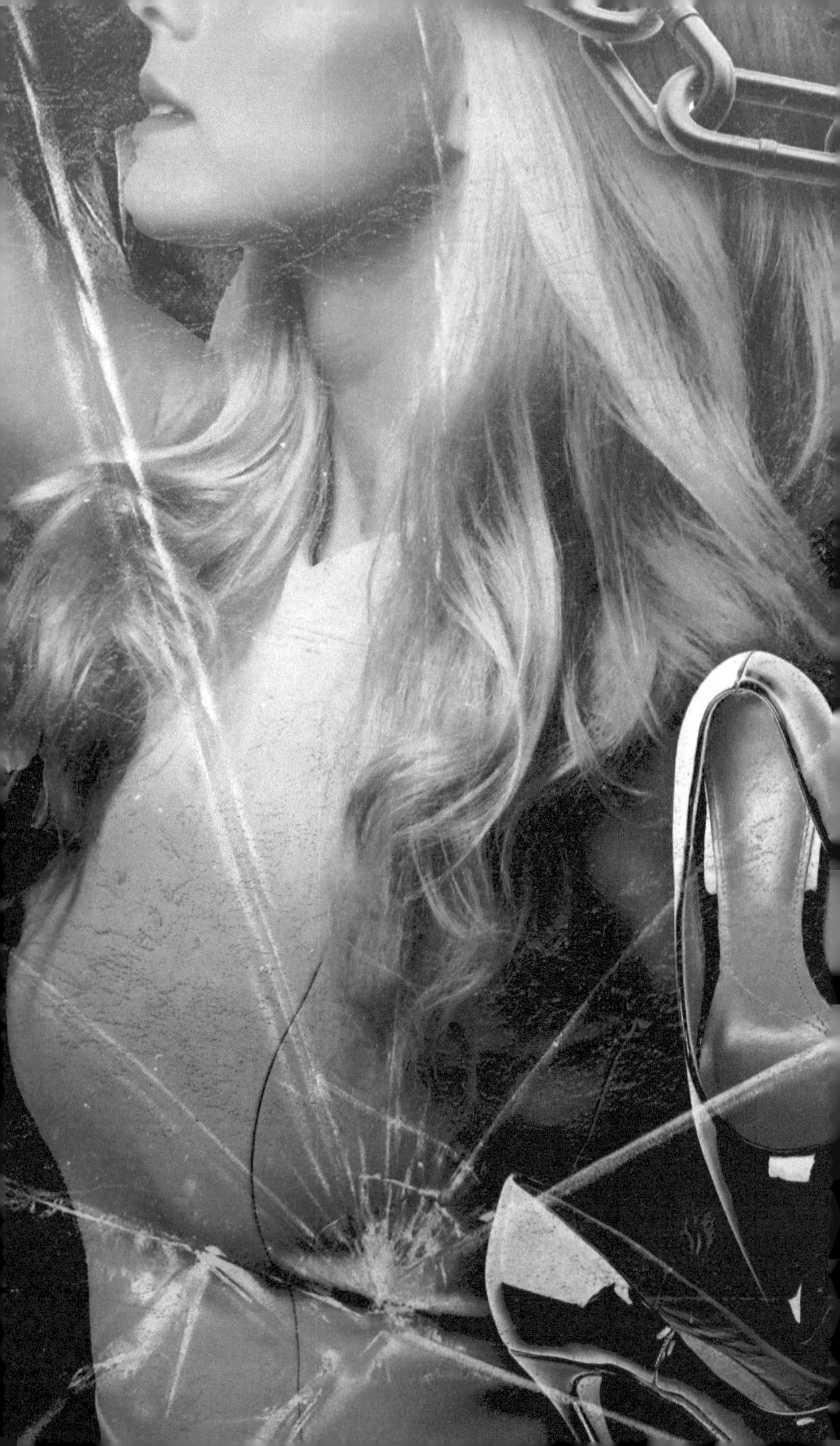

HELEN
CHAPTER 33

1,460 days in captivity

Hot, stale breath washes over my face. With a frown, I try to twist away from it, not wanting to leave my dreams behind just yet. It's getting harder and harder to conjure up Cora's face, and it's near impossible to remember what being held in Jonathan's arms feels like. The urge to burrow deeper into them while I can is a physical ache that nothing can alleviate.

"Rise and shine, 103," Kyle taunts, tugging the ends of my hair. Reluctantly, I pry open my eyes, only to choke on a startled scream at his proximity. His face is mere inches from mine; so close, I can count the freckles across the bridge of his nose and pick up on the flecks of gold in his brown eyes. The smell of stale coffee and bourbon clings to his breath as he sneers at my horrified expression.

"Ah, there's my pretty pet. Come on, today's a special day." He tells me as he frees my wrists from their restraints before moving lower and freeing my ankles. Pins and needles race through the muscles as sensation floods back in. Rotating my wrists to alleviate the pain, I keep my eyes trained on Kyle as he keeps up a steady stream of condescending small talk, gathering a length of rope before turning back to me.

Tutting at the fact I haven't moved, he yanks me up by my shoulder before looping the rope through the 'o' ring in my collar. Standing back, he smiles at the sight before tugging the rope, forcing me to my feet. I don't so much as flinch when he squeezes my ass, pulling my body into his and grinding his hardness against me.

"Come along. There's no time to waste." His sickly happy, slightly manic tone has the hairs on the back of my neck standing up. It's been a while since our last visitor, and I hope that's not about to change. My ribs have seemingly healed, but the thought of playing the role of punching bag so soon has them twinging with phantom pain.

"What's today, sir?" The words taste like ash as I grit them out, but prolonged silence on my end only serves to rile him up. The last time I let him prattle on with no input resulted in a fractured wrist that still twinges. The time before that, he burned off my pubic hair. Needless to say, I've learnt to pick my battles now.

"I'm so glad you asked, pet. Today's our anniversary. Four years together, isn't that wonderful?" He turns to face me, a cocky smile painted on his face. The implication is clear: anything other than an enthusiastic yes is the wrong answer. And yet, how can he expect me to say four years of daily abuse, rape, and captivity is wonderful?

Four years I'll never get back, even if I do find a way out of here.

Four years of scars I'll carry with me forever.

Four years of nightmares disguised as reality.

My silence drags on, and slowly, his smile fades and twists into something ugly. A twisted sneer would unnerve me if I weren't so used to seeing it by now. But what never fails to unnerve me is just how quick he can flick the switch. In an instant, the slightly manic but chipper man is gone, and in his place is a man with evil behind his eyes and a snarl on his face as he backs me into the wall.

Boxing me in, he leans so close, I can smell the bourbon on his breath as he snarls, "I. Said. Isn't. It. Wonderful?" Spittle hits my cheek with every word, and the revulsion crawling through me makes keeping a straight face even harder than normal.

"Y—yes," I manage to choke out, doing my best to force a smile on my lips when all they want to do is curl back and flash my teeth at him. What I wouldn't give to rip his throat out with my bare teeth, to feel his blood splatter on my skin and know with every fibre of my being that I'm free, to watch the life drain out of him slowly, to repay every awful thing he's done to me in kind. Would that make me a monster? Or would my actions be just and pardoned in a court of law in a way his never would be? Would my bloodlust be sated, or would it unleash a side of me born from agony and fear? These questions plague me daily, but the answers never come.

"That's more like it. Now, come along." In a blink, he's back to his chipper if not manic persona as, with a tug to the rope, he continues leading me out of the dark, dank basement and up to the main house. For a moment, my feet are frozen in shock, eyes firmly glued to his back, waiting for him to realise his slip up. Only, he never does, and I stumble to follow him before he clocks the fact I haven't moved.

For the first time since I've been here, he's forgone the blindfold. Swallowing down my shock, I catalogue every inch of the house as we pass through a sparsely decorated living room towards the kitchen. Seeing the front door covered in a maze of locks and the bars across each of the windows, my heart kicks up a notch. Looking over his shoulder, he flashes me a smirk. Biting my tongue against the retort he's clearly waiting for, I plaster a demure smile on my face instead and flick my eyes to the floor as we get ever closer to the heavenly smell of food. My mouth waters and my stomach grumbles, but I know better than to get my hopes up. One of his favourite forms of torture is to tease me with what I can't have.

An open door I'll never exit.

Food that will never cross my lips.

A gun that will never enter my grip.

Freedom that will never be mine.

Or so he thinks.

Prior to my time here, I would have rolled my eyes at something so basic being a form of torture. But when you're robbed of your basic rights, served scraps of often out-of-date food, it's surprisingly effective. I'd do close to anything for even the smallest plate of the greasy food on offer or the luxury of having a bubble bath.

"As a treat for being such a good pet, I've decided to let you feed me. And if you're lucky, I might even give you a taste. Now, come here," he demands, taking a seat at the head of the table and patting his lap. I eye the table full of more food than one could possibly consume, and a small, dangerous kernel of hope unfurls in my gut before I can stomp it out—hope for a kindness that might not come, but maybe if I do what he wants, he'll allow me a few bites. After all, he did say today was special…

Taking a deep breath, I shuffle closer to him. When I come to a stop at his side, he quirks an eyebrow at me in silent challenge. Swallowing my pride, I perch on his knee and pretend I can't feel his eyes crawling over me.

"That's my good pet," he croons huskily, his enjoyment evident as he wraps an arm around my waist to pull me closer to him. The tips of his fingers brush against my mound, and it's all I can do not to throw up on his shiny black loafers. That touch sets the tone for the rest of the meal. As I scoop up the food and feed him, his fingers dip ever closer to my entrance, and never once does he follow through on letting me have any. Once he's had his fill, he uses his grip on my pussy to forcefully turn me so I'm straddling him.

"You like that, pet?" he taunts me as he plunges his fingers inside my dry channel. While I wish I could spit in his face and claw his eyes out, I can't, not if I want to make it out of this alive. So instead, I shove how I truly feel into a box and nod my head, praying he'll just think I'm too wrapped up in feeling good to speak. With a smirk, he reaches up with his other hand to twist my nipple. "I think it's about time we pierce these. A pair of matching Ks dangling from these rosy tits would look perfect, don't you think?"

The mere thought of him modifying my body to fit his sick desires has a scream fighting its way out. Biting it back to a whimper, I let him think what he wants as I pray to a God I don't believe in anymore that this will be over soon, one way or another. There's only so much one person can bear, and I'm fast approaching my end. Something needs to give before I do. Smirking at me, he reaches between us, his hands going for his belt. Ice trickles down my spine as dread settles into my bones. But before he can make good on his intentions, a sharp ringing stops him in his tracks. With a curse, he deposits me on the chair, muttering to himself as he ties the length of rope around the back of the chair.

"Fucking cock blocker cunt. What does she want?" Glaring at his phone screen, he paces the length of the kitchen as he picks up.

"What?" he snaps, crossing his arms over his chest as he stares at mine. "Now's not a good time. Can't this wait?" A pause. "Suspicious? Isn't that what you're there to stop?"

He scowls. "Well, get to work then. You know the drill. If Ciaran isn't working, then move on to Jonathan. I don't care what you have to do, just keep them busy. Pit them against each other if it comes to it." Hearing Jonathan's name coming out of Kyle's mouth has me straining to hear more over my pounding heart, but as the person on the over end continues, he lets out a groan and leaves the room, slamming the door shut behind him.

Flicking my eyes around the kitchen for any clue to help unpack what I just heard proves futile. Bits and pieces of how I ended up here have glued themselves together, thanks to Angus' big mouth, but never in my wildest dreams did I anticipate Kyle to have any kind of tie to Jonathan. Maybe it's just a coincidence—it's not like Ciaran or Jonathan have overly unique names, but given the context…

Jonathan might not be mine anymore—and he may never be again—but I'll be damned if I don't do everything I can to protect the father of my child, the only man to ever make me feel safe and treasured.

Little does Kyle know, his little phone call has relit the fire of determination inside me just as hope was slipping from my grasp.

JONATHAN
CHAPTER 34

"**T**alk about a shitshow." Shooting a glance at Seamus, I grunt in agreement. Angus going off the deep end, while not unexpected, is a ball ache I could do without right now. Between our daily dealings and watching out for Cora while ensuring there's no ties linking me to her, this is the last thing I need. Cracking my neck to relieve some of the tension, I lead the way to collect our weapons.

"You can say that again," I sigh as we collect our guns before making our way out to the car. The sooner we're on our way out of Scotland, the better. Every second inside their compound, surrounded by mindless soldiers, is a second too long. The contrast between home and here is always glaringly obvious in the most unsettling way.

"What's our next call of action?"

"We go home," I answer wryly, knowing full well that's not what he's asking me. When a scoff is all the answer I get, I crack my neck before muttering, "And then we get to work. Things are heating up. Think Owen is ready to step up and earn his place?"

"I'll make him ready." His words hold more conviction than I think he truly has, but I let it drop for now. His son's softheartedness isn't high on my list of worries. After all, he'll either shape up to be the man the Four Points needs, or he'll be cut loose. After Angus' outburst, my biggest concern is making sure he has no reason to suspect I have a daughter, because despite the code of honour that's meant to exist, I don't doubt for a second he would exploit her existence in a heartbeat. If one hair on her head is touched because of me, I'll never forgive myself. Perhaps now's the time to stop outsourcing her security and get someone I can trust instead.

Hours later, I'm still weighing my options as we pull up to the penthouse. With a gruff thanks, I make my way inside. I stride through the lobby as the answer comes to me in the form of an overheard conversation.

"Come on, man. You know I can beat your ass." Glancing over at the commotion, I see one of our newest recruits stepping up to Owen. With a roll of his eyes, Owen pushes him back before clipping him around the back of the head.

"Bullshit. Liam Finlay trained me himself. You do know that asshole is a black belt?" His scoff is met with a protest from the new kid. With a fond shake of his head, he looks around the lobby, only to meet my gaze. He tips his chin in greeting, a lopsided smile on his face, but I'm already entering the lift with little more than a half wave.

Turning my attention back to the issue at hand, I mull over that name. Liam Finlay, one of three brothers, if memory serves. Never one for bringing trouble across my doorstep, and yet notorious for getting results. Quiet fucker. Big on not asking unnecessary questions. Perfect qualities for a guard.

Pulling out my phone, I shoot off a text to Jack to send them over. Entering the dark penthouse, I use muscle memory to make my way over to the drink cart. When the elevator dings with their arrival, I'm looking out at the city below. The sight of London twinkling below would be relaxing if it didn't fill me with a sense of overwhelming responsibility. Without the Four Points' careful rule, this city would be nothing, and they don't even know it.

"Jack said you wanted to see us, boss man?"

"What did I tell you, Cole? Shut the fuck up. Sorry about him, sir. He's new to this," Liam grunts, sounding frustrated with his younger brother. Biting back a smirk, I turn to face them. Liam has taken a couple of steps in front of his brothers, and if the dark scowl on his face is anything to go by, he'll be ripping them a new one once we're done here.

Looking past him, I take in his brothers. The younger one, a kid with bleach blond hair, looks like a cocky little shit on the surface, but if his constant shuffling and fidgeting is anything to go by, he's seconds away from shitting himself. Good. A healthy dose of fear will keep him in line. Beside him must be Aidan, the middle brother. He's wisely keeping his gaze steady on me, showing no sign of fear, but the way his chin is dipped conveys respect. Looking over the three of them, I weigh them up.

When it comes to protecting my daughter, I can't afford to cut corners. The time for outsourcing her protection has come to an end. It just doesn't make sense anymore, not when the threats she needs protecting from are deep rooted in this life. Outsiders are woefully underprepared, uneducated on the risks and threats out there. Using some of my own guys takes away that risk factor, but in its place, it increases the chances of questions and suspicions. The epitome of a rock and a hard place.

"I've a job for you three. Discretion is a must." I raise my eyebrow, and at their confused nods, continue. "It's a guard position, but your charge won't and can't know you're on her tail. Neither can anyone else. If you breathe one word about it to anyone, it'll be the last thing you do, understand?"

"We can do discreet," Liam reassures me with a firm nod.

"Good. Show me you can be trusted, and maybe we can talk about a more permanent promotion. Don't worry about explaining things to Jack. I'll handle telling him," I reassure them, indicating for them to follow me through the dark living room to my office. Flicking the light on, I make my way to my desk, perching against the front of it as I watch them file in. The differences between the three of them couldn't be more obvious: whereas Liam is clearly shut off and just here to do a job, Cole is practically a kid in a candy shop, taking everything in with wide eyes. Aidan rounds the trio out with untrusting eyes that haven't left me for a second.

"Your charge is a twenty-year-old female. She currently works for O'Neill's and lives in a rundown flat with her boyfriend. I need you three to keep an eye on her, tail her without her knowing. If any threats appear, handle them. Give me daily reports. That kind of thing," I inform them, watching as confusion darts across their faces and they exchange a look.

Clearing his throat, Liam answers for them. "Consider it done."

With that, I give them the dossier I have on Cora with strict instructions not to repeat or share this with anyone. They're bound to have their suspicions about why a bartender at O'Neill's warrants this kind of protection, but, wisely, they keep their questions to themselves. Placing my trust in these three to guard the single most important person to me is a hard pill to swallow, but needs must be met. And right now, I need to be able to hunt for answers without worrying about her safety. The time for her to flounder on her own is fast running out, and the sooner I can bring her home where she should always have been, the better.

HELEN
CHAPTER 35

1,825 days in captivity

At some point in our lives, we're all afraid to die. We worry about what comes next. We worry about leaving our loved ones behind and wonder, will it hurt? Will it be quick? How will it happen? It's human instinct to have those worries, those questions. But what's not so normal is to long for it to hurry up.

If he'd just kill me already, it wouldn't hurt so much.

Please, someone put me out of my misery.

Things I never thought I would long for, but time is a cruel mistress, and as days stretched into months with no signs of an escape, the hope I clung to steadily got smaller and smaller until it's just a distant glimmer now. Paying close attention to Kyle's phone calls did little more than fill my head with more questions—questions I'm not sure if I want to know the answers to. Maybe, in this instance, ignorance is bliss.

"Rise and shine, 103," Kyle greets as he unshackles me. The feeling of his grimy hands on my skin has me flinching back into the mattress, only to freeze when his grip on my ankles tightens to the point of pain.

Stupid. You know better.

"Enough. We have a very special guest coming today, so if I were you, I'd behave." The unspoken threat hangs in the air between us. If I don't do as he says, he'll ensure my life isn't worth living. Jokes on him. My life is *already* not worth living. I've already lost my freedom, my daughter, and the love of my life. He's made sure I don't even have my dignity. What more do I possibly have to lose?

"Fuck you," I spit, unable to hold myself back a moment longer. For a brief second, satisfaction curls in my gut, only to be snuffed out a moment later when he lashes out. His fist connects with my cheekbone, and blinding pain races through me as my vision goes hazy.

"Ungrateful whore. After everything I've done for you, this is how you repay me? Just you wait. I'll give you something to curse me for." He keeps up a steady strain of bullshit as he drags me through the house, shoving me to my knees on the living room floor and wrapping his belt around my wrists and ankles. Once I'm hogtied, he crouches in front of me.

Gripping my chin, he forces me to meet his gaze. "Today was supposed to be a treat for you, but you had to go and piss me off. This is your fault, whore. Remember that." Spitting on my face, he watches it drip down my cheek with a smirk before rising to his feet. As he disappears from my line of vision, I try to calm my racing heart.

Panicking won't do me any good. Panicking won't get me out of here and back to my baby girl. Panicking won't change my fate, but maybe I still can.

With resolve sinking into my bones, I force myself not to flinch as the purr of an engine gets closer. As the door opens and booming laughter washes over me, I brace myself for whatever fresh hell is coming my way. I don't have to wait long to find out. A shocked gasp wrenches my eyes from the floor, only to feel my heart lodge itself into my throat.

Blood-stained curls. Glassy blue eyes wide with horror. Features so similar, it's like looking in a mirror. A collar around her throat, the leash tightly held by the monster at her side.

"Helen?"

"Freya?"

God, please, no. It can't be.

I can only watch in horror as she stumbles a half step towards me, only to be yanked back. The flash of pain on her face has me wanting to tear that damn thing off her neck. Before I can move an inch, my hair is wound around Kyle's fist. Yanking my head back, he glares down at me. His expression promises a world of pain if I so much as *think* about moving, and while every instinct I have is screaming a giant "fuck you" at him, it's not just my fate that rests in the balance anymore.

"What do you think of your surprise, pet?" he taunts. When all I do is glare back at him, he lets out a dark chuckle before turning his attention to the man at Freya's side.

"You'll have to excuse my pet. She's still got a bit of fight left in her."

"Impressive. It's been, what, four years? Mine crumbled about a year in."

"What can I say? I like it when they fight back. You're welcome to take her for a spin, assuming the offer goes both ways."

"Of course."

Hearing them talk about us so callously—like we aren't even human—is disgusting, but not surprising. Watching the colour drain from Freya's face, knowing I can't save her from Kyle or her captor, burns, but I can't tear my eyes from her. Cataloguing all the changes since I last saw her twenty years ago, knowing everything was in vain, is like a knife to the heart. Tears trail down her cheeks as her silent agony bleeds between us. Her hand twitches at her side, but with a soft shake of my head, she clenches her jaw instead, visibly forcing herself to shove her emotions down.

"I got a call the other day. Apparently, Jonathan is sniffing around again," Kyle casually comments.

"Is that so? I'll tell Jen to work on him. Does Angus know?"

"Do I look stupid? Fuck no. I quite like having my balls and my pet intact, thank you very much." He snorts. The other man just quirks a brow before tugging Freya into his side. His dark eyes remain focused on me as he whispers something to her. Terror dances across her face even as she reluctantly nods and strips out of her paper-thin summer dress.

"Fuck, look at those tits," Kyle groans, reaching for my own even as his eyes stay glued to my sister's. "I've been thinking of piercing my pet's. Want to join me?"

"You got the right tools? I'm not botching these beauties."

"Yeah, in the basement." He nods towards the hall, and then we're on the move. Kyle makes quick work of freeing my ankles so he can yank me to my feet. As soon as we're in the basement, they secure us to two chairs, so close, we could hold hands, if only our wrists were free. I lock eyes with her, seeing the raw pain and fear there, and pain slices through me. I swore to protect her; I sacrificed knowing her to do so. And for what? For Angus to marry her anyway? For him to sell her to the highest bidder when he grew tired of her? It was all for nothing, and that thought burns worse than the poker, leaving a scar deeper than any Kyle could ever dream of inflicting on me.

"I'm so sorry, Frey." My voice is barely more than a whisper, but it reaches her all the same.

"None of this is your fault, Hel. Mother and Father shouldn't have let this happen." She sobs, and not for the first time, I'm reminded just how ill-suited for this life she is. She never stood a chance, and fuck our parents for not doing more to shield her, to protect her as a parent should.

"I should have taken you with me," I argue, shaking my head.

"It wouldn't have changed anything. Were you happy, Hel? Please say one of us got a happy ever after."

"I was," I confess, my heart breaking at the thought that she might never get her happy ending. "And you?"

"I had a beautiful son; you would have loved him. Promise me you'll find him one day?"

"I promise, *we* will find him." Blinking back my own tears, I implore her to believe me, to trust in me despite how badly I've let her down. Before either of us can say anything more, we're interrupted by approaching footsteps. When I glance at Kyle, the smirk on his face has my skin crawling.

"Guests first, Benedict." He passes a needle to the other man before coming to stand before me. Benedict advances on Freya with a look so cold, it chills me to my bones. With sharp precision and without a moment's hesitation, he pierces her, ignoring her shrieks of pain, sliding the shiny metal bars into place before tossing the needle to Kyle.

Making short work of sanitising it—small mercies—I'm soon treated to the same white hot pain racing through me. Only, instead of plain silver bars, mine have a little bedazzled 'K's dangling from the ends, which makes me want to vomit. Who the fuck does he think he is?

"What a beautiful sight. What do you think, pet?" he croons from his position in front of me. I meet his brown eyes, and my lip curls back in disgust that I know I will pay for later. With a smirk, he pinches the sensitive flesh in retaliation before rising to his full height and making his way over to Benedict.

"What do you say? Want to test out my pet for yourself?" Kyle offers me up as easily as a glass of water. My stomach drops at the implications of what's to come. As one, they turn to pin me under their evil stares. My skin crawls as they look at me, but that's a small price to pay if it keeps their eyes on me and off Freya.

Eyeing me up and down like I'm cattle being weighed for my worth, Benedict dips his chin before advancing on me. Once he's within touching distance, he wastes no time in grabbing my chin and tilting my head back.

"This is going to be fun," he taunts before shoving his free hand between us, grabbing my pussy in the palm of his hand. When he tightens his grip to the point of pain, my head lolls to the side, and

I meet Freya's gaze. Anchoring myself to her, I pretend this is all a nightmare. Soon, I'm going to wake up, and we're going to be far from the horrors of this basement, far from this cruel reality I would never wish on my worst enemy.

If it's the last thing I do, I will get us out of here and reunited with our children.

So help anyone who dares try to stop me.

JONATHAN
CHAPTER 36

Watching the security footage from O'Neill's is a guilty pleasure of mine. Once darkness has descended, the day's dealings are done, and I have a glass in hand, I flick open the footage and settle in. If the closest I can get to Cora is watching her shifts at O'Neill's, then well…consider me the most security-conscious business owner you've ever met.

As I watch her mix drinks with a smile on her face and tip her head back as she laughs with her co-workers, a sense of pride fills me. She could so easily have crumbled when her Mum died, but instead, she picked herself up and came out of it stronger. Letting her shoulder that alone when I should have been by her side, offering her comfort and strength when she needed it most, is just another reason I'm determined to make Angus pay. He alone bears the weight of keeping me from her side, for Helen being vulnerable in the first place.

Before my thoughts can spiral too far, my phone pings with a text. With a sigh, I pause tonight's footage before picking up the damn thing. So much for business being done for the day.

Liam:

We have a situation. There was a code red with our charge—it's been handled, but she's a bit shaken up.

Jonathan:

The next words out of your mouth better be that you're already en-route

Liam:

Already halfway there

Reading over Liam's text does little to ease my anxiety. A code red with my daughter? Un-fuckin-acceptable. Heads will roll. What the hell are these three idiots doing? Sitting around gossiping while someone makes moves to attack her? If one hair on her head is harmed…

Pacing the length of the living room does little to alleviate the anxiety clinging to me. Everything is about to change, and the timing couldn't be worse. Angus is still a thorn in my side with no evidence to back up my suspicions, we're constantly on the verge of war, and I'm up to my neck in power struggles with wannabe gangs. The idea of bringing Cora into the middle of things now scares the shit out of me, but at the same time, getting to meet her is something I've dreamed about for over twenty years. God, this is going to be messy, and she might hate me—fuck, she has every right to—but I'm minutes away from having my daughter within arm's reach, and nothing can dull the spark that lights inside me.

I promise, I'll look after her, sweetheart.

By the time my phone chimes with a heads up that they're on their way up, I've managed to get a grip on my emotions long enough to force my face into something welcoming. Spinning to face the lift as it pings open, for a split second, I'm transported back to the past. Blonde, wavy hair, five foot nothing, with enough attitude to land a man on his ass, Cora is the spitting image of her mother. Her eyes, though, they're the trademark O'Neill blue, a shade or two darker than Helen's, and the smattering of freckles across the bridge of her nose are all me. Fuck, how did Helen look at her every day without breaking down? She's the perfect blend of both of us in the most heart-breaking way.

"Welcome home, Cora." The words slip out without a second thought, and as confusion darts across her face, I take a few steps closer. As she opens her mouth to let a tirade of sass loose that's all Helen, I know I must look like an utter fool as I stand there, smiling at her. Sue me—I'll happily listen to her go off if it means she's standing in front of me.

When she finally takes a breath, I take the opportunity to dismiss the brothers. The room is pin-drop silent as Liam, Aidan, and Cole file out, a range of emotions from confusion to suspicion flickering across their faces. Soon, everyone will know, but for now, for a few blissful moments, this moment is ours, free of expectations and questions. But the fragile peace doesn't last long.

"You wouldn't happen to know an Angus, would you? Because if so, he says hello." Thank fuck my back is to her as those words land like a missile between us. Fucking Angus—as if costing me Helen wasn't enough, he's dipping his hand into messing with my daughter? I bloody well don't think so.

Five Months Later

Before we can even catch our breath, things go from bad to worse. The news of her existence spreads like wildfire and the guys are far from impressed that I kept them so far out of the loop for so long but soon that's the least of our worries.

Between break ins, safe houses, and kidnappings… It's a fucking miracle she's still here in one piece. And if what she needs is Owen—who has more than proven how much she means to him—then fine. I can live with that.

"What a shit show," Jack groans from his seat in my home office. Humming in agreement, I pour us both a drink while we wait. After everything that went down with Angus kidnapping Cora, and Logan doing the honours of killing that fucker, I was anticipating his call. What I wasn't expecting was for him to be looking for a wife. None of what's been going on in the Clan over the past few decades makes sense, but this almost takes the cake. Why would a newly crowned leader need to align himself with us?

"Tell me about it. It's been, what? Five months since that first attack on Cora? Christ, I need a break," I groan, cracking my neck to ease some of the tension. "At least that bastard has been dealt with. Dealing in the skin trade, who does he think he is?"

"And you're sure the son is nothing like the dad? Because I swear, if you've handed my Abbie off to a piece of shit, I won't just sit by." The dark promise in Jack's words should have my guard up, but I'd be saying the same thing if I were in his seat. Before I can reassure him, a knock on the door interrupts us. Seeing Owen, I motion for him to take a seat.

"Any update on getting the girls reunited with their families?" he asks, referring to the unfortunate souls stuck in that house of horrors with Cora.

"Brennan has been working on it night and day. Last he checked, he was down to the last one," Jack fills him in.

"Good. I can't believe that bastard would stoop so low." For once in his life, Owen looks positively furious, his lip curling back as he spits the words out. I don't blame him. What Angus was doing—stealing and then selling helpless girls—is abhorrent. It goes against everything we stand for, all the values we make sure to instil in our children and soldiers.

Spying the alert on my phone that Logan's on his way up, I excuse myself to go greet him. Stifling a chuckle at his complete disregard for wearing a suit to this meeting, I lead him back into my office and nod to the empty chair before handing him a whiskey.

"Thanks for agreeing to meet with me so soon. I'm sure you have things to sort out on your end, which is why I thought it important to share what I know about my father's activities before proposing this... arrangement." Watching as he struggles to dance his way around the word *marriage* has me once again questioning just why he's pitching this idea. Still, none of that matters in comparison to getting answers about his cryptic remark he made before killing his father.

"The girls believed they were going to be auctioned off. What I'd like to know is what you meant when you said he was probably doing what he did to your mum, what he tried to do to Helen." The thought of Angus having anything to do with Helen has rage simmering in my veins. That bastard doesn't deserve to breathe the same air as her, never mind anything more.

"My father was a pathetic excuse for a man. He got a huge power kick out of hurting women and children. He beat Mum for the entirety of their marriage, but he would rant and rave about how she was just a stand-in. He was mixed up with a lot of scumbags who had more money than morals, and eventually, someone came up with the idea of hosting these auctions—which was the worst idea ever, if you ask me. That led to him attempting to kidnap Helen and later selling Mum off." As Owen and Logan continue talking about Logan's mum and reasons for wanting this arrangement, my mind goes a million miles an hour with all the possibilities. For the first time since that dreaded phone call, I cling to the hope she really is dead.

Cutting in, I ask, "What's in this for you? You can't want a bride that much."

"Resources. I have a hunch that could be explosive if true, but so far, I've had no luck proving it. I'm going to need the help of one of your Butcher Brothers and Owen for it."

"Well, come on, man. Spit it out," Owen mutters, his desperation to get back to Cora's side evident.

"I have reason to believe the hit-and-run that killed Helen didn't *actually* kill her. The driver was on our take and a close friend of Angus', who mysteriously disappeared afterwards. From what I understand, when Cora had to identify the body, there was too much burn damage from the explosion, and they had to use dental records, leaving ample opportunity for it not to be her."

Logan's theory lands like a blow, stopping me in my tracks as my mind races with worst case scenarios. If what he's suggesting is true….

I'm so fucking sorry, sweetheart.

The beast inside me rattles at its cage, demanding to be let free, demanding vengeance and blood. White noise rings in my ears as my vision zeros in on thoughts of Helen, where she would be now if what Logan is saying is true. Would she even still be alive after all this time in their clutches?

I swear, if it's the last thing I do, I'll find you, sweetheart.

I'll bring you home no matter the cost.

HELEN
CHAPTER 37

2,190 days in captivity

Perspective is a funny thing. I thought I knew what the worst thing Kyle could throw at me was. I thought I knew pain, that nothing he could do would surprise me after so long with him, and yet Benedict's visits are a whole new beast. They compound the physical torture of what was done to me with the mental torture of witnessing the same horrors being bestowed onto my baby sister. It's hell on Earth. Every time I close my eyes, all I can see is her face, etched in pain as they take what they want and leave no inch untouched. My own injuries felt like *nothing* in comparison to watching her shatter before my eyes.

I'm constantly on edge, dreading the day Kyle taunts me with their next visit, and at the same time, he seems to be unravelling before my eyes. It started small—the odd day without coming down to the basement, tossing me slightly more food than normal. But over the last few weeks, he's got steadily laxer with the privacy of his phone calls. I've managed to catch snippets of numerous conversations, and adding them together paints a picture so ugly, I don't know if I can stomach being right, if it's something I can handle without the fragile shards of my sanity shattering completely.

We've got his daughter.

The last shipment was stolen.

He's dead. We need to get a new leader in place.

Arranged marriage.

A new heir.

The missing context haunts me with the what ifs, but unless I want to face Kyle's wrath and ask questions, there's not much I can do except file it all away for later and keep my ears open, as much as it pains me. The mere fact that some rat is feeding him this information has my stomach churning with the implications. Do they know about my ties to Jonathan? About Cora? The thought of any of this kicking back on her has what little fight I have left notching up into high gear. So, with every trip upstairs, I search for a way out, a weapon, anything I could use to my advantage when the time comes. But while he might slip up in a lot of ways, he always makes sure to tie me up before leaving the room.

"Wakey, wakey. We're going on a field trip." At first, I just blink at him, convinced I've heard him wrong. Field trip? As in, leave this hell hole? It's more than I ever dared hope for. Crossing his arms across his chest, he cocks a brow at me. Clearly, my shocked silence isn't the response he was hoping for.

Rotating my wrist in its cuff, I cock an answering brow as I drawl, "A little help here?"

"Watch the attitude," he grumbles, ambling over and twisting my nipple until I let out a hiss of pain. Satisfied he's proven his point—that he can, and will, hurt me at any given moment—he works on freeing me before leading me over to the bath in the corner. Grimacing at the griminess and the coldness, I grit my teeth as he hoses me down with ice cold water.

"If I were you, I'd be on my best behaviour. Wouldn't want to give Benedict any reason to take him temper out on poor little Freya, would you?" Turning the water off, Kyle turns his attention to taunting me with what's to come, but the reality is, nothing he says will even scratch the surface of what's waiting for me there.

With me blindfolded, restrained, and stuffed naked into a boot of a car, the journey to Benedict's passes without much fanfare. For a while, I try to keep track of the route, but soon, the lefts and rights blur together in a way that's impossible to keep track of. What *is* easy to note is that the distance between the two can't be much more than an hour.

Sooner than I'm ready for, Kyle is dragging me out of the boot, shoving me in front of him with a hand firmly fisted in my hair while the other grips my shoulder. Only once we're inside does he free me of the blindfold. Wincing at the sudden brightness, I glance up, only to be met with Benedict's leer mere inches from my face. It's like looking the devil in the eyes, but I refuse to back down.

"Any news?" Kyle grunts, shifting Benedict's focus to him—for now.

"Other than the stepson being a pain in the ass? No. Same shit, different day. Apparently, Jonathan's too wrapped up in the reappearance of his daughter, he thinks Angus' death means there's nothing more to dig into." He snorts, disdain dripping from every word. It's clear they think Jonathan a fool, and it's also clear they have no knowledge about my ties to him. Either that, or they're so sure I'll never make it out alive. Schooling my features, I pretend to be zoned out in hopes they'll talk shop a little more.

"Fucking idiots. As if something this big could be run by one man." Kyle scoffs before tugging me closer to him. Feeling his hardness dig into my lower back, I swallow down my instinct to lash out—the fear of not knowing where Freya is or what they have in store for us has me in a death grip. As sweaty palms grope and their excited conversation floats around me, I focus on the fact that if they're hurting me, they're leaving her alone, and for that, I would happily sell my soul.

"Where's your little pet? I've been hard as steel thinking about getting a taste of her again."

"Downstairs. The cunt threw up on me this morning, so I left her down there. Ungrateful whore."

"All the more reason to pay her a visit. Put her in her place."

"Be my guest. I've got all I need right here." With that, Benedict thrusts two fingers inside my underprepared body. Hissing out in pain only gains me a cruel smirk as he keeps up his ministrations.

"Be a good pet, and I won't hurt your sister…much." With that parting hiss, Kyle leaves me in Benedict's clutches to find Freya. Thousands of scenarios rush through my head in a matter of seconds—ways to get out of this unscathed, ways to get Freya away from this monster, what I could do or say to stop the hurricane of pain rushing towards us. But in the end, I come up blank. The reality is, men like these will never listen to reason. They like getting their kicks this way—in fact, I'd wager it's the *only* way they can.

My mouth has dried, my tongue stuck to the roof of my mouth. Instead, all the moisture has made its way to my eyes in the form of unshed tears I don't dare let fall. Showing that kind of weakness won't help anyone. Prying my tongue free, I push out some words, useless as they'll be.

"Please, don't let him hurt her," I choke out, my eyes downcast and shoulders slumped forward. The sight of his hand between my legs tests my willpower not to also vomit all over him.

"Stupid girl. Why would I do that?" he hisses, using his free hand to force me to meet his hard eyes. His disgusting breath invades my senses, further testing my stomach's resolve. As his cold, dead eyes glower at me, a piercing shrill deafens me. *Danger,* it screams at me. Pushing this monster is something to be avoided at all costs, lest I want to suffer the consequences. In a split second, he wrenches his hand free from my body and seizes me by the throat, lifting me clean off the ground. Instinctively, I claw at his hand as the need for air balloons inside me. Benedict doesn't flinch—instead, he tightens his grip with a smirk. The edges of my vision darken and, slowly but surely, the fight fades out of me as my lungs scream for air. Distantly, I hear a scream, though it sounds worlds away.

Snarling, he tosses me to the floor. I grunt from the impact, gasping for breath, landing awkwardly on my left wrist. Before I can even comprehend what just happened, I hear a guttural scream that has me scrambling to sit up. Before I can, Kyle is climbing on top of me, pinning me under his bulk. Realisation lashes through me seconds before my eyes process what they're seeing, and my survival instincts kick into overdrive. Twisting beneath Kyle, I try desperately to dislodge him, but truly, what chances do I have at knocking someone easily double, if not triple, my weight off me?

"Get the fuck off her! Leave her alone!" I screech, bucking my hips as the scene beside us unfolds. Benedict has Freya pinned down in a similar position, his hands working frantically between them. With a groan, he thrusts himself inside my protesting sister. Her screaming and futile attempts to stop him do little more than rile him up.

"Such a tight whore, even after all this time. Too bad you had to interfere. I've had enough of your insolence," he snarls, his fist clenched tight around her throat. Her head lulls towards me, her eyes holding me captive as the fight drains out of them. She stops fighting, stops moving, even as he thrusts himself inside her repeatedly. Her skin turns pale, all the colour bleached out of it as her eyes grow hazy. Through it all, I can't look away. My desperation turns rabid. I'm an animal backed into a corner, willing to tear flesh from bones with my teeth if it means saving her. I will do anything—absolutely *anything*—to save her. But in the end, there's nothing I can do. I can only lie there and watch as that monster snuffs my sister's life out under his fist as he reaches his finish inside her still form. Something inside me snaps in that moment, even as my body shuts down, all fight or flight instincts abandoning me as they turn their attention to me.

"What the hell happened down there?" Benedict demands as he

stands, crossing his arms across his chest and not caring his dick is still out. Pig.

"As soon as I opened the door, the bitch lunged for me. Near took my damn eye out."

"What, and you couldn't contain her?" he snorts.

"Fuck off. You're the one who left her unchained. Are you fucking stupid?" Kyle grumbles as he stands before reaching down to drag me to my feet. I can't tear my eyes away from the sight of Freya: blonde hair a mess of matted curls, skin and bones, bruises littering every inch of her. Even as they continue to argue amongst themselves, my eyes stay glued to her as thoughts of what I should have done differently race through my mind.

I promise, they'll pay for this, Frey.

HELEN
CHAPTER 38

2,250 days in captivity

How's it feel to be a failure?
God, you're pathetic.
You couldn't even save your own sister.

I jolt awake, clawing myself away from my nightmare's clutches. Images of haunted blue eyes clog my headspace on the daily, and the sudden movement has sharp needles of pain shooting up my wrists and ankles as I aggravate my restraints. The echo of my sister's voice berating me, along with the memory of her lifeless eyes, remind me where I am, alongside the dull throb in my wrist and between my legs. As if I could forget.

"Good morning, pet. I've a special treat in store for you today. Are you excited?" The sardonic smirk on Kyle's face as he enters the basement speaks of things I'd rather not experience, not after the last time he dangled something *special* in front of me.

"Of course," I manage to mutter, but my lack of enthusiasm is enough to flip the ever-present switch in him. In a blink, he's across the room, the door wide open behind him as he pins me to the bed.

His harsh breath fans across my face as he snarls, "I've had enough of your shit, 103. Do you realise how lucky you are to be mine? How good you have it?" Reaching between us, he grips my chin, pinching my jaw to the point of pain as he glares down at me. "I'm going to show you just how lucky you are to have me, you ungrateful slut."

Reaching over, he undoes the ties, freeing my wrists. I don't have more than a second to enjoy being free before he's yanking me up, only to shove me to my knees in front of him. My stomach drops at the implications. There's something about being forced to take him into my mouth that feels like an even worse violation. Maybe it's because this act forces me to partake, to be a willing participant in a way.

With a hungry look, he demands, "Take my cock out."

My hands are shaking as I reach up to undo his belt. My stomach twists into a million knots as I undo his button and fly, dreading the part that comes next.

"I said take it out, not edge me," he snarls when I don't move fast enough. Letting out a breath, I reach in to pull his cock out from behind his fly.

"That's a good pet. Now, kiss my cock and show me how grateful you are." The glee in his tone has my stomach revolting, but flicking my eyes up to his, I maintain eye contact as I lean forward. Slowly, I press a kiss to the tip of it, fighting against the urge to vomit. You'd think he'd wash this damn thing before demanding a blowjob, but no. The stench of piss and body odour greets me.

Pushing past the urge to gag and the horrific idea of putting him in my mouth, I swallow to try and get some saliva in my dry mouth. And then, still maintaining eye contact, I slip my lips around him. His head tips back on a groan as he reaches down to thread his fingers through my hair. Slipping him deeper into my throat, I pay close attention to his face. With his eyes closed and my mouth at the base of his pathetic cock, I take one sharp inhale before scraping him with my teeth, lulling him into a false sense of security.

"Fuck, just like that, slut," he groans, holding me even tighter to his base. Lightning quick, I clamp down, and for a split second, he freezes in shock before, with a howl, he shoves me off him. Or, well, he *tries* to shove me away. Unfortunately for him, my teeth are my only weapon, and I'm not about to lose this opening. So, with sheer determination, I clench down harder, ignoring the metallic taste of blood as it pools in my mouth.

"You fucking bitch," he shrieks at a pitch only dogs can hear as he finally succeeds in shoving me away. But it's too late to save his so-called manhood. Spitting out the lump of flesh, I rise to my feet as he howls, cupping himself and spewing vitriol at me. I lunge for the branding iron in the corner. After my branding session all those years ago, he thought it was a 'nice reminder to behave'. Instead, that damn thing has taunted me daily with thoughts of *if only I could get my hands on it, he'd never get his hands on me again.* Turns out, today's the day to make that dream a reality.

Feeling more powerful than I have in years, with the taste of freedom on the tip of my tongue, I use his distraction to my advantage. Putting every scrap of strength into it, I swing the iron above my head and aim for his skull. With a curse, he crumbles to the ground on impact, lunging for my ankles. Dodging his grasp, I follow him down, straddling his back and fisting his greasy hair in my hand.

"This is for ruining my life." *Thunk.*

"For taking what wasn't yours to take." *Thunk.*

"For every moment you stole from me." *Thunk.*

"This is for Freya." *Thunk.*

Soon, I'm seeing red, unable to stop bashing his head into the floor. Again, again, again, until his whimper fades and his blood has joined mine in every crevice of this room. Until I'm covered in it and brain matter. Until he stops moving, stops whimpering, stops breathing.

"Take that, asshole," I spit, landing one final hit with a grunt before rolling off him. It's not until I'm watching his blood swirl down the drain that the implications of my actions hit me. I killed a man, and not just any man—the piece of shit who's kept me captive for six years and helped murder my sister. I'm *free* for the first time in close to a decade, but at the same time, am I really? I have no idea where I am, with no means of getting back home. Do I even still have a home to go back to? And Cora—what will she make of her mum being a murderer? And God—Jonathan. He needs to know about the potential rat, but will he even want to see me? Can I stomach seeing him? So many questions, so few answers, and no time to waste pondering them.

Shelving my worries for now, I finish getting cleaned up the best I can before venturing upstairs to start my hunt for answers and freedom. Being free to roam the house that has been my prison for so long doesn't feel right. Each second spent snooping upstairs feels like a second wasted. I should just run before I'm caught. Logically, I know it's just me and Kyle's corpse, but fear leaves no space for logic, so it's with shaky hands and a pounding heart that I flick through random papers on Kyle's desk, not really processing what I'm looking at until a name jumps out at me.

Benedict Murphy

My lip curls as I read that bastard's name, and the bloodlust that was sated comes roaring back. Scanning the letter full of all kinds of boasting bullshit, I look for any information I can use, only to hit the jackpot when an envelope falls from between the pages. Bending to pick it up, I flick it over, and there, in black and white, is a return address.

With as much cash as I can find stuffed in the pockets of my borrowed hoodie and sweats and a destination in mind, I make my way downstairs. Eyeing up the door that taunted me far more than an inanimate object should be capable of, I can't help but feel a twisted sense of accomplishment. *Finally*, after six godawful years, I'm about to cross its threshold once and for all.

Freedom is a basic human right, yet inhaling that first breath of fresh air feels foreign, like any minute, someone is going to track me down, strip me naked, and throw me back into that basement. Keeping my eyes peeled and my head down, I work to find a way out of the grounds surrounding the house, but every time I so much as hear a twig snap, I freeze, terrified that this is it. My brief escape is over. Then, I have to work on reminding myself I do deserve this. Being free shouldn't feel like something earnt. It should just be a given.

Making it out to a main road, I quickly determine I'm not in London anymore. Nothing looks familiar, and none of the street names are ones I recognise or have even heard of. I might be free, but I have no idea how to get home or where to even start. Looking down at the oversized hoodie and joggers I stole, it's also clear it'll be a miracle if I don't raise a few eyebrows.

Following the winding road, I keep an eye out for any clues as to where I am. It's not until I stumble across a sign for a town I could swear was in Northern Ireland that I realise just how far from home I am. The soft barking of a dog draws my attention up ahead. An older lady is walking her poodle, and as much as I'd rather not draw attention to myself, if I'm going to work on getting home, I need to know where I am.

"So sorry to bother you, but I'm a tad lost. Is there any chance you could point me in the right direction?" Painting a friendly smile on my face, I approach her slowly so as not to startle her.

"These country roads will do that to you, won't they?" She smiles as she talks down to her dog before turning her attention back to me. "Where is it you're headed?"

Rattling off the address from the letter, she frowns to herself for a moment, repeating it before, with a click of her fingers, giving me some directions and landmarks to look out for. Thanking her, I head the way she pointed.

Time to take out the trash once and for all.

Following the directions given to me, it's not long until I'm cloaked in darkness at the bottom of a driveway, looking up a gravel path towards a derelict-looking house. Swallowing down the fear threatening to swallow me whole, I think about Freya, about the life lost for no reason, her son left without a mother, all the hopes and dreams snuffed out in the blink of an eye, all because she wanted to save me from the same fate. Steel straightens my spine and rids me of any lingering hesitation.

Crouching and blending in with the shadows as much as possible, I edge towards the house while keeping my eyes peeled for any movement. I can't afford to be caught now, not when freedom is within touching distance. Slowly, I make my way around the side of the house, heading for the back. The French doors make me freeze in my tracks, but when a minute or two passes without any signs of life, I ease them open. Flinching at the creek, I duck and roll behind the nearest item of furniture: a sofa. Straining to hear over my pounding heart, I don't dare move a muscle for the longest time.

After a while, I crawl out of my hiding space and slowly make my way through the house, heading towards the basement. Given how still the house is, my money is on him being there. Shoving down the emotions that want to rush to the surface at the thought of going down there, I force myself to head down the stairs, holding my breath and hoping none of them creak. Spying the light pooling under the door, I tighten my grip on my borrowed knife. Once I hit the landing, I take a deep breath, brace myself for the worst, and slowly inch the door open.

Blinded by the sudden light, it takes a second to realise what I'm seeing: Benedict hunched over a porcelain tub alone. Questions as to what the fuck he's doing down here when I'm sure he's got a fully functioning bathroom upstairs hold me captive for a second before I shrug them off. At the end of the day, what he's doing doesn't matter. The only thing that matters is what I'm about to do.

"If you're here to kill me, you may as well get it over with." His words freeze me in my path, one foot over the doorway with the knife raised. Flicking his eyes from the bath to me, he raises an eyebrow. The silent challenge is evident, even if the reason for it is not.

"Come on, then. Get it over with." His words are void of all his usual cockiness. Part of me wants to demand answers, but bloodlust clouds my rationale. The need to make him pay for what he did far outweighs any curiosity about him as a person. And so, with a guttural cry, I lunge at him, driving the knife straight into his artery and watching as he slumps into the bath face first in a pool of his own blood. But it's not enough—it's nowhere near enough. Pulling the knife free, I thrust it into him over and over again until I can't anymore, until I'm once again covered in the blood of a monster.

I hope you can forgive me, Frey. I should have saved you, but instead, all I can do is avenge you.

Getting to London was almost too easy once I had the cash in hand and a ferry ticket in my pocket. But ease doesn't mean peace. Not when your soul is fraying at the edges. The moment I arrived, I caught whispers—soft, cautious ones—about a gang member's funeral. The kind people didn't speak about unless they had to. The kind that carried weight. Meaning. Power.

With my heart lodged in my throat and dread coiling sharp beneath my ribs, I followed the murmurs to the cemetery, each step heavier than the last. I didn't know what I was hoping to find. I just knew I couldn't stay away.

It's been twenty-three years since I last laid eyes on Jonathan O'Neill—but standing at the edge of the crowd, it's as if no time has passed at all. Even from behind, I'd know him anywhere. That broad frame. The set of his shoulders. The quiet command of space.

Time has been kind to him—the same way it's been merciless to me.

I glance down at myself—blood-stained, broken, barely stitched together—and something in me twists. What would he see if he turned around? A ghost? A stranger? A woman too far gone to be loved again?

Before I can disappear, he turns.

His eyes lock on mine. And in a heartbeat, I forget how to breathe. Those eyes—God, those eyes—I used to dream about them. But memory failed me. They're more vivid, more alive, more him than I ever remembered. His lips part. His head shakes, like he can't quite trust what he's seeing. Then the moment shatters.

A sob. Raw. Shaking. It cuts through the silence like a blade.

Cora.

Her face crumples, and before I can move, she's thrown herself into my arms. And then—Jonathan. He's there too, one arm around each of us, holding us all up like he's the only thing keeping the world from falling apart.

I let myself feel it. Just for a second. The warmth of him. The solidity. The safety I once knew like the back of my hand.

Because when I tell him the truth—what I've done, what I've lost—I know that warmth will vanish.

I'm safe now. But somehow, it still feels like I never left Hell.

JONATHAN
CHAPTER 39

After twenty-three years of separation—and six years believing her dead—my cold, blackened heart never dreamed I'd be reunited with Helen.

My sweetheart.

The mother of my child.

There's no universe where someone like me should end up in the same place as her. Not with the blood on my hands. My soul is too stained to be anywhere near hers.

As much as the choice we made was the right one—for Cora's safety, for her survival—it cost me a piece of myself I'll never get back. The part that dared to dream.

So when I turned to leave Cole's funeral, the weight of his death dragging behind me like an anchor, I thought I was seeing things.

It wouldn't be the first time her ghost haunted me.

Despite Logan's suspicions and Owen's cautious hope, I never dared to believe she might still be alive. Dreams and happy endings are luxuries men like me aren't afforded. Second chances don't come to those whose hands are soaked in blood.

But then Cora let out a sob—raw, broken, and gut-wrenching—and I knew I wasn't the only one seeing her.

She's a shadow of the woman I once held. Pale. Bruised. Haunted. But still—undeniably, devastatingly—*my* Helen.

As I move closer, the bruises on her skin burn into my memory. And the hollowed-out look in her eyes? It tears something open in me.

And in that moment, I make a vow so deep it rewires my bones:

I will erase that look.

I will destroy whoever gave it to her.

Pulling her and Cora into my arms feels like coming home. Like something real anchoring me in the chaos.

I'll slay every demon that haunts her.

Whatever it takes to help her heal from the hell she's survived—I'll do it.

Even if she never lets me hold her again, *nothing* will stand in my way.

Reckoning

JONATHAN
CHAPTER 40

Sometimes, you can feel chaos lurking in the shadows before it hits. You can taste it on your lips, feel it coating your skin. It's like a little warning light flashes on and off in your peripheral vision. As I sit in my penthouse with the shell of the woman I love sitting opposite, her secrets and horrors a vast ocean between us, that warning bell is thrumming in the air as chaos mingles with the anguish of today.

Today should be a day for mourning the life lost. Cole was a good soldier, loyal to a fault, and will be missed by more than just his kin. His death was a harsh reminder of the risks we take each and every day. I feel like an utter bastard for the relief coursing through me while Liam and Aidan are consumed with grief, but how can I not? I never dared hope Logan's theory was right, so to have Helen in front of me, after all this time, is almost more than I can fathom.

"Is anyone going to answer me?" Cora spits, hands on her hips as she stands between us. Other than confirming what we'd come to suspect—that she's Logan's aunt—and refusing to see Doc, Helen hasn't said a word. As much as I would love to hold the answers to Cora's questions, I don't. None of us do. I may have my suspicions, but the only person who truly knows what's going on is Helen. One look at her pale face and trembling hands makes it clear she won't be talking anytime soon. God help anyone who tries to force her. They'll have to go through me first.

"Cora, come sit down. Please," Owen tries to convince his wife, but she's having none of it. If the circumstances were different, I'd be proud of her stubborn streak. She truly is her mother's daughter, for better or for worse.

"No! It's clear as shit you all know something I don't. I am sick and tired of being kept in the dark. You saw how well that worked out last time. Now, can someone please tell me how the hell my mum is sitting here alive?" she begs, all anger draining from her as tears well up in her eyes. Her voice breaks on the last word, and she throws her hands up in frustration.

"Darling, I'm so sorry," Helen chokes out, her face pinched at Cora's reaction. She reaches towards her, and, with a sob, Cora throws herself into her mum's arms. I look at the two of them, at the bruises littering Helen's arms, and red clouds my vision. How dare some fucker put his hands on her? Tear mother and daughter apart? Rob them of precious memories that can never be recreated? Anyone responsible for one iota of her suffering will receive it back tenfold by the time I'm through with them.

"Why don't we all get some sleep and revisit this when we're a bit calmer, yeah? It's been a long day for all of us," I suggest, rising from my seat to tug Cora into my arms. Seeing her cry is like a fucking knife to the heart every time. It's my job to make sure she never has reason to, and yet at every turn, I've failed her. Hell, I nearly lost her for good last year. When I lock eyes with Helen over Cora's shoulder, the haunted look in her eyes has me scared she's still as lost as she was before today. She might be less than ten feet from me, but she looks like she's miles away, mentally stuck in whatever hell she physically escaped.

As Owen wraps Cora in his arms and leads her out, silence so thick it should be awkward descends on the now-empty penthouse. If it was anyone else, it would be. But with Helen, I'd sit in silence for a hundred years if that's what it takes. Sharing the same air with her is more than I ever thought I'd get.

"This place hasn't changed a bit," she finally rasps, breaking the silence.

"I couldn't bring myself to alter anything," I confess, watching as she flinches at my words. With a frown I continue, "I really think you should let me get Doc to check you over."

"I know…just not yet. I can't face it. Letting another man look at my body…." she whispers, looking up at me through her lashes, imploring me to understand. Her words slice through me. Even without saying the words, she confirms my worst fears, and the need to do something is like a physical itch. Someone needs to pay for putting that look on her face, and they need to pay *now*. Grinding my molars and swallowing back the urge to demand names, I let it lie with little more than a stilted nod.

Whoever laid hands on her is going to fucking pay. But for now, her safety is top priority, and blowing the lid on my temper isn't going to help in the slightest. Neither is pushing her to lay her soul bare before she's ready. The last thing I want to do is send her running before we've even had a chance.

"Come on, then. Let's get you settled." As much as I'd rather have her back where she belongs, I'd be a fucking fool to think we can just snap back to how things were. She might be back from the dead, but it's clear as day that whatever evil she endured still has its claws buried in her marrow. Patience might not be my default, but if anyone can draw it out of me, it's her. She's not on her own anymore, and I'll do whatever it takes to show her that.

My resolve to give her all the time and space she needs is tested when days go by without so much as a peep from her. If it weren't for the fact the trays of food I've been leaving at her door have been cleared, I'd have knocked the damn door down by now.

"Any changes?" Cora sighs, sounding more defeated than I've ever heard her. It's easy to forget this isn't just about my selfish needs. While I might be longing for the woman I love to let us help her, Cora is faced with the reality that the mum she grieved was never really dead, but it may have been better off if she was. It's a clusterfuck to say the least.

"Nothing. I'm running out of ideas here. I want to help her, but at the same time, I'm scared pushing her will backfire. How much space is too much, you know?" I sigh, rubbing my temples as I stare out at the city below. Questioning if I'm making the right move—wondering if I shouldn't be doing more—is driving me insane. Remaining stationary is far from my norm, and knowing the bastards responsible for putting that haunted look in her eyes might still be out there…. It's unbearable.

With a sigh of her own, Cora answers, "I don't know, Dad. My instinct is screaming that space is the last thing she needs, but none of us know what she's been through over the last six years. Maybe there's a middle ground between space and suffocating."

Humming to myself, I weigh up what she's saying. It's true there are a lot of gaps between what we know and what we suspect. She might not be the woman we knew or have the same reactions to things. All I want to do is take that look out of her eyes and hold her so tight, she never questions her safety again, to hunt her demons down, to do onto them what was done to her, and then present her with their heads on spikes.

"Anyway, I have to go. I promised I'd help Liam and Aidan pack up Cole's things. I'll grab some more of Mum's things from the storage unit while we're up there." The reminder of the life lost and the shit-storm brewing elsewhere does little to settle my bloodlust. Cole was a fucking kid. He had his whole life ahead of him.

"Give them my best. Remind them anything they need is theirs." The stubborn fuckers might not speak up, but I'll be damned if they're left floundering in their grief alone. This is a family, in good times and bad. While the person responsible for Cole's death may have been dealt with, this shit goes so much further and the second I have names they'll be my first call. If anyone deserves a chance at revenge, it's them.

"Of course. Give Mum my love if you can." With that, Cora hangs up, and I dial Ciaran. Just because Helen isn't ready to talk yet doesn't mean we can't start digging in the meantime. We have enough crumbs to go off, and after Logan and Owen's discovery in Belfast, we have a body and a house to turn over for answers.

"Yeah?"

"You ready to get your hands bloody?"

"You know I was born ready." He lets out a dark chuckle before asking, "Who's on the shit list this time?"

"That's the question of the day. It's time for a little recon over in Belfast."

"I'll get Bren and a few runners gathered up. We can be on the next ferry out." Never one to waste time or words, he hangs up, and I brace my palms on the glass window. The sooner we have answers and names, the better, and if sending the Butcher Brothers to Belfast is what it takes, so be it.

I will not rest until every sick fucker involved in Angus' sex trafficking ring is six feet under.

HELEN
CHAPTER 41

I thought killing Kyle would alleviate my fears. I thought seeing him lying there, dead, feeling his blood splatter against my skin and watching the life bleed out of his eyes, would quiet my fight or flight instinct. For a minute, it seemed to. But the second the lift opened into the achingly familiar penthouse, something in my brain switched. All the fear I managed to shove down and hold at bay came crashing back with a vengeance.

Every little noise has sweat trickling down my back, my heart pounding and fear lashing at my every nerve ending. Anytime Jonathan knocks on the door to let me know he's left a tray of food has me panicking someone is going to come crashing through the door to get me. It's fucking exhausting. I want to be normal, to enjoy my freedom that never should have been stolen from me. I need to share everything I managed to overhear, down to the smallest detail, in hopes to save more souls from the same fate. But anytime I try to force myself to, the fear of Jonathan's reaction, of everyone knowing, has my throat tightening and the words refusing to come out. Even scrubbing my skin raw in the shower, and ripping those bastard piercings out, did little to erase the crawling sensation of my skin not being my own.

Once they know just how damaged I am, how broken, why would they want to keep me around? How could Jonathan or Cora ever look at me the same way?

Not to mention, every time I try to sleep, the past claws its way into my mind, dragging me back to that basement of horrors, to the hands taking what they wanted from me as I struggled to keep my sanity. It's like a constant replay of the worst moments until I wake up in a cold sweat, normally on the floor with a scream lodged in my throat and my heart pounding so fast, my ribcage aches.

This time, when my fear lurches me into awareness, I'm greeted by the sight of a frantic Jonathan crouched beside me, sleep rumpled, shirtless and backlit by the hall light. My racing mind can't work out what's reality and what's my nightmare. Am I still dreaming, and he's about to be ripped away from me, or is he really here, seeing me at my weakest with fear in his eyes? My racing thoughts can't pinpoint which would be worse.

"Sweetheart, breathe with me. You're okay, I promise. In and out," he coaches me, locking eyes with me and making a show of breathing until my racing pulse slows down. But in its place come the tears I've been holding back for far too long. Scooping me into his arms, he settles us on the bed, my head on his chest as he rubs soothing circles on my back. I break apart in his arms, the one place that always felt like my safe place amidst all the secrets and fear.

"Can you do me a favour?" I croak, my head still buried on his naked chest now damp from my tears.

"Anything."

"I know I'm not the woman you knew, and there's no changing that. But can you lie to me and tell me what our future could have been?"

"Helen…" The pain in that one word has fresh tears escaping.

"Please?" I whimper, the need to hear what could have been feeling like a physical ache somewhere behind my ribs.

"Somewhere…" he whispers, stroking my hair in smooth, slow motions. "Somewhere, there's a world where we never parted ways. You wake up in my arms every morning, you feel my heart beating against your cheek, and I kiss you good morning despite your protests about morning breath. Then, I slip out to make you coffee, which is always served with a kiss. We shower together, and I wash your hair before heading into the office. We live every day to the fullest—full of laughter and love. So much love, sweetheart. You're mine, and I'm yours, and we are so, so happy."

I drift back to sleep, yearning for the picture he's painting to be our reality, soundtracked by his hopes and dreams for a different us, a version that wasn't destroyed by tragedy, one that wasn't cursed from the start, cloaked in secrets and lies.

How lucky are they to have what we never can.

HELEN
CHAPTER 42

Something shifted between us after that. When I woke up the next morning, tucked under the duvet with a pillow clutched in my arms and no Jonathan in sight, some jagged part of me settled a little, at least enough to venture out of my room. Bypassing the familiar pictures of his dad and Sheila mixed in with newer photos of Cora's wedding day and a baby April sleeping on Jonathan's chest, I head down to the kitchen before fear digs its claws in again.

Having the freedom to wander, to eat and drink what I want, *when* I want is something I can't quite wrap my head around. God. To think, I'm in my forties, excited over something so mundane, so basic. Making my way to the Nespresso machine and looking at the overly complicated device, I'm biting my lip in concentration when I feel his presence behind me.

"Need a hand?" he offers, coming around slowly. Giving me time to move, I realise. God damn this man and his considerate ways. It's more than I can handle these days. Is he trying to kill me? Because if so, mission success.

Stepping back and letting him work, I take him in. He was always unfairly handsome, and time has only served to enhance that. His dark hair is greying slightly at the temples in a sexy way. There are lines on his face that weren't there before, evidence of a life well lived. His skin is still tan despite living in dreary England, and his cologne is the same as it always was. He might be taller and broader, but he's the same man at his core.

The man I was helpless but to fall in love with.

The man I longed for, day in and day out, for years.

The man I don't deserve.

I'm a broken mess of a human, barely able to function, with more baggage than an airport belt. I'm holding him back from his life. I shouldn't be here. I can't bear witness to him living his life while I'm struggling to get out of bed each morning. I refuse to hold him back. He doesn't deserve to be cursed to living half a life because of me.

"Thank you." I take a sip of the coffee, letting it warm my bones before continuing. "I was thinking, I'm going to start looking for a job so I can get out of your way."

Leaning against the counter, he sips his own coffee. Closes his eyes. Exhales. Pins me under his unwavering stare. "No."

"Excuse me?"

"You heard me. No. You're not going anywhere, not until you're good and ready. *If* you're ever ready, that is. There's no rush."

"It's hardly fair," I scoff.

"Fair?"

"You have a life to live. I'm sure me being here isn't helping." I roll my eyes, setting my cup down before taking a seat at the breakfast bar and rubbing my hip. Standing for long periods tends to make old injuries flare up, reminding me they aren't to be ignored. His sharp eyes miss nothing, zeroing in on my hip with a cocked brow and clenched jaw.

He scoffs, downing his coffee and crossing the kitchen to lean against the other side of the breakfast bar. "I want you here, end of discussion."

Before I can come up with a response, the lift behind me pings, and I can't control my flinch at the sudden noise. Seeing it, he raises his eyebrow, as if I've just proven his point. Rolling my eyes at his stubbornness, I twist to see who arrived, only to inhale sharply at the sight of Cora with a toddler perched on her hip. Hearing about April and seeing my baby with a baby are two very different things, and the reminder of everything I missed is just another blow. Those bastards robbed me of so many life events, so much time I can never get back, milestones I can never witness firsthand.

"Hey, Dad –" With a sharp inhale, she cuts herself off, her eyes frozen on me. I hardly even recognise myself these days, so I can only imagine what she sees.

"Hello, darling." With sweaty palms and a racing heart, I close the distance between us. With a watery smile, she passes me April. Looking down at my grandchild—her green eyes the spitting image of her father's but the blonde curls are all Cora, all me, all Freya— wetness trickles down the side of my face as my heart splinters. My finger gripped in her tiny fist, she coos up at me, bright eyes full of innocence, an innocence I pray she never loses. "Hi, precious girl. I'm your Nanny, and I'm so happy to meet you."

"I thought you'd like an April day, but I think Mum has laid claim," Cora jokes as Jonathan comes to stand beside me. In this moment, it's easy to picture what should have been. I look up at him, the pain that beats inside me like a drum reflected on his face. We lost so much, and for what? Angus still got me. He still got Freya. I still lost her. And what did we gain? Who did our sacrifices save? Certainly not us. It's hard not to think it was all for nought.

"While I would love to fight for some April time, there's a few things I need to attend to today. Why don't you have a girls' day?" he suggests, pressing a kiss to the top of April and Cora's heads as he makes his way to the lift. Such a familiar move that I wish I had been around to see develop.

"Sounds good," Cora responds before turning her eyes to me. They're eyes so like her father's, it was like he was haunting me every time I looked at her, a blessing and a curse at the same time.

"Hey, Mum." Her voice breaks but her eyes stay dry, and her hands twitch at her sides. Closing the distance between us, I wrap my free arm around her and pull her in for a hug. Instantly, I'm transported back to simpler times, when a hug could fix everything, and our biggest issues were things like high school heartbreaks. Fuck, I'd give everything to go back to those days, and yet seeing her and Jonathan together, the idea of ripping father and daughter apart is too cruel to stomach.

"I missed you so much, darling," I tell her. Pulling back, I take her in, cataloguing how she's changed, how she's aged. Gone is the softness to her features and the wide-eyed look of innocence, and in their place stands a woman sure of herself. As April starts to fuss, she takes her back, getting her situated on the living room floor with some toys before taking a seat to play with her.

"Being a mum suits you," I comment, crossing the room to join them. Seeing this bachelor pad turned into something more homey, with family photos and kids' toys scattered about the place, just strengthens my resolve to get caught up on everything I missed. I've lost more than enough time, and I'll be damned if I don't treasure being reunited with my family. I owe it to Freya to make the most of this for both of us.

"I learnt from the best." Cora's softly spoken words jerk me from my thoughts. "Anytime I questioned myself or got overwhelmed, I'd ask myself what you would do. It's worked for me so far, I think. I just wanted to make you proud."

"Darling, you've made me proud every single day of your life, even without knowing the ins and outs of the last few years, I can guarantee you that," I reassure her, reaching over to grasp her hand. The fact there's even room for her to doubt that cuts me in half.

"So, tell me—how did little April here come to be? What happened to Corey?" Corey was her now ex-boyfriend who I never thought was good enough for her. Something about him always set my instincts on edge, like a sharp sensation in your teeth you can't quite explain.

"I don't even know where to start," she laughs, shaking her head. Then she dives in—telling me about how she caught him cheating, how it finally pushed her to end things for good. Her voice is animated, her hands moving as she talks about Owen.

It's obvious—he's the one for her.

She lights up just saying his name, and as the day passes with stories and stolen smiles, one thing becomes clear: this world fits her.

While I've always felt like I was trying to survive the mafia, she was born to lead it.

As morning fades into early afternoon and April falls asleep in Cora's arms, she takes her leave with promises to do this again soon. The second they're gone; the silence turns eerie and stifling. The flat feels almost haunted by my mistakes, my fears, my worries, the impending doom looming over my head with every second.

"Fuck," I mutter to myself, pacing the length of the room while my mind races. The guilt at keeping what little I know to myself is eating me alive. But how do I even begin to piece everything together without reliving my worst memories? No matter what I do, I can't shake the gut instinct that shit is going to blow up. I'm seconds away from working myself into a panic attack when the lift opens to reveal a familiar redhead. With her trademark red lipstick, a bottle of chardonnay from one of Don Salvatore's vineyards clutched in one hand, and her hip cocked to the side, she looks as much of a boss bitch now as she did all those years ago.

"I thought you could do with some wine time," she explains as she grabs two wine glasses and makes her way over. Setting her haul on the coffee table, she turns her feline-like eyes on me. Tutting, she says, "We have a lot of work to do, don't we?"

"I guess so." I laugh. God, I missed her and her frank nature. Quirking a brow at her choice of wine, I drawl, "Speaking of, are you looking for trouble?"

"Helen, darling, you should know the answer to that. Regardless, with a wedding on the horizon, we're practically allies." She waves off my concerns, and before I can even question the second half of that sentence, she's pouring us both a glass, toeing off her heels and curling her feet underneath her as she swiftly changes the subject. "A little birdie told me you've been hiding up in that spare room. And while I can't say I blame you—those sheets are heavenly—it's time we nip that in the bud."

"Says who?"

She laughs like it's actually funny. "Me, darling. Jonathan, bless his soul, would let you take your sweet time until he's in the grave because that man loves you. He's scared of sending you running for the hills. I, however, do not share the same fear. I thought we lost you, and now, we have a ghost back. While it's an improvement, it's nowhere near enough. So, I come with a pep talk in hand."

"Oh yeah? Let's hear it, then."

"It's simple, really. That man hasn't so much as looked at anyone in all the time you've been gone. He mourned you like a widower and wore his grief like a badge of honour. You can trust him; you know that, right? Even when Logan came spitting facts about you not being dead, when they went down a rabbit hole of unravelling your secrets, he never once cared about your ties to the Clan. And you should know how much that means coming from a man like him. So, whatever it is that's eating you alive? You can trust him. You can trust *me*."

Her words land like the well-aimed attack to my defences she means them to be. Tears stream down my face by the end, and all the hurt, all the damage I've been trying so fucking hard to keep behind the damn spills over.

"I think I need to get tested," I confess. Donna's shocked inhale reaches my ears a moment before the sound of glass shattering has me whipping around to find Jonathan standing mere feet behind us, a broken glass at his feet and a look of anguish painted across his features.

JONATHAN
CHAPTER 43

Since Helen returned, it has been nothing short of a mindfuck. She's here, and yet she's not. I still have more questions than answers, and she's still refusing to see Doc or let me take her to the hospital. Hell, until last night, I'd barely even seen her. I refuse to be another person who takes her choices out of her hands, as much as it hurts me to do nothing. Hearing her cry out in her sleep, seeing her thrash around as if she was mid attack, only for her to ask me to lie to her, just about tore my heart out, but getting to hold her… That is something I would happily carve out my heart to do.

Everything outside the penthouse is equally as fucked. Ever since the last table meeting, Salvatore has been breathing down my neck daily for updates on the rat problem, threatening to call off the marriage between Matt and his granddaughter if we don't get our shit ironed out. But no amount of investigating or torturing has led us to any answers. And that's not to mention the mess in Scotland that Logan is trying to get to the bottom of. With Angus and Peter both dead, so should be the sex trafficking ring they were running, and yet Brennan's deep dive on the dark web indicates otherwise.

Which begs the question: what the fuck is going on?

So, coming home, only to catch the tail end of Helen's confession and seeing her tear-stained face—it's the straw that breaks the camel's back.

"What the hell happened?" I growl, crossing the room as quickly as possible, only to about die when Helen flinches at the bite in my tone.

Fucking stupid asshole, I curse myself out.

"Sweetheart, are you okay?" I ask gently as I crouch in front of the sofa, not touching her despite the urge crawling along my skin to do so. She lifts her tear-stained face, looking at me in a way that has my heart shattering into a thousand pieces at her feet. I don't need her to tell me her story to know it's an ugly one. I tuck her hair behind her ear, letting my knuckles graze her cheek. She leans into my touch, closing her eyes.

"I think that's my cue," Donna mutters, extracting herself from Helen, pressing a kiss to her cheek before she leaves with a weighted look tossed my way. It's my turn to look after our girl, and that's something I'm happy to do. Opening my palm, I cup her cheek, running my thumb over her cheekbone as I debate what to say, where to even start. Thankfully, she beats me to it.

"There are things I need to tell you…but I don't know where to start. Talking about it, reliving it like that, feels like it'll make it real, like there's no going back once I open that Pandora's Box. But I know you deserve answers, the truth," she confesses, her eyes still closed. Taking a fortifying breath, she continues, "My real name is Helen Campbell, and when I was eighteen, I ran away from the Clan. I was meant to marry Angus and provide him with an heir, but I couldn't face it. The rumours surrounding his previous wives' deaths, the way he looked at my sister… I couldn't do it. So, I ran, and I buried that part of my life in hopes it would mean Freya was safe."

My heart breaks for this woman, whose selfless actions were in vain.

"I should have told you… There were so many times when I nearly did, but…" She finally opens her eyes, meeting my gaze.

"But you were scared about what would happen."

"I know I should have trusted my gut, trusted you, but I couldn't shake knowing what Angus would do if the shoe was on the other foot. If someone from a rival faction so much as dared set foot on the compound, never mind someone meant to marry his enemy, it would be a blood bath." The pain in her confession lashes at my insides.

"Sweetheart, I don't hold that against you. How the hell could I? You did what you needed to. You were trying to protect your sister from a monster. At the end of the day, it's a name, and it means nothing in the face of that. I swear, it changes nothing," I reassure her, stroking the silk of her skin and enjoying the privilege of being allowed to touch her.

"Sometimes, I wonder if I had just told you, would the same fate await me? It drives me mad, Johnathan, to know I might have escaped all the pain and hurt and heartbreak if only I hadn't been such a coward. But at the same time, I don't think Angus would ever have given up until he got his hands on me," she confesses, her voice breaking at the end.

"We thought Angus was behind the hit and run, but we couldn't find any evidence," I murmur.

"That doesn't surprise me. What he was doing…. It was an extremely sophisticated operation. From the moment of the accident until I was…sold, I was blindfolded and kept disoriented. I couldn't even tell you how long I was kept in that holding cell or where I was before I ended up in Northern Ireland. Jonathan, he had to have people in government paid off to move us so seamlessly." The spark of fire burning in her eyes is the most life I've seen from her since she showed up, and it's almost enough to distract me from the words she's saying—what she's confirming.

"I swear to you, we will get to the bottom of this sick and twisted web one way or another. Things are already in motion to get to the bottom of it, and sure, it might take us longer without whatever insight you have, but no one is going to force you to talk before you're ready, okay? I can promise you that," I vow, watching as she lets out a shuddering breath, tears leaking down her face as she nods.

"I want to confess it all, but I just…can't yet. I'm sorry." I'd do anything to rid the broken tinge to her words, if only she'd let me.

"You have nothing to be sorry for. I thought I lost you forever, and if the price to pay to have you back is a bit of patience, then sweetheart, call me a saint. I don't care how long it takes you to feel safe—I'm going nowhere, and anyone who has an issue with that will have to go through me." With a watery laugh, she lets silence fall between us. I'd happily sit like this forever, pain at being hunkered down and all, if it means being close to her. Eventually, her stomach lets out a loud noise, and we both burst out in fits of laughter that deflates the heavy atmosphere, if only for a moment.

"Someone hungry, huh?" I ask her, rising with a wince and holding out a hand to help her up.

"Apparently." She laughs, a blush coating her cheeks as she lets me help her up.

"Let's see what we can do about that," I say, making my way to the kitchen and spying the ingredients for chicken parm. Her favourite, the last I checked. Perfect.

"Why don't you go get a shower while I get this ready, hmm? And then tomorrow, I'll take you to the clinic," I tell her. Her shaky inhale and quiet thanks are all the response I get, but it's all I need. The last thing I want is for her to think her need to get tested is an awkward thing, and I'll be damned if I let her sneak off to do it alone.

The sooner she accepts that I'm here for the long haul, the better.

Hours later, with her safely tucked in bed, dark thoughts swirl as I sit in my darkened office, whiskey in hand. Sitting in here late at night seems to be the norm these days. I can't remember the last time I went to bed at a reasonable time. Too much to do, too little time.

It's after midnight when soft footsteps alert me to Helen's presence moments before she knocks lightly on the open door. Another nightmare has clearly chased her down here, if the haunted look on her face is anything to go by.

"Can't sleep?" she asks, curling up in the chair opposite my desk.

"Something like that. Nightmares haunting you?" I ask, quirking a brow at her in question.

"Something like that," she sasses back, and that brief flash of the Helen I know and love so dearly has my chest tightening.

"Care to share with the class?" I ask, getting up to make her a drink. Handing her the wine, I lean back against the front of my desk, inhaling her sweet scent that clings to every corner of my flat these days.

"Thank you. It was just the same old shit, but it did prompt me to remember something I need to share with you. Towards the end, I started overhearing a lot of phone calls. From the bits and pieces I managed to overhear, it seemed like there was a rat from here, filling him in." She frowns as she mulls over her words, and my stomach drops. Fucking hell; this is the last thing we need.

"What makes you say that?"

"They would tell him things like you had been reunited with your daughter, or you were suspicious about something. They were the ones to tell Kyle Angus was killed, which was odd to me. It makes me wonder if Kyle wasn't such a random player in this whole set up after all." She frowns, looking up at me with confusion painting her features.

This is the last thing we need to add to the already piled high shitshow, but her slip of the tongue has me latching onto that name. *Kyle.* Sounds like an absolute wanker who needs an introduction to how we dish out justice over here.

HELEN
CHAPTER 44

After another fitful night of sleep, the morning comes all too soon. I'm grateful to be able to broach this subject in my own time, but the thought of what awaits me has dread curling in my stomach. Yet, at the same time, leaving the house and letting a stranger be the one to do the examination is a far easier pill to swallow than calling Doc, even if that would mean I could stay in the penthouse. I doubt I'd ever be able to look the man in the face again. Jonathan's steady support means more than words could ever convey.

"Are you sure about this?" I can't help but ask as we step into the lift. He's looking unfairly handsome this morning: dark suit, clearly tailored to flatter his every muscle, silver watch glinting in the early morning sunshine, stubble-covered jaw. His familiar cologne invades my senses; he's my every fantasy wrapped into one six-foot two man I can't have. Not anymore.

"Of course. When have you ever known me to go back on my word?" He cocks a dark brow, giving me his full attention. Time has done nothing to take the headiness out of that action.

"Touché. But no one would blame you for not wanting to be a part of this. It's humiliating."

"Helen, nothing could keep me away. I want to be here for you in any way I can. If that means giving you your space, then that's what we're going to do. If that means driving you to the clinic, then we'll do that too. None of this is a chore, and it sure as shit isn't humiliating." His unflinching gaze holds me in a way I wish I could let him physically, heating me up from the inside in a way I haven't felt in years. Letting the silence blanket us, I offer him a shaky smile before following him to his car. A laugh escapes me as I take it in.

"Truly nothing has changed, huh?"

"I told you—I couldn't bare it," he murmurs, holding the door open for me. The leather seat holds memories of all the times I sat in this very spot. Swallowing back the emotions fighting to take over, I watch Jonathan round the car before sliding into the seat beside me.

The drive passes in comfortable silence as I take in the once-familiar-now-foreign sights of London. So much has changed, and yet our old haunts line every street. Where we had ice cream in the middle of winter. The little café I spent hours in with Donna. O'Neill's restaurant.

"It's strange, isn't it?" he asks.

"Hmm?"

"How time moves so slowly and yet at the speed of light. Nothing changes, and at the same time, everything does." Looking across at him, at his hand resting on the steering wheel with his veiny forearms on full display, I flush before averting my eyes back to the road.

"Sometimes, I feel like I lost more than six years, like I'll never be up to speed or make up for all the missed birthdays and holidays. Hell, I missed our daughter's wedding. Her pregnancy. The birth of my granddaughter." The list of missed milestones is too long to even comprehend. It's like a stab in the gut to even think about how much has changed, how little I know.

"Sweetheart, we're all here for you. Cora has a million photos and videos of the wedding and pregnancy and April to share with you, and

I'll do anything I can to help you. All we want is for you to feel like you can lean on us when you need to." His words soothe an ache inside me that has been bleeding out for far too long. Letting out a shaky exhale, I reach across the car to link hands with him on the gear stick.

We remain like that for the rest of the drive, and sooner than I'm ready for, we're pulling up to the clinic. Squeezing my hand, he gets out and makes his way around to open the door for me. With a hand on my back, he guides me into the clinic. The friendly receptionist takes my details without a trace of judgment and instructs me to take a seat. I can't stop my knee from bouncing while we wait, and before I know it, I'm called back. The nurse takes all my samples with a no-nonsense attitude, and once I've been poked and prodded for every test under the sun, I'm sent on my way with instructions to look out for a call in the next week.

Knowing the first step to taking back ownership over my body is underway feels like a weight off my shoulders, one that's been nearly suffocating me. Back in the waiting room, my eyes automatically drift to Jonathan. In typical mafia man style, he has his back to a wall, eyes constantly scanning the room. The moment he lays eyes on me, he's out of his seat and meeting me halfway.

"Everything go okay?" he grunts, scanning me as if he can see the results for himself.

"As okay as it can." I shrug, adjusting my bag strap as it starts to slip down my shoulder.

"Fancy getting some food before we head back?" When I nod, he leads the way back to the car, helping me in before making his way around to his side. I watch the roads blur as we pass them, and it's not long before we're winding our way down an old, familiar road.

"No way. This place is still here?" I can't control the shocked gasp as I eagerly get out of the car.

"Sweetheart, what have I told you about letting me get the door?" he grumbles, quickly catching up to me with a scowl on his face.

"Can you blame a girl? I've been dreaming about Angie's milkshakes for twenty years." I laugh as we make our way in. With a fond shake of his head, he holds the door open for me, leading me to the same booth we sat in all those years ago. It's comforting to see that, while a lot of things have changed, this place hasn't aged a day. Taking in the familiar sights and smells, I'm transported twenty years into the past, to better times, more carefree times, though I would have scoffed at the idea if you had dared suggest that to me then.

"Johnny, what did I tell you about—" Angie cuts herself off midstream as she lays eyes on me with a gasp. Before I can blink, she's closed the distance between us, pulling me into a hug. With a laugh, I hug her back, unaware just how much I needed to be held, to feel the kind of love and safety only a mother's embrace can provide.

"Oh, sweet child, let me look at you," she tuts, pulling back and framing my face between her palms. As she takes me in, I do the same to her. Her hair has greyed, and there's a few more wrinkles, telling the story of a life filled with love and laughter. She frowns as she takes in my sunken features. No matter how much I've been eating, the weight I desperately need to gain doesn't want to stick to my bones.

"Johnny, what are you feeding this girl?" She huffs, spinning on her heel to level a glare at him. I bite back a laugh at the sight of this five-foot nothing woman ripping the Boss of the Irish Mafia a new one without a trace of fear or hesitation. Slipping back into my seat, I join her in chiding him.

"Yeah, Johnny. What *are* you feeding me?"

Kicking back in his seat, arm draped over the back, he rolls his eyes. "I should have expected this from you two. Ganging up on an old man is so unfair, don't you think?"

"Oh, hush. Now, what will it be? Two vanilla milkshakes and two loaded cheeseburgers?" Just the thought of the delicious burgers has my mouth watering. Angie laughs at the expression on my face before she leaves to place our orders with a squeeze of my shoulder.

"This place is like a time warp," I observe, unable to keep the awe from my voice as I look around before turning my focus to the man across from me.

"I thought you'd appreciate somewhere familiar amidst all the change." He shrugs like it's no big deal when it is, in fact, a huge deal to me. It's another nail in the coffin of the reasons why Jonathan is single handedly the best man I've ever known. The fact that he'll never be mine again cuts deep. Dropping my eyes to the table, I fiddle with the cutlery as I fight back the emotions threatening to choke me.

Before I can think of a response, Angie comes back with our drinks. The second I take a sip, my taste buds light up with desire, and I let out a moan, only to be jerked back to reality by his groan.

"Sweetheart, you can't make noises like that. Please. I'm only a man." The tortured look on his face would have me laughing if the heat in his words wasn't making it hard to think past them. We're caught in a heated staring contest until our food arrives.

It's only once our plates are cleared that the tension eases enough for me to focus. Tearing my napkin into small slivers, I open the lid on Pandora's Box just enough to tell him about my suspicions.

"The man who had me, Kyle, would invite visitors. There was one, Benedict, who had my sister. I'm pretty sure Benedict's ties to the rat ran deep," I confess, looking up at him. Confusion darts across his face before he clears his throat and sits forward, closing the gap between us. "What makes you say that?"

"Little things he would say—comments about how he vouched for them, how he had pull over them. Saying it out loud, it doesn't sound like a lot; it's more like a gut feeling, I guess." I frown. Putting my finger on why I think Benedict and the rat were tightly connected has been driving me crazy.

Letting out a breath, he holds eye contact. "If I'm honest, that would explain a lot. It feels like everywhere we look is a dead end, but if we turn our gaze inwards, well…"

"I'm sorry."

I watch him across the table. The weight of the betrayal, the secrets, the uncertainty—it's all carved into his expression. His handsome face is drawn tight with frown lines, and the spark that once lived in his eyes is gone, replaced by something harder.

Someone's pissed all over the core values of the Points—family and honour above everything—and now he's left to pick up the pieces.

Someone is carrying tales to the worst kind of people, and the fallout's going to be ugly.

I can already hear the outrage. The demands for blood.

JONATHAN
CHAPTER 45

The days blur together as I hit dead end after dead end. After Helen confided suspicions that our rat problem might be internal, I compiled a list of who it could be, of people who raise my hackles and those who are a tad too innocent. Perhaps now is the time to follow Logan's lead and give the whole organisation a shakeup. Just because we're family doesn't mean anyone's spot in the Points is guaranteed—if you fuck around and find out, that one's on you.

I can already picture my brothers' reactions. Seamus will no doubt be pulling out his hair as he comes up with a plan of action. Meanwhile, Declan will do little more than grind his teeth as he stews in the corner. Jack will likely start drafting his own list of names with Brennan's help—who will do little more than push his glasses up his nose and sigh at the inconvenience, leaving Ciaran to be the one to blow his fuse and turn as red as his hair. It's a shit storm waiting to happen.

"Fucking hell," I grunt to myself as I stare at the list of names glaring back at me. The second I hit send and ask the twins to start looking into these fuckers, there's no taking it back. Once the seed of suspicion is planted, it can't be undone. Even if we're wrong, the damage—the broken trust—will be irreversible. Picking up my phone with a sigh, I bite the bullet.

"Yeah?" Brennan answers, sounding less than impressed at being interrupted. God knows what the fucker is up to at this time of night—probably hacking his way through the government's security systems for the fun of it.

"I'm about to send you a list of names to look into for me. This little rat problem might be a bit closer to home, so we need to keep this on the down low for now, yeah?" The silence on the other end of the line does little to reassure me that this is the right move, but I forge ahead. "There's every chance I'm wrong, but we can never be too careful. If anyone gives you pause, work with Ciaran to bring them in, yeah?"

"Christ, Johnny. This shit is nuclear."

"You can say that again. Have any luck across the water?"

"No, Logan and Owen turned this place over pretty thoroughly. It looks like whoever killed the fucker knew what they we're doing. No signs of a struggle, but the place has been raided, either by the kids or the murderer," he muses, frustration bleeding into his tone at the wasted trip.

"Or both. Get the runners to dig up the back yard. All signs point to that fucker being the last to see Freya alive…"

"You think she might be buried here…" he fills in the blanks.

"Maybe. Either way, we should check." Helen's sister—Cora's aunt and Logan's mother—deserves more than being forgotten about in some garden in Belfast. If she's still there, she needs to be brought home where she can rest in peace. It's the least she deserves.

"Roger that." As he hangs up, I send across the list with a pit in my stomach. Shaking it off, I switch gears to deal with the next thing on tonight's agenda. Ever since Logan and Abigail's wedding and the subsequent merger, we've been trying to get the Clan cleaned up while also working out who exactly is behind the sick and twisted sex trafficking ring. But much like me, Logan has had his fair few setbacks and dead ends. Pouring myself a whiskey, I log onto Zoom and wait for him to join.

"Jonathan, good to see you. How're things?" he greets me, and even through the computer screen, I can see the way his eyes dart to the sides.

"She's not here," I mutter with a roll of my eyes. "If you want to get to know your aunt that bad, there are these things called phones. Ever heard of them?"

"And just how do you propose I get her number? Not all of us have IT geniuses on the take, and I don't see you handing it out."

"Bloody right, you don't. But that doesn't mean you can't ask around—I'm sure someone would be willing to play messenger for you. Now, back to business: any news?" As fun as it is to wind him up, I steer us back on track. The sooner we get this shit worked out, the sooner I can focus on the important things. My woman. My family. Our future.

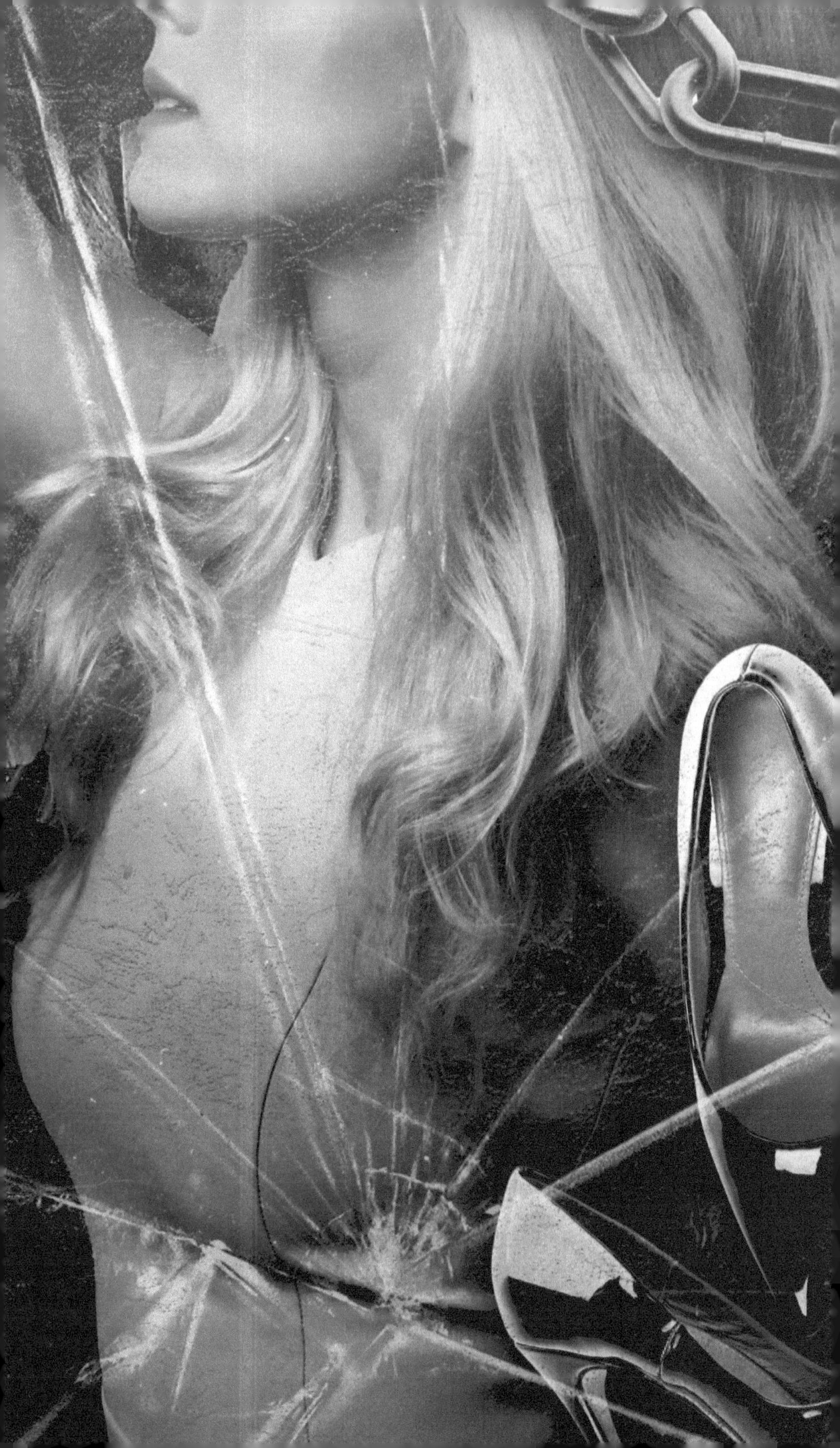

HELEN
CHAPTER 46

The next few weeks blur together as I slowly but surely get caught up on everything I missed. Our lunch that day only served to remind me of everything I missed, everything stolen from me, which I was determined to rectify. One phone call later, and Donna and Cora were enroute, ready to give me a crash course on the last few years, with receipts to back them up in the form of camera rolls.

Seeing videos of Jonathan walking Cora down the aisle, of their father daughter dance, knowing I should have been there to witness it, relights the need for revenge inside me. Yes, Kyle and Benedict may have been dealt with, but the fact remains—there are still more monsters like them out there, preying on the vulnerable. Clinging to that rage and using it to bolster my strength, I've shared as many details as I can with Jonathan without laying myself bare and picking at the barely scabbed over wounds.

I'm sure he's worked it out for himself, but the thought of putting those horrors into words isn't something I can stomach just yet. Getting the all clear from the clinic was a miracle that nearly brought me to my knees with relief. They might have tarnished me in a hundred different ways, but at least they didn't give me something that would linger forever.

"What's going through that pretty head of yours?" Looking up at Jonathan, I bite back a whimper. The man wears the hell out of a suit, but seeing him in a tight tee and sweatpants? Lord have mercy.

"Hmm? Oh, nothing. Just looking at the photos Cora left," I answer, gesturing to the wedding album Cora had dropped over on her way to the airport. Apparently, Logan wants to give Abigail the proposal she never had, and that includes getting her nearest and dearest to meet them on his private island. It's incredibly romantic, yet more evidence he is Freya's son through and through. Holding up a bottle of wine in question, he pours us each a glass before coming to join me. The heat of his thigh pressed against mine burns through my thin leggings.

Passing me a wine glass, he gently takes the album and lays it on the table between us. Twisting to face him better, I ignore the jolt that goes through me as his knuckles brush my bare shoulder. Quirking an eyebrow at him, I wait for him to say what's on his mind.

"I've been thinking –"

"Careful you don't strain yourself," I quip.

"Smartass," he says fondly before continuing, "Why don't you join Donna and the others at one of their girls' nights?"

"Trying to kick me out? See, I knew you wanted your space back."

He scoffs. "Don't get it twisted. I'm glad you're here. You bring life to this place, which has been lacking for a long time. But it would be good for you to ease yourself back into the swing of things."

"I've been weighing it up, trying to get the courage. Going from being confined in a nasty basement, chained nearly every hour of the day, it's quite a shock to the system to be free again. To come and go as I please. I can't help but doubt it will last, that someone won't drag me back to that hellhole the second I drop my guard."

"Helen…please. Who hurt you? Give me a name," he begs,

dropping his forehead to rest against mine. Agony bleeds from his every pore, lashing at me, making me bleed all over again as I stumble through baring my soul to the man I never stopped loving. Even when it hurt to do so.

"Angus. Kyle. Benedict. Rodger. Too many to count, in more ways than I could ever have imagined. Johnny…I'm ruined. They made sure of that," I sob, squeezing my eyes shut. "It hurt so bad. Not a day went by without someone raping me, torturing me, not to mention my punishments. Please. I can't."

"Hush, you're safe now. I swear, no one will ever touch a hair on your head again. They'll have to go through me. I should have been there; I shouldn't have let you go. Sweetheart, can you ever forgive me?" His strong arms pull me into his embrace, and the safety of being in his arms cause the last of my walls to crumble between us.

"It was never going to be that easy. Angus said as much when he…" I trail off, unable to put into words what was done that day. I'm shaking uncontrollably when he gently pulls back to cup my face between his palms, rubbing circles on my cheekbones as soothing words leave his lips.

"Johnny, he…. they… God, it was awful. It hurt so much; I wanted to die. Death would have been a kinder fate. There's nothing they didn't do, didn't ruin. How can you possibly sit there and look at me as anything other than ruined?" I sob the words like acid as he holds me tight to his chest. It's like opening a dam I can't close as I purge the last of my horrors to him, laying myself bare at his feet and hoping he doesn't crucify me for it. I pray he doesn't look at me differently. Eventually, he encourages me to open my eyes and release the death grip I have on his wrists.

"There's my pretty girl. Give me those baby blues. You never need to hide from me, understand? Their actions are their burden to bear, not yours. You survived. That's the most important thing, and if it takes you twenty years to feel safe, then that's what it takes. I'm not going anywhere. Nobody and nothing will ever change that," he vows, imploring me to understand.

The intensity in his eyes should scare me, but instead, it strengthens me.

"I never stopped dreaming about you," I confess on a shaky exhale, watching as my words land like a blow. He bows his head, kissing my forehead, letting his lips rest there for a moment.

"I never stopped loving you." His words are so quiet, I don't think I'm meant to hear them.

But I do, and they change everything.

JONATHAN
CHAPTER 47

I've been angry before. I've felt rage. But as Helen's confessions slice through me, the blackness inside me reaches a whole new level. Its uncharted territory—this violent, thundering urge to hunt and destroy anyone who dared touch what's mine. It's overtaking every logical thought and leaving me in a red filled haze. This is more than mere anger. It's colder, sharper, a rage that sears everything in its path.

I knew her story wasn't going to be pretty, that it would have my blood lust kicking up a notch, but fuck me. Hearing the utterly devastating tale from her lips lashes at me with more efficiency than a barbed whip. The only thing keeping me somewhat sane is feeling her heart berating against mine, her breath fanning across my neck, and the way her nails dig into my wrists. Clinging to her, I remind myself she's safe now. No one will ever get their hands on her again. Over my dead fucking body.

"I'm going to run you a bath, and you're going to let someone else take care of you for once, okay, sweetheart? It's okay to need help, to break down when you need to. You are safe here, I swear it. On my life," I vow, wishing I could go back in time and undo all her hurt. I might not be able to, but I sure as fuck can seek vengeance and lay all her abusers at her feet in a bloody trail fit for a queen. For that's what she is: a queen. My queen. And it's about time everyone knew that.

"That sounds nice," she whispers and it's all the permission I need. Placing a kiss on her crown, I head upstairs. Bypassing her room and en-suite, I head for the master bath. I turn on the tub, testing the water before adding some bath salts and pulling out my phone while I wait for it to fill up.

"Yeah?" Brennen grunts as soon as the call connects. A man of few words, but words aren't what I'm after tonight. Action is, and if anyone can get this ball rolling, it's him, even if he is currently in the middle of a recon mission.

"I need you to run a few new names for me. This trumps the previous list."

"Are heads going to roll?"

"Maybe. Check through that server and start with a Kyle. He would have made the *purchase*," I spit the word out, disgust curling in my gut, "around six years ago. No purchases that I know of since then. Then, cross check for mentions of visits from Angus, Peter, a Roger, and a Benedict. Keep digging until you get me all the names you can."

"Got it. Want me to get Ciaran to start hunting them, or should we wait and dial you in?"

"He can start, but those fuckers are mine. Get them in the Pit or get me addresses, yeah?" At his grunt of agreement, I hang up and take a deep breath. Cracking my neck, I try to shove my rage beneath the surface. It won't serve me to unleash it now. Knowing we have things in motion to find these sick fuckers makes it a tad easier to force a sense of calm I don't feel onto my face as I head back down to get Helen. She's exactly where I left her, a haunted look on her face that I'd sell my soul to erase. Making my steps heavier so as not to startle her, I make my way over.

No words are needed as I guide her up to the bathroom with a hand between her shoulder blades. With a frown, I note she's still too skinny, too fragile, for my liking. I shouldn't be able to feel her bones through her clothes. Making a mental note to ask Fiona for some recipes, I lead her through my room to the master bath.

"You meant it when you said you couldn't change anything, huh?" she remarks, taking in the uncaged room where we spent so many, and yet nowhere near enough, nights.

"What can I say? I didn't want to move on when I knew what heaven was." Ignoring her sharp inhale, I open the bathroom door. "There's towels on the rail. I'm going to get some dinner started. If you need me, just call, okay, sweetheart?" At her nod, I leave her, offering her privacy. It's the least I can do.

Leaving her to it, I assess what we have in the kitchen. Spying the ingredients for lasagna, I quickly throw it together and pop it into the oven before heading back upstairs. I softly rap my knuckles against the door, waiting for her to give me the go ahead before letting myself in.

Seeing her with her skinny knees curled up to her chest, blonde curls damp around her face, and glassy eyes has an ache burrowing its way between my rib cage. In that moment, all her hurt, all her scars, are a physical thing between us that I wade through to edge closer to her. Once I'm close enough, I grab the bottle of conditioner, the same one she used to keep here. At her tentative nod, I settle on my knees beside the bath and guide her head back as I lather the conditioner into her soaked curls.

"You remembered," she mutters, looking up at me as I tip her head back to rinse the conditioner out, taking care not to tangle it in the process.

"Of course I did. There's not a thing about you that ever left my mind."

"Hmm, yeah? How'd I take my coffee?"

"With far too much sugar and a dash of milk, but your preferred drink was an iced caramel latte with an extra shot and a bucket full of cream and caramel drizzle." I wrinkle my nose at the memory of the sugar overload. Seeing her spark come back is worth it all. Once the last of the conditioner is rinsed out and the bathroom smells like coconuts, I hold up a big, fluffy towel for her and avert my eyes as she wraps it around herself.

"Thank you," she murmurs, eyes solely focused on the floor. Slowly, I reach for her, tilting her head up so I can capture her eyes with mine.

"Queens don't look at the ground." I back away, taking a seat on the bench and patting the seat beside me. Hesitation lines her face, but she comes over, and when she spies the detangler in my hand and microfiber towel beside me, her face softens into a look of wonderment.

"How…"

"I've done my homework. I wanted to be able to help with April's hair, since it looks like she's inherited your curls." Offering her a crooked smile, I indicate for her to turn around. Once she does, I get to work gently taking the dampness out of her hair and detangling it. I've spent more nights than I care to admit dreaming about this. Her shocked hiss as she inhales and the way her back quivers is her only answer, but it's all I need. Pressing a kiss against her shoulder, I reach for one of her hands and offer her what comfort I can while she lets me.

HELEN
CHAPTER 48

Opening up to Jonathan, sharing the ugliest parts of me with him, only for him to turn around and practically fall on his knees in his attempts to reassure me has me wanting to try. To prove I'm more than what they did to me—what they stole from me. To let him in even though the thought of doing so fills me with a fear so intense, it stops me in my tracks most of the time.

So, when Donna floated the idea of a girl's night at hers, for once, I didn't hesitate. If anyone can help me sort out my conflicting emotions, it's her. Seeing Fiona after all this time—especially factoring in the fact that our kids got married—feels long overdue. The way all our lives have ended up intertwined thanks to our children feels fitting in a 'what a small world' kind of way.

"Will Una be there?" I ask, phone wedged between my ear and shoulder as I flick through my wardrobe for something to wear. Cora's sentimentally stopping her from getting rid of my belongs sure came in handy. The thought of starting from scratch and building up a whole new wardrobe right now sounds like hell.

"Una? Absolutely not. That bitch had the nerve to cheat on Ciaran and then accuse him of being the cheater. The only reason she's even somewhat relevant is because she managed to get knocked up before all that." She sniffs, and I can positively feel her disgust bleeding through the line. "His new wife should be coming, though. Jen's…harmless."

An uneasiness settles in my stomach, but I shake it off. I can't let fear of the unknown stop me from taking steps towards healing and moving on, or those bastards will have won, and my escape will have been for nought. With promises to be there soon, I hang up and focus on getting changed before I can change my mind. Slipping a simple shift dress and some heels on, I do my best to channel my most confident self. Applying some makeup and spraying some mist to de-frizz my curls, I take a couple of deep breaths and give myself a pep talk before heading downstairs.

The sound of my heels on the hardwood floor echoes in the otherwise-silent penthouse as I make my way to Jonathan's office. I'm sure he'll be over the moon I'm making steps to improve and leave, to branch out and rebuild. Rapping my knuckles on the door to his office, I push it open and lose my breath. The sight of him behind a desk still sends me bat shit crazy, even after all this time. The man is designed for this look. The businessman who's hot as shit and knows it. The mafia leader through and through. Looking up at me, he runs a hand through his dark hair as he blesses me with a smile.

"Hey there, sweetheart. You look beautiful."

"Thank you. I'm heading to Donna's for a few with the girls," I tell him as I watch his small smile turn into a blinding one.

"That's great. Just let me grab my keys, and I'll take you." He's already rising as he says the words. As he rounds his desk, his smile slips for a second as he looks down at my feet. "Why do you insist on wearing those death traps? Especially when we both know how much you detest them."

"You know what they say: beauty is pain," I tease him, biting my lip as he shakes his head and mutters to himself. Making our way to the living room, he pulls me to a stop.

"Wait here for a second," he commands, dipping down to press a kiss to the side of my forehead before disappearing upstairs. With heat racing through me, I do as he asks, only to blink back tears as he reappears with a pair of ballet flats in hand. Reaching me, he slowly drops to one knee and holds eye contact as he switches my shoes. Feeling his touch on my ankles as he slowly helps me step out of the heels and into the flats, combined with his unflinching eye contact, has me biting back a whimper as he presses a kiss to ankle before rising to his feet and cupping my face between his hands.

"You'll never suffer one more moment of pain, Helen. Not on my watch." Speechless, I can't do much more than blink back tears and swallow down the emotions threatening to choke me. With a hand on the middle of my back, a touch I'm growing to not just tolerate but crave, I let him lead me down into the garage and over to his car. The ride passes in a heated, weighted silence, and as he pulls into their driveway, his next words do little to snuff out that heat.

"Call me when you're ready to come home."

Home. The word still echoes in my head as he rounds the car to help me out, placing a hand on my waist as he guides me up the steps. Tipping my chin back to look at him, I open my mouth to say something—God knows what—when all of a sudden, the door is ripped open, and our bubble bursts.

"Helen, lovely to see you again," Fiona gushes, her dimples shinning as she grins at me. I can tell she wants to pull me in for a hug but is restraining herself for my benefit, which just makes me even more determined to overcome my fears.

"And you," I tell her, closing the distance between us and hugging her for a second. She freezes in shock before gently squeezing me. Clearing her throat, she steps back and ushers me in. With a glance over my shoulder, I see Jonathan watching us with a heated look; when he catches me looking at him, he winks before dipping his chin and heading back to the car.

Lord help me.

Following Fiona through the house to the kitchen, I see more than one framed photo featuring our girls. Knowing Cora had Donna and Abigail in her corner helps ease some of the sting. Entering the kitchen to the sight of Donna elbow deep in cookie dough, I stifle a laugh at the look on her face. I glance around; it seems like we're the only ones here right now.

"Need a hand?" I offer, slipping my jacket off and draping it over the back of a chair.

"Absolutely not. Sit down and relax," she protests, hip checking me when I come round to see what she's trying to do.

"Are those meant to look like that?" I laugh at the misshapen cookies. It looks like she tried to make them heart shaped without a cutter, resulting in some interesting cookies.

"Hush and drink up, would you?"

"Where's Jen?" I ask Fiona, taking a seat beside her at the table and smiling as she passes me a wine glass filled to the brim. My kind of girl.

"She should be here any minute. Apparently, her daughter, Lily, was causing a bit of trouble, and she got held up," Fiona answers with a roll of her eyes. It doesn't take a genius to read between the lines and sense what Fiona thinks of that.

"So, tell me: do we like her, or is she an Una 2.0?"

"She's not an Una, but she's also not…perfect," Donna answers diplomatically just before the doorbell goes off. With a look, Fiona lets out a sigh before she leaves to let her in. Clearly, she drew the short straw. Taking a sip of my wine, I raise a brow at Donna in silent question. With a shake of her head and a tip of her chin at the doorway, I shelve my questions for later. Swivelling in my chair just as the girls appear in the doorway, I take Jen in. At first glance, she's nothing special and radiates ice queen energy by the bucketful. My hackles are instantly up and as she turns her nose up at the wine Fiona offers her that feeling only strengthens

Going by the look on Donna's face, I'm not the only one taking offense with her attitude. The tension in the air doesn't dissipate as the night passes in a blur of small talk, wine, and cheese. Just as it's wrapping up, something Jen says catches my attention, and not in a good way.

"Sorry, what did you say?"

"I asked what Belfast was like. That's where you were, right?" She frowns. Sure, I know Jonathan and Co. had been looking into my disappearance and trying to find me, but that doesn't explain how she knows. And if she *did* know, posing the question like that, like it was a nice little vacation, is beyond insensitive.

Donna, sensing the tension, wraps things up by making a show of looking at the time and declaring it late. In a flurry of stilted goodbyes, Jen leaves, Fiona hot on her tail, a blush coating her cheeks as Seamus picks her up. His gaze is heated, and it's nice to know at least one of us will be getting lucky tonight. Once it's just me and Donna, I turn my focus on her.

"Okay, fess up. What's the story there?" I ask as, with a groan, she flops beside me, kicking off her heels and running a hand through her hair.

"I've tried to keep an open mind with that woman, but the way she treats her daughter doesn't sit right with me. And the ways she's so cold just isn't right. You got that vibe, didn't you?" She frowns, pursing her lips.

"By the bucket. What's the story of how they met? Her accent doesn't sound local." I frown.

"Well, after Una cheated and then tried to paint him as the one in the wrong, he went a bit off the rails. They had to get a whole new host of girls at Albi after he'd done the rounds and things got a tad awkward. Jonathan sent him to Belfast for a job, and next thing we knew, Jen and Lily were moving in with him, and there was a ring on her finger. I'd call her a gold digger if she didn't come from money of her own."

"Something doesn't add up. Did you see the way she asked me about my time in Belfast? As if it was some holiday?" I scoff, downing the rest of my wine to chase away the memories.

"Speaking of, how did she even know that's where you were? I don't even think *I* knew that." Donna frowns. The more titbits she shares, the more I think about things, and the more red flags go off. Something about her truly isn't sitting right with me.

"I don't know, but I don't like it."

"Oh, hell no. I know that look in your eyes, and it spells trouble with a capital T."

"Please, help me look into her. I'm sure it's nothing, and I don't want to point fingers without facts. I promise, the second it gets too much, I'll bring it to Jonathan," I plead, trying to appeal to the Donna who was never was able to resist a good mystery.

"Fine, but I swear the moment this blows up, I'm blaming you." She teases me with a roll of her eyes before topping our wine glasses up and grabbing her laptop from the coffee table. As she fires it up, I send a text to Jonathan to let him know the change in plans.

Helen:
Slight change of plans. Donna has pulled out a few photo albums and another bottle of wine. I think I might just crash here and get her to drop me off at Cora's in the morning.

Jonathan:
As long as you're sure. You know I don't mind coming to get you, no matter how late it is.

Helen:
I think it might do me some good. Baby steps, you know?

Jonathan:
Yeah. Well, if you change your mind, I'm only
a text away, sweetheart.

HELEN
CHAPTER 49

After a long night of hitting dead end after dead end, Donna dropped me off at Cora's house—our old home. Stepping through the front door is a weird mix between stepping foot in a time warp and seeing her little touches sprinkled everywhere. But even the cuteness of April and their tuxedo kitten, Socks, batting a ball back and forth on the living room floor can't distract from the pit of suspicion and unease that's taken root.

Cora is mid-way through telling me about her own brush of danger with Angus when her phone rings. Shuffling closer beside me, she answers the Facetime call with a beaming smile, and a redhead pops into view.

"Cora, babe, you'll never believe –" Abigail cuts herself off mid-sentence with a gasp when she spies me beside Cora. "Helen, oh my God. It's so good to see you." The last—and first—time I saw my daughter's best friend, she was spitting mad on her behalf. My kind of woman; it's clear she takes after her mother in more than just the looks department.

"I was calling to show you the progress on the makeover, but now I want to know how things are going with you guys." Abigail sets her phone up against something so we can see her sitting cross legged on a bed while she pets the golden retriever curled up against her.

"It's an adjustment for sure, but it's just nice to be able to have days like this." I indicate with a swivel of my hand to the peace that is having family moments, moments that, in my darkest days, I never thought I'd be lucky enough to experience again. Cora's sharp inhale beside me says it all.

Abigail, sensing the fragility of the moment, offers us both a small smile as she tries to change the subject to something lighter. "Speaking of family…how about the fact Logan is technically Cora's cousin?"

"Meaning we're basically family."

"Please, as if we weren't already sisters," Abigail scoffs with a roll of her eyes before turning to me. "Speaking of the devil—any chance you'd be up to talking to my husband?"

The thought of seeing him, even through a phone screen, and being slapped in the face with his resemblance to Freya is almost too much to stomach. At the same time, though, I owe it to her to offer him whatever sense of closure and answers I can. She would do it for me if the shoe was on the other foot.

"Sure. I'll get Cora to give you my number, and you can pass it along to him." The visible relief on her face at my concession tells me all I need to know about how important this is to her—to him. With promises to do so, she hangs up just as the doorbell rings. With a frown, Cora heads to answer it while I watch April and Socks. The sound of footsteps alerts me to Cora's reappearance, but as I turn around, the sight of a curvy brunette with tears in her eyes and heartbreak bleeding from her every pore wipes the smile clean off my face.

"Are you okay, honey?" I ask, making my way over to her. When I'm close enough, I place my hands on her heaving shoulders. Her wide, panicked hazel eyes look at me in shock before she starts sobbing.

"Hey, it's all going to be okay," I hush her, running my hand over her hair, pulling her into me. Cora joins me in trying to soothe the clearly distraught girl by rubbing circles on her back.

"Lily, babe, what's wrong?" she asks, shooting confused looks at me over her friend's shoulder. Not knowing what's going on any more than she does, I shrug and continue to soothe her, offering what little bits of comfort I can. Eventually, we get her to calm down a bit and move her over to the sofa.

"How about I make us all some hot chocolate, hmm? Chocolate fixes everything." Leaving Lily curled up beside Cora, I make our drinks the way I used to for Cora when she had a bad day at school: boiling the milk on the stove, melting a chocolate bar down over boiling water, and combining both in a mug before topping a dollop of heavy whipping cream and a sprinkle of marshmallows. Taking the mugs back over to the girls, I catch the tail end of their conversation.

"I thought we talked about this. He's just going to break your heart." Frustration bleeds from Cora's every word. It's clear this is a conversation they've had a million times.

"I know, but I can't help loving him, Cor. Don't you think I've tried? Of course I'd save myself from this if I could." She sobs, burying her head in her hands. Even with missing information, that kind of pain, of heartbreak, is universal enough that my heart goes out to her. Taking a seat beside her, I pull her into my side and hum a lullaby, trying to soothe her before she works herself up even more. Just as her breathing calms, we're interrupted by the sharp click clack of heels on the wooden hall floor. Twisting to see who the hell has decided to let themselves into Cora's home, I spy the frosty blonde from last night. Jen's here, and she doesn't look pleased to see her daughter here with us.

"Lily Jenifer Murphy, what on Earth are you doing here?! We are supposed to be halfway across town by now, and thanks to you, we're going to be late. God, can't you do anything right, you ungrateful brat?!" She ends her tirade with a shout before narrowing in on the hot chocolates.

"And what have I told you about consuming stuff like that? God, as if you aren't big enough as it is. This is going to take weeks of dieting to correct." With a huff, she grabs Lily's arm without so much as a word to anyone else and drags her away. Lily's tear-stricken face might be out of our line of sight for now, but not from my memory. It'll take more than a closed door to erase a sight like that, or to erase the absolute venom clinging to Jen's every word.

"Well, that was…" Jonathan frowns, having let himself in somewhere in the middle of Jen's tirade.

"Interesting," I offer, and he snorts.

"You could say that again," Cora mutters, darkness clinging to her words as she glares at her front door. It's clear Jen is making bad impressions left, right, and centre. My main question is, what kind of woman—what kind of mother—can treat her own daughter like that?

JONATHAN
CHAPTER 50

Ever since Helen started spending more time with Donna and Cora, taking steps towards healing, every moment we spend together feels even more charged. Watching a movie with her thigh touching mine has me fighting back the urge to pull her into my arms. Having family dinner nights with her and Cora has me dreaming of what our life could have been, of what I'm determined to make it into. It's like there's an electric current in the air. With every breath we take, every move we make, it feels like it's going to shock us.

It's not just thrumming in my veins anymore—it's palpable in the air. Anytime we're in the same room, it's all I can do not to act on it, to touch her, kiss her, show her I mean it when I say it's always been her and always will be. She's it for me, but she's not ready for the weight of that yet. Once I make her mine, there's no going back. I made the mistake of letting her go once, but never again. I'm playing for keeps this time. The only way this ends is with the ring that has lived in my dresser for two decades being slipped on her finger with vows of forever and I do's.

"You know the thing that got me through that hell hole the most?" Looking up from my laptop, I see she paused the movie and cast aside her book. Evil never sleeps, but that doesn't mean I can't multitask and spend time in her presence while answering the never-ending wave of emails.

"Hmm?" Shutting the lid of my laptop and setting it aside, I give her my full attention.

"The thought of being back in your arms," she confesses, twisting to face me. "Every time they would touch me, I'd think of you, of us. It's the only way I managed to stay sane." Her confession rips at my restraint, and in seconds, I'm across the room on my knees before her, resting my forehead against hers.

"Sweetheart, knowing what you went through is killing me," I confess against her skin. "I missed you so much. I never got over you. The guys didn't understand my sudden celibacy, but I couldn't stomach the thought of being with anyone who wasn't you. Now that you're back, I'll give you all the time in the world, but just know, I still want you, Helen. I've wanted you since I first laid eyes on you, and that's never changed. I want you so much, I'd give up everything to go back and change the path we took. I'd lay myself at the altar to save you from that if I could."

"Johnny, I…" She trails off, tears wetting her cheeks. I kiss them away, ignoring the burning in my own eyes. She reaches up to cup my cheek, scanning my eyes for who knows what before bridging the distance between us. Kissing her feels like coming home, and as she wraps her arms around my neck, tugging me closer, the last shreds of my restraint snap. Her breathy moans are like an aphrodisiac that have me following her lead blindly, ignoring all thoughts of taking things slow.

"I want to feel alive," she confesses against my mouth before tugging me closer. Fuck, how I hate anyone who made her feel less than alive. Following her lead, I rest my weight on my elbows as she blinks up at me. Being so close to her, feeling the heat from her skin and tasting her desire in the air, has me feral with need. Yet at the same time, as I look down at the woman beneath me, I want to treasure every single second she blesses me with.

"It will always be you, sweetheart. Do you understand that?"

"Please, I just want to be yours."

"You have me, baby, I swear. You always have, but there's no going back from this. Do you want that?" I ask, nipping at her neck and making my way down to kiss the swells of her breasts her tank top can't contain.

"God, yes," she moans, twining her fingers through my hair and tugging me back up so she can kiss me again. Biting her lip at her impatience, I pull back enough to look at her. Blonde curls splay over my sofa, pupils blown wide and not an ounce of hesitation or fear in sight. Instead, raw need has her arching her back and digging her nails into my neck. Slowly moving down, I help her strip, taking care to kiss every inch of skin exposed to me. Soon, she's tugging my shirt off, and when she sees the tattoo, her eyes grow wide and damp.

"Jonathan…"

"I told you, sweetheart. I carried you with me always," I confess as she takes in the portrait of her eyes I got inked over my heart, right where she belongs. Leaning down, I claim her mouth as mine, and as she arches her back, moaning into my mouth, it feels like all the missing pieces slot together. *This* is what's been missing for the last twenty odd years, this feeling of being loved and loving in equal measure, of having someone to confide in, to love, to worship with every fibre of my being.

"Please, Johnny. Make me forget," she begs in a whisper, clutching me like she's scared I'm going to disappear. Like hell. I have her back, and nothing and no one can tear me away from this woman ever again.

I'd like to see them try.

I kiss my way down her neck, nipping at the delicate flesh and relishing in her whimpers that light my soul on fire. Her hands in my hair, clutching me for dear life, urge me lower. Locking eyes with her, I mouth her breast through her bra, taking great joy in the glazed look on her face. Euphoria suits her.

"Please, Johnny."

"Tell me what you need, sweetheart. Name it. What my pretty girl wants, she gets; you remember that, don't you?"

"Please, I want to feel your mouth," she whimpers, fisting my hair with desperate moans.

"Hmm, I think you can do better than that." I smirk. With a frustrated whine, she struggles to remove her bra, freeing her marvellous breasts to my hungry eyes. With a groan, I suck one into my mouth, lapping at the dusky pink flesh like a starved man. Fuck, I've missed these. I've missed her taste and moans and the way she shatters under me so perfectly.

"God, I dreamed about these," I murmur, letting my words roll over her as her whimpers grow, each one a plea I feel deep in my chest.

My hand slips between us, sliding beneath her shorts to find her— hot, wet, and trembling. At her sudden gasp, I freeze.

Panic grips me.

Did I go too far?

I look up, an apology already forming, ready to pull away and drop to my knees if she asks—if she even looks uncertain.

But her eyes…

They're locked on mine, wide and burning with hunger. No fear. No hesitation.

"Please," she breathes, her voice shaking but firm. "Don't treat me like I'm broken. I want more. You know I can handle it. So don't you dare stop."

With a curse, I claim her mouth once more, collaring her throat with my free hand as I work her pussy over like a man on a mission. Only when she's positively drenched and begging for more do I rip myself away from her long enough to shuck my trousers and shrug off my shirt.

"I need you, sweetheart," I confess, coming back to her and helping her remove her shorts and underwear. Once she's naked below me,

I go to lean back and take her in, only for her to dig her nails into my back, hauling my attention back to her face. With a stiff shake of her head, she lays her boundaries without words. If she's not ready to be laid bare in front of me just yet, that's fine. I can still worship her in the way she deserves blindfolded if that makes her feel more at ease.

"I need you, Johnny. I need to feel you inside me, claiming me in the way only you can. Please, erase their touches." Her words slice through me, but with a heated kiss and locked eyes, I slide home. The feeling is like none other. I've missed this more than words can convey, and goddamn, was she worth every second of the wait.

"That's my perfect girl. My gorgeous, perfect girl," I rasp, driving my hips into hers as she claws at my back. Fuck, I'm not going to last long, not when she feels so good wrapped around me like this, arching herself closer to me and begging for more with every breath. Dropping my forehead to her shoulder, I mouth at the flesh there as she digs her nails into me.

"Oh, God," she whines. "I'm gonna…"

"That's right, come all over my cock. Show me how much you missed it. Be my good girl, and I'll fill you up. You'd like that, wouldn't you? Covered in my scent so everyone knows who you belong to," I growl, reaching between us to circle her clit.

"Come with me. I want to feel it," she begs before dragging my face to hers and claiming my mouth. With a moan, I lose myself in her, feeling her walls clench around me. I follow her over the edge with a groan. Fuck, what I wouldn't give to pull back and look at the sight between her thighs, us mixed together in the most sinful way. Instead, I hold her gaze as I pull out and push my cum back inside her, where it belongs.

I love this woman, and I think I always have.

JONATHAN
CHAPTER 51

It's amazing the effect waking up with Helen tangled around me has on me. For the first time in years, I wake feeling lighter, ready to face anything that comes my way. Nothing can take this spring out of my step. Last night was worth all the waiting in the world, and I'd do it again tenfold, but I hope I never need to. With regret, I disentangle myself from her sleep-heavy limbs. She lets out a soft grunt of discontent, a frown marring her pretty face as she burrows deeper into the duvet. Pressing a kiss to her forehead, I smooth out the frown lines that should never be there before quietly getting dressed and leaving.

As much as I would love nothing more than to be there as she wakes up and have a repeat of last night, business calls. The twins are finally back with a full report and have managed to get a lead on our rat situation. The sooner we get to the bottom of this mess, the better. The last thing we need is a rat bleeding our secrets out.

Making my way into the Pit, I stop by the chest freezer to grab supplies before making my way to where the piece of shit soldier is chained up. His panicked screaming only increases as he lays eyes on me and the ice cube in my hand. Jerking my chin at Declan, he makes quick work of stripping the fucker as Ciaran holds him. With a smirk, I shove the ice cube up his ass and take great joy in the way the whites of his eyes show. He squeals as realisation sets in.

"If I were you, I'd start talking before that melts. If you please us, we can remove it… If not, well…you'll get a nice surprise soon enough," I drawl, stepping back and folding my arms as I watch him squirm. He's spitting mad, but still, he clenches his jaw as defiance bleeds form his eyes.

Turning to Ciaran, I ask, "What makes you think it's him?"

"The fucker was caught on that server. Bren was able to track an IP and name to him, but the asshole won't speak."

"Even if he's not the rat, he's scum," Declan spits.

"What makes you think looking into sex trafficking would float with us, you wanker? Do you not remember your oath? Family above all else!" I snarl, landing a punch. Still, he clenches his teeth, offering us nothing.

Sharing a dark look with Ciaran, he dips his chin before heading to grab supplies. Meanwhile, I roll up my sleeves as I prowl around the shrivelling peace of garbage chained to the ceiling. Declan catches my eye, and, with a subtle dip of his chin, he zeros in on black ink on the man's stomach. In this life, ink is very rarely meaningless or random.

"What've you got there?" Declan mutters, advancing towards our captive, who stubbornly clenches his jaw and fixes his gaze on a spot on the wall. Clicking my tongue, I slide up behind him, resting my chin on his shoulder as I taunt him.

"Now, now, is that any way to save your skin? It's a simple question, but maybe we need to make this even easier for you." In a flash, Declan pulls his knife from his boot and uses it to slice the man's shirt off. Flinching back from the blade just delivers him into my grip. Wrapping my fist around his throat, I hold him still as Declan traces the tattoo with his knife.

"Trust you fuckers to start the party without me," Ciaran grumbles as he comes back with his hatchet slung across his shoulders.

"You took your sweet ass time," Declan fires back. "Look at this and tell me that's not some twisted version of the Clan's tattoo." Like our four-leaf clover tattoo, the Clan has their own initiation tattoo, and for this asshole to bear both ours and theirs… *Fuck*. With a shove, I release my hold on him to look at the ink for myself. There, in black and grey, is a badly covered Celtic cross tattoo just above his left hip. With a clang, Ciaran drops his hatchet to his side in shock.

"Well shit, looks like my twin needs to do some more digging into Jimmy here," he mutters. Jimmy chooses that moment to start fighting his restraints again, clearly not as checked out of the conversation as we thought. Or maybe the ice cube has started to melt, and he's feeling the effects of having barbed wire shoved up his ass.

We work him over until he's a bleeding, scowling mess. Even when the ice cube melts and barbed wire is in his rectum, he still refuses to say anything. Getting nowhere, we shove him into the Pit with plans to come back and assess the situation once he's had a little time to starve and dehydrate. Maybe then, he'll be more willing to talk. Maybe a few days with barbed wire cutting into his ass will loosen his tongue. For now, I've more important matters to attend to.

"You heading to meet with Salvatore?" Ciaran asks as we tidy up. Glancing at him out of the corner of my eye, I debate answering him. Matt's impending nuptials with the Don's granddaughter is a bit of a sore spot between father and son.

"Yeah. Any idea if Matt will be joining us?"

"Not a fucking clue. That kid is testing me, out drinking every night like he has no purpose."

"Like father, like son," Declan chimes in, joining us in front of my car.

"As if you can talk. At least I have a kid and a missus," Ciaran fires back, all ice and venom despite Declan meaning no harm.

"Christ, you two argue like an old married couple. Any word from the runners of their little digging mission?" The sooner we can lay Freya to rest, the better.

"Nothing good. I'm heading back over there today to see if we can't get this sorted," Ciaran answers me. Clapping him on the shoulder in thanks, I dip into my car and make my way to O'Neill's HQ for today's next order of business. Since stepping into Da's shoes, my days here have been fewer and far in between, but any chance I can take to come back is always a godsend. Nodding at the people I pass, I make my way into my office, running my hand over what was Helen's desk. I wonder what she'd think if she saw even this place was like a shrine to our brief time together.

I've barely got the contracts printed and the drinks poured when a heavy fist pounds on my door. *Show time.*

"Testing the strength of my door, Salvatore?" I quirk a brow as I let him in. Brushing past me, he surveys the room as if it's beneath him before taking a seat and sniffing one of the whiskeys I'd prepared. Pinching the bridge of my nose and praying for patience, I take a seat behind my desk.

"Did young Mathew decide not to join us?" He sniffs, looking less than impressed—probably as impressed as Matt would be to be called Mathew.

"No, Matt is busy. You know how it is." I shrug. The reality is, if I could escape this pointless meeting, I would. Even with three or so years before his granddaughter is of age to marry, Salvatore has been breathing down my neck to get things ironed out. Where they will live, who's getting a cut, how much—it's all so fucking tedious.

I can only hope Matt is up for the challenges that lie ahead.

HELEN
CHAPTER 52

Hiding the worst of my scars from Johnathan wasn't a conscious decision as much as it was instinct screaming at me to do so and circumstance making it easy. My left hip was against the back of the sofa, so hiding the worst from him was easy enough, and then sleeping in his shirt made it easy to hide at night. But now, sitting in the bath with bubbles up to my chest while he takes such great care in washing my hair while I hug my knees to my chest has me wanting to take that last leap of faith.

The care in his every action, the utter devotion he's shown me, has me wanting to share it all with him: the good, the bad and even the ugly. As he massages conditioner in my scalp I feel the last part of my resistance crumble. Taking one of his hands in my own with a squeeze, I place it on the ruined flesh of my hip. He freezes beside me, fingers lightly tracing the marks there. I can feel the fury bleeding into him as he growls, "Who did this to you?"

And so, with a shaky breath and my heart in my throat, I lay my soul bare to him. The words are slow and stilted, and with every sentence, I can feel him grow tenser and tenser at my back. "After the accident, I woke up in a cell. It wasn't long before I was sold off. For a while, I thought my new owner was the worst fate that awaited me, but then Angus paid us a visit…"

As the words spill from my lips, as I share every inch of depravity and heartbreak, part of my soul knits itself back together, the damage lessening with every word.

"After what they did to Freya…I couldn't cope anymore. I'd reached my breaking point, and with nothing left to lose, a part of me just snapped. I killed them, Johnny. I'm a murderer. God, I feel so filthy. They ruined me in ways I don't think I'll ever recover from. He branded me, pierced my nipples… Jonathan, there's nothing he didn't do," I sob.

"Helen…I'm so fucking sorry," he rasps, resting his head against mine. We sit there in silence, him still gently tracing the ugly mark that ensures I never forget what happened.

103 might be free, but she's far from buried.

Eventually, he breaks the charged silence to get me to tip my head back so he can rinse the conditioner out. At the same time, it feels like he's rinsing away some of the hurt clinging to me. Helping me out of the bath, he keeps his gaze firmly locked with mine as he drops to his knees before me.

"What are you doing?" I whisper.

"Showing you just how perfect you are to me, scars and all." He places a kiss on first one foot, then the other before making his way up my legs. Seeing this powerful man on his knees for me takes my breath away. As he works his way up my body with an endless stream of reassurance and praise, I'm a mess by the time he's standing in front of me again. As he cups my face in his palms, tears blur my vision.

"You are perfection, Helen, and you always have been. It was always you, sweetheart; *it will always be you.* I want you exactly as you are. Nothing is ever going to make me want you or love you less. You're my beginning, middle, and end. When I thought you died, a part of me died with you. The only reason I didn't chase death was because I knew our daughter needed me, but God, sweetheart. It was agony living in a world without you. I want to spend a lifetime by your side, helping you heal, watching you flourish and making up for what was stolen from us." Tears stream down both our faces at this point.

"I always loved you, even when it hurt to do so," I confess on a broken sob. With a choked noise, he drops his forehead to rest against mine. I'm captivated by his eyes, eyes I dreamt of, eyes that haunted me as I raised our daughter without him. With his hands under my ass, he lifts me, and I wrap my legs around his waist. In that moment, Jonathan's kiss is a rough claiming as he reassures us both that this is real. It strips away the last of my control, pulling me deeper and deeper into him until the only thing I can think about is him and the burn of his mouth on mine.

I cling to him as he steps out of the bathroom and into the bedroom. The world around us blurs, shrinking to focus on the heat between us. All that matters is our raw need to be one. The whole world could burn down around us right now for all we'd notice. Setting me on my feet in the middle of the room, he takes me in with heated eyes.

"Every inch of you is mine, from the top of your pretty head to your toes, and I think it's about time I remind you of that fact. What do you say, sweetheart?" The promise in his words has me shifting my weight, desperate for some relief from the low throbbing in my core. My mouth is dry, so with a nod of my head, I go to move closer to him, only to stop when he tsks.

"Words, pretty girl. I need to hear you say it."

"Pretty please," I sass, rolling my eyes at him.

His lips twitch into a smirk, and for a heartbeat, the air between us softens—less fire, more warmth. But then his gaze drops to my bare body, and a low groan escapes him as he shifts, adjusting himself.

I watch him, heart pounding, the air thick between us.

"I don't want you to go easy on me," I say, the words raw and real. "I need this—I need *you*. You're the only one I trust to help me take my body back."

The hunger in his eyes flares hotter, but it's tempered by something deeper. Something reverent. His jaw tightens, and for a beat, he doesn't speak—just watches me like he's memorising this moment.

"Be a good girl," he murmurs, voice low and reverent now, thick with restraint. "And crawl to me."

I don't hesitate this time. I lower myself, deliberately, onto my hands and knees, and meet his gaze as I move. There's no fear in my chest now—only fire. Only him.

Each step forward is a quiet rebellion against the years I was forced to flinch, to shrink, to obey out of fear instead of desire. With every inch I close between us, I reclaim something.

The act of crawling should have me outraged. Humiliated. But the way he looks at me—like I'm something sacred—and the way he doesn't command, just *waits*, has me desperate to close the space between us.

When I finally reach him, he kneels too, meeting me eye to eye. One hand rises to cradle my face with aching gentleness.

"You're sure?" he asks, voice low and hoarse with restraint. "If you say stop—"

"I won't," I whisper. "Not with you."

His breath catches. Something flickers in his eyes—fierce, protective, awed.

"I don't want you to go easy on me," I add, barely more than a breath. "I need this—I need *you*."

He nods once, his thumb brushing over my cheek, like he's anchoring himself with the weight of my words.

"Then let me give you everything," he says softly. "Let me show you what it feels like to be wanted without fear."

And there's no hesitation when he leans in to kiss me—slow, reverent, claiming in a way that feels like a promise.

As the kiss deepens, his hands move with aching control, one sliding down to my waist, the other unfastening his belt with a quiet click that sends heat curling low in my belly.

When he breaks the kiss, his eyes darken.

"You want a taste?" he murmurs, teasing a bead of precum over my bottom lip with the pad of his thumb.

I don't answer. I don't need to.

I part my lips and dart my tongue out, offering myself in the most deliberate way.

With a groan, he gives me what I want.

Rising to his feet, he frees his cock and thrusts into my mouth—slow, deep, deliberate—and my moan vibrates around him. My eyes flutter shut, body tingling with every roll of his hips. His hand anchors in my hair, his other resting protectively on my shoulder.

And in this moment, there's no shame. No fear.

Only *trust*.

Only *him*.

And the beginning of something that feels like healing.

"Good girl," he groans, thrusting in and out slowly, letting the head almost pop out from between my lips before guiding himself to the back of my throat again. Reaching down to squeeze my throat, he lets out a curse as he feels himself there.

"Such a pretty girl on her knees for me. Did you miss my big fucking dick, huh? The way it stretches you, fills you up." Leaning over me, his palm cracks across my bare ass, and I whimper around his cock. He does it to the other cheek, spanking me hard enough to have fire chasing across the tender skin. Arching into it, I whine as I take him even deeper, moans and spit slipping out around him. He spanks my ass again before slowly sliding between my thighs and palming my pussy.

"God, look how needy you are," he groans, holding my face against his abs as he teases my pussy with the other hand. As he sinks two thick fingers into me, I moan, arching into his touch, desperate for more, all while I hollow my cheeks around his cock.

Soon, he's thrusting his fingers in and out in time with the movement of his hips as he fucks my mouth. It's lewd and messy and oh so fucking hot as he fucks me from both ends, turning me into a puddle of need at his feet.

With a low, throaty sound he pulls away. His fingers stroke my lips, making me taste myself before slipping lower to squeeze my neck, then stepping back to look at me. "Such an eager slut for me."

"All yours," I vow, my voice coming out raspy after being thoroughly face fucked. With a hum, he circles before crouching in front of me.

"The question is, will you let me show you what eager little sluts get?" A million possibilities flick through my head at his words, but the only thing any of them make me feel is excitement.

"I'm yours to fuck how you see fit, Sir." I bat my eyelashes at him, and with a dark chuckle, he rises to his full height again.

"Oh, sweetheart, you're going to regret that." He mutters before helping me to my feet. Leading me to the bed, he pushes me down face first. As he slowly and meticulously wraps silk restraints around my wrists and ankles, binding them together, my pulse races—not from fear, but from anticipation. Pure, unfiltered lust courses through me as Jonathan binds me into a present for himself. By the time he's done, I can't move a muscle. All I can do is take what he gives me. Everything feels heightened, and as he glides his fingers over the backs of my thighs and up over my ass, I gasp.

"I wish you could see what I see right now," he murmurs. "My perfect, needy little slut, all her holes open to me. Which one should I stuff full of my cock first, hmm?"

Suddenly, warm air teases my bare pussy, making me gasp. Without warning, I feel his tongue dragging up between my lips to circle my clit. I try to thrust back against him, only to get a sharp slap to my cheek before he drags his tongue towards the rosebud of my ass instead.

Slipping his hand underneath me, he thrusts two fingers inside my pussy as he eats my ass like a starved man. The dual sensation has me crying out, choking on my pleasure as I strain against my restraints, my eyes rolling back in ecstasy. My moans mix with his growls, my thighs starting to shake as, suddenly, Jonathan yanks my head back by my hair, and the triple whammy of sensations sends me hurtling over the edge with a sharp cry.

I'm still gasping for breath when he stands, withdrawing his fingers, using his grip on my hair to pull me back into him as he blankets my back. "I'm not done with you yet, sweetheart."

That's all the warning I get before I feel him pressed against my pussy. With a curse, he tugs my head back to lock eyes with me as he thrusts his cock inside me. Instantly, I feel like I'm split in half as he rams every inch of himself in to the hilt.

"Christ," he mutters, pressing a kiss to my shoulder blade as he stills, like he's savouring the moment. My knees shake with the pressure as he grinds his hips into me. "Fuck me, your pussy is trying to strangle me. Such a greedy little hole. She missed me, didn't she?"

"God, yes," I cry. My eyes roll back into my head, my jaw going slack as everything ceases to exist. Another guttural sound rips from me as he shoves my head down into the mattress, using the leverage to truly fuck me. Sharp, fast thrusts have me clenching down on him, desperate to keep him inside me. I dig my nails into my ankles to ground myself as his hips roll into mine. When he said he was going to show me what eager sluts get, he wasn't kidding. Fuck, does it feel good to be so free.

I'm so fucking wet, I can feel it dripping down my thighs as Jonathan fucks me with single-minded determination. In this moment, the only thing that matters to him, to me, to us, is *this*. The harder he fucks me, the more firmly he reclaims me, the more at his mercy I become, the closer I get to coming all over his dick and reminding him who owns it.

"That's it, sweetheart," he grunts as his cock rams into me. "Bounce on my fucking cock. Show me how much you missed it. Coat me in your cum. Do it." The tight coil inside me reaches its breaking point. "Fuck, you're going to make me come. Be a good girl and take every drop."

The combination of his filthy words and the feeling of his dick swelling inside me does it. Everything blurs as my shaking body arches back into his thrusts, and needy whines fall from my lips. I'm shaking as Jonathan slams into me one final time, his abs hitting my ass as he buries himself deep and groans. His cock twitches, pumping me full of his cum just as he promised. He pulls my head up, twisting my face around before his mouth crashes to mine, kissing me like he's claiming me.

As if he hasn't already claimed me soul-deep.

JONATHAN
CHAPTER 53

Having all the pieces to Helen's story is all I wished for from the moment the seed was planted that she might be alive. But now that I have them…I wonder if it would be easier if she was dead. I'd much rather shoulder that pain than have her go through what she did, what those sick motherfuckers put her through.

How can she stand to let me touch her? Hell, how is she even still *standing*?

In the morning, I'll get to work tracking down every sick mother-fucker who had anything to do with her time in Belfast but, for now, I'll hold her and do all I can to absorb her pain. A listening ear is the very least I can offer her.

"I feel like all we've done since I got back is talk about me. What's happened in your world? Catch me up, please. I'm sick to death talking about me and my trauma. I'd much rather talk about you. What ever happened to Sheila? To your dad's house?" She tilts her chin to look at me from her place on my chest.

"The house is still there, but it never felt right moving into it. I pay for it to be looked after, but it's empty. As for Sheila, she passed a year or two after Da." Running my hand down her back, I play with her hair as she blinks up at me with sorrow-filled eyes.

"She loved him, didn't she?"

"She did. I like to think they're together now," I murmur, squeezing her closer.

"I bet they are." She kisses my chest before switching subjects. "And business? What's been happening there?"

"It's a shit show, if I'm honest with you. I thought when Logan killed Angus, things would settle down, but if anything, things got worse. We learnt about the dark web, which led us down a rabbit hole. Logan overhauled the entire Clan; we lost one of our own, and we thought we'd gotten to the root of the problem, only to discover the damn thing was still running. It's like a damn viper—cut off one head, and another grows, no matter what we do." Frustration bleeds from me as I summarise the last few months.

With a frown, she hums as she processes. This is another thing I've missed: how we could bounce ideas back and forth off each other and conquer whatever issue plagued us. After a few moments of consideration, she snaps her fingers and props herself up a bit to look at me better. Her hair falls round her face in a sex-rumpled mess that has my ego standing tall.

"Have you considered instead of actively hunting them down, maybe blending in? Making up some fake profile and gaining their trust until you're invited to the next auction? Instead of having a rat in your midst, be like a rat in theirs, ideally without telling anyone. That way, the chances of it leaking are as low as possible."

"It's worth a shot," I muse before pulling her into a kiss and ending all conversation. Business will still be here in the morning. For now, I want to enjoy the feeling of my sweetheart being back where she belongs.

HELEN
CHAPTER 54

With Jonathan's concerns gnawing at the edges of my thoughts, I ask Donna to come over the next afternoon while he heads out on business. There's a tension in my chest I can't shake — like something vital is about to snap.

As soon as she steps through the front door, I don't even give her time to take her coat off.

"Please tell me you've got something," I say. "Something we can use."

She raises an eyebrow at me, but there's no bite behind it. Just tired understanding.

"Oh, honey," she says, exasperated but kind. "Do you even remember who you're talking to?"

"Then quit edging me and cut to the damn chase," I huff, though my voice lacks its usual fire. My nerves are frayed raw.

Donna grins—sharp and unapologetic, just like always. "Some things never change."

She settles in, flipping open her laptop with a flourish. "I started with Lily's birth certificate. No father listed, but the hospital was in Belfast. That led me down the rabbit hole of old hospital staff logs, cross-referencing birth records, background reports... and then I found this."

She turns the screen toward me.

I freeze.

The air disappears from the room. The blood in my veins turns to ice.

Because there, staring back at me in black and white, is a man I've spent every waking moment trying to forget.

My sister's rapist. Her killer.

And beside him—Jen. A much younger Jen, barely more than a girl herself, with a swollen belly and vacant eyes.

"Oh my God," I gasp. The words feel foreign, like someone else is saying them. My legs buckle, and I grab the back of the nearest chair to stay upright.

"I know," Donna says, her voice softening. "She was so young— too young."

"No, Donna... it's not that." My voice breaks. "I know that man."

She goes still, brows knitting together. "You *what*?"

I can't answer.

I push away from the table, panic clawing at my chest. Pacing the length of the room like a caged animal, I fight the rising tide of nausea. Every beat of my heart feels like it's thudding against something hollow.

The past is no longer buried—it's clawing its way up, screaming.

"Helen—breathe," Donna says urgently. "Come on, you've got to breathe. Don't you dare pass out on me. If you make me tell Jonathan I broke you, he'll kill me. Then Jack will kill him. And then the kids will kill all of us. Is that what you want?"

A breathless laugh escapes me despite the tremor in my hands. I collapse onto the couch beside her, head in my hands. My lungs feel like they've been wrapped in barbed wire.

"He was Freya's owner," I whisper.

Silence crashes between us. Donna goes completely still.

"Holy shit."

"Yeah."

"Jesus, Helen…" she breathes, her voice low and stunned. "This is going to change everything."

"I know."

"We have to tell them."

"Have you told Jack?"

"Not yet. I wasn't sure you'd believe me until you saw it. But now… God, Helen. What if Ciaran doesn't know who she really is? What if none of them do? That photo… It's damning. Doesn't matter what the truth behind it is—it's enough to burn everything to the ground."

"Ciaran needs to know," I murmur, each word a lead weight in my mouth. "And Lily… what if she has no idea? What if she's just collateral in all this?"

"That's what scares me most," Donna admits. "She's just a kid. But she's tied to this now—by blood, by proximity. And if Jen's up to something, it might already be too late."

"I'll talk to him tonight."

After she leaves, I pull myself together and head to Cora's house—desperate for a moment of normalcy, some kind of emotional anchor.

Lily opens the door, beaming, with April perched happily on her hip. She greets me with a laugh, her cheeks flushed, completely unaware of the inferno that's coming.

I try to match her energy. I really do. But my mind keeps spinning.

Does she know what her mother's done? Is that why she's afraid of her? Or is she just another girl who's never had a real chance?

I look at her—so young, so warm—and all I can do is hope.

Hope that when the truth comes out, she isn't the one who pays for it.

Because if I've learned anything… it's that the sins of the parent have a long reach.

And too often, it's the children who bleed.

JONATHAN
CHAPTER 55

From the moment someone first uttered the word "rat," I knew this would turn into a mess. But I never expected *this*.

One of the inner circle's wives?

It's unthinkable. Unimaginable. The kind of twisted scenario no one dares to consider because it would mean rethinking everything.

But now, with what Helen's uncovered—what she *felt* in her gut before she ever had proof—I can't ignore it anymore. The more I dig, the more I realize how little we actually know about Jen. Her past. Her family. Her loyalties.

Maybe we never should've assumed her innocence came so easily.

Fuck. This is about to become an absolute disaster.

Calling an inner circle meeting without Ciaran feels like sacrilege, and the tension in the room reflects it. Jack and Declan exchange a wordless glance as they sit, while Brennan stays standing, posted up against the wall like a ticking time bomb. His arms crossed, his jaw flexing. Even behind the lenses of his glasses, I can see the storm building in his eyes.

The twins might be fire and ice, but splitting them like this isn't just risky—it's *unnatural*. But bringing Ciaran in now, before we have anything solid, would be like lighting a fuse with no exit strategy.

"What's going on? Where's Ciaran?" Jack asks, voice wary.

"He's not coming. Johnny here won't let him," Brennan snaps, cracking his knuckles like he's already prepping for a fight.

"Christ," I mutter. "I'm trying to *protect* him, for fuck's sake. Since when is that a crime?"

I sweep the room with a glare. They don't get it. They can't.

"It's the rat, isn't it?" Declan says quietly, already piecing things together.

I nod once. "I have reason to believe… it might be Jen."

"Says fucking who?" Brennan explodes, launching out of his corner. He looks one second away from tearing someone apart.

"Helen," Seamus says, his voice steady beside me.

"What the *fuck*?" Jack's eyes darken. "And what proof does she have?"

"It's her story to tell," I growl, steel in my voice. "But I believe her. That's enough. And let me be crystal clear—if anyone thinks about pressing her for answers, you'll deal with *me* first. Got it?"

That shuts them up.

For a beat, the room holds its breath.

"We need *proof* before we do anything drastic," Brennan mutters. His voice is lower now, but he's shaking. "Ciaran… he's not gonna survive this if it's true."

After Una, we all watched him unravel. Seeing him find stability again with Jen gave us hope. If this blows up? He won't come back from it.

"Agreed," I say. "Bren—bug her house. Every device. Her phone, Lily's phone. Plant audio in the cars. I want everything."

He nods, but I can see it in his face—he already knows where this is heading.

A part of me hoped Brennan would come up empty. That Jen was just misunderstood. That we were chasing shadows. But when is anything ever that simple?

With a frustrated sigh, I kiss Helen's forehead before leaving her curled in my bed, safe and warm. A rare moment of peace—one I don't deserve, not when this kind of storm is brewing.

The city is barely waking as I drive, the sunrise doing nothing to warm the cold knot in my gut. I pull into the Pit and make my way through the biometric security. This place has always felt like a bunker—part prison, part sanctuary. A home for our darkest work.

Liam's already waiting.

"He expecting me?"

"Yeah," Liam nods. "He told me to wait for you before heading down."

"Typical," I mutter. "Fucker loves building suspense."

Clapping my hand on Liam's shoulder, I step through the doorway, letting him close the door and lead the way. As the sounds of wet work get louder, so too does the stench. "Jesus," I rumble, grimacing at the foul odour. That shit never gets less offensive. We round the corner and there he is—Jimmy. Still hanging, still taped up, still painted in pain.

"You work fast," I mutter.

"No time to waste when kids are getting sold off." Ciaran spits the words like venom. The blood on his shirt is fresh, his hair a mess, his whole body humming with rage.

"What brings you down here?"

"Liam, why don't you take over interrogating Jimmy here for a second?" I toss over my shoulder as I steer Ciaran away from prying ears. While I trust Liam with my daughter's safety, and I can't see Jimmy ever making it out of here alive, one can never be too careful.

"What?" Ciaran barks, impatient. Looking him over, taking note of the way his once pristine white shirt is splattered in blood, at the bags under his eyes and the way his normally slicked back hair falls across his forehead, I let out a breath before meeting his eyes.

"I need you to breathe. Just… for a second." He glares.

"It's Jen." His face stills.

"She's on the server. We're still confirming how deep it goes, but…"

The silence stretches. Then, in the blink of an eye, he shoves me back, turns, and punches straight through the wall. Plaster rains down as he whirls around, grabbing his hatchet off the table.

"Ciaran—wait—"

He storms back into the room before I can stop him.

Liam barely has time to get out of the way before the hatchet swings.

Jimmy doesn't scream. Not through the duct tape.

But I do.

"*Ciaran!*"

He doesn't stop. Blow after blow. Blood spraying. Rage uncontained.

I stand there, useless, watching my brother fall apart with every strike.

And deep down, I know—this isn't about Jimmy. Not really.

This is only the beginning.

And God help us when the rest comes out.

JONATHAN
CHAPTER 56

Seeing the puzzle pieces finally lock into place should feel like relief. Like progress.

But instead of peace, all I feel is pressure. A heavy, suffocating sense of responsibility settles in my chest as I look around the penthouse. The room is alive with fury and heartbreak—raw, undiluted chaos bubbling just beneath the surface.

"I fucking told you she was a no-good, gold-digging whore!" Matt explodes.

He's been a live wire since walking in with Owen and Cora, his fury eclipsed only by his heartbreak. He's never hidden his contempt for Jen, but now it burns with bitter vindication.

For years, everyone brushed him off—said it was just loyalty to his mother. That he'd get over it. But now? Now it's obvious he was right.

And it's about to cost us more than we ever imagined.

"Enough. We can play the blame game all night long, but that's not going to solve jack shit." The room stills. "Matt, you're with Bren. Seamus, Owen, and Jack, look after the girls. Ciaran, Dec, Liam, and

Aidan—you're with me," I snap, putting a stop to the bickering before we waste even more time. While Matt looks ready to argue, jaw clenched and eyes blazing, he holds it in. He dips his head, his red curls falling forward to hide the grief etched across his face.

I've stood in this room a hundred times. Blood-slick floors. Metal tables. The heavy silence before a scream. But tonight feels different. The air at the Pit crackles with tension, thick with anticipation and something darker—*dread*.

The Finlay brothers sit across from me, Declan pacing by the wall, and not one of us speaks. We don't need to.

We all feel it.

For an organization that values family above all else, interrogating a woman—*one of our own*—cuts deeper than we'd ever admit. It makes monsters of us. And still, we can't walk away.

"Cole would hate this," Aidan mutters, his voice low and raw, eyes locked on a spot of dried blood on the floor.

I cross the room and sit beside him, placing a steadying hand on his shoulder.

"He'd hate what she's done more," I say quietly. "Think of what's at stake—how many lives we might still save."

"Boss is right," Liam adds from across the room, flipping his knife idly through his fingers. "If we get names, we get to go hunting."

The promise in his voice is quiet but unmistakable.

Aidan exhales slowly and rises, rolling his neck as he shifts into something colder. Sharper.

"Then let's get it done."

"Showtime," Declan murmurs, sliding his phone into his pocket just as the steel door creaks open.

Ciaran enters like a phantom—silent and seething. Jen hangs limp over his shoulder, unconscious and pale.

No one says a word.

We move as one, securing her to the metal exam table like we've done a hundred times before—but this time, it feels like betrayal.

When the bucket of ice-cold water hits her, she jerks awake with a gasping sputter, her eyes wide and wild.

Ciaran stands before her, unmoving, shoulders squared and jaw clenched. The room is heavy with his rage, thick and electric.

"You know," I say calmly, clicking my tongue as I step forward, "this doesn't have to hurt. All we want are a few answers. And you do love to talk, don't you, Jen?"

She groans behind the gag, fury and defiance burning in her eyes.

"We're going to take that gag off now," Declan says smoothly, arms crossed. "You can cooperate, and this ends fast. Or you can be difficult… and learn why they call your husband and brother-in-law the Butcher Brothers."

Ciaran steps forward and loosens the gag.

She spits in his face.

The room freezes.

"You fucking *cunt*," he snarls, trembling with rage. "I should have listened to my boy. All this time, you were leading me around by my dick."

Her mouth curls into a smile—mocking and cruel. "It was all too easy."

Ciaran's hand flies to her throat, fingers digging in.

She doesn't flinch.

"That's enough," I say quietly, nodding to Liam and Aidan. They pin her arms and legs as Declan steps in, pulling out his knife.

There's no mercy in the room now.

If she thought being a woman would spare her, she's about to learn just how wrong she is.

HELEN
CHAPTER 57

Sitting idle while others interrogate Jen has my skin crawling. I need to be *doing* something, not just sitting here, but anytime I so much as look at the lift, Seamus or Jack shift closer to it, as if I'm a flight risk. Okay, maybe I am, but that doesn't mean they have to act like it.

"Penny for your thoughts?" Cora asks, coming to join me in the kitchen. If I can't help with the interrogation, the next best thing is making sure everyone has a drink in hand while we wait. Handing Cora a glass of wine, I pour my own before turning to lean against the counter.

"Just wondering how things are going, you?" I mummer.

"I still can't believe Jen is connected to Angus," she confesses.

"We don't know that for sure."

"No, but we know she was on that same sex trafficking server. We know she has ties to at least one of the bastards who hurt you. What more do we need?" The note of defeat in her voice and the slump of her shoulders pulls me closer. I wrap an arm around her without hesitation.

One day, she'll be the one standing in Jonathan's shoes, expected to carry herself like steel. But right now, she's just a twenty-four-year-old girl bearing far too much.

And if anyone has a problem with her needing her mother's arms tonight, they can come through me first.

"If anyone can get to the bottom of this, it's your dad. We just have to trust him and wait, darling," I comfort her, running my hand over her hair as she releases a loaded sigh. "What's really got you this worked up?"

"Lily." One word weighted down with a hundred different questions. Does she know? Is she involved? What about her ties to Benedict? I can't imagine the girl I met—so clearly terrified of her own mother—had any willing involvement, but from the way Cora bites her lip and wrings her hands, it's clear she's not so sure. Or perhaps she's worried the others won't listen to reason, and she'll be forced to choose between her friend and her responsibilities.

Our weighted moment is interrupted by her phone. Slipping it out of her pocket, she answers the Facetime call from Abigail with a forced smile. Squeezing her shoulder, I leave her to it and head to Jonathan's office to make a call of my own.

"Hello?" The confused, gruff voice on the other end of the line is so like his father's, it takes my breath away for a moment. That Scottish lilt haunts my nightmares, but I owe it to Freya to push through.

"Logan, this is Helen," I manage to choke out around the lump in my throat. For a moment, his shocked inhale is the only response I receive, and then like a damn breaking, a torrid of questions spill down the line.

"How are you? Shit, that was stupid. What I meant was, how are things going? Can we meet? Do you know anything about what happened to my mum?"

"Your mum was the single strongest person I know. She loved you so much. All she wanted was to fight her way back to you…" Through my tears, I spend God knows how long in that office, sharing every little detail about Freya with him as he breaks down on the other end of the line. I know this man is nothing like his father; he's every inch the caring soul Freya would have wanted him to be. While she might be gone, she lives on in him.

The click of the door opening jolts me awake.

At some point, after everyone had cleared out—once it was obvious Jonathan and the others wouldn't be back anytime soon—I must've passed out from the emotional overload. Now, as light from the hall spills into the room, I'm groggy, tense, and completely disoriented.

Squinting against the glare, all traces of sleep vanish when I spot a blood-soaked Jonathan in the doorway. "Jonathan, what happened?" Sitting up, the sheet pools around my waist, and I flush when I remember I'd decided to forgo clothes.

Letting out a tortured sound, he closes the distance between us in seconds, and then his mouth is on mine, and who needs words or answers? He kisses me like he was born to do so, stealing the air from my lungs. This isn't a simple kiss—no, this is a claiming.

He follows me down, bracketing me between his hips and arms as we get lost in each other. All I can feel is the silk against my skin, his tongue against mine, the tightening in my core, the sudden wetness between my legs. With a groan, he pulls back, staring down at me with molten eyes.

"Do you want me to stop?" His breath is harsh, his voice utterly wrecked, as if even the thought of stopping was more than he could stomach.

That's the last thing I want, and I tell him as much. "Fuck no."

"I'm not in the mood to be gentle right now, sweetheart."

"Good thing I'm not breakable, then, isn't it?" My words are a challenge—one he gladly meets. With a curse, he claims my mouth as his once again as he reaches between us to palm my breast, pinching my nipple in the process. Hissing at the sensation, I arch up into him.

"That's my pretty fucking girl. Look how good you are for me. You like that, don't you? These are my fucking tits." Dipping his head, he gently tugs one of my nipples between his teeth, and the instant pain has me whimpering, fisting his hair. With a click of his tongue, he leans back.

"Did I say you could touch me, sweetheart?" The heat in his gaze has me clenching on nothing as I shake my head. "That's right. I didn't." With one hand, he deftly undoes his belt, and I bite back a whimper at the sight. Something so simple shouldn't be so hot, but as he uses that same belt to secure my wrists together, I'm practically a puddle of need.

"Now, you're going to lie there and let me worship you. And only once I've had my fill will I move on." With that dark promise, he stands and slowly removes his shirt and trousers. Seeing this man strip will never *not* affect me. As each inch of skin is revealed to my hungry gaze, my need ratchets up another notch.

"Fuck," I whisper, looking up at him with heavy eyelids. Smirking, he joins me on the bed again, this time kissing his way from my chest to my ankles, but skipping the places I need him most. With a whine, I arch my hips.

"Shh now, pretty girl. Good things come to those who wait. You can be good for me, can't you? After all, you want to be pumped full of my cum, don't you?" His dirty words set me on fire as he feathers light kisses across my inner thighs, eyes locked on mine. Finally, his tongue flicks where I need it most, swirling around my clit as he pushes a finger inside me. Instantly, all words flee my head, and in their place is a series of moans and whimpers as he uses his knowledge of my body against me.

"Fuck." I circle my hips as he reaches up to twist my nipple, and the dual sensation has everything inside me tightening, my eyes squeezing shut. "Jonathan—"

Suddenly, he withdraws his fingers, and my eyes snap open in outrage. "Eyes on me when I make you come," he demands before thrusting his fingers back inside me. With a shout, I clamp down around the digits as I explode. I'm still trying to catch my breath when he frees my wrists before moving to stand at the edge of the bed.

"Come show me those pretty holes. Show me what's mine," he orders, stroking his hard cock, arching a brow when I don't move. "Or have you changed your mind?" That has me moving in a heartbeat. Once I reach the edge of the bed, I reach down to spread myself open for him, earning a groan of approval before his hands wrap around my thighs, spreading me even wider.

"Look at that gorgeous cunt. So tight and wet for me, clenching around nothing. You need to be filled, don't you, baby?" I bite my lower lip as he pushes two fingers inside me before removing them, centring the head of his cock at my entrance instead.

"Oh God," I gasp as he pushes inside me.

"That's right, baby. I am your God," he grunts as he begins to fuck me relentlessly. The sound of skin slapping against skin echoes around us, mixed with our moans like a symphony. If I ever doubted how much Jonathan O'Neill loved me, all it would take to rid me of that thought is the vision of him above me: the love and need radiating from his every pore, the tattoo of my eyes over his heart, the way he worships me every damn time.

His movements are familiar, and as he collars my throat, I hitch my left knee higher on his hip to deepen the angle.

"Please, more," I whimper.

With a cocky smirk, he positions my leg over his shoulder and tightens his grip on my throat. I dig my nails into his shoulder as my vision gets fuzzy and everything tightens inside me.

"Harder," I mouth, my voice stolen from me. With a curse, he fucks me even harder, not even pausing when the bed slides across the floor.

"That's a good girl. Fuck, you're choking my cock. Do you need my cum that bad?" he growls, reaching between us to pinch my clit. In seconds, I'm shattering around him with a breathless cry. Cursing, he releases his grip on my throat as he follows me over the edge, flooding me with his cum. Pulling free, he collapses beside me, pulling me into his arms and kissing my forehead.

"You're perfect, you know that?" he asks, running his hand down my back. Snuggling further into his chest, I press a kiss to his chest before tilting my head back to look at him.

"How I ended up here after all the chaos and darkness, I don't know, but I'm so glad I managed to fight my way back to you. To us."

JONATHAN
CHAPTER 58

After the shitstorm that was dealing with Jen—the bitch biting off her own tongue to avoid talking, followed by Ciaran killing her in a blind rage—the last thing any of us wants to do is face *whatever* Brennan and Matt have dug up.

But here we are.

"I still can't believe she'd rather *die* than talk," Declan mutters, shaking his head like he still hasn't quite processed it. If it wasn't so fucking frustrating, it would be impressive.

"I can't believe five grown men got played by one lying little woman," I spit. "If word gets out…" I don't even finish the thought. The shame would outlive all of us.

Dec snorts. Jack glances at his watch, clearly over this entire ordeal.

"Got somewhere better to be?" I snap, irritated by his indifference.

"Yeah," he shoots back with a wink, "between my wife's thighs."

I roll my eyes, but it's barely enough to lift the tension weighing on us all.

"Enough. Where the fuck is Bren?" Ciaran growls. He's been a powder keg since he stumbled out of the lift—edgy, sharp, ready to blow at the smallest spark. He's testing every last bit of my patience, and going by the way Dec is grinding his teeth, I'm not the only one.

"Christ. For the fifth time, he's on his way," Jack mutters before the lift finally dings open, spitting out Brennan, Seamus, and Matt.

The three of them look wrecked. Matt in particular—he all but folds into the nearest chair beside his dad, face drawn and pale. Looking at father and son, it's hard to say who looks worse.

"Nice of you to join us," Jack snarks.

Brennan just rolls his eyes while Seamus beelines for the vodka, pouring a shot like it's water.

"Some of us were flying back from *Belfast* at the ass-crack of dawn," Bren says.

"Belfast? Why the fuck were you over there again?" Ciaran grumbles, looking somewhat alive for the first time all morning.

"Gathering evidence." His voice is rough, and when he drags his hands through his hair, I notice the tremor in them. Whatever they found, it's bad.

Brennan hands me a few sheets of paper—printed emails, records, things I'd hoped we'd never see. I scan them. Once. Twice. A third time, hoping they'll change. They don't.

"You're shitting me."

"Wish I was," Bren sighs, rubbing the bridge of his nose. "She knew, Johnny. There's no way she *didn't* know what Jen was involved in. And even if that didn't seal her fate, this will."

"Christ," I mutter, reading the email from Jen to Benedict.

This isn't just messy. This is a nuclear-level fuck-up. I pass the pages to Declan, watching as his jaw tightens while he reads. No matter how we spin this—no matter what we do someone is going to be left feeling hurt and betrayed.

"Tell me we at least have a body to bury," I mutter. Declan curses under his breath. The rest of the room goes still. I look to Brennan. He shakes his head.

"Fuck."

"You have to be *joking*," Cora snaps. "No. No way. This is *Lily* we're talking about!"

The fire in her voice doesn't surprise me. If anything, it hurts more. Because I know what I'm about to do is going to feel like betrayal. But what choice do I have?

"I know it's hard," Helen says gently, stepping in to try and soften the blow. "But I'm sure your dad has a plan. He wouldn't do this without one."

Right. A *plan*.

"You said it yourself," I tell Cora. "Before the wedding. She wanted to study abroad. She wanted to go—"

"Don't," Cora cuts in, her voice trembling. "Don't twist that into something it's not."

I sigh and scrub a hand over my face. "Listen. There's solid evidence she *knew*, Cora. That she kept quiet. And there's the birth certificate—Benedict listed as her father."

She flinches like I hit her.

"So we just cut her off? Exile her?" she whispers.

"It's the best option we have," I say. "She's safe. She's getting what she wanted, and this buys us time. Enough time to find the truth. But she can't stay here. Not with the men whispering, not with Matt ready to explode, and definitely not with Ciaran seeing red every time her name comes up."

I watch my daughter fight to keep herself together. Her jaw trembles, but she refuses to let the tears fall.

"When it comes out she was innocent..." she whispers, voice breaking.

"If she is," I say softly, "we'll make it right."

I cross the room and kneel in front of her, resting my hand gently over hers. "I *promise* you—I will find who's behind this. And when I do, they won't walk away."

Across the room, Helen nods. Her eyes meet mine, and the fire burning behind them is the same one that's been driving me for weeks now.

We're hunting this truth together.

And we won't stop until we drag it into the light—no matter how many heads we have to cut off to do it.

HELEN
EPILOGUE

Walking through the glass doors of O'Neill's HQ is like slipping back in time. The minute they close behind me, the outside world fades. Gone is the chaos, the heartbreak, the bloodshed. In here, there's only polished floors, sharp suits, and the thrill of walking familiar halls with new purpose.

For the next hour or so, I'm not a survivor, a mother, or a woman piecing herself back together. I'm an assistant again—and Mr. O'Neill expects nothing but first-class service.

As I bypass the reception desk and head straight for the private lift, anticipation coils hot and tight in my belly. I tug at the hem of my skirt, suddenly hyper-aware of how short it is, how bare I am beneath it.

The lift climbs, slow and steady, every passing floor tightening my pulse.

When it spits me out at the top, I'm practically vibrating.

Slipping into my old office, I head straight for the connecting door and enter the code. As soon as the door unlocks, I drop to my knees, crawling towards his desk as he watches me with a phone pressed to his ear, keeping up his conversation with a hungry gleam in his dark eyes.

He doesn't say a word. Just watches.

And God, do I feel *seen*.

It feels like it takes years to cross the distance between his door and desk. Sliding his chair back, he leaves just enough room for me to slip in, raising a brow in challenge. Invitation or command—I don't care. I crawl between his legs like I belong there. Because I do. Before I can even begin to catch my breath, he's closing the distance between us. Suddenly, I'm trapped.

Just as suddenly, his hands appear below the desk, unbuckling his belt and freeing himself from his trousers. God, just seeing it makes my mouth water. I must be too slow for his liking, because his hand darts out to grab a fistful of my hair. Pulling me towards him, he angles his hips towards my mouth, and who am I to refuse?

I suck him down, swallowing around him as he keeps talking like nothing's happening. It's filthy. Intimate. And so fucking *hot* I nearly come from the act alone. The knowledge that, any second, we could be found has me worshipping his cock like my life depends on it. I use everything I've got—hands, lips, tongue, hollowed cheeks, gentle moans. I worship him with my mouth like it's my calling.

His grip tightens. His hips flex. But his voice stays level. Calm.

Until the line goes dead.

I'm so wrapped up in what I'm doing, I don't hear him ending his call. One minute, I'm blissfully sucking his dick like it's my job, and the next, he's shoving his chair back and staring down at me, nostrils flared and a dark expression on his face that screams trouble.

Game fucking on.

"Do you have any *idea* how distracting you are?" he growls.

I fight a shiver. "Mhm, but isn't that what you wanted, Sir?"

"You needy little slut. Get the fuck up here." I crawl out with a deliberate sway to my hips. Before I can rise fully, he grabs me by the hair and hauls me to my feet, then tosses me onto the desk. Papers fly.

He doesn't blink.

"My, you really are a whore, aren't you? Who else would turn up to work without underwear?" He tsks, taking my thighs in his hands and spreading them further apart. "And what's this?"

Pressing a hand to the butt plug, he goes to take it out, drawing a whine from my throat.

"Please, Sir. I don't want to be empty," I beg, spreading my pussy open for him and dipping my fingers into my own wetness.

With a curse, he leaves the plug and slaps my hand away. "These are *my* holes. You want something? You ask." Grinding his fingers against my clit, he proves his point. I squirm, trying to get more friction where I need it most, but he's having none of it. He moves his hand away, sucking on his fingers as he watches me squirm before he takes his cock in hand with a smirk.

"Let's see how well you can take me." Slapping his cock against my pussy, the wet sounds echoing around us, he teases us for a brief moment before slamming inside me. With one hand braced beside my head and the other wrapped around my throat, he pins me to the desk as he drives his hips into mine. All I can do is wrap my legs around his waist and moan for more as I hold on for dear life.

"You're fucking dripping for it," he growls.

"Please," I whine, undone already.

"You'll take what you're *given*." He pulls out of my pussy, pulls the plug free, and presses the head of his cock against my ass.

My breath catches.

"No... I can't."

"Yes, you fucking can." He coats himself with lube—when the hell did he even grab that?—and starts inching his way in, bit by bit, until I'm so full, I can feel him in my throat. Just when I think I've adjusted to the feeling, he pulls out, only to thrust back in to the hilt, and holy *shit*. When he thrusts two fingers back inside my pussy, stars explode behind my eyes as he claims my ass at the same time.

"See? I knew you could take it. Such a pretty fucking ass. Look how good you are for me." As filth drips from his lips, I climb higher and higher until, with a shout, I clamp down on his cock.

Stars explode behind my eyes. My entire body trembles.

"Shiiiit," he groans as I pull his orgasm from him, flooding my ass with his cum. For a moment, we stay like that, him buried in my ass, his face in my neck. With another groan, he pulls himself free, and before I can blink, he's feeding the butt plug back into my ass. Rising up on my elbows, I quirk a brow at him.

We stay like that—connected, breathless, wrecked. Finally, he eases out and, before I can even breathe, slips the plug back into place.

I raise an eyebrow. "Seriously?"

He grins, wild and unapologetic. "What can I say? I like seeing my cum where it belongs."

He helps me off the desk and pulls me into his lap. One hand strokes my hair; the other cradles my thigh. He kisses my temple.

"Was that everything you wanted?"

"And so much more," I murmur, smiling against his lips.

Life's still a storm. We're still hunting monsters.

But in his arms, in this moment?

I finally know what peace tastes like.

And it's damn good.

WHAT'S COMING NEXT?

The next book in The Four Points will be Matt and Lily's story. It Can't Be You will be coming in early 2026 and you can expect high heat packed into this stepsiblings romance where the MMC is going to crawl and beg for forgiveness.

In the meantime you can check out the first two books in this series and follow me for updates!

ACKNOWLEDGMENTS

Somehow this section gets harder to write every time and for that I am so grateful.

To Adam and Padfoot, thank you for your endless patience and support as I chase this dream. One day we will look back on all the hours I spent locked away with fondness and gratitude but for now thank you for believing in me.

To Sam, my ride or die. You've been my loudest cheerleader since day one and none of this would be possible without your listening ear and encouragement of my delulu goals. Here's to being one step closer to our writing cabin dreams.

To Paris, Eima and Chelsey. From spreadsheets to slugs in bikinis our origin story needs its own book but for now – thank you from the bottom of my heart. Each and every one of you has went out of your way to offer support and your enthusiasm means the world to me. You guys are the definition of hype women, and I struggle to remember how I did this without you.

To Paris, yes you deserve a second mention, you are my very own simp extraordinaire and devil on my shoulder. You're combination of beta reading proofreading for me so last minute was a life saver and I can not wait to see your reactions to what's coming next!

To Elizabeth, my proofreader and extra set of eyes – thank you for taking the time to read over Jonathan and Helen's story for me. You made so many correct guesses about what would happen, and I hope this lived up to your expectations!

To Aurelia, I'm once again blown away by your ability to understand and deliver exactly what I'm looking for in my covers. Your patience is endless and I love working with you.

To the babes at Luna, you are angels, and I can't wait to work with you again!

Last, but certainly not least, the biggest thank you has to go out to my readers. In a world where there is an endless array of options you picked up my book and that means the world to me. Seeing your reactions and the love you show my books makes my heart grow three sizes every time.

ALSO BY SHANNON JADE

The Four Points Mafia

It Was Always You

It Shouldn't Be You

It Will Always Be You

It Can't Be You

ABOUT THE AUTHOR

SHANNON JADE

is a full-time cat mum, part-time coffee addict, and a readaholic who resides in Northern Ireland. She has always wanted to write the stories in her head and loves an obsessed hero.

She can be found on TikTok, Instagram and Threads
@authorshannonjade

9 781068 750328